STAR TREK®
MIRROR UNIVERSE
SHARDS AND SHADOWS

STAR TREK®
MIRROR UNIVERSE
SHARDS AND SHADOWS

Edited by Margaret Clark and Marco Palmieri

Based on *Star Trek* and *Star Trek: The Next Generation*®
created by Gene Roddenberry

Star Trek: Deep Space Nine®
created by Rick Berman & Michael Piller

Star Trek: Voyager®
created by Rick Berman & Michael Piller & Jeri Taylor

Star Trek: Enterprise®
created by Rick Berman & Brannon Braga

POCKET BOOKS
New York   London   Toronto   Sydney   Tantalus Colony

Contents

Contents

Nobunaga

Dave Stern

HISTORIAN'S NOTE: *"Nobunaga" takes place in early 2156 (ACE).* The Terran Empire has possession of a powerful weapon, the twenty-third-century Federation Starship Defiant *("In a Mirror Darkly,"* Star Trek: Enterprise; *"Mirror, Mirror,"* Star Trek). *The Empress Sato, having mercilessly destroyed the usurpers to her rule (*Star Trek Mirror Universe: Glass Empires—Age of the Empress*), now seeks to eradicate any rebellion.*

Dave Stern has written/edited/collaborated on multiple previous works of *Star Trek* fiction, as well as the *New York Times*–bestselling biography *Crosley*. He lives in a creepy old house on a hill in Massachusetts, kept company by his family and a lawn of immense and ever-growing size.

He dreamed of T'Pol.

Not the Regent she had become but the woman she had been. The woman he had loved, out of duty at first and then with all his heart. He pictured her as she had looked ten years ago, at the time of the Empress's ascension, wearing the uniform she had taken from the *Defiant*'s stores, a blue skirt that let her long legs show, that left the curve of her neck bare.

He pictured himself kissing that skin, felt her long hair brush against his face, felt his hands moving over her body, her yielding to him. He luxuriated in the moment, stayed with T'Pol as she had been for as long as he could stand the memory.

And then the memory faded, and for a second, he saw T'Pol as she was now, T'Pol the Regent, hard, harsh, close-cropped hair. He pictured her standing over him, her face blank, expressionless, emotionless. Alien. Vulcan. As if they had shared nothing. As if he were nothing more to her than another cog in the Empress's machine.

He saw her hands reaching for him. Her fingertips on his forehead. Her mind invading his. Her strength forcing him to yield.

He shot up in bed, suddenly awake. Drenched in sweat.

Completely disoriented.

He wasn't aboard *Defiant*. He was—where?

Wearing a hospital gown. A hospital bed. Dim lighting in the room, a small room, no windows, a door at the foot of his bed, ventilators humming . . .

The door cracked open. Lights—dimmed, thank God for that— came on.

Dr. Phlox walked in.

"You." Tucker hated the Denubolan with a passion. "Where am I?"

"I'd take it easy if I were you, Commander. Your body needs time to recover from the—"

"Answer the damn question."

Phlox smiled.

"You're in a private medical facility. On Earth."

"Earth? How did I get here?"

Tucker shook his head. Images flashed through his mind. He was out on *Defiant*, near the Neutral Zone, hunting the rebels. Hunting Archer.

"I want that man caught!" Robinson yelled, slamming his fist into the padded armrest of the captain's chair. "I want more speed!"

He turned and glared at Tucker.

"I want my ship!" he screamed, and his face morphed into Hoshi's. The Empress's.

Tucker blinked, returning to the here and now.

"There was an accident," Phlox said. "In engineering."

"I don't remember that at all."

"Not surprising. It was rather a large explosion. You've been unconscious for some time."

"Some time."

"Three weeks."

"Three weeks? What about the ship?" Tucker asked.

"The ship is functional."

"Functional. What does that mean?"

"There is time to worry about the ship later," Phlox said. "For now, I need to examine you."

The doctor moved closer to the bed. Tucker flinched.

"I'd rather have another doctor."

"You don't get a choice. The Empress has personally charged me with your care."

Ah. Tucker could guess how that conversation had gone.

Heal him, or else.

He gritted his teeth, and endured the doctor's none-too-gentle probing. His machines and his tests. At the end, Phlox stepped back.

"So?" Tucker asked. "How am I?"

The doctor shook his head. "Dying," Phlox said.

Something to do with delta rays and radiation. The *Defiant*'s warp engines and the explosion that had occurred. Impending CCB—catastrophic cellular breakdown.

A more extreme version of the energies that had scarred his face at Bozeman, at the warp training facility, twenty years ago.

"Fix me," Tucker said. "The Empress charged you with my care, right?"

"Believe me, I am well aware of that fact. There is nothing I can do, however."

Tucker sat up. Frowned. "I don't feel any pain."

"It will be minimal at first," Phlox said. "As the nerve endings deteriorate, however, you will begin to—"

"Spare me the gory details." Tucker glared, rubbed the small of his back. "I hope this isn't another one of your sick jokes."

"Hardly."

"Maybe I should get a second opinion."

"A second opinion." Phlox burst out laughing and, just as suddenly, stopped. "Get all the opinions you want, Commander. The Empress would certainly love to have you with us for as long as possible. But the data are irrefutable. Machines do not lie."

There was a rolling cart next to the bed; on it, a case lay open. A machine lay within the case, the last machine the doctor had used. He popped a data chip out of the machine and put it into Tucker's hand.

"So, what kind of time frame we talking about?" Tucker asked.

"A few weeks. Perhaps longer. Depending."

"On what?"

"On the speed of the breakdown. How fast the effect travels through your system." The doctor retracted cable, folded sensors, snapped the case shut. "If I were you, I would get my affairs in order. Sooner rather than later."

He picked the case up by a handle, nodded, and left.

Tucker got out of bed. A mirror, three feet square, occupied one wall of the room. He went and looked at himself in it.

His body was scarred all over, burned. New scars to go with the old ones, the ones running down the side of his face. Souvenirs from Bozeman and the years he'd spent slaving next to the reactor chambers of various starships. *Enterprise. Defiant.* And—

Pain stabbed into his head. Sudden, sharp, debilitating. He groaned, lowered his head, waited for it to pass. Eventually, it did.

He stood up, and the room stopped spinning after a moment.

He'd never felt pain like that before. Not even after Bozeman.

Dying. Maybe Phlox was right.

He went to a terminal on the other side of the room. He popped in the data module Phlox had given him and reviewed what was on it. Started to, anyway. He was no doctor. He couldn't make heads or tails out of what he was seeing; it was highly unlikely, though, that Phlox had been lying. The Empress would have his head. Tucker was important to her—or, rather, the knowledge in his head was important.

His stomach growled. He walked out the door and into the hall.

There was a guard there, of course. There were guards everywhere.

This one was a good half-meter taller than he, built like a walking mountain.

"You don't leave the room." He drew his weapon and motioned Tucker back inside.

"Food," Tucker said, and went back into the room. Ten minutes later, a tray showed up. Hospital crap. He ate it anyway.

He lay back on his bed, hands behind his head, and closed his eyes.

Dying.

When he'd never really had a chance to live.

• • •

He slept, and dreamed again. Of T'Pol at first, not the T'Pol he had loved but the Regent, standing over his bed. Her fingers probing. Her mind probing.

The Empress stood next to her. Watching. Glaring. Fury written all over her face.

The pain in his head returned, stronger than ever.

The dream shifted.

He was back on *Defiant*. Back in his quarters. Staring at a red light flashing on his console: message waiting.

Message? Who would be sending him a message?

No way to know without opening it, of course.

His fingers danced above the input screen. Curiosity and fear warred within him.

Curiosity won.

He tapped the screen; it came to life.

The past came to life with it.

"Trip."

The message was from Jonathan Archer.

"I won't waste words," Archer said. "You can't do it. You can't let her—"

Tucker stabbed at the screen.

"Delete!" he shouted. "Delete, delete, delete!"

If the Empress found out . . .

He awoke, his heart thudding in his chest. His head ached. His body stank. He needed a shower. He needed to get back to *Defiant*. Whatever life he had was back on that ship. Correction: whatever life he had *was* that ship. He had no friends; his family had long ago abandoned him. His work was his legacy.

He took care of the washing up first, then went to the terminal. He opened a comlink, and after almost an hour of waiting, got through to his ship. To the captain.

"You're awake." Robinson looked neither pleased nor displeased. "What can I do for you?"

"How's the ship?"

"The ship is fine. How are you?"

"Ready to get back to work."

Traces of a smile flitted across the captain's face. "I heard you were dying."

"So they tell me. But I'm not dead yet." He leaned forward. "And I'm sick of this place already."

"I can understand that. I hate hospitals myself. But . . ." Robinson shrugged. "I can't help you."

"What?"

"Orders."

From whom? Tucker was about to ask, and then realized that, of course, there was only one person Robinson took orders from these days.

Right at that second, he heard footsteps in the hall. He turned in time to see the door open.

A woman stepped in.

The Empress.

She wore a black robe styled like a uniform and boots that added half a foot to her height. Bodyguards crowded the doorway behind her.

Tucker went to one knee, gritting his teeth the whole way down. "Empress."

"Commander. Rise—please. There's no need for such formality between old friends."

Which was an out-and-out lie, of course, Tucker thought as he got back on his feet, a lie that Travis Mayweather's component atoms—wherever they were—would happily attest to.

Hoshi entered the room. Two of the bodyguards followed her in—hulking monsters, bigger even than the man-mountain who'd shooed Tucker out of the hall before. *Augments,* though if what Tucker had heard about the Empress was true, she hardly needed them these days. The word was, she'd augmented herself as well, her strength, her recuperative powers . . . other things. Image-projection fields, allowing her to disguise herself. Telepathic abilities. The rumors were legion. Three-quarters of them were false, no doubt, but they all added to her mystique.

The Empress. Some said she would live forever.

Tucker wouldn't bet against it.

The bodyguards stayed put, flanking the door. Hoshi walked closer, put a hand on his shoulder. "I'm so sorry."

"So am I, Your Majesty." The first time he'd had to mouth those words, he'd almost choked on them. Now they slipped out like snake oil.

She sat down on the edge of the bed and patted a spot next to her. Tucker sat as well.

"How is the pain?"

"Tell you the truth, I don't feel it very much."

"That's good, at least. A minor blessing." Her face smiled; her eyes stayed cold. "You'll have the best care, of course. We'll make you as comfortable as we can."

He took a deep breath. "I'd be more comfortable aboard *Defiant.*"

"*Defiant* is on the line. In harm's way. You—"

"I can take a courier. Be there in three days." He turned back to the monitor, to the image of Captain Robinson watching them. "I can help you, Captain. You know I can. Morowski is good, but nobody knows those engines like I do."

Rather than respond, Robinson looked at the Empress.

She smiled again. Rattlesnake smile. "The ship is in good hands. Engineering is in good hands—isn't that so, Captain?"

Robinson bowed his head. "We stand ready, Empress, to serve your will."

She nodded. "So you see, Commander—"

The frustration boiled over inside him. "Empress, please. I—that's my life out there. That ship—I rebuilt those engines from parts, remember? That's my design out there—that's my—"

"Enough!"

Her grip tightened on the mattress frame. The steel snapped.

Some of those rumors about the augments were obviously true.

The Empress stood. "*Defiant* is mine to staff as I see fit."

Tucker lowered his head. "Of course, Your Majesty. Forgive me."

She nodded. "Your service to the Empire has been long and meritorious, Commander. It will never be forgotten."

"Thank you."

She looked him in the eye then and smiled. "I brought you something," she said. "A gift in honor of that service."

She reached inside her robe and pulled out a badge. It was shaped like a starship. There was writing on it, Japanese characters. Tucker couldn't read the language, and yet . . .

They looked somehow familiar to him.

His head began to ache. "Thank you, Your Majesty," he managed.

"Of course." She took his hand and put the badge in it. Closed his fingers around it. "A memento," she said, "of your greatest achievement."

"Yes," Tucker said, just to say something, because all at once, his head was pounding even harder, pounding as if it would split.

She leaned closer to him. "*Nobunaga,*" she whispered. "You remember."

No, he was about to say. *I don't.*

But then, all at once, he did.

Five years ago, he'd been summoned to Kyoto, to the palace, to the Empress's presence. T'Pol was there, the Regent, at the Empress's side. Her hair cropped close to the skull, her face a mask, her eyes looking right through him.

Tucker went to his knees in front of the throne. "Empress," he said.

"Rise, my old friend. My old comrade." Hoshi sat on her throne, her robes gathered around her, bejeweled, the imperial crown of old Japan restored to her brow.

Tucker rose and, for a second, felt dizzy. She smiled at him.

He felt sudden desire.

Pheromones.

Word was she continually spiked the air with them, rendering her visitors—her supplicants—compliant. Suggestible. Putty.

"I want you to build me a ship," Hoshi had said. "A sister to *Defiant.*"

Tucker remembered the feelings that had gone through him then.

Terror. Honor. Above all, apprehension.

Defiant's technology was decades ahead of anything the Empire had. Her warp drive, her weapons systems. Tucker had spent the last ten years probing those systems, teasing their secrets out. He understood them as well as anyone.

He was not sure he understood them well enough to replicate them.

He said as much.

"We can replicate the weaponry—the torpedoes." T'Pol spoke for the first time. Her expression was unreadable. "But the warp engines—"

"We require your assistance in this matter, Commander. This ship must be built. We must show all that the way forward—the way toward lasting peace—is under our dominion." Hoshi leaned forward. "Do you not agree, Commander?"

It was as if she were daring him to mention the rebels. Or the man who led them.

He lowered his head. "I am yours, as always, Empress."

"Of course you are." Her smile was dazzling. "Who else's would you be?"

The Empress left, vowing to return. Empty words; Tucker knew it, and she knew he knew it. She would never be back.

He managed to stay on his feet long enough for her to depart. Then he lay down on his bed and waited for the pounding in his head to stop.

Nobunaga.

How had he forgotten? That ship had been as much a part of his life for the last five years as *Defiant*. Even when he wasn't in Spacedock, overseeing her construction, he was on the subspace to Hess, or another of his subordinates, making sure things were done the right way. And they had been. The ship was a masterpiece. The ship was . . .

He frowned. He could remember virtually nothing to do with the ship since it had been constructed. The last he could recall of *Nobunaga* was months ago.

He went and got the guard. The guard went and got Phlox.

The doctor didn't even need to unpack his machines. "Memory loss is not surprising. Neural tissue is particularly sensitive toward delta radiation."

"Yeah. I know that." It was delta radiation, after all, that had scarred Jonathan Archer's mind, as it had scarred Tucker's face. "But this seems like a pretty specific set of memories being affected."

"Ah." Phlox smiled. "Memory. A fascinating phenomenon. Its acquisition, its retention . . . the mechanisms are still so poorly understood. How are specific memories grouped within the brain? How are they linked? Recalled? How—"

"I get the point."

"I am conducting experiments. Some show great promise. Perhaps you would like to participate?" Phlox's eyes glittered with pleasure. "The remunerative value is relatively small, but consider the legacy you would be leaving to—"

"No, thanks." Tucker knew a little too much about how Phlox conducted his laboratory ever to enter it voluntarily.

The doctor's eyes narrowed. "Of course, I will have to notify the Empress of this latest development, Commander."

"Of course you will."

"There can be no question of your returning to duty now. What other portions of your memory have been affected? Your knowledge of warp systems? Proper intermix procedures?" Phlox almost smiled. "It would be irresponsible to allow you anywhere near such valuable machines. You understand."

"Sure." Tucker managed a smile himself. *Ha-ha. Funny joke.* "I understand."

Phlox bowed and left the room.

Tucker stood there a moment, arms folded across his chest.

Dying was one thing, but to go out a drooling, raving mess, who couldn't even remember his own name—

He looked across the room at his image in the mirror. The image stared back.

It was as if it spoke to him.

You're going to die here, it said.

You're going to die all alone.

An overwhelming wave of despair washed over him.

No one would mourn his passing. No one would remember him when he was gone. No one, more than likely, would even come to say good-bye. And he would never be allowed to leave. Mixed up as it was, the knowledge in his head was too valuable to the Empire to risk losing it to . . .

He stared into the mirror, and an idea came to him.

An idea, he realized, that had been drifting around in his mind for a long time. Years, even. Twenty years. Ever since he and Jonathan Archer had first met.

The mirror.

The Tucker who could have been. The Tucker who was, in some alternate place, somewhere. The universe that was. Not an Empire but . . .

He shook his head. It was a stupid idea, all things considered. It was a dangerous idea.

But it was his only chance, he realized. To leave a legacy of some kind.

To live before he died.

He bided his time.

He ate the hospital food. He did his exercises. He contacted *Defiant* daily, spoke to those who had been his staff, when they could spare the time. Which was less and less often. He was irrelevant. Which was no more than he expected.

He read his journals, and in between, he read the news reports. They were unfailingly optimistic. Inevitably censored. The war was going well. The rebellion was doomed to fail. Same old story; for a while it had even been true. Those first few years following the Vulcans' about-face, their leaving the rebellion to ally themselves with the Empress, had been hard ones for the rebels. Their cause had seemed defeated.

And then came Archer.

And now the tide had turned again; reading between the lines of the news stories, he could sense it. The rebellion was growing, spreading. More systems, more races joining with the Tellarites, the Andorians, the Klingons . . .

Of course, there was nothing in the news reports about that. Or his old friend, for that matter. That was to be expected as well.

A week passed.

Mornings he spent dealing with the pain, the pounding in his skull, which came with renewed vigor. Days he spent reading and thinking. About the past and the present and the future. What had been, what could yet still be. He continued to dream at night and to work at the bed railing the Empress had snapped.

On the seventh day, he managed to break it at the other end. Ended up with a metal rod about a foot long, jagged edges. He hid it in the sleeve of his gown.

He went out into the hall.

"What?" the guard asked.

"I want out," he said. "I want to smell some fresh air."

The guard sneered and stepped closer. "Get back in there. Before I—"

Tucker drove the metal rod into his throat.

Blood gushed everywhere. The guard gagged and tried to pull the rod free. Tucker drove forward with his legs, slamming the guard up against the wall. The man gagged some more. Hospital white, on the walls, on Tucker's gown, blended with sticky red.

The guard reached for his communicator and then his weapon. Tucker slapped his hands away each time.

The man gagged one final time and went stiff.

Tucker let go of the rod; the body slumped to the floor. The guard's uniform was soaked with blood, stained. That wasn't part of the plan. The plan was to put on the big guy's uniform, walk out the front door. What was the plan now?

Improvise.

He stole the guard's weapon, stole the guard's money. He found a laundry room, the door half open, beckoning him inside. A spare medical uniform—pale green jumpsuit, white coat. A stairway that took him out to a lobby and out onto the street.

He recognized the skyline immediately. Kyoto. The Empire's capital, the Empress's home turf. No big surprise; Hoshi was keeping him close. He was surprised she hadn't chained him to the bed.

They'd be looking for him by now, have all the spaceports locked down. Have all the harbor facilities and rail stations watched. There was only one way out for him, one way to get off this planet, out of the Empress's clutches, live the last few weeks of his life in peace. Go to his grave knowing he'd done something to justify his forty-odd years of existence.

He made his way to the seediest part of town he could find and went into the seediest-looking bar. He sat on a stool and ordered a beer.

Time passed; the bar filled up.

He started conversations, started asking questions. Leading questions, questions designed to lead him to a particular kind of person. He got a few nibbles, no bites. He finished his first beer and nursed a second. He kept asking questions.

He decided the plan wasn't working; he needed to improvise again. He finished his beer and went out onto the street.

He sensed movement behind him and turned.

Everything went dark.

When he woke, he was in a small, windowless room. Two men were leaning over him.

One was hawk-nosed, unshaven, dark-haired; the other was squat, balding, sallow-eyed. Robin Hood and Friar Tuck.

"You've been asking a lot of questions," the thin one said. "Why?"

Tucker hesitated.

They could be spies; the Empress had scores. Or they could be exactly what he was looking for.

If he was wrong, he was screwed. Of course, if he was wrong, he was screwed anyway.

He took a deep breath. "My name's Tucker. Archer is a friend of mine."

The two men looked at each other.

"Archer who?" the thin one asked. "I don't know what you're talking about."

"I'm talking about the rebellion," Tucker said. "I want to join it."

They asked more questions. They left the room for a good five minutes. Only the fat man came back.

"My friend has gone to check out your story," he said, sitting. "If you're lying, you're a dead man."

"I'm not lying."

"We'll see, won't we?" he said, and that was the last either of them said for the next hour or so.

Finally, the thin man returned. Robin. He handed Tuck a sheet of paper.

The fat man read it, looked at Tucker, and nodded.

"We have to hurry," he said, standing.

They blindfolded him. They bound his arms behind his back. Shoved him into a surface vehicle. A bumpy road, a long ride— several hours. Tucker's bladder almost burst. Finally, a stop. Tucker heard noises around him, familiar noises. Machinery. A spaceport.

He was pulled from the vehicle. Marched up a ramp, down a curving corridor, into a room. A metal door slammed shut. The blindfold, and then the ropes, came off.

Tucker was looking at a stranger. A woman. In the blue dress from his dream, the one that T'Pol had worn, a lifetime ago.

The rebel uniform. The uniforms they'd found aboard *Defiant*.

Uniforms from a mirror universe, symbols not of Empire but Federation. The world that could be. Uniforms Archer had made his own.

"Commander Tucker," she said. "I'm Leandra. Welcome aboard."

He looked around the room. It was a metal box, six by six. No windows. A cot, a sink, a toilet.

"Aboard what?"

"The *Ulysses*. You're safe. In good hands."

"That's good to hear. We're going to see Archer?"

She smiled. "I'll be back soon. We can talk more then."

"All right." He smiled back. They weren't telling him. They still didn't trust him completely. He found that reassuringly familiar.

He lay down on his bed. The stress of the last few hours suddenly caught up with him.

He closed his eyes. He was too keyed up to sleep. Instead, he let his mind wander. To the past, recent and not so. Phlox, Robinson, T'Pol, Archer. The world as it had been before Hoshi became Empress. How she came to power, which had all started with Jonathan Archer and *Enterprise*.

Archer had been first officer; he'd picked up message traffic from Tholian space, images of a ship the Tholians had captured. An Earth ship but unlike any anyone had ever seen before. A ship from a mirror universe, a ship from a mirror future, *Defiant*. A starship somehow catapulted into the past, a starship so powerful it could render the entire Imperial fleet obsolescent. Archer had mutinied, led *Enterprise* and her crew into Tholian space to capture that ship, which eventually they accomplished. *Enterprise* had been destroyed, most of its crew killed in the process. Returning to Earth, a second mutiny, this one led by Hoshi with Mayweather's assistance, had resulted in her seizing control of first *Defiant* and then the Empire itself.

She used the ship—its weapons, its power—to cow those opposed to her into submission. The forces loyal to Cochrane, the forces intent on liberty. A relative calm descended on the quadrant. The calm before the storm.

Before the rebellion began growing in strength again. Before—

"I want you to build me a ship," the Empress had said. "A sister to *Defiant*."

Nobunaga.

Tucker's head pounded.

Nobunaga.

He blinked, and suddenly he was there. At the engineering console, on her bridge. Reed stood next to him; stood over him. Malcolm Reed, chief of the Imperial Guard. The most feared man in the Empire.

"Explain this to me again," he said.

"It's called a prefix code," Tucker said. "Think of it like a last line of defense, for the Empress. It enables her to take personal control of this vessel, anytime she likes. From anywhere within subspace range."

"And who else besides the Empress will know this code?"

"No one."

"That's not exactly true, is it?" Reed smiled. Not a pleasant smile. "You'll know it, won't you?" He leaned closer. His features morphed into T'Pol's. "Won't you?"

Her hands reached for his forehead.

Tucker screamed out loud and shot awake.

He was back in his bed, on *Ulysses*.

The door to his room was open. A man stood in the light from the hall.

He moved into the room; his features came into focus.

"Trip," he said. "You all right?"

Trip. No one had called him Trip in twenty years.

Tucker looked at the man.

The rebellion's new leader.

His old friend.

Jonathan Archer.

Hoshi killed him and took his command. Took *Defiant* and, with it, the Empire.

And then she changed her mind. She decided she needed Archer alive, needed his expertise, his skills, to further her goals. Phlox had done the medical work, the cloning. T'Pol had done the dirty work. Gone into Archer's mind, once the man was healthy enough, and conditioned him to obey the Empress's orders.

Phlox's work took; T'Pol's didn't.

Two years into his service to the Empire, Archer turned. Went over to the rebellion. Became the bane of the Empress's existence.

"Find him." Trip remembered her image on *Defiant*'s main viewscreen, spitting at Mayweather. Spitting at Robinson. "Catch him. Kill him."

Neither man had been able to do it. And now—

"A nightmare." Tucker swung his legs over onto the floor and stood. "Been having a lot of those lately."

"Haven't we all."

Archer looked thinner than Tucker remembered; his golden uniform shirt hung off his body. He had a full beard, shot through with gray. He had a long scar running across his temple, at the hairline, courtesy of Dr. Phlox's tender ministrations, no doubt.

The two men shook hands.

"It's good to see you again, Trip."

"You, too, sir."

"Even better to have you here. With us."

"I didn't want to die in Kyoto. I didn't want to die without doing something about the way things are."

"Good," Archer said. "You've come at a very opportune time."

"Oh?"

"We're in the middle of an operation. A plan that—if we can pull it off—will make things a lot harder for the Empress. For the Empire."

"I'll do what I can to help."

"I have the feeling you can do a lot."

"Really?"

The captain nodded. "Let's get you something to eat. Then we'll talk."

They went to the ship's mess—a second windowless room, half again as big as Tucker's quarters. Three tables, twelve chairs, dehydrated rations, purified, lukewarm water. Tucker wasn't hungry; his head was still pounding. Continuous, low-level pounding.

"You're not eating," Archer said.

"I'm getting my sea legs." Tucker forced a smile; Archer returned it.

They weren't alone in the mess; Robin, the thin man from the bar who'd brought him there, was at the next table, along with Leandra. They were talking. They were also watching him and Archer. Probably making sure he didn't harm the captain.

"So, you gonna tell me about this mysterious plan of yours?" Tucker asked. "What I can do to help?"

"Sure. It's a pretty simple one, actually."

"Simpler ones always work the best. Less to go wrong."

"My feelings exactly."

"Go on."

Archer smiled. *"Nobunaga."*

The pounding in Tucker's head grew louder.

The room around him blurred.

"He was a visionary."

That was Hoshi's voice. The Empress's voice.

He was no longer aboard *Ulysses.*

He stood in an observation lounge, looking on the skeleton of a huge starship.

Hoshi stood next to him.

"He brought muskets to the army. Western trade to the empire. He sought to open Japan to the world. To open the empire to a better future. What better name for our vessel? What better way to represent the future we desire?"

She placed a hand on his arm, smiled her dazzling smile. Tucker inhaled her scent.

"Trip?"

Tucker blinked.

He was back on *Ulysses.* Back in the mess hall.

Archer was standing. Leandra was standing, too, just behind him. Staring.

"You all right?" the captain asked.

"Fine."

"You went away there for a minute."

"Sorry. It's been a helluva couple days." He willed the memory— and the pain—away. "What about *Nobunaga*? What's your plan?"

The captain smiled.

"We're going to steal it."

Tucker let out a long, slow whistle. "Steal *Nobunaga*?"

"That's right."

"Steal a whole starship?"

Archer's smile grew broader.

"Simple, right?"

"That's a mighty tall order, Captain. The security at Beta Nairobi is tighter than a drum. Believe me, I know. You can't get within a parsec of that place without some sort of alarm going off. Not to mention the patrols they have."

"Beta Nairobi?" Archer shook his head. "Trip, they moved her from Beta Nairobi a long time ago. Don't you remember?"

Tucker frowned. "No," he said. "No, I don't remember that at all."

A drooling, raving mess.

Was it happening already?

"*Nobunaga* is at Vulcan now," Archer said. "Showing the flag. Cowing the locals."

"Wait a minute." Tucker shook his head. "The Empress—the Empire—Vulcan is an ally. Hell, half the army these days is Vulcan, they—"

"Propaganda. Believe me. Most of the people on Vulcan are very dissatisfied with the present state of affairs. A lot of them have been helping us—directly, indirectly. You'd be surprised at who."

Tucker waved a hand. "I don't doubt it. But still . . . getting to Vulcan isn't going to be easy either."

The captain smiled again. "Like I said . . . we have a plan."

Tucker frowned. "Yeah. I heard. Only . . ."

Steal *Nobunaga.*

His head began to pound.

The room wavered.

He was back in his quarters. On *Defiant.*

The message light was blinking.

"You can't let it happen, Trip," Archer said. "You can't let her have that much power."

"Delcte," he said. "Delete, delete, delete."

But the message kept playing.

"Remember Bozeman?" Archer said. "Everything we talked about? Everything the space program stood for, once upon a time?"

"Delete!" Tucker screamed.

"How many digits is it?" Reed asked, and now he was someplace else, Tucker realized. The agonizer. Reed's home-built torture chamber.

"How many digits?" Reed asked again. "Surcly, if you simply give me that number, it's not the same as telling me outright. No one could blame you for just giving me a clue . . ."

Tucker shook his head.

Reed smiled, showing all his teeth. He pressed a button.

Tucker opened his mouth to scream.

T'Pol put a finger to his lips.

"Shhh," she said, but her lips didn't move. "Be strong."

She was wearing the dress she had taken from the *Defiant*'s stores, the blue one, the one that let her long legs show, that left the curve of her neck bare. Her long hair brushed against his face.

He leaned forward to kiss her . . .

Restraints held him back.

He was in a hospital bed. Bound hand and foot. Dim lighting in the room, a small room, no windows, a door at the foot of his bed, ventilators humming . . .

He was back in Kyoto.

The same hospital room he'd escaped from earlier.

"No," he said, starting to shiver. "Oh, no."

The door opened. Phlox entered, pushing a cart before him. A cart with all sorts of gleaming metal instruments on top of it. Sharp edges, shiny surfaces . . .

The doctor rubbed his hands together. "Shall we get started?" he asked.

Tucker blinked.

He was back on *Ulysses*. Not in the mess but in the room he'd first been taken to. His bedroom.

Archer leaned over him. The captain held Phlox's data chip in his hand.

"How long has this been going on?" Archer asked.

"Since the accident. However long that's been." Tucker sighed and shook his head. "It's getting worse."

"When were you going to tell me?"

"When I had to."

"When you had to." Archer cursed. "Come on, Trip. How long have we known each other? Why didn't—"

."Because what's the point? There's nothing you can do. There's nothing anyone can do."

The captain went to one of the walls, leaned against it. He was silent for a moment.

"I want to help," Tucker said. "That's why I didn't tell you. I was afraid that if I wasn't a hundred percent, you wouldn't—"

The comm sounded.

"Bridge to Captain Archer."

The voice came from a comm unit on the wall; Archer crossed to it and pressed a button.

"Archer here."

"Our visitors, sir. They've arrived."

"Good. I'll be right there. Tell them to . . ." He looked at Tucker. "No. On second thought, send them down here. Commander Tucker's quarters."

"Aye, Captain. Commander Tucker's quarters."

"Good. Archer out."

The captain closed the channel.

"Visitors?" Tucker asked.

"That's right. Allies. People who are going to help make this possible."

"Stealing the ship."

"That's right."

"So—you going to tell me what the plan is?"

"I'll wait. Till they come. Part of the plan is theirs. They should get the chance to explain it."

"I'm all ears," Tucker said.

Archer laughed.

"What's so funny?"

"You'll see."

A minute later, he did. The visitors walked into his cabin.

They were Vulcans. The first two were male, one older, one younger.

The third was T'Pol.

Tucker was utterly flummoxed.

He got to his feet. He looked from T'Pol to Archer, and back again, and shook his head.

"No. She's—" He pointed at T'Pol and looked at Archer once more. "She's the Regent, for God's sake. She runs the government, more than Hoshi does. She's the one who—"

"You're wrong, Trip." Archer stepped up next to him. "She's one of us. On the side of the angels."

Tucker shook his head. He wanted to believe, but . . .

He looked at T'Pol.

She looked exactly as she had in his dream. The blue dress. The long hair, the eyes—

"Commander," she said. "It is agreeable to see you again."

"Is it true? You're with the rebels, you're not—"

"I am allied with the rebellion," she said. "But I do also run the government. The two are not mutually exclusive propositions."

Archer smiled. Everyone smiled. Tucker smiled, too.

"That is the best news I've heard in years," he said.

"Many happy reunions," Archer said. "For all of us. But if we want to get that ship, we ought to talk it through now, people. So, if you all don't mind following me . . ."

Tucker's room was too small to meet in; Archer took them down the corridor, heading for the mess. He watched T'Pol, a step in front of him. The Regent, a rebel. It all made sense now; no wonder the rebellion always seemed to be a step ahead of the Empire. No wonder *Defiant* could never find, much less catch, *Enterprise*. T'Pol, one of them.

She turned at the doorway to the mess. Her hair turned with her. Her long hair, cascading down her back. How had it gotten so long so quickly? The last time he had seen her—

He frowned. He couldn't remember the last time he'd seen her.

"Is something the matter?" she asked. "Are you all right?"

"Fine," he said. "I'm fine."

They entered the mess. The tables had all been pushed together, the chairs arranged in a rough horseshoe shape around them. Everyone sat, everyone except Archer, who stood in front of a viewscreen, three feet square, that hung on one wall of the room. A star chart was projected on it, a map of the space in Vulcan's immediate orbit. The moons, the space stations, the orbiting weapons platforms.

Nobunaga.

"This is how we're going to do it," the captain said.

Tucker listened as Archer outlined his plan.

A manufactured emergency on one of Vulcan's moons that would siphon off security personnel. An automated maintenance shuttle sent shortly thereafter to resupply *Nobunaga*'s food synthesizers, a shuttle that would contain not raw foodstuffs but live people.

A Trojan horse kind of thing. Everyone discussed the details; as they talked, Tucker saw a flaw in the plan.

"They'll have shields up," he said. "*Nobunaga*. It's standard operating procedure on all Imperial ships. You sure they'll lower them for your shuttle?"

"They have in the past," Archer said.

Tucker shook his head. He still didn't like it.

His uncertainty must have shown.

"You have a better idea?" Archer asked. "Another way to get those shields down?"

His head began to ache. He tried to fight past it.

Another way to get those shields down.

There was something there . . . something in the back of his mind . . .

"Any thoughts?" T'Pol asked. "Commander?"

She looked at him. Everyone was looking at him.

Nobunaga.

Nobunaga.

His heart hammered in his chest. His head was pounding.

"Lower their shields," he said.

Archer nodded. "Yes. That's the point."

He blinked.

Everyone was still staring at him.

"I don't know," he managed. "I guess that'll have to work. The maintenance shuttle. I can't think of anything else."

Which was the truth. His head was pounding so hard he could barely think of anything at all.

The meeting broke up. T'Pol left with the other Vulcans. Tucker managed a quick good-bye but no more. All of the things that had been in his head so long, the things he wanted to say to her, they were suddenly gone. All he wanted to do was go lie down, stop the pain.

He found himself back in his quarters, without even knowing how he'd gotten there.

Leandra leaned over him. She smiled. "You should rest," she said.

She smelled nice. A familiar smell. He couldn't place it.

He looked over her shoulder, at the mirror on the wall, and

realized the whole time he'd been on this ship, he had yet to see the stars. Had yet to see anything other than this tiny room and the bigger one down the hall.

"How long till we reach Vulcan?" he asked.

"Soon enough."

"You'll wake me. I want to be there. I want to help."

"Of course. I'll wake you." She smiled again.

Tucker closed his eyes.

Images flashed through his mind. The hospital room and Phlox leaning over him. Reed and his agonizer. The Empress.

"You are a gentle lover, Commander."

He was in her bedchamber. In the palace in Kyoto.

She propped herself up on one elbow. "Tell me again, what you were saying before . . ."

"They built it into all their ships," he said. "I found a reference in *Defiant*'s computer banks."

The Empress's eyes flashed. The Federation—the mirror universe—these were dangerous topics of conversation. She'd wiped *Defiant*'s computers clean long ago, had only made the old records accessible to Tucker and his staff recently, for them to refer to during *Nobunaga*'s construction.

He hurried on with his explanation. "It lets one ship's computer take control of multiple vessels. So you can have split-second battlefield coordination—attack runs, that sort of thing. We build it into *Nobunaga;* it would enable you always to have ultimate control of the vessel."

Her eyes flashed again, this time with pleasure. "I begin to see your point, Commander."

"Of course, it only works over relatively short distances. But still—"

"Still." She smiled. He felt as if he could read her mind, for a second.

What happened long ago with Archer, and *Enterprise,* would never happen again.

"You are a gentle lover, Commander."

He smiled. "You said that already."

"*I, however . . .*"

She raised herself above him. Straddled him.

He couldn't move.

He was in the hospital again, in Kyoto. Strapped to his bed.

The door opened. Phlox entered with his cart.

He looked up and shook his head.

"She's not happy with you," the doctor said. "The Empress. Not happy at all."

Phlox came closer; metal gleamed. He flipped switches; electricity sparked.

An alarm sounded. All quarters.

Tucker sat up in his bed. In his room, on *Ulysses*.

The door opened.

A figure stood in the light from the hall. A woman. She moved into the room; her features came into focus.

T'Pol.

"Come with me," she said. "Hurry."

"What's going on?" Tucker sat up, still disoriented.

"Hurry," she said again.

She took him by the hand, pulled him out of his quarters, down the corridor into the mess.

The two older Vulcans were there. So were Robin and Tuck from the bar, back in Kyoto. They had all been staring at the viewscreen.

They all turned to stare at him now.

"Your concern was justified, Commander," Leandra said. "*Nobunaga* is not lowering her shields."

Tucker sat, trying to get his bearings. "So, what do we do?"

The hawk-nosed man—Robin—stepped forward.

"Whatever we decide, we have to do it quickly. They're sending over a boarding party, to check out the ship. To make sure it's safe."

"If they board that shuttle, they'll find the captain. And the others. They'll kill them," Leandra said. "T'Pol will die."

Tucker frowned. "But—" He looked over at T'Pol. "T'Pol's here."

"Of course." Leandra smiled. "I misspoke."

There was silence.

"So, what do we do?" Tucker asked again.

Leandra stepped forward. "I have an idea," she said. "What about the prefix code?"

Tucker blinked.

The prefix code.

"Right," he said. "I don't know why I didn't think of that before."

"It doesn't really matter, does it?" Leandra smiled. "The point is, with the code, we can lower the shields ourselves. We can take over the whole ship."

"That's right." Tucker nodded. That's how it worked—the prefix code. He'd programmed it into *Nobunaga* at the Empress's command. So that she would have ultimate control of the vessel, in case . . .

He frowned.

"Tell it to me, quickly," Leandra said. "They're on the way."

"They're almost there." The older Vulcan stood next to the viewscreen and pointed at it. "See?"

Tucker followed the man's arm, looked where he was pointing.

For a second, the wall itself seemed to waver. Instead of the viewscreen, he saw —he thought he saw—a mirror.

And then the star chart appeared and gave him a view of the tactical situation. The shuttle and the starship. *Nobunaga.*

Nobunaga.

The message light was blinking.

"I hear you're building a ship," the captain said. "As powerful as *Defiant.*"

"How did you hear that?"

"You can't do it, Trip. You can't let her have that much power."

"So what am I supposed to do?"

"The right thing," Archer said.

"Destroy it?"

"Unless you have a better idea."

Tucker frowned.

No, he was about to say.

And then he remembered.

The code.

"Tell it to me." Leandra gritted her teeth. "So we can transmit it."

She was on the verge of losing her temper, Tucker saw. He should tell her the code. There was no reason not to tell her the code.

Was there?

He looked up at the viewscreen and frowned.

"Why aren't we on the bridge?"

Leandra walked around in front of him, put both her hands on his shoulders, leaned into his face.

"What does it matter where we are? We can transmit from anywhere. Now tell me the code! Before it's too late."

"We were fired on." The hawk-nosed man stepped forward. "Some structural damage. That's why the all-quarters alarm."

"Ah." Tucker nodded. That made sense.

"Access to the bridge is temporarily blocked," the man continued.

"So tell me." Leandra's eyes blazed fire. "The prefix code."

He inhaled her scent. It was so familiar . . .

His head began to pound. Harder than ever before.

He looked up at her again, and something stirred at the back of his mind.

The truth.

"No," he said. "Oh God no."

The room around him began to waver.

The hawk-nosed man cursed.

"Look at him," he said. "Look at his eyes. He's coming out of it."

The fat man nodded. "Without a doubt."

"The code!" Leandra screamed. "Tell me the code!"

Her hands were still on his shoulders; she shook him. Tucker felt something snap.

The pain there, though, was nothing compared to the pain in his head. The pounding in his skull.

He screamed too then.

His head felt like it was going to explode.

T'Pol stepped forward. "Let me," she said, and put her hands on his forehead.

The pain stopped.

She looked him in the eye.

And then her voice was in his head.

Courage. Be strong.

She stepped back, which was when Trip became aware that everything around him had changed.

He was no longer aboard *Ulysses*. He was in his hospital room, at Kyoto.

He had never left.

The hawk-nosed man was Reed.

The fat man, Phlox.

And Leandra . . .

"What did you do?" the Empress demanded, glaring at T'Pol.

"His mind was breaking down. The image projectors, the consistent mental intrusions. I feared we would lose him entirely."

"I don't care about him!" Hoshi screamed. "I want my ship. Where is my ship?"

Tucker watched her rant and barely—just barely—kept himself from smiling.

He remembered everything now.

Building *Nobunaga,* embedding the prefix code. Chasing the rebels. Archer's message. Changing sides. Giving the captain the key to the Empress's brand-spanking-new starship. Giving the rebels a weapon that, at last, could match *Defiant.*

Being captured. Being tortured. Physically, first, and then—

"Rip it out of his mind," the Empress said. "Get me that code. Now."

T'Pol nodded. "I will do as you wish, of course. However, if we cause permanent damage—"

The Empress let out a scream of frustration and left the room.

Reed started to follow, then stopped at the door. He looked at Phlox first and then at T'Pol.

"Let's do it again, shall we? Until we get it right?"

T'Pol and Phlox nodded.

Tucker felt his stomach turn over.

Again? How many times—

He tried to catch T'Pol's eye. She wouldn't look at him.

"Progress reports every hour," Reed said.

"Every hour." Phlox nodded. "You're saying we shouldn't sleep?"

Reed glared at him and left the room.

The doctor shook his head. "No sense of humor, that man." He walked to the far corner and pulled his cart forward. He looked up at T'Pol.

"Do you want to go first, or shall I?"

"You," T'Pol said. "I have had quite enough for the moment."

"Really?" Phlox smiled again. "Not going soft on us, are you?"

She reached up and pulled off her wig.

"Of course not," she said.

Her face was blank, expressionless, emotionless.

Courage. Be strong.

Oh God, Tucker thought. Had he imagined that, too?

Phlox stepped forward. His eyes glittered.

Metal gleamed.

"Memory," he said. "Such an interesting phenomenon. Don't you agree?"

Tucker closed his eyes and braced himself.

Ill Winds

Dayton Ward & Kevin Dilmore

HISTORIAN'S NOTE: *"Ill Winds" takes place after
2245 (ACE) and before Captain Christopher Pike takes command
of the Terran Empire Starship Enterprise in 2251 (Star Trek).*

Dayton Ward is a software developer, having become a slave to Corporate America after spending eleven years in the U.S. Marine Corps. When asked, he'll tell you that he joined the military soon after high school because he'd grown tired of people telling him what to do all the time. If you get the chance, be sure to ask him how well that worked out. In addition to the numerous credits he shares with friend and co-writer Kevin Dilmore, he is the author of the *Star Trek* novel *In the Name of Honor* and the science fiction novels *The Last World War* and *The Genesis Protocol,* as well as short stories that have appeared in the first three *Star Trek: Strange New Worlds* anthologies, the Yard Dog Press collection *Houston, We've Got Bubbas,* DownInTheCellar.com, *Kansas City Voices* magazine, and the *Star Trek: New Frontier* anthology *No Limits.* Though he currently lives in Kansas City with his wife and daughters, Dayton is a Florida native and still maintains a torrid long-distance romance with his beloved Tampa Bay Buccaneers. Visit him on the web at www.daytonward.com.

Kevin Dilmore for more than eight years was a contributing writer to *Star Trek Communicator,* penning news stories and personality profiles for the bimonthly publication of the Official *Star Trek* Fan Club. On the storytelling side of things, his story "The Road to Edos" was published as part of the *Star Trek: New Frontier* anthology *No Limits.* With Dayton Ward, his work includes stories for the anthology *Star Trek: Tales of the Dominion War,* the *Star Trek: The Next Generation* novels *A Time to Sow* and *A Time to Harvest,* the *Star Trek: Vanguard* novel *Summon the Thunder,* the *Star Trek: Enterprise* novel *Age of the Empress,* and ten installments of the original e-book series *Star Trek: S.C.E.* and *Star Trek: Corps of Engineers.* A graduate of the University of Kansas, Kevin works as a senior writer for Hallmark Cards in Kansas City, Missouri.

Captain Nathan Thorpe stood at rigid attention in the center of his own quarters aboard the *I.S.S. Indomitable,* fighting the urge to vomit.

Bile rose in his throat, and he swallowed, forcing it down for the moment. Feeling a line of sweat trickling down the left side of his face, Thorpe dared not reach up to wipe it away. Despite the lack of personal guards to stop him, the idea of attempting to draw the phaser or dagger on his belt seemed ludicrous. While the reputations and martial prowess of many high-ranking Starfleet officers were fraught with exaggeration—if not outright lies—Thorpe knew from firsthand observation that such was not the case with the officer now standing before him, a man whose very name evoked fear throughout the Terran Empire's Starfleet.

Commodore Robert April.

The commodore was an imposing man with thinning brown hair swept back from his face. His physique was trim and athletic, with lean yet still-muscled arms extending from his sleeveless gold tunic. In one hand, he carried the data slate Thorpe had given him upon his arrival, which contained updated reports on the damage *Indomitable* had suffered during its recent encounter with Klingon warships, as well as the current status of the crew's repair efforts.

"Your crew is to be commended, Captain," April said, standing before the teak curio cabinet Thorpe had placed near the bed in the far corner of his quarters' sleeping area. "The progress they've made in such a short time is noteworthy."

"Thank you, Commodore," Thorpe replied, feeling his throat tighten.

Without looking away from the cabinet, April added, "Of course, none of that effort likely would've been necessary if you'd made wiser decisions." He said nothing more for several moments, engrossed in the collection of books, photographs, and other keepsakes arrayed atop the curio's six shelves—mementos Thorpe had accumulated during his Starfleet career. April seemed particularly interested in the pictures of Thorpe's wife and family.

"You're a widower, Captain," the commodore said after what to Thorpe felt like an eternity. "Is that correct?"

Swallowing again, Thorpe replied, "Yes, sir. My wife and children died some years ago in a shuttle accident." Of course, he knew precisely when they had been killed, just as he remembered the exact date and time he had been informed of their deaths.

"A tragedy, to be sure," April said, turning from the cabinet to face him, and Thorpe felt the commodore's cobalt-blue eyes boring into him. "And you've never wavered in your service to the Empire." He began pacing the quarters' narrow confines. "Your record shows you to be an exceptional officer, with almost limitless potential." Pausing before the sheathed Japanese katana sword mounted on the wall over Thorpe's desk, he reached up and ran a finger along its length before looking over his shoulder. "A gift from the Empress Sato herself, yes?"

Again, Thorpe nodded. "Yes, Commodore." While serving years ago as part of Sato II's personal security detail, he had single-handedly thwarted an assassination attempt by one of her senior military advisers, killing the duplicitous admiral and sustaining severe injuries in the process. In addition to the sword, the Empress had awarded him accelerated promotion and an eventual fast-tracking to starship command.

None of that seemed to matter at the moment.

April turned from the sword. "Your loyalty is irrefutable, Captain, which is why it saddens me to be here today." As he stepped closer, the commodore's expression changed for the first time since entering the room. Now his chiseled features darkened as he frowned. "I trust you know why *Constellation* and I were sent?"

Here it comes.

Thorpe replied, "I failed in my mission to learn about the new weapon being developed by the Klingons." There was no sense trying to deflect blame or mitigate the circumstances surrounding the bungled assignment. His only chance here was open honesty and candid acceptance of responsibility for his actions.

Pursing his lips, April shook his head. "It's not merely that, or that your clumsy efforts resulted in the destruction of one starship along with heavy damage to your own. More important, the Klingons now know we're aware of their activities."

Though he stood absolutely still before the commodore, inwardly Thorpe flinched. The Klingons had caught on to the covert surveillance being conducted by *Indomitable* and her companion ship, the *I.S.S. Thermopylae,* launching an ambush attack on both vessels before either starship could bring weapons or defenses to bear. *Thermopylae*'s warp core had breached within the first moments of the assault, the resulting matter/antimatter explosion consuming the ship as well as one of the Klingon cruisers. Thorpe had guided *Indomitable* and her crew through the battle well enough to make an escape, but not before the vessel sustained considerable damage and more than one hundred casualties.

That alone would justify my execution.

"Even as we speak," April continued, "that pack of rabid animals is at this very moment collecting their research and materials and burrowing into a hole to hide. We'll have to track the Klingons again, only now we've lost the element of surprise. By the time we find them, they may well have developed a working model of this new weapon." He stepped closer, until mere centimeters separated their faces. His hard blue eyes peered into Thorpe's own as if trying to pierce his very soul, even as his voice maintained its even tenor. "Your failure may well end up costing countless lives, Captain."

It required physical effort on Thorpe's part to keep his knees from buckling.

Just when it seemed that April would continue to lean in so that Thorpe might have to move to avoid physical contact, the commodore abruptly stepped away, making a show of examining his fingernails before crossing the room and returning his attention to the curio cabinet. "The Admiralty only dispatches me for particular types of missions, Captain—those that prove beyond the capability of other commanders."

Thorpe nodded. Despite the commodore's composed demeanor, he had acquired a reputation for ruthlessness when the situation called for it, particularly when addressing failure. Among his peers and within the ranks of Starfleet, Robert April had come to be known as "the Quiet Tyrant."

Drawing a deep breath, April sighed. "Like you, I am a loyal servant of the Empire. Though my orders afford me wide latitude, there still are some things that are beyond my control. For that, Captain Thorpe, I truly apologize."

Behind him, Thorpe heard the sound of his door sliding open and someone entering the room. Remaining at attention, he waited until the new arrival walked into his line of sight. Her lean figure reminded Thorpe of a dancer, the provocative cut of her blue uniform skirt and matching top accentuating her long legs, toned arms, and flat stomach. She was armed with a dagger in her left boot and a phaser attached to the wide gold sash wrapped around her waist. Her brown hair was short yet still had a feminine style, with one long lock drooping down to cover her right eye.

"I'd like you to meet my trusted personal assistant, Captain," April said, "as well as my wife, Dr. Sarah April." Of her, he asked, "I trust everything is in order, my dear?"

The woman said nothing for a moment, choosing instead to study Thorpe from head to toe, her gaze seeming to alternate between clinical detachment and wanton lust. Thorpe felt a new rush of discomfort as she finally nodded toward her husband. "Repairs continue on schedule. *Indomitable*'s first officer is an efficient taskmaster." As she spoke, she walked around Thorpe until she passed beyond his peripheral vision. Then he felt a gentle hand on his neck, the doctor's long, slender fingers playing across his skin. "I think she'll do just fine, at least until our mission is complete."

The commodore nodded. "Very well."

Instinct commanded Thorpe to move, guided his right hand to the phaser at his belt. April stood still, hands behind his back and not even flinching as Thorpe brandished the weapon.

The movement was halted as a staggering jolt of energy coursed through his neck, radiating outward to consume his entire body. His muscles contracting, every nerve ending was aflame, and his sharp cry of pain echoed within the cramped room. He was powerless to move, to defend himself or even to push away the source of his torment. The pain stopped as abruptly as it had begun, and Thorpe fell to his knees, the phaser dropping from his hand.

He reached for his neck an instant before a booted foot slammed into his rib cage, forcing him to the floor, upon which he rolled onto his back. Looking up, he saw Sarah April standing over him. In her right hand was an object that he did not recognize. Behind her, the commodore observed the proceedings with cold dispassion.

"I want to thank you for volunteering to help me test this, Captain," she said, holding up the object for him to see. "I've been working on it for months. It stimulates nerve clusters in the body, transmitting signals that translate to varying levels of pain, so far without causing permanent damage. You have the honor of being my first human subject." With that, she offered a seductive smile.

The hum of the agony-inducing device was the last thing Thorpe heard.

"Congratulations on your promotion, Captain."

Erin Stone had not even blinked upon entering Thorpe's quarters and seeing the body of her commanding officer lying on the floor, leading Robert April to wonder if *Indomitable*'s first officer might have been expecting this turn of events. Perhaps she had been waiting for the opportune moment to enact a similar ploy of her own. Maybe she was not easily affected by death, or it could be that she simply possessed a formidable poker face. She did not even pause to clear her throat before replying.

"Thank you, Commodore. I won't let you down." Stone was a striking woman, April decided, slender yet toned like a swimmer or gymnast. Her dark skin contrasted nicely with her gold uniform skirt and tunic—which he noted was not quite so revealing as the design usually favored by young female officers hoping to catch the eye of a superior. She wore her straight black hair short in a style that exposed the nape of her neck while a few locks drooped across her forehead. Wide, expressive brown eyes offered no hint of emotion as she regarded him.

April smiled from where he sat at the desk, one hand resting near the desktop computer terminal. "Rest assured, Captain, that any disappointment I feel will last only a short while." To emphasize his point, he gestured with his free hand toward Thorpe's body.

"Understood, sir." Stone then reached for the phaser on her left hip, drawing the weapon and aiming it at the remains of her former commanding officer. The confined room echoed with the phaser blast as the orange beam enveloped the corpse, dissolving it in the space of a few heartbeats. Apparently satisfied with her work, Stone nodded as she returned the weapon to her hip. "Will there be anything else, Commodore?"

April shook his head. "I need this room for a time, but rest assured I will be out of your way in short order," he said without an iota of sarcasm. To occupy the sanctuary of *Indomitable*'s captain— which, by all rights, now belonged to Erin Stone—was a decision made of efficiency. He possessed the codes and protocols necessary to gain access to Thorpe's personal log and mission orders, but such action still required interfacing with the quarters' secure computer terminal, which operated independently of the network of similar interfaces throughout the ship and was inaccessible via outside means.

"At your leisure, sir," Stone replied before offering the traditional imperial military salute—tapping her right fist to her chest before extending her arm and hand ahead of her. After April returned the salute, she pivoted on her heel and headed for the cabin's lone door. The portal opened, and she was almost into the hallway before the commodore stopped her.

"Captain?"

"Yes, sir?" she asked, her expression quizzical.

With a wry grin, he replied, "You're out of uniform."

For the first time, Stone smiled. "I'll correct that immediately, Commodore. Thank you again." With that, she was gone, the door sliding closed behind her.

"I'll just bet you *want* her out of uniform," a voice said from the room's sleeping area, beyond the divider screen. Rising from his chair, April moved to see his wife, Sarah, lounging on the bed. Her head propped on a pair of pillows and with her legs crossed at the ankles, Dr. April had drawn her dagger and was using it to pick something from beneath the nail of the ring finger on her left hand.

Leaning against the low cabinets to the right of the bed, April folded his arms across his chest. "I still might, once all of this is behind us."

"You know my rule," his wife replied, holding up the dagger and pointing it at him for emphasis. "You can't have her if I know about her. Otherwise, I'll be forced to kill her."

April chuckled. "Maybe you want to keep her for yourself?"

"I've got my eye on that bodyguard of Thorpe's." Rising from the bed, she returned her blade to the scabbard in her left boot, the top of which came to the midpoint of her thigh.

"Well, then, perhaps I can persuade you to make an exception, but now's not the time." Moving back into the front room, he reclaimed his seat behind the desk and swiveled the computer display to face him once more. "Computer, access captain's personal log and current mission orders, voice-print override authority April Zeta Five."

"*Working,*" replied the mechanical male voice of *Indomitable*'s main computer. Under ordinary circumstances, the personal logs of a starship's commanding officer, as well as anything else they might protect under their own voice-print lockout, were sacrosanct information, requiring special authorization from the Admiralty or even the Empress herself for others to gain access. Fortunately, April was one of a trusted few officers within Starfleet who held such sanction.

"What do you know about the Penemu?" he asked after a moment of perusing Thorpe's mission orders.

Sarah shook her head. "Not much. Their planet was subjugated by the Klingons eight or nine years ago."

"Right," the commodore replied. Given his position and security clearance, he knew a great deal more than his wife on this and many other topics. "According to the communiqués Starfleet's intercepted, the Penemu are rather advanced, technologically speaking. Energy generation and distribution, propulsion, medical and other science applications—they apparently are quite a remarkable people." He shook his head. "A pity the Klingons got to them before we did."

"And now they're being forced to build this new weapon for the Klingons, whatever it is." As she leaned closer, April's wife frowned while reading the data displayed on the computer monitor. "Some sort of missile? For ship-to-ship combat?"

April grunted. "If only it were that simple. These missiles are designed to carry warheads containing chemical compounds that, when detonated within the atmosphere of a Class M planet, initiate a fusion reaction that literally burns away oxygen and other gases to create a massive global fireball."

Neither April said anything for a moment, the only sound in the captain's quarters being the faint, omnipresent thrum of *Indomitable*'s massive warp engines. Despite himself, the commodore paused as he pondered the mental image of a world cast aflame as a result of such an attack.

"Dear Lord," Sarah finally said, her voice barely a whisper. "If those savages build an arsenal of those things, the Empire could be doomed."

April nodded, knowing that the Empire's position of power in the galaxy was not as absolute as the propaganda broadcasts might lead citizens to believe. It was true that the Imperial Starfleet was unmatched and had been so for more than a century, thanks to the mysterious and timely acquisition of the *U.S.S. Defiant,* the starship from the future and the so-called "alternate universe."

Regardless of its origin, there had been no denying the vessel's tactical superiority, which Sato I had commandeered and used to solidify her ascent to power. Later, she would use the advanced ship to put down the rebellion plaguing the Empire at that time and ensuring its supremacy for decades to come. That accomplished, Sato had assembled a team of experts to study the *Defiant* so that its technology could be replicated, giving rise to a fleet of warships whose supremacy in the quadrant remained unquestioned.

However, as far as April was concerned, the Empire had rested on its laurels in recent years rather than continuing to press its advantage, while the Klingons, as well as other races that had refused Imperial rule, had been marshaling their resources and closing the technological gap. There was no way to be sure when the Empire might face all-out war with adversaries on multiple fronts, but April was certain that day was coming.

And with a weapon such as that created by the Penemu, that day may be sooner than anyone thinks.

April used the controls on the front of the computer workstation to page through the most recent entries of Captain Thorpe's personal log. "According to this, Thorpe followed Klingon vessels to the Donatu system and observed the detonation of a prototype missile on the system's fifth planet. *Indomitable*'s sensors recorded most of the atmosphere being torn away, though it did not ignite as originally intended."

"So, it performed below expectations?" Sarah frowned. "Still enough to decimate a planet's population, though. What do we do?"

"Our orders are to capture the weapon, along with all available data and materials."

He felt Sarah's fingers tracing a path along his bare arm.

"Imagine such weapons at our disposal. There would be no questioning the Empire's rule throughout the known galaxy." When he did not answer, she leaned closer, whispering into his ear, "Better yet, imagine the power you could command with those weapons under your *personal* control."

Seeing the lusty smile on Sarah's face, April smiled back, if for nothing else than to temporarily sate her desire to know what he was thinking. While the prospect of acquiring the Penemu technology for his own purposes was tempting, April knew he would not be alone in recognizing what it could offer toward shaping history from this point forward.

"For now," he said, "we'll follow our orders and learn everything we can about this weapon, but we certainly won't squander any other opportunities that may present themselves."

Though her smile remained fixed, April noted a slight yet familiar narrowing of her eyes, as though she remained unconvinced. "I trust that we won't."

No sooner did *Constellation* enter the Donatu system than April knew something was wrong.

"Commodore," said Commander Lorna Simon from the science station, without turning from the hooded viewer that was the console's prominent feature. Pale blue light played across her face and caused her salt-and-pepper hair to appear even grayer beyond her nearly seventy years. "Your information specified the *fifth* planet as our destination?"

"That's right," April replied. "Why?"

Turning from the viewer, Simon settled into her chair. "According to our star charts, Donatu V is Class M, but my sensors say otherwise." She eyed him with a withering gaze. "Bob, what the hell kind of weapon do the Klingons have?"

For a moment, April smiled at the slip in protocol. Easily the oldest officer on his staff, Simon also was one of the few people who could get away with addressing him in such an informal manner. She had long ago earned such latitude and was one of his most trusted confidants.

"That's what we're here to find out," he said, seeing the genuine concern in Simon's eyes. Though she and the rest of the crew were aware that they had been ordered to investigate a possible new Klingon weapon, they did not yet know specifics. Therefore, he knew that their sense of shock would only increase in the coming minutes. "Maintain sensor sweeps, Commander."

He said nothing more as the *Constellation* continued its approach, a sense of dread beginning to take hold of him as the starship entered orbit. The planet now dominated the bridge's main viewer, its distinct lack of cloud cover, swirling gases, or any discernible contrast within its atmosphere making it appear barren. Nothing in Thorpe's logs had prepared him for the sight of the bleak, dying world now displayed on the screen before him.

Simon's voice broke the silence hanging over the bridge. "The planet's atmosphere is being deconstructed at a molecular level, Commodore. Oxygen levels are at seventeen percent of normal for a Class M planet and declining, while levels of ammonia, argon, and sulfur are on the rise. What vegetation hasn't been scrubbed away by wind and rain is being baked by unfiltered solar radiation." April glanced toward her as she stepped away from her console and looked to him. "I'm also picking up traces of other chemical compounds that I don't recognize. Whatever the Klingons have, it pretty much set fire to the atmosphere. And you're telling me this was a *failed* experiment?"

"Partially successful experiment, Commander," April countered, offering the dry rebuttal before returning his attention to the viewscreen. The stark, ruddy pallor of the planet's defoliated landmasses matched that of a fresh bruise, and he likened the sight before him to a hapless living being, one beaten and bleeding and left for dead. He imagined he could hear the mortally wounded world attempting to cry for help yet silenced by the unmatched agony inflicted upon it, its suffering made all the worse by why it had happened.

From a purely tactical viewpoint, the results were staggering. Wars, the fates of entire civilizations, the history of the very galaxy, might well be decided in seconds if a key imperial world were targeted with just one weapon such as that unleashed upon Donatu V. This planet had been subjected to its fate at the whim of those hungry for power much greater than they ever should be allowed to control.

Does that apply to the Empire as well?

"Any signs of life?" April asked, pushing away the unwelcome questions.

Pausing to consult her sensor readings, Simon replied, "Here and there. Pockets of survivors in many of the major cities. Most of them are underground, probably inside survival shelters or other subterranean structures. Based on the population figures I could dig out of the computer, I'd estimate less than three percent survived whatever the hell happened, and they won't be lasting much longer, either."

April said nothing at first, before realizing that most of the bridge crew had turned from their stations to look at him. He noted their varying expressions of puzzlement and uncertainty, perhaps not so much because of what had happened to Donatu V but rather his own obvious reaction to it. Did they sense his unease at what they had found here? Though he never had wavered in carrying out his duty to the Empire, he also had prided himself on avoiding the use of violence for its own sake in order to do so. He had conducted himself with integrity in that regard, well above most other starship commanders and Starfleet officers, including, admittedly, his own wife. Still, that he might be perceived as weakening in the face of what they now were witnessing, particularly when it involved a relatively insignificant alien species, did not sit well with him.

"The Klingons have a weapon that's responsible for this," he said, his voice loud and forceful enough to echo across the bridge. "What you're seeing doesn't even represent this new weapon's full potential." He waved toward the viewer. "Forget this irrelevant ball of baked mud and the parasites who once called it home. Our focus is the weapon that caused their extinction. Only one force in this galaxy is worthy to wield such power, and that force is the Terran Empire. The Klingons cannot possess it, and Empress Sato has charged me with ensuring that does not happen."

"Speaking of Klingons," Simon said, "I'm picking up Klingon life signs down on the planet. They're coming from an underground structure beneath one of the larger population centers. The area looks to be protected by a force field, and the energy signature is definitely Klingon."

"A hidden base?" April asked.

Simon shrugged. "That, or maybe an outpost to observe the effects of the test detonation." She shook her head. "Hell of a way to gather data, but I suppose they could have been left behind after *Indomitable* came calling."

Leaving the command well, April moved to stand next to Simon at her console. "Can our sensors penetrate the field?"

"A bit," the science officer replied, "but not enough to get any kind of conclusive look inside the structure. If we channel additional power from the warp engines to the transporter circuits, we might be able to beam through." She said nothing else, allowing the suggestion to hang in the air between them.

Intrigued by the notion of seeing firsthand the effects of the experimental weapon, as well as getting an early look at any equipment or research data that might be contained within the Klingon outpost, April nodded in agreement with his friend's idea. "Meet me in the transporter room in ten minutes, along with a security detail," he said before turning to the communications station. "Lieutenant Copowycz, notify *Indomitable* of our status and that they are to maintain course and speed."

Despite his presence to provide new motivation to *Indomitable*'s engineering crew, repairs to the starship's antimatter inducer had proven more difficult and time-consuming than he had hoped. With time an issue, and rather than push the ailing vessel beyond its limits—thereby finishing the job of sacrificing *Indomitable* that the late Nathan Thorpe's ineptitude had initiated—April had ordered Captain Stone to trail *Constellation* at its fastest yet safest possible speed.

A moment later, the dark-haired communications officer replied, "*Indomitable* acknowledges, sir, and estimates her arrival in one hour and seventeen minutes."

April nodded at the report. "And have my wife join us in the transporter room." To Simon, he added, "If we do find a Klingon or two down there, her particular talents will prove rather useful."

As he headed toward the turbolift at the rear of the bridge, April could not help stopping for one final look at the image of Donatu V displayed on the main viewer. Watching the dying world rotate slowly beneath *Constellation,* he sensed dread brewing deep within him.

Will this godforsaken planet be remembered for what happened here or only that it happened here first?

"All clear, Commodore."

Gripping his phaser, April entered the corridor and saw that his security detail had cleared it of Klingons—there was no way to tell how many they might have disintegrated during their advance—and now were moving farther up the passageway. He waved for the rest of the landing party to follow him as he set off down the hall. Simon and Sarah, shadowing his movements, each drew their own weapons.

"Commodore," Simon said, pointing up the corridor with her tricorder, "the concentration of life signs is twenty meters in that direction."

Ahead of him, the security team leader, Lieutenant Elizabeth Ryckert, held up her hand, signaling a halt. The tall, leggy woman then turned and ran back to April's side, sweat already matting her closely cropped blond hair to her head.

"They're holed up in what looks like a lab," Ryckert reported. "What's left of them, anyway."

"Take the lab," April ordered, "but leave at least one of them alive for interrogation."

Ryckert nodded in acknowledgment before returning to lead the security team up the corridor. Reaching a closed door at the end of the passageway, she aimed her phaser at it and fired. The harsh blue beam lanced out, opening a hole in the door's thick metal. She kept her finger on the weapon's firing stud, widening the gap within seconds to a size large enough to allow entry. Ryckert plunged ahead, leading the way for her team to follow as the three of them rushed into the room beyond.

Charging after them, April entered the lab in time to see one of his personal guards, a well-muscled and dark-skinned man named Malhotra, slammed into a nearby bulkhead by an attacking Klingon. The savage had shunned his disruptor in favor of the massive knife in his right hand, which he plunged into Malhotra's chest. The security guard cried in pain and shock as the blade sank into his heart, his screams growing louder as the Klingon twisted the knife within the ghastly wound. April, incensed by the brutality of the attack, aimed his phaser and fired, its burst washing over Malhotra and the Klingon. Both warriors writhed in momentary agony before they dissolved into nothingness.

A beam of ruby-tinted energy flashed from the lab's opposite corner, missing him by a wide margin to strike a nearby computer console. Sparks and the tinge of ozone filled the air as a second disruptor burst gouged another gaping hole in an adjacent bank of electronic equipment. April saw another Klingon—this one wearing what to him looked like a lab coat—and ducked for cover, suddenly realizing that he was not at all the target.

"Stop him!" he shouted. "He's destroying the computers!"

With practiced ease, Ryckert drew a dagger from the sheath in her left boot and hurled it in the direction of the disruptor fire. The expert throw buried the blade in the Klingon's shoulder, and he growled in pain as he dropped his disruptor, reaching for the knife embedded in his body.

Without waiting for orders, Ryckert and the remaining guard,

Pearson, rushed to subdue the Klingon. April turned to see the rest of the landing party enter the room, which looked to him as though it might have been an emergency shelter commandeered by the Klingons as a place from which to observe the test of their deadly new missile.

Stepping past him, Sarah looked around the room before crossing the floor on her way to an adjoining chamber. Stopping in the doorway, she turned back to him, indicating the other room with a nod of her head. "You'll want to see this."

April followed her into what resembled a makeshift hospital ward, including the patients it now housed. On a dozen beds rested unmoving forms, natives of Donatu, he presumed, all of whom appeared to have been burned almost beyond recognition. Taking in the scene, April was struck by how the room seemed more like a hospice than a place of healing.

Moving to stand beside one of the beds, he looked down at the patient. It was a female, were he to hazard a guess, struggling to draw even the faintest of breaths. Her dark hair lay plastered onto a bloodied scalp, while her face, neck, and other exposed areas of skin were mottled with radiation lesions. Studying her cracked, dry lips, April found himself running a tongue across his own.

He heard movement and turned to see Sarah strolling past the beds on the opposite side of the aisle, her expression one of clinical dispassion as she regarded the ward's hapless patients.

"There's nothing to be done for any of them," she said. "Their lungs are seared from the superheated air, and several dermal layers suffered acute sunburn." She shook her head. "Why they're fighting the inevitable, I'll never know."

Despite himself, April could not help feeling some measure of compassion for these beings and their plight, and his wife's words of casual dismissal gave him a chill. It was an odd sensation, one to which he was not accustomed and yet could not deny. Millions of their friends and relatives already had succumbed to conditions on the planet above, and uncounted billions across the galaxy might well follow them should the Klingons be allowed to proceed unchecked.

Them, he reminded himself, *or anyone else.*

Sarah was examining a nearby desktop computer terminal, and April noticed the frown darkening her features. "What?"

"There's more to these patients' injuries than simple exposure to the weapon's effects," she replied. "It's almost like . . . a secondary experiment."

April was puzzled. "What kind of experiment?"

She waved one hand toward the rear of the room. "There's a decompression chamber installed back there. I think the Klingons were monitoring the effects of various levels of atmospheric exposure."

Scowling, April asked, "Why? Surely the weapon's effects are obvious?"

"If you really want answers, we should go to the source." Sarah offered a small, sly smile as she strode past him and back to the front room.

The balance of the landing party was there, and April saw that Ryckert now stood next to the bound and seated Klingon. Pale pink blood streamed from the wound in his shoulder, as well as from a long gash on his head, just to the left of the prominent ridges enhancing the crown of his skull.

"Report," he said as he moved toward the Klingon.

The security chief shrugged. "He appears disinterested in cooperating, sir."

From the other side of the room, Simon added, "He did a hell of a number on the computer banks. We can probably reconstruct their research data, but it'll take time."

April glared at the Klingon researcher. "Anything you'd like to add?"

The captive snarled in reply. "What more do you need, Earther? We now possess a weapon that will wipe the galaxy clean of your filth."

Shrugging, April asked, "What good's a planet that you can't use? Are you planning to live inside pressure domes or bunkers on every world you conquer? You can't have an empire if you're hiding underground everywhere you go."

"For now, it works well enough!" Gesturing toward the other room with a nod of his head, the Klingon added, "Look at those *petaQ,* wasting away in their beds. The Penemu's initial failure has led us to a solution even more desirable than we could imagine. We need not destroy a planet's atmosphere. With just the right manipulations of the original formula, we can poison it only to the point that it proves deadly to native life."

April nodded in comprehension. "And leave the planet and its resources relatively intact."

The Klingon sneered. "It's only a matter of time before we perfect the process, but even now, the weapon is more than enough to slaughter our enemies. You may well live long enough to see Klingons plant their flag on your homeworld, Earther."

Waving his hands to indicate the room and the rows of destroyed computer consoles and other support equipment, April said, "But here you are, with all of your newfound knowledge lost." The Klingon said nothing, holding his gaze without so much as a blink. "Of course, it's not truly lost, is it?"

Behind him, Simon said, "He wouldn't sacrifice his research and findings so easily, not without some kind of backup. I'm betting he and the rest of his team have been sending regular reports to his superiors, and wherever they are, that's where the real weapons research is being performed."

That was when the Klingon blinked.

April smiled, watching the prisoner squirm—if only slightly— in his seat. "Dr. April, perhaps you can persuade our new friend to pinpoint that location for us?"

Ordering Ryckert and her team to wait outside, Sarah stepped forward. She reached to her belt, the fingers of her right hand playing across the small device that had become one of her favorite toys. "I've only just begun to experiment with physiologies that differ greatly from humans," she said, removing the device from her belt. "Tellarites usually provide excellent baselines when it comes to pain thresholds, but I think a Klingon would be even better." She leaned closer to the bound prisoner. "It's not often I encounter Klingons, so I do thank you for this opportunity." She then placed the appliance to the Klingon's neck and pressed its activation control.

The response was somewhat surprising to April. An electrical crackle pierced the air, and while the prisoner obviously registered the targeted pain being inflicted by the device Sarah wielded—as evidenced by the flurry of muscle spasms and the way his eyes bulged and how his hands clenched into fists—there was no overt audible concession to the agony he must surely be feeling.

"Where is the weapon being developed?" Sarah asked, her tone neutral, almost relaxed, as she touched a control. April heard the device's pitch rise in response, doubtless now unleashing an even greater level of discomfort. Despite that and the obvious effect it was having on the Klingon, he remained silent save for dull moans of pain forced between gritted teeth.

Sarah's brow knitted in confusion. "That's the agonizer's highest setting."

"It's not working," April said before turning to Simon. "Check the equipment again. There has to be a record or log of communications. Maybe there's something that'll help us find who they're talking to."

"Wait," Sarah said, holding up her free hand. Deactivating her tool of choice—her "agonizer"—she straightened her posture, regarding her subject with something approaching genuine admiration. "I applaud your strength, Klingon. A pity it's wasted on such an inferior animal." Glancing over her shoulder, she held up the device. "Obviously, this still requires some fine-tuning to account for more robust humanoids. For now, though, we'll have to go back to basics."

With that, she drew her dagger and jammed it to its hilt just below the Klingon's left knee.

This time, the captive's response was immediate, as he loosed a howl of shock and distress unlike anything April had ever heard.

He could not help wincing himself, feeling his hand moving to the phaser on his belt as the Klingon's body jerked so violently that it appeared he might break free from his bonds. His anguished cries only intensified as Sarah twisted the knife.

"Sometimes more traditional methods offer the desired results," she said. Bright pink blood streamed from the wound as, with almost surgical precision, she angled the slim blade upward, its tip exploring beneath the Klingon's kneecap. When he drew a deep breath in an effort to combat the pain, Sarah reapplied the agonizer to his neck. "Where are your superiors?" When she asked the question this time, her voice was sharp and taut, echoing within the room's confined space.

Feeling his gorge rising, April shared an uncomfortable glance with Simon. As Sarah turned the embedded blade and the Klingon jerked yet again, the commodore was certain he saw something new in the prisoner's eyes. His mouth moved, though no words came forth. April rested his hand on his wife's shoulder; she seemed consumed by her current task. "Sarah! He's trying to say something."

Deactivating the agonizer, she pulled away the device, at the same time extracting her dagger from the Klingon's knee. He groaned in response, flicks of spittle flying from his mouth as he struggled to speak. Finally, he forced out a single word. "H'atoria."

April looked at Simon, who already was consulting her tricorder. "H'atoria is the Klingon name for the Strelluf star group. It's only a few hours away at high warp."

Nodding at the report, April turned his gaze back to the Klingon, who appeared drained from his ordeal. Though all haste in this situation had been necesssary, the commodore wanted to pity the prisoner. They had what they needed now, and he saw no reason to prolong the proceedings any longer. Drawing his phaser, April aimed it at the Klingon and fired, the weapon discharging a harsh blue-white beam that washed over the prisoner, enveloping him in a shroud of energy and ripping his body to atoms that promptly dissolved into oblivion.

"We should take the specimens with us," Sarah said, wiping her bloodstained dagger with a towel before returning it to the sheath in her boot. "I may be able to glean something from them."

"There's nothing here of any use," April snapped, increasingly irritated at the pleasure his wife was taking in her particular talents. Was he actually taking pity on members of a lesser alien species? He had never cared before, so why now? Could it be fatigue? Had this mission revealed something about her, or perhaps even himself?

Forcing away the troubling thoughts, April returned the phaser to his side and reached for his communicator. "Stand by to return to the ship. We'll destroy whatever's left from orbit."

There still were larger issues that required attention, after all.

Sitting in the center seat, April felt the *Constellation* drop out of warp drive seconds before his helmsman, Lieutenant Ran Armstrong, turned from the helm.

"We've entered the Strelluf star group, sir. Slowing to impulse."

April nodded at the report. "Where's *Indomitable*?"

At the science station, Simon replied, "They should arrive in about fourteen minutes, Commodore."

"Excellent," April said, pleased with the progress Captain Stone and her crew had made with repairing their damaged ship even as they coped with following him all over the sector. "Notify them of our status. Meanwhile, let's have a look. Full sensor sweep."

"The planets in this star group are reportedly uninhabited," Simon said, adjusting the controls on her console before turning her attention to her viewer. "Klingons aren't exactly known for their subtlety, so finding them won't be hard, but what do we do after that?"

"I don't know yet," April conceded as he rose from his chair and stepped up to join her at her station. "For the moment, all we can do is be prepared."

The turbolift doors opened to admit Sarah April. "Assault troops are assembled for deployment," she said, a satisfied grin curling the edges of her mouth. "They'll be ready for transport within two minutes of your order, Commodore."

"Thank you," April said, trying not to dwell on the fact that his wife seemed most pleased to deliver her report.

"Well, that's what I call being prepared," Simon said.

April released a tired sigh. "It'd be simpler just to destroy the base," he said, glancing toward his wife, "but if we're going to take it, then I'm not leaving anything to chance."

"We take it, Bob, and then what?" Simon asked.

"Whatever the Empress commands," replied Sarah.

Simon ignored her. "So, what? We hide it until someone comes to take it from us? Or maybe we start using it?"

"All questions I've already asked, Lorna." Avoiding the eyes of both women, April returned to the command well. "For now, we follow our orders."

An abrupt beeping sounded from Simon's console, and she turned to consult her instruments. "Bingo. Sensors are picking up indications of a base on the moon orbiting the fourth planet. I'm also reading high levels of inorganic compounds matching those we found on Donatu V."

"Life signs?" April asked, already feeling the surge of adrenaline in response to the report and what it meant.

Simon nodded. "Hundreds. Klingon and Penemu. This has to be it."

Settling into his seat, April said, "Red alert. Armstrong, close to maximum transporter range." To his communications officer, he said, "Lieutenant Copowycz, notify the assault teams to stand by for beam-down." It would still take time for Simon to determine the best points for infiltrating the base, but he wanted them to be ready the instant that information was provided.

Another alarm echoed across the bridge, and this time, the large wedge-shaped indicator on the center of the helm and navigation console flashed an angry crimson.

"Our shields just went up, Commodore," Armstrong called out. "Unidentified vessels on an intercept course."

"Lorna?" April asked.

Bent once more over her viewer, Simon replied, "Four Klingon light attack cruisers, coming at us at full impulse with weapons hot. Sneaky bastards were hiding beyond the far side of the moon."

"Stand by for evasive," April ordered, seconds before something slammed into the *Constellation*'s shields. Klaxons pierced the air, the overhead lighting flickering in protest as the shields bore the brunt of the attack. Feeling an impact against the back of his chair, April looked up to see Sarah gripping the backrest for support, and he reached to steady her.

"Full power to the shields!" he ordered. "And give me some maneuvering room! Stand by all weapons!"

He felt Sarah's hand on his arm and turned to see her regarding him. "They know we're here now. They might try to destroy the weapon and anything else of use. You've got to send down the assault teams."

"No time," April countered, his attention divided between his wife and the rapidly evolving tactical situation. "Find a seat and hang on. This is going to get bumpy."

Alarms wailed across *Indomitable*'s bridge in wholly unnecessary fashion, given that the starship's entire crew had been at battle stations since well before entering the Strelluf star group.

"Feel free to shut that off," said Erin Stone, leaning forward in her command chair. "Report."

"We're closing to maximum effective weapons range, Captain," replied Lieutenant Jason McNally from his position at the helm.

On the bridge's main viewscreen, Stone could just make out the five telltale points of light standing out from the other stars that formed the backdrop for the battle they were approaching. "Give me a tactical plot."

The image on the viewer shifted to depict a computer-generated schematic. A pale green grid appeared, over which was displayed a large blue circle to represent the barren moon. In proximity to the lone satellite, four red circles—each symbolizing a Klingon attack cruiser—moved around a single green arrowhead, the *Constellation*. Though the four cruisers were smaller and more maneuverable than their lone opponent, the *Constitution*-class starship's weapons were nearly a match for its enemies.

"What's *Constellation*'s status?" Stone asked.

From the science station on the bridge's starboard bulkhead, Lieutenant Kisho Akamatsu replied. "Her shields are down to sixty-five percent, Captain. Aft torpedo launcher appears damaged." Looking up from his workstation, the science officer added, "Considering the odds, Commodore April's holding his own."

"Let's try to even those odds a bit," Stone said, before tapping the communications control on the arm of her chair. "Engineering, route all power from nonessential systems to weapons and shields."

From the intercom bridge speaker came the harried voice of *Indomitable*'s chief engineer, Commander Leslie Collins. *"We're holding things together down here with spit and prayer, Captain. Main power's only back to eighty-seven percent."*

"It'll have to do. Take power from wherever you need it, but keep us in the fight."

Stone knew that *Indomitable*, despite the past days of frantic repair work, still had not regained peak operating efficiency, and Commodore April had shown surprising understanding. Rather than execute her for her failure, he instead had ordered her to continue repairs and to follow *Constellation* at her best possible speed. It had galled Stone to have to accept such a concession from the commodore while he traveled ahead to the Strelluf star group in search of the new Klingon weapon. Now, his generosity had resulted in him venturing alone into a fight when she should have been at his side, earning the trust he had placed in her by giving her command of *Indomitable* in the first place.

Now's your chance, Captain.

"Weapons are online, shields at full intensity," reported her new first officer, Thomas Blair, from where he sat at the engineering station, behind Stone's left shoulder on the bridge's upper deck.

For just the briefest of moments, Stone thought she could detect anxiety in the just-promoted lieutenant commander, but it passed quickly, if indeed it was there at all. A young officer on the fast track, Blair had—like Stone herself—barely been given the opportunity to adjust to his promotion and change of duties before being thrown headlong into the current situation. Still, he was good at his job and, more important, utterly loyal to Stone, both on and off duty. She could think of no one else she would rather have watching her back as she took command of *Indomitable*.

Akamatsu suddenly released a triumphant war cry. "One of the Klingon ships has just lost all power!"

"Split screen," Stone ordered. "Keep the tactical view." The image on the viewer divided into two sections, adding a display of *Constellation* and its four adversaries. While three of the attack cruisers bobbed and weaved as they fired, attempting to stay out of reach of the starship's weapon, the fourth was adrift, all ports and running lights dark. Energy spewed from its port warp nacelle as the cruiser fell away from the battle in a slow arc.

Then a pair of brilliant yellow orbs launched from *Constellation*, crossing the void between predator and prey to strike the Klingon vessel's secondary hull. With no shields to protect against the attack, the photon torpedoes punched through the heavy plating before detonating, shredding that section of the cruiser from the inside out. Seconds later, the entire ship disappeared in a massive ball of exploding gases and energy, flinging debris in all directions. All around her, Stone listened as her bridge crew cheered on the fatal blow Commodore April had dealt their enemy as *Constellation* changed course, bearing down on its next target.

"Two of the enemy vessels are breaking off," Akamatsu reported. "Changing course to intercept us." The science officer's update was punctuated as Stone saw four new blips on the viewscreen's tactical plot, the computer's way of signifying torpedo launches from the oncoming enemy vessels. "Incoming fire!" he called out.

The torpedoes struck seconds later, and though the bulk of

their energy was absorbed by *Indomitable*'s shields, Stone still felt the starship shudder in the face of the assault. Overhead lighting and various display monitors around the bridge flickered as the shield generators called upon more power to reinforce the ship's defenses.

"Return fire!" she shouted. On the viewscreen, bright orange beams of phaser energy lanced across space, hitting the shields of both approaching vessels. At the helm, McNally pressed the attack, following his initial volley with a quartet of photon torpedoes. Guided by *Indomitable*'s fire-control computer, the weapons charged after their intended target, also striking the deflector shields protecting the Klingon ships. Seemingly undeterred, the enemy continued to advance, unleashing its own fresh barrage of disruptors and torpedoes. The ship trembled again, more pronounced this time.

Behind her, Blair called out, "Shields at twenty-four percent and dropping. I'm reading power fluctuations in the generators!"

Stone punched the comm switch on her chair. "Engineering! Collins, route all available power to the shields!"

"It's no good, Captain!" shouted the chief engineer through the speakers. *"All our jury-rigging is coming down around our ears. You need to give us some breathing room."*

"We'll all be breathing vacuum if you don't keep those shields up!" Severing the connection, Stone rose from her seat, reaching forward to grasp the top of McNally's chair for support. "Blair," she called out over her shoulder. "How bad is it?"

"Shields for the upper primary hull are below fifteen percent," replied the first officer. "They'll probably go altogether with another hit."

"Keep firing," she said, "and get us on an evasive course to the *Constellation!*"

McNally's hands moved across his console, struggling to implement the new orders. Thanks to the compromised inertial dampening system, Stone felt the ship lumbering to starboard as the helmsman changed course while loosing new salvos at the enemy vessels. From the tactical view on the main screen, she could see that the Klingons had separated, tracking after *Indomitable* from opposite directions and working to catch the starship in a deadly crossfire.

"Direct hit!" reported Akamatsu. "One ship's shields are down, and I'm detecting damage to their forward torpedo launcher. They're pulling back!"

It was welcome news, but Stone knew there was no time for celebration. The tactical display showed the second Klingon ship closing in for another strafing run, approaching *Indomitable* from a point above it.

From the science station, Akamatsu shouted, "Computer shows its attack vector is the primary hull! Our shields!"

Tightening her grip on the helmsman's chair, Stone ordered, "McNally! Evasive!"

Then the Klingon vessel fired. On the viewscreen, the tactical plot tracked a new quartet of torpedoes, stalking the wounded and fleeing starship with unrelenting menace.

This is it. Stone could feel it in her gut. Her muscles tensing in anticipation, she closed her eyes, counting down the seconds until the end came.

"Brace for impact!"

April watched all four of the Klingon torpedoes rip through the remnants of *Indomitable*'s shields, enveloping the starship's bridge and a significant portion of her primary hull in a hellish maelstrom.

Pointing toward the viewscreen, he shouted, "Target that ship, full spread!" In response to his orders, a fresh barrage of photon torpedoes chased after the Klingon vessel that had just dealt *Indomitable* its deathblow. Energies collided as the strikes slammed against the enemy ship's shields, but one torpedo managed to make its way to the cruiser's hull. April nodded in satisfaction as the weapon

62 **Dayton Ward & Kevin Dilmore**

pierced the heavy metal plating and detonated, the new explosion flinging debris into the void as the ship lumbered away from the new attack.

"Report!" he ordered, gripping the arms of his command chair and unable to tear his eyes from the scene of the wounded *Indomitable* on the screen.

"*Indomitable*'s lost all main power," Simon replied. "Impulse engines are still online, but primary power distribution circuits are fused. The bridge and the majority of decks three through six are gone. I'm also picking up fluctuations in the antimatter-containment system."

"What about auxiliary control?" April asked. "Was that damaged?"

Simon shook her head. "Deck eight looks to have been spared the brunt of the attack, but I'm not picking up any attempts to route power there. Engineering probably has their hands full right now."

Damn it!

Indomitable was crippled, April knew, probably dead in space, unless its engineering crew could craft a miracle and somehow gain control of the wounded starship via its auxiliary command center. As for *Constellation*, it, too, had sustained significant damage, though both vessels had to this point held their own during the brief yet vicious battle. *Indomitable*'s timely arrival had helped turn the tide of what he at first had considered a small yet distinct mismatch.

Irrelevant, he reminded himself. The only thing anyone would remember was that someone had won and someone had lost. April had no intention of being the latter.

"Commodore," said Lieutenant Copowycz from behind him, and he turned to see the communications officer regarding him with concern and even fear in her eyes. "I'm picking up multiple distress calls from *Indomitable,* including one from her chief engineer."

"Put her on audio," April ordered, and seconds later, the bridge's intercom system blared to life with a burst of static that faded, allowing the garbled words of the wounded starship's chief engineer to be heard.

"... *der Collins. Constellation, if you can hear this, we've lost all main energizers, and reserve power is already failing. We're losing antimatter containment, and I may have to jettison the warp nacelles. Captain and first officer are dead. We need to abandon ship!*"

"Commodore," Copowycz said, the expression on her face now one of worry, "I'm also picking up a distress call coming from the moon. They're signaling for any available ship to render assistance."

"Reinforcements," April said, feeling his jaw clench as he parsed the new information. "How long?"

Simon shrugged. "Sensors are clear, but based on what we know of Klingon patrol patterns, maybe half an hour. The other ships are pulling back. Assessing damage and waiting for the cavalry, I guess."

Constellation's maneuvering had brought the moon into view once more, and April snarled as he searched the barren surface for signs of the outpost and top-secret research facility, which were all but invisible from this distance. Somewhere down there, the secret he sought lay in hiding, waiting for him to seize it for the greater glory of the Empire. It seemed so tantalizingly close, yet April knew that under the current circumstances, it might as well be half a galaxy away.

"Even if they abandon ship," April said, "we won't be able to get them all before *Indomitable*'s warp engines blow."

"There's no time for an evacuation," said Sarah April from behind him. He turned to where she stood at the back of the bridge, in the turbolift alcove and next to his own personal guard, Lieutenant Pearson, and saw the determination in her eyes. "You can't help them now," she added, "and our priority is the weapon."

April was nearly beside himself in the face of the outburst, and he noted that even Pearson appeared shocked by what he was hearing. His wife had remained out of the way as the battle unfolded, saying nothing. To hear her speak now, so openly questioning his decisions? If it were anyone else, he would have killed them where they stood.

I understand my priorities. The statement burned in his mind even as he glared at his wife, hoping his expression conveyed the unspoken message.

"What about a tractor beam?" Armstrong asked.

"We'd be defenseless while towing them," April countered. Taking his eyes from Sarah, he looked to the viewscreen and its image of *Indomitable,* drifting in high orbit above the moon. Given sufficient time, the dying starship would likely fall from its trajectory until it hit the moon's surface.

The Klingons aren't likely to wait around for that.

Rising from his seat, April moved to the railing separating him from Simon. "Lorna, can you access their main computer?"

Pausing to consider the question, Simon nodded. "If its external interface isn't damaged. I'll need its prefix code."

"Computer," April said without hesitation, "release the command override codes for the *I.S.S. Indomitable* to Commander Simon. Voice authorization April, Six Four Zulu Delta." To Simon, he said, "Patch in, and give navigational and maneuvering control to our helm."

"What are you doing?" Sarah asked. Her tone was hard, almost accusatory, but to her credit, she remained near the turbolift.

Stepping away from the railing, April tapped the shoulder of the ensign seated at the navigator's station. "Let me have the console, son," he said. The ensign's eyes widened in fear; he no doubt wondered what he had done to incur the commodore's wrath. Seeing the younger man's expression, April shook his head. "Relax, Ensign. I just prefer to do this myself." It took a quick moment to reacquaint himself with the console's layout before he looked to Simon. "Ready?"

The science officer nodded. "I've accessed their main computer and routed navigation to your station, Commodore."

Still seated at the helm, Armstrong asked, "Orders, sir?"

"Lay in an evasive course out of the star group at maximum warp, and stand by for my command," April replied. His fingers moved across the navigation console's rows of multicolored buttons, initiating the command string from his ship to *Indomitable*. It seemed to take forever for the wounded starship's taxed computer system to respond to his queries, during which he verified the coordinates he wanted. Seconds later, the indicators on which he was waiting finally flashed green.

Leaning over her hooded viewer, Simon called out, "*Indomitable* is moving, Commodore. I'm picking up fluctuations in the impulse engines, but its orbital track is leveling off, and it's responding to course corrections."

His attention focused on his console, April entered a new command. On the viewscreen, *Indomitable* accelerated, now oriented toward the moon.

"Track is . . ." The words seemed to die in Simon's throat, and she looked up from her viewer, her gaze locking with April's. "It's on a direct course for the base."

"You're destroying it?" Sarah asked. "You can't do that! Your orders were explicit!"

"We can't leave here with the weapon," April replied, his voice quiet yet firm. "There's no time to locate and retrieve anything of use. We can't allow the Klingons to leave here with it, either. They'll just relocate to some other, more secure location. The only option is to make certain there's nothing for them to take." To emphasize his point, he jabbed another control on the console.

On the viewscreen, *Indomitable*'s trajectory arced until the starship was aimed downward, its speed increasing as it responded to the commands April had given it.

"Commodore," said Copowycz, "we're getting new distress calls."

"No response, Lieutenant," April replied, his mouth pressed into a thin line. He tried not to think of the hundreds of lives aboard that ship, which he was sacrificing with this bold, unilateral decision. On numerous occasions, he had ordered subordinates to their deaths or had caused such deaths by his own hand, but never before on this scale. He now told himself this action was necessary, not only to stop the Klingons' immediate threat but also to secure the long-term security of the Empire. He wanted to believe that everyone aboard *Indomitable* would understand and agree with his decision, confident that their sacrifice was a worthy one.

Not that it matters, really.

He watched the wounded starship's course pull it ever closer to the moon. Gravity, inertia, and whatever power remained in the vessel's flagging impulse engines had sealed its fate. No one on the bridge said anything as *Indomitable* dove for the surface, the viewscreen updating its imagery to compensate for the gap growing between the two starships. Structures and other components of the Klingon base now were visible, and April saw the telltale flashes of land-based defensive systems coming online, tracking and firing after what essentially had become an incoming missile.

"Impact in five seconds," Simon reported. "Three. Two. One."

A new sun appeared on the surface of the moon as *Indomitable* plowed into the base at full impulse power, its antimatter-containment system rupturing at the point of impact. The resulting colossal detonation swallowed the starship in the first instant, taking with it the base and a significant portion of the valley in which it had resided. April and everyone else on the bridge flung up their hands to shield their eyes, the viewscreen lagging as it fought to compensate for the sudden, intense brightness change. Within seconds, the flash had faded, leaving behind a rapidly expanding cloud of ash, soil, and debris hundreds of kilometers across.

"Dear God," April heard Simon say, her voice low and choked.

Rising from the navigator's station, he turned away from the image of the moon and the dreadful secrets it once had harbored. He caught sight of his wife, still standing at the rear of the bridge, and he was certain he saw incredulity and even shock burning in her eyes. She said nothing, instead turning on her heel and marching into the turbolift. The doors closed behind her, leaving Lieutenant Pearson to regard April with an expression bordering on relief.

"Set a course for the nearest starbase," April said as he returned to the command chair. "Engage at maximum warp."

"No sign of Klingon pursuit," Simon reported. "Looks like we're clear."

April nodded, taking some measure of comfort in knowing that his ship still possessed superior propulsion systems, one of the few advantages the imperial Starfleet still held over most of its enemies.

There's no one to follow us where we're going, but what waits for me once we get there?

Despite failing to acquire the weapon the Klingons had labored to create, April also had denied them their opportunity to use it against the Empire. He knew his actions to be tactically sound, but would the Admiralty, or even Empress Sato herself, view such facts in a similar light? Or would their lust for power blind them to all but the immediate consequences of what he had done?

Such answers would not be long in coming. Of that, April was certain.

His eyes gritty with fatigue, the knot in his lower back nagging him for sitting in one place too long, April studied the mission report displayed on his desktop viewer. It read well enough, he decided, but would it convince his superiors?

In a rare breach of protocol, April had sought Lorna Simon's counsel, despite her not holding the required security clearance for reading any reports sent to the Admiralty or Empress Sato. Still, she possessed the objectivity he needed in order to craft a report that would stand up to the scrutiny for which this one was destined. With her assistance, he had honed his argument to one he hoped would justify the destruction of the Klingon facility along with the loss of *Indomitable* and her crew, as well as every detail relating to the Penemu weapon. Still, one question lingered.

Had Thorpe written such a report, would I have seen through it?

He heard the door to his quarters open. He smiled without looking up, immediately recognizing the scent of his wife's preferred perfume. "I'm almost done," he said, straightening in his chair. "Want to read it?"

Sarah's hand touched his neck, her nails gently raking the exposed skin, and he felt her chin rest on his shoulder. "Eventually." There was no mistaking the intent behind the single word. Her other hand moved to caress his chest, beneath the fold of his tunic. Smiling again, he reached up to place his hand over hers.

Then he felt cool metal against the back of his neck, an instant before every nerve ending in his body exploded.

Each heartbeat and breath was agony. His muscles jerked, beyond his conscious control, and April crumpled out of his seat to the deck. It took several tortured seconds before he could even attempt to regain control of his breathing, his body still protesting the memory of the onslaught it had endured. Even sitting up proved impossible, and it took all of his energy simply to refocus his attention enough to see Sarah towering over him, her phaser aimed at his chest.

"I've finished a report as well," she said, returning the agonizer to her belt and extracting a green data card from the top of her left boot. "I think my perspective on your recent decisions will prove most interesting to Her Majesty."

"Your . . . perspective," April repeated, each word a knife in his lungs as he felt motor control returning to his body.

Smiling, she moved to sit in his chair, keeping her phaser trained on him. "You may be able to justify your actions to a room of doddering old admirals light-years away from here, and convincing the Empress is certainly no great triumph. But to someone who's stood by your side for as long as I have, you might appear weak, maybe softening in your advancing age, but still capable of undermining the advancement of the Empire."

Despite the lingering pain, April almost laughed at his wife's unleashed ambition, one of the qualities that had drawn him to her all those years ago. Of course, he could not ignore the irony, in that his own conflicted conscience had enabled her to take such bold action. The question now was: What would Sarah April do with the opportunity she had seized?

These ill winds, they bode no good. The errant thought—a quote from something he had read long ago—mocked him as he fought to regain control of his body.

"What do you want?" he asked, forcing the words past his lips.

"To re-create the Penemu weapon, of course," Sarah replied. "You upset my original plans for that, but I can afford to be patient. Between Donatu and Strelluf, we gathered enough basic information to start over. It'll take time, but it will give me plenty of opportunities for research, particularly when we're ready to test the weapon's effects on living beings. Lorna Simon would make an excellent specimen, don't you think?"

April's eyes widened at the name of his closest friend. "I'll kill you first." Even as he spoke the words, the fingers of his right hand twitched, already seeking the comforting grip of his phaser yet knowing he would never reach the weapon.

"Doubtful," Sarah said, holding up the data card. "A copy of this is in trusted hands. They'll stop at nothing to avenge my death, and don't think you'll suffer alone, my dear. Family, friends . . . even trusted confidants." Leaning closer, she added, "She'll beg for death."

His body still aching, April felt his throat constrict as he envisioned Sarah moving her final game pieces into position. Closing his eyes, he gritted his teeth and tried to sit up, but a gesture from her phaser hand was enough to stop him.

"Of course," she said, "none of that has to happen. Pledge loyalty to me, and you can keep your reputation and your life relatively intact. Cross me, and anyone who's ever called you friend or lover will suffer for your treachery."

"Why not just kill me?" he asked, still struggling for breath. "Assassinations have been carried out for less. Get rid of me, and earn yourself a commendation for being a loyal officer at the same time. Empress Sato would be proud."

"It would be stupid to kill you," Sarah countered, rising from the chair, "especially given my own unique position. I'd waste years regaining a similar advantage." She crossed to the door, which slid open at her approach. Pausing at the threshold, she turned and regarded her husband one final time. "For now, at least, you're more valuable to me alive than dead."

She exited the room, and the door slid shut, leaving Robert April alone to contemplate all the ways in which his universe had changed, and how long "the Quiet Tyrant" might be allowed to continue occupying it.

Ill winds, indeed.

The Greater Good

Margaret Wander Bonanno

HISTORIAN'S NOTE: *This tale is set in 2264, three years before the events of the second-season* Star Trek *episode "Mirror, Mirror."*

Margaret Wander Bonanno is the author of over twenty works of fiction across several genres and the co-founder of Van Wander Press. She lives on the Left Coast, and very much enjoys being a grandmother.

Please visit her website, www.margaretwanderbonanno.com.

Every creature, James T. Kirk thought as Lieutenant Spock contemplated the untenable position of his king's knight, *has its weaknesses. It's only a matter of discovering what they are and exploiting them.*

"That was a most illogical move, Mr. Kirk," Spock said finally, extricating his knight, but not easily.

"All the same, Mr. Spock," the newly promoted lieutenant commander said with the winsome grin that got him what he wanted almost as often as coldblooded murder did, "it had the desired outcome."

When this game was invented, Kirk thought, *the loser usually forfeited his life. Simpler times then. But Mr. Spock is worth more to me alive.*

Three moves later, Spock tipped his king over, conceding defeat. It was an unusual enough event to have drawn a crowd in the officers' lounge on Earth's main spacedock. The background noise was just sufficient, Kirk thought, to block their conversation from the listening devices that were everywhere.

He was inordinately proud of his self-control. Not only had he just beaten one of the best chess players in Starfleet, but he'd managed to do so despite the fact that the great love of his life was watching through the floor-to-ceiling window just beyond Spock's shoulder. She seemed more beautiful every time he saw her.

Enterprise! Kirk had to stop himself from whispering the name aloud. She stood alone in Spacedock, sleek and resplendent, her yearlong refit nearing completion before her next five-year mission under Captain Pike. Only the fact that there were others in the room stopped Kirk from going to the window and pressing his hands against the surface so that he could be closer to her.

His ship. She had to be. His attraction to her was almost visceral. He had adored her from a distance for years, because she belonged to another man, a man who didn't deserve her. But someday he would have her, no matter who tried to get in his way.

Concentrate! he warned himself. *Think three moves ahead. This is only the first step . . .*

"Must be difficult finding players at your level," he ventured, tearing his eyes away from the window and watching Spock carefully. "I gather Captain Pike doesn't play?"

"Indeed, he does not," Spock said with a slight frown as he reset the board, indicating that he was still trying to figure out where he'd gone wrong. Then he seemed actually to hear what Kirk was implying. "I am curious how you ascertained this."

"Just gossip," Kirk said disarmingly. There was nothing as easy as lying to an honest man. There was a strange, feral gleam in his eyes, the kind of hyperfocus one saw in predators when the prey appeared suddenly over the rise and they began to stalk.

"Spock's the key," Marlena had said casually, tossing the information over her shoulder the way she was in the habit of doing with her luxuriant dark hair. "Others will grumble about life under Pike, but they're cowards, or lazy. Spock's ambitious, but not the way you think." She yawned and stretched like a cat. "Are you coming to bed?"

"In a minute," Kirk said distractedly. "How do you know all this? Don't tell me you managed to seduce a Vulcan?"

Was that jealousy, Marlena wondered, *or just enlightened self-interest?*

"Not the way you're imagining," she said, yawning again and giving him her most appealing look. "Vulcans thrive on *intellectual* foreplay."

"Intellectual—you?" Kirk started to say, then saw her eyes narrow and changed his tune. He owed her for getting close to Spock in ways he couldn't, and if he angered her, she wouldn't tell him anything more. "I'm sorry, that was low. I'd be interested in what you found out."

"I seem to have a knack for the sciences," was how she had begun her conversation with Spock, holding back the kittenish sexuality that usually got her what she wanted. "My sponsor . . ." The word *lover* didn't seem appropriate in this context. ". . . has promised to pull the necessary strings to get me into the Academy, but I thought I'd do most of the work by remote, complete the labs aboard ship, then finish out the last year on Earth."

"A reasonable approach," Spock had said. "A starship offers far more opportunities to examine as-yet-uncategorized species and phenomena."

"But I was wondering," Marlena had said before he could ask why she'd brought this to him. "*Farragut*'s an older ship, and even if she weren't being held over to investigate what happened with that horrible vampire cloud . . ." She managed an appropriately sad face for the two hundred dead crewmen, including Captain Garrovick. "Would it be better for me to request a transfer to a newer ship? *Enterprise,* for example . . ."

"He assigned someone from his department to show me around," she told Kirk now. "You'd be amazed what a girl can find out if she knows what questions to ask."

He'd finally come to bed, and she was caressing him, though her words seemed to excite him more than her touch; not only Vulcans were stimulated by intellectual foreplay, apparently.

"Spock and that—woman, if you can call her that—that machine masquerading as a woman, Number One, apparently don't get along. More than once, she's given Pike recommendations that could have gotten them all killed. Spock's second-guessed her and gotten reprimanded. He won't say it, but he thinks he'd be a better first officer."

"And then captain," Kirk suggested. "All he's got to do is work up the courage to eliminate Number One and then go after Pike."

"I don't think he wants that," Marlena said, feeling him pull away from her. "And there's something else . . ."

"What? The drinking?" Kirk said impatiently, out of bed and pacing now. "I know all about that. How Pike's ship's surgeon feeds him martinis in his quarters where the crew can't see, keeps him not quite drunk all the time, makes him easier to manipulate? And Number One probably covers up for him. Which, if I know my Vulcans, is something Spock wouldn't do."

"Something bigger than that," Marlena suggested.

That got Kirk's attention. "What?"

She shrugged. "Something about a rescue mission that went wrong. Whole ship was sworn to secrecy afterward; that's all I could get. There's even supposed to be a general order involved." She rolled over, genuinely sleepy this time. If Kirk was going to sit up plotting all night, well, she had an exam tomorrow. "Guess you'll have to do the rest yourself . . ."

Chess as metaphor for life, Kirk thought, watching Spock set up the board again. *And while he won't admit it, Spock's bothered by losing that last game. Let's see what I can do with that. Learn his weaknesses, work with his strengths . . .*

Marlena had seen the feral glint in Kirk's eye during the *Farragut* debriefing. Some might have taken it for grief or posttraumatic shock; in fact, the brass had recommended that Kirk take extended leave and visit a therapist. But Marlena knew him too well. She wasn't quite sure how he'd steered Garrovick and the rest of the crew into the path of the vampire cloud, but it had gotten him another rung up on the ladder, and that had been the goal all along.

"You actually enjoy killing," she said over dinner the evening after the debriefing.

Kirk was startled at the thought. "No, I really don't. It's an awful lot of work. I wish there were some other way. But you know what they say. 'If you're going to make an omelet, you have to break some eggs.' I was only after the command crew. The enlisted men just . . . got in the way."

"And now you're going after Pike," Marlena marveled. "How many of *Enterprise*'s crew do you figure will 'get in the way'?"

"Only those who resist me," Kirk murmured, lost in thought. "Besides, look at it this way—Pike's a liability. His sloppy judgment could get his entire crew killed. A more competent commander would actually *save* lives. Pike's death would be for the greater good."

Marlena shook her head. "My hero!" she said wryly.

"I cannot tell you what happened on Talos IV, Mr. Kirk," Spock said solemnly. "To do so would be a violation of General Order Seven, and I do not wish to be executed for treason. However . . ."

He handed off the data disk so quickly it took Kirk a second or two to realize what it was and wonder where he could hide it. He started to say something, but Spock's raised eyebrow silenced him.

"I have *told* you nothing," the Vulcan pointed out.

"I'm aware of that, Mr. Spock. But how you got access to this information—"

"—is not for you to know."

"What if it's traced? Every download leaves a signature."

Spock's expression might almost have been pitying. He was, after all, an A7 computer expert. Kirk finally relaxed.

"And in exchange?"

"Number One is an excellent first officer," Spock observed casually.

"But you think you'd be a better one." Kirk got up from the chessboard. "Thank you for an excellent game, Mr. Spock."

As he left their meeting, it occurred to Kirk that having a second in command who preferred to let others do his killing for him might be a liability. A captain would never know where the potential attack was coming from.

Worry about that once you're in the chair, he told himself, the data disk weighing him down.

What he found on it lifted his mood considerably.

"That's it!" he said, almost shouting.

"What is it?" Marlena was reading over his shoulder, but not as quickly, as she was massaging his neck at the same time.

"Incredible," Kirk said. He didn't know what outrageous revelations he'd hoped to find on the disk, but this surpassed his expectations. "A telepathic species with this kind of power . . . and he let them live! Pike *let them live.* I don't have to tell you what the Empire thinks of telepaths."

No, he didn't. Everyone knew the Empire's policy toward telepathy. The talent, so rare in Terrans, was deemed too dangerous if found in the possession of other species.

"But *why?*" Marlena was puzzled. "And more to the point, why did *they* let *Pike* live? Someone should have tried to kill him."

"You'd think so, wouldn't you?" Kirk mused. Then the part of his brain that enabled him to think three moves ahead, or piece things together three moves backward, kicked into gear. "Of course—that has to be it!"

Marlena stopped massaging his neck and squeezed his shoulders. "What is? Tell me!"

Kirk spun his chair around, mischief on his face. "Uh-uh. You're a smart girl. Figure it out for yourself!"

"Don't tease me!" She pouted. "My mind doesn't work like yours. Tell me!"

"Your mind has more steel traps than mine ever will," he replied, grabbing her by the waist and moving her toward the bed.

An hour later, she was still trying to worm it out of him. Sated and content, he told her.

"There's only one reason the Talosians didn't crush Pike and his crew like cockroaches. They wanted something more . . ."

. . .

What they'd wanted were eyes and ears inside an Empire that they knew would eventually attempt to surround them, absorb them, and learn their secrets.

Given your terror of telepathy, you humans will simply attempt to destroy us and pillage our world for its resources, the Keeper had mused in Pike's mind. *We have seen in your mind what they have done to others, and they will do the same 'here, if we do not act.*

Weak, sick, every bone in his body aching, aware that his mind had been violated and he had given up information he didn't even know he possessed, Pike glared at the Keeper balefully.

Not a day ago, he'd hoped they'd simply kill him. That had seemed to be their intention when he refused to "mate" with that insipid human female. How could he survive if they let him go? If his own crew didn't kill him in the state he was in, Command would see through whatever explanation he gave for his escape and have him executed.

We will give you the skills to prevent this, the Keeper was saying now, but Pike wasn't listening. Without Boyce and his concoctions to kill the pain, he had been to the core of himself, a weak-willed pretty boy pushed to the front of his graduating class at the Academy ahead of far more capable men, not on the basis of achievement or guile or even family connections but because he was charming and he photographed well, and Starfleet needed a wholesome-looking poster boy to counter the stories of corruption at every level, officer assassinating officer, incompetence leading to ships lost with their entire crews.

In any case, Pike thought, facing the awful truth in a subterranean cage on an alien world from which there now seemed only two means of escape—death or betrayal—his whole life to this point had been a sham. A glory-filled sham, to be sure, and if he hadn't survived assassination by wit and guile, at least he had survived. That was the law of the universe, wasn't it, survival? Faced with the possibility that he might not have to die, Pike discovered another truth about himself. He wanted to live, no matter the cost.

Besides, what would he be betraying? A fleet that considered its members expendable? An Empire built on betrayal and counterbetrayal? A philosophy that dictated, above all else, "Save your own skin"?

"What do you want from me?" he asked the Keeper now.

We wish you to be our early-warning system, the Keeper explained. *Our . . . canary in the coal mine, if I understand the metaphor correctly.*

"Meaning—?" Pike staggered to his feet for the first time in days, half starved, filthy, unshaven, but suddenly repossessed of the will to live. He felt the pain leaving his joints. So, that had been an illusion, too.

"Meaning," the Keeper said, speaking aloud for the first time. Its voice was feeble, old-womanish. "We will free you, and the women. Oh, yes, we captured two more of you. They're being held separately. We intended to go forward with our original plan to use you as breeding stock. But a larger plan suggested itself.

"You will be returned to your ship, and your ship will return to your Empire. You will tell your superiors essentially what happened here, and they will quarantine our world until they feel they have the strength to vanquish us. When that time comes, you will let us know so that we can prepare."

"How will I do that?" Pike demanded, as close to the barrier between himself and the Keeper as he could get. He rubbed his arms to get their strength back, wished he could do the same for his mind. *Think!* he told himself—never his strong point at the best of times, but now, with this creature hearing his thoughts almost before he thought them, what was the point? He was trapped. But he would live. *Focus on that,* he told himself. *It's all you've got.*

You have already begun, the Keeper said in his mind.

Forever after, Pike would try to rationalize what he did next or, rather, what he didn't do. He should have filled his thoughts with rage—the only thing they couldn't read through—turned the ship around, and destroyed them. Instead, against all of his training and his experience, he had simply taken back his pitiful life and run.

It was, he told himself, because he couldn't trust his crew to do the same, fix their minds on a single angry thought that would serve as a more powerful weapon than a laser cannon. It was, he told himself, because he was physically weakened, disoriented, a prisoner of war newly released into the sunlight and trying to get his bearings. It was because he was thinking of his crew and what would happen to them if he guessed wrong . . .

It was, he finally admitted in the dark and solitude, because he was no leader but a coward, just as he'd always known he was.

How was it that pitiful female had described her captivity by the Talosians?

"They own me!"

They owned Christopher Pike as well, and he would regret it every day of his life.

"What would a species so powerful possibly want with us?" Marlena wondered.

Kirk shrugged. "Control over the Empire? Maybe the entire quadrant? Pike's classified report indicates that they're dying out on their world. They lack physical strength. Their technology is in ruins. There must be a reason they didn't destroy Pike and the ship with him."

"You think he's a spy?" Marlena guessed, stroking his chest.

"Or something else," Kirk mused. "There's something beyond being able to buy off the right people that protects him—some power these Talosians gave him—but what?"

"Let's say these creatures gave him some sort of magic, some sort of power," Marlena said. "It would make him a formidable opponent."

Kirk's eyes had taken on that feral look again. "That just makes it more fun, doesn't it?"

. . .

But how to do it? Kirk wondered. Pike didn't know him, didn't fraternize with mere lieutenant commanders, in fact rarely left the ship even when she was in Spacedock. Aboard, he was surrounded by his cadre of loyal officers and those who would kill anyone if the credits were right.

Was that it? Kirk wondered. Find out whom to bribe and bribe them? And how was he supposed to go about finding who was willing to kill Pike without tipping off the others? Even if there were some way to get close to him, one-on-one—rumor had it Pike used to box in his prime; if they were peers, that might work, but no— how was it possible to know the limits of the powers these Talosians had given him?

The data Spock had given Kirk were meticulous, insofar as what the Vulcan knew. But he hadn't been on the planet with Pike; only the women had. Send Marlena to talk to them? Not the frigid Number One, certainly, who would treat an officer's woman like something she'd tracked in on her shoe, but the other one, what was her name—Colt? No. Probably clinging to some silly infatuation with Pike, willing to give her life rather than betray him, hoping he'd choose her as his woman. Kirk had known a few of those, even had to eliminate one, as he'd worked his way up the ranks.

Besides, Marlena had done her bit. Now it was his turn. Still, try as he might, he couldn't think of a way to get to Pike alone. Maybe he should just let it lie for now.

But all things come to him who waits, often from the most unexpected sources. And sometimes fortune favors the foolish.

In the meantime, he was still on medical leave following the disaster aboard the *Farragut,* and regulations would not allow him to return to duty until he'd been debriefed by what was euphemistically known as a "grief counselor." Kirk knew what that meant, and he didn't want Starfleet shrinks poking around in his head. Their drugs and devices would uncover the truth about how he'd led the crew into the path of the vampire cloud, and while Command would not discipline him for what was essentially within the rules of promotion in this man's fleet, the survivors of some of the dead crewmen might have other ideas, not excluding bribing the shrinks to learn what role Kirk had played in their loved ones' deaths.

He knew he couldn't avoid a psych debriefing entirely, but he suggested an alternative to SOP. Would Command let him do his required sessions with an old friend, a vetted former Academy member, now second in command at the most prestigious psychiatric facility in the Empire?

They would. Remembering to look properly solemn, Kirk felt the grin spreading across his face as soon as he was out of HQ and away from the watching devices.

"Pack your things," he told Marlena. "We're taking a little vacation."

Command had still not decided who would replace Captain Garrovick, and it was clear to Kirk that lieutenant commander was as far as he could push that envelope. *Farragut* was in Spacedock, her crew on extended leave until everything was sorted out.

"A vacation, in a mental hospital?" Marlena wrinkled her nose when he told her. "That sounds . . . thrilling!"

"Come on, where's your sense of adventure?" Kirk said. "Simon's an old friend from the Academy. Did I ever tell you how he helped me solve a little . . . problem I was having with another upperclassman?"

Finnegan, he thought fondly. *You bullied the wrong man. Even death couldn't wipe that stupid grin off your face.*

Simon van Gelder had decided Starfleet wasn't for him, dropped out of the Academy and gone into psychiatry, and rose quickly by the usual methods to assistant director of the Tantalus Penal Colony. But now he was the one who needed a favor.

"Don't want to say too much on subspace, even on scramble, Jim," van Gelder said, his rough-hewn face filling the comm screen. "But I could really use your help."

He'd owed van Gelder since the Academy; it was a debt he'd

like to have paid off. In exchange for handling his little "problem" (which Kirk assumed meant "disappearing" someone who stood between van Gelder and something he wanted), he'd wangle a nice, bland psych evaluation stating that Lieutenant Commander Kirk showed no long-term *sequelae* from the trauma of watching his crewmates die and being helpless to save them, was fit to return to duty, and scored high in leadership potential.

"So, while you're getting therapy, what am I supposed to do?" Marlena pouted. "Sit in a padded cell and do my nails?"

"You can watch them 'reprogram' the inmates," Kirk suggested. "It's great entertainment. Dr. Adams is actually responsible for the latest refinements in agonizer technology. He holds several demonstrations a year, and people come from all over the Empire to watch."

Marlena's eyes lit up as he described some of the creative torture techniques developed in Tristan Adams's personal bedlam. "Actually, that does sound like fun." She relented finally. "The better to refine my own techniques, darling." She gave him a little pinch for emphasis, just hard enough to make him wince. "But you have to promise to take me shopping first."

Kirk groaned theatrically. "I'll have to make captain just to keep you in shoes! Not that you need an excuse to go shopping, but why now?"

Marlena batted her eyelashes at him. "Well, a girl has to be prepared for all contingencies. I've never been to an insane asylum before. I don't have a thing to wear!"

Doctors see their patients at their most vulnerable, learn things about them that no one should ever have to know. It was why the suicide rate in the profession was so high.

Nightly on his rounds, Philip Boyce saw Pike as no one else— not even Pike himself, who had removed all mirrors in his quarters— could see him.

The crew saw a handsome, virile man, younger than his years, with a pleasant voice and a sparkle in his eye, a man no less cruel than any other senior officer, but at least when he sentenced you to the Booth, he did it with a smile.

Boyce saw the man behind the mask, a man ruined by alcohol and other bad habits that only gilded his essential dissolution of character. The doctor straightened his shoulders, bracing himself for the nightly horror show that transpired in the captain's quarters as the bloom of youth faded from Pike's features because he couldn't maintain the illusion all the time.

Only in the privacy of his darkened cabin were the true ravages Pike's double life had visited on him apparent.

Boyce was the only one permitted to see him this way, aged to his chronological age plus the effects of long-term alcohol abuse. The once luxuriant dark hair with the widow's peak was reduced to thinning strands of gray. The sparkling blue eyes were dulled and red-rimmed, the whites crisscrossed with the broken capillaries of the habitual drunk. His skin was slack, his neck wattled. There was a tremor in his hands that only Boyce's magic potions could cure.

Boyce didn't know how this shipwreck of a man managed to sustain his youthful appearance whenever he stepped beyond the door of his cabin, and he didn't want to know. He'd run some medical tests on the sly once; they showed nothing unusual, and Boyce had left it at that. He knew *when* Pike had changed; he didn't want to know why.

It had begun on that accursed planet no one could talk about on pain of death. Where before Pike had been as ruthless as the next man, crushing his adversaries, stepping over his peers, he had come back from Talos IV a changed man—hesitant, soft, indecisive, and a drunk.

His ship's doctor managed him on a delicate chemical highwire act between the amount of alcohol he needed to ingest to get through his day and the amount of counterbalancing pharmaceuticals that would keep him from staggering and slurring his words while at the same time not showing up on random tox screens.

More often than not, Boyce had to err on the side of caution.

More often than not, Pike seemed off his game, occasionally stupid. Mistakes were made, errors of judgment that sometimes got his ship into difficulties from which only a command crew accustomed to covering up for him could extricate it.

There were hearings on the worst blunders, but the charges never stuck. The few crewmembers foolish enough to file them found that somehow their accounts of what happened conflicted with the ship's logs and with their shipmates' versions. Pike skated every time. And the luckier of his complainants only found themselves transferred off his ship.

But Boyce dreaded his nightly visits to the captain's cabin almost as much as Pike dreaded letting him in.

"Here you go," Boyce would say gruffly, trying not to stare at Pike in the darkened cabin as he poured him the first martini of the night.

Boyce was a well-read man. He remembered an ancient story about a dissolute man who kept a painting of himself as a young man hidden away in an attic; the portrait aged while the man stayed young, until the very end, when all of his crimes revisited him, and he instantly crumbled to dust.

Boyce had only read the story because it was forbidden, written by some centuries-dead fop during a more permissive age.

Having read the illicit story, passed around furtively during his med-school years, he'd thought it was silly. Now he confronted the man in that portrait nightly. Christopher Pike was only forty-five, but he looked nearly twice that age.

Once upon a time, the two men's sharing a drink had been a welcome nightly ritual, a chance for old friends to relax and enjoy a conversation away from the rigors of rank and command and the long knives in the shadows.

Now neither man spoke, and only one of them drank. After about an hour, Boyce would inject Pike with what he hoped was a sufficient amount of time-released protoacamprosate and other drugs to allow him to keep the buzz from the alcohol without tripping over his own feet when he arrived on the bridge the next morning.

When the martinis were gone, Boyce went, too, knowing that Pike would sleep at least until the gin wore off, then start his careful daily ritual of Saurian brandy and other substances he had cached all over the ship to sustain him throughout the day.

Pike wasn't the only ship's captain with a serious alcohol problem. In fact, in this man's fleet, it was hard to find a sober one. It was no job for a man with a conscience. Not that Christopher Pike could be accused of having such an impediment, but something was eating his guts out.

"They won't leave me alone," he muttered on this particular night. "I keep telling them there's nothing to worry about. All they have to do is look through my eyes to see. If the Empire was going to make a move on them, I'd tell them. Why don't they trust me, Phil?" he pleaded, a look of genuine terror in his faded blue eyes. "Why don't they trust me?"

He'd made similar outbursts before, and Boyce had always put him off. He did not want to know who "they" were, whether "they" were real or just delirium tremens. He knew himself well enough to know he wouldn't do well under torture. One burst from an agonizer, and he'd sell his own mother. The less he knew about anything, the better.

"I don't know, Chris," was all he said.

"Have to trust me . . ." Pike murmured. "Have to trust me . . ."

He'd been sitting on the edge of his bunk at the start of this round. Now he shut his eyes and started to list. Boyce heard him snoring and realized he'd fallen asleep sitting upright. A trickle of drool formed at the corner of his slack-open mouth. Gently, Boyce pushed on his shoulder until Pike tipped over, took his boots off, and lifted his legs onto the bunk.

He was about to let himself out, but he forced himself to look back one more time. As happened every night, Pike was somehow transformed from broken old man to pretty portrait once again. No matter how many times he watched it happen, Boyce couldn't turn away.

He was lost in deep and troubled thought, or he'd have checked the corridor first. Instead, he almost collided with Spock. How long had the Vulcan been lurking in the shadows, and why?

"We need to talk, Doctor," was all Spock said, his grip on Boyce's bicep indicating that it was not a request.

There were advantages to having a brother who was a famous research biologist, Kirk thought as he eased the sleek little shuttle out of the section of the Planitia Yards reserved for privately owned craft. George Samuel Kirk—*Dr.* George Samuel Kirk, if you please—had only the year before been granted the Z-Magnees Prize for his work in precision frontal lobotomy, a refinement of an ancient technique to excise "bad" brain cells and render patients docile, if slow-witted—in other words, perfect for work in mines and factories where robotics weren't suitable.

The advantage to his brother was twofold. One, Sam had no interest in a military career, and Jim had no interest in science unless he could manipulate it to make his life easier. Neither brother had to worry about the other getting in the way of his career and having to be eliminated.

Two, the prizes and grants and prestigious appointments Sam earned had made him a wealthy man, and an indulgent one. He owned a fleet of shuttles, some with no serial numbers—the better to transport abducted political enemies to his experimental labs unnoticed—and if his kid brother wanted to take one out for a spin to impress the young lady, well, Sam was only too happy to oblige, no questions asked.

Because Simon van Gelder had been adamant about one thing.

"Come as a civilian, Jim. If this thing backfires, I don't want Starfleet implicated, and trust me, neither do you."

There was a third advantage to arriving in orbit around Tantalus in a big-ticket private shuttle. It impressed the hell out of the director of the colony, Dr. Tristan Adams.

The Tantalus Penal Colony was the last stop for those deemed intractably criminally insane. Technically, there were no longer any such persons in the Empire, now that modern medicine had eliminated the kind of "insanity genes" that made some Imperial citizens incapable of obeying orders.

"However," Dr. Adams was saying as he showed Kirk and Marlena around, his high forehead furrowed with seriousness, "while no one is born insane anymore, there are still some mutations which evidence in adulthood and, since insanity per se is not a crime, these people are not eliminated but sent to us for long-term treatment."

Trying to look interested, Kirk suppressed a yawn. Marlena didn't even bother. Bored with peering into the individual padded cells where inmates either lay immobile on their narrow beds or sat upright staring off into the distance, she wanted to see the "reeducation" chambers and had said as much.

Adams looked at her curiously and stopped lecturing. "We'll discuss that over dinner," was all he said, then moved on down the seemingly endless maze of corridors.

Deliberately lagging behind Adams in the hope of communicating with van Gelder, who tagged along but so far had said nothing beyond the usual exchange of pleasantries when their shuttle docked, Kirk gave van Gelder a puzzled look. Van Gelder gestured with his chin in Adams's direction, as if to say, *Wait for it!*

Coming to a bend in the corridor, Adams stopped abruptly and turned to face his guests. "Dr. James, you know why these patients are here?"

"No, sir, I don't," Kirk said, suppressing a smile. He'd given himself an entirely new identity, and a doctorate, on his way there.

"Most of them simply crossed the wrong person," Adams said. "Standard procedure. But the others are suffering from something known as 'sluggishly progressive schizophrenia.'"

He was looking at Kirk expectantly.

Say less, Kirk told himself, *and you won't give yourself away.*

"I've heard the term," he lied carefully, "but I can't say I'm familiar with all of the symptoms."

Adams seemed about to say something else, then changed his mind. "If you and your lady will join me for dinner, I'll elaborate further."

"What's going on?" Kirk demanded as soon as he was reasonably certain that he and van Gelder were alone. Marlena was in the shower; he could hear her singing.

"There's only one genuine psychotic on this planet," van Gelder said hurriedly, his voice low as if he expected to be overheard. "Adams used to be as orthodox as any man. But something changed. He lost his nerve, started saying that what we were doing was evil. Over dinner, he'll start babbling about how it's possible to rehabilitate people, put them back into society. You'll see!"

"So?" Kirk didn't see the problem. "Report him to his superiors. You've kept records, I'm sure. It should be easy enough to—"

Van Gelder was shaking his head. "Don't you think I've thought of that? But if I do, they'll eliminate him and put me in charge."

Kirk was puzzled. "Isn't that what you want?"

"Hell, no! I want to get as far from here as I can travel. Change my identity, disappear. Buy myself a little planet somewhere, go native, find the secret to immortality—I don't know. But you know the security arrangement on penal planets. The supply ships stop by twice a year, and Adams has put a stop to his 'special performances.' You're the first outsiders who've been here for months. He'll get caught eventually, but I've got to get out of here before he implicates me in this lunacy. Just get me as far as the nearest Orion space hub. I'll keep your name out of it."

All he wanted was transport? That made Kirk's blood boil.

"You brought me here to be your chauffeur?" He seethed.

"Keep your voice down!" van Gelder warned him. "Listen to me. You'll go back to Earth and tell them the inmates have killed Adams and taken over, and there was nothing you could do with a lightly armed shuttle. Starfleet will send a force to liquidate the entire planet, and I'll have disappeared, ostensibly killed by the inmates as well."

"What's in it for me?" Kirk asked.

"Your psych evaluation, for one thing."

"And?"

Van Gelder's eyes flickered over every surface in the guest quarters, as they had when he'd first arrived, looking for listening devices. The man's paranoia was palpable.

"When the inmates are remanded here, most of them are allowed to bring their personal possessions with them," he said. "Weapons, jewelry, rare artifacts, some newfangled currency called gold-pressed latinum. They never get any of it back, of course. Adams has all of it stashed away. Get me out of here, and half of it is yours."

"I'll think about it," Kirk said, somewhat mollified, wondering how easy it would be to kill van Gelder once they'd gotten rid of Adams.

It was easier than he could have imagined.

Just as van Gelder had predicted, Adams droned on throughout dinner about "rehabilitation" and "mainstreaming these unfortunates back into society." Marlena sat silently, looking decorative, listening for any nuances Kirk might miss so that they could compare notes later.

"There's no such thing as 'sluggishly progressive schizophrenia,' Dr. James," Adams was saying. "It's a phony designation for political prisoners, nothing more. Their families are too powerful for them to be killed outright, so they're kept here, drugged and tortured, for the rest of their very short lives. They'd be better off dead!"

Adams looked as if he were about to cry. Van Gelder was right. Kirk listened for as long as he could stand it. Van Gelder excused himself just before dessert, and Kirk wondered what he was up to.

"You can't expect your colleagues to concur with this," he suggested to Adams, if only to shut him up.

"Oh, but they will eventually, Dr. James. I intend to educate some of the brighter inmates to act as models of what rehabilitation can do. We have some very powerful people interned here . . ."

Yes, I know, Kirk thought. He'd done his homework, knew how many contrarian voices had been stilled in the last purges. Most disappeared without a trace; some "lucky" few ended up here.

". . . I intend to turn this planet into a showplace," Adams was saying, a look of messianic fervor on his face. "It will become a model for all future—"

"Forgive me," Kirk said. Enough was enough. If he had to listen to that voice much longer, he was going to explode and blow his cover. "But as soon as the Bureau of Mental Hygiene finds out what you're up to, you may find yourself an inmate here instead of the director."

"Ah, you think I'll allow myself to be led like a lamb to the slaughter?" Adams shook a cautionary finger at him, then finished his wine. "I'm prepared for resistance. Tomorrow, after morning rounds, I will show you my secret weapon."

But there were no morning rounds. Sometime in the middle of the night, no doubt with van Gelder's help, the inmates staged a revolt. Kirk was awakened by shouts and the thunder of running feet, dozens of them, in the corridor outside. Moments later, van Gelder was pounding on the door.

"Adams is dead. Let's go!"

"Wait here," Kirk started to say to Marlena, but she had already slipped into a practical jumpsuit before he'd adjusted the setting on his phaser.

"Oh, no, you don't!" she said, raking her fingers through her hair, managing to look beautiful even shaken out of a sound sleep. "Whatever you two are plotting, I want in!"

Kirk grinned, watching her slip her favorite knife into one thigh-high boot. "Glad you're on our side!"

They found van Gelder rifling through the desk in Adams's office.

"Coder," he explained, holding up a small device in one hand, a silencer-fitted phaser in the other. "Unlocks the safe."

They hurried down the labyrinthine corridors away from where the noises were coming from—inmates freeing other inmates, killing the guards who had tortured them, Kirk assumed. Van Gelder led the way, apparently so intent on getting to the pilfered goods that he didn't realize how vulnerable a target the back of his neck made.

For a moment, Kirk was tempted to take him out just for the hell of it, but, for one thing, he couldn't find the safe on his own. For another, Adams had said something about a secret weapon. Something powerful enough to defend his mad schemes against a military come to reclaim his little planet? Kirk wasn't leaving until he learned whether there was a grain of truth to Adams's raving.

The "safe" was, in fact, a good-sized storeroom filled with unimaginable riches. Kirk's eyes roved over an entire weapons wall—antique knives and swords, Imperial devices, and alien objects whose purpose he would love to learn. Van Gelder had no time for such niceties. He was too busy stuffing loose gemstones and ancient coins into his pockets, loading whatever he could lay his hands on onto a small antigrav sled he must have had stashed away for years in anticipation of this moment. Marlena joined in the fun, grabbing at rings and necklaces, trying them on, giddy as a child.

Kirk glanced out into the corridor. The inmates hadn't come this way yet, but he could hear them shouting, and what sounded like doors being broken down, echoing from several directions. He tried to remember where the minuscule transporter room was from here—on this level, up or down, left or right?

"Simon," he said tightly. "We really should go."

Still madly scavenging, van Gelder wasn't listening. "Come on, Kirk, grab your share! I don't want you claiming I didn't give you what you've earned!"

Something in the clutter caught Kirk's eye then. When they'd come in, it had been hidden behind an ornate armoire that van Gelder had knocked over in his enthusiasm. At first glance, it was some sort of visual monitor, though it didn't look at all like the others almost everywhere in the complex. Kirk retrieved a once-beautiful silk robe, trampled under van Gelder's feet, and wiped a layer of dust off it. "What's this?"

"Some sort of monitoring device," van Gelder said over his shoulder, distracted. "Belonged to a scientist from a colony world, some odd species I'd never seen before. Worked on weapons technology until he balked. They trashed his laboratory, remanded him here for some of Adams's special interrogation techniques." Van Gelder paused for breath, scanning the room to see if there was anything else of value he could fit on the antigrav.

"He died in transit," he said after a final inventory. "Never did say what that thing was for, but it was what he was trying to conceal when Starfleet moved in. Adams was convinced it was important, but as far as I know, he never made heads or tails of it. Time to go!"

"We'll be right behind you," Kirk said, transfixed by the alien device. It was nothing but a screen and some primitive knobs and lights and buttons, but something about it whispered *Power!* Could this be Adams's "secret weapon"?

More than a dozen necklaces around her delicate neck, her fingers glittering with rings, Marlena staggered over to him giddily. "What does it do?"

"I'm not sure yet," Kirk murmured, absently fiddling with things until he managed to activate the screen. The visual showed the corridor outside, where van Gelder was making sure the coast was clear. Kirk followed his movements onscreen. Van Gelder came back for the antigrav, loping out into the corridor without looking back.

"Come on!" Marlena said, tugging on Kirk's arm. When he didn't seem to hear her, she started for the door.

"Wait!" He stayed her. On a hunch, he touched the button shaped like an inverted teardrop, set apart from the others as if to emphasize its importance.

Halfway down the corridor, Simon van Gelder vanished, faster than any transporter beam could have taken him.

With a jolt, Kirk realized exactly what he had discovered. It took Marlena a moment longer. Staring at the empty corridor, one hand over her mouth, she giggled. "Oops!"

Kirk recovered himself. "Oh, well. Simon did say he wanted to disappear."

The device was self-contained, merely hung on the wall like a picture frame, unconnected to any power source. Amazed at their good fortune, Kirk dumped van Gelder's loot out of the antigrav with a rueful look and set the alien device down in it almost reverently. After a few wrong turns, he and Marlena finally reached the transporter room, only to find it blocked by a crowd of inmates.

"Dr. Adams was a good man!" one of them, a disheveled gray-haired woman with the marks of shackles visible on her wrists and ankles, shrilled at him. "You killed him!"

"We had nothing to do with that!" Kirk said impatiently, but the crowd showed no signs of moving. Below her line of sight, he focused the alien device on the ringleader and pressed the button. Like van Gelder, the woman disappeared.

"What you do once we leave is your business!" Kirk shouted at the now confused and agitated inmates, "but my woman and I are walking out of here unharmed. Do you understand me?"

They did. Some of them ran. The others silently stood aside and let them pass.

When he and Marlena returned to Earth, Kirk found a message from Spock waiting for him.

"Mr. Kirk, *Enterprise* will be leaving Spacedock in ninety-four-point-three hours. I would appreciate a final chess game before we do so."

They were abandoning him.

You are no longer of use to us, Christopher. We shall have to let you go.
The voices were in his head, as always, but more and more

lately, he found himself answering them aloud. "I've told you everything I know! I've protected you! My report said there was nothing of use on your world; I made the recommendation for General Order Seven." He could hear his voice rising, couldn't stop himself. "What more do you want from me?"

Nothing. That is precisely the point, Christopher. You are not close enough to the centers of power to know what is being planned at the highest levels. We should never have let you live.

"And I should have recommended the Empire send a fleet to destroy you!" Pike shouted with the last shred of anger he possessed.

He was answered with silence, and for a moment, he thought that might be all there was to it. In truth, he wanted to be rid of them more than anything in the universe, but he had been in their thrall for so long he wasn't sure he could trust his own mind to obey him. As for his body . . . without the illusion they had given him, he was convinced he would crumble into dust.

"How soon?" he asked the voices, hoping they would kill him outright, because with what he knew, they certainly would not let him live.

He could still feel their presence, but there was no answer. He dared a glance in the mirror, waiting for the transformation to take place. There was a touch of gray at his temples that hadn't been there before, but the illusion still held. Perhaps if he kept his promise not to betray them, they would let him go gradually. He wondered if it was worth it, but he could no longer think it through. Christopher Pike did the one consistent thing he still remembered how to do: poured himself a shot of Saurian brandy and headed for the bridge.

"How did you find out?" Kirk asked, trying not to wince as Spock captured his king's bishop.

"Dr. Boyce was most cooperative. A single touch of the agonizer persuaded him to tell me that the man we see is not the man Christopher Pike has become. And there is something more." The Vulcan seemed to hesitate. "Captain Pike's aberrant behavior has become too blatant for his superiors to ignore. It is rumored he is to be . . . eliminated."

Kirk couldn't sleep that night. It all seemed too easy. Why was Spock feeding him all this information, stepping out of the way to give him the means to get at Pike? It had to be a trap. Unless the Vulcan meant what he said about not wanting command, a mindset Kirk simply could not understand. And if Starfleet wanted Pike out of the way, would Spock be the only one they'd approach? Why didn't they just bring him up on charges and execute him themselves? They were, as Spock would say, playing most illogically.

Kirk broke out in a sweat, slipping out of bed so he wouldn't disturb Marlena, who slept the sleep of a child—or someone with no conscience at all—and began to pace. Maybe Pike was actually the aggressor here instead of the victim. Maybe Pike was working with Spock to eliminate anyone aspiring to his job. Maybe . . .

You've got the Tantalus device! Kirk reminded himself, slowing his breathing, calming down. Spock probably expected him to rush headlong into some confrontation with Pike in which either or both of them might be killed. Then Number One would get command and Spock would be promoted to first officer, which was all he claimed he wanted.

But the Tantalus device would make all the difference.

Starfleet Command had scheduled a gala send-off for *Enterprise* on the eve of her next five-year mission. Knowing what he knew, Kirk wondered if they could be more blatant. The ship would be crawling with brass and visiting dignitaries, all eggs in one basket. An assassin in or out of uniform could lose himself in the crowd, and an assassin who knew the layout of a starship could easily find his way to the captain's quarters, if he could get past the extra security.

A handful of junior officers had been invited as well, Kirk among them. It was just too convenient. He wondered if Command hadn't sent several people to remove Pike, and if they happened to kill one another off at the same time . . .

He would simply have to get there first.

"Let me come with you!" Marlena pleaded, tossing one outfit after another out of the closet onto the bed, trying to decide what to wear.

"No . . ." Kirk started to say, but she didn't let him finish.

"I understand, my darling. You don't want me implicated in case anything goes wrong." She touched his face tenderly. "I appreciate that, I do. But with you in charge, how can it possibly go wrong? You'll at least take me to the gala with you? The invitation did say 'Lieutenant Commander Kirk and Guest.'"

"Actually," Kirk said, taking both of her small hands in his. "I had something else in mind."

How one man managed to overcome four of Pike's personal guards, more heavily armed than usual and stationed at intervals outside his quarters for extra security with so many civilians onboard, would be a tale told down the years and exaggerated with each telling. Kirk's characteristic guile and skill were augmented by his knowing that, back in their rooms, Marlena was monitoring with the Tantalus device.

"Keep an eye on me," he ordered her, his face more serious than she had ever seen it. "But don't intervene unless I get in trouble."

"You're giving me an awful lot of responsibility," she said, reluctant to touch the device this time, even though they'd practiced it together. "How do you know I won't kill you?"

Even as she said it, Kirk had to remind himself, for all the trappings and sophistication, just how young and vulnerable she really was.

"Because I think you like to watch, but you don't really want to kill personally," he said. "Besides, if anything happens to me . . ."

She nodded. She knew. Without him as her protector, she would have to start anew, perhaps with someone less appealing, more willing to cast her aside. She had seen what happened to other officers' women when the officers grew tired of them.

So it was with relief that she watched as Kirk took down each of the guards all by himself.

It was too easy, Kirk thought, again wondering if he was, in fact, the intended victim. Maybe it was someone's revenge for the death of Captain Garrovick or a host of other actions from his past come home to roost. The hair on the back of his neck prickled ominously as he pressed the buzzer outside Pike's door.

"Come," said a voice that sounded as if it were coming from the bottom of a well.

Despite his reclusiveness, Kirk had expected to find Pike at least going through the motions of dressing for the festivities, which were already starting on the main rec deck. The absolute darkness he encountered once the door closed startled him, and he prepared for an ambush that didn't come.

"It's all right," the voice said, as the lights came up slowly. "I've been expecting you."

Kirk wasn't sure what he would find in that darkened room, but the sight of the real Christopher Pike took him aback. He recovered himself.

"How did you know it would be me?"

"I didn't," Pike said wearily. "I just knew it would be tonight. You haven't brought a phaser. A knife, then?"

Kirk shook his head. "I promise it will be quick. There's a little something I need you to do for me first . . ."

Pike gave Kirk what he wanted. As he did so, his shoulders began to heave. He was weeping openly.

"I can't sustain the illusion. Don't let anyone see me like this!"

"Don't worry," Kirk said with a compassion he didn't know he possessed. Why would anyone care what he looked like after death? Apparently, the only thing Pike still had left was his vanity. "No one will see you at all."

Pike sat with his hands in his lap, a man defeated, awaiting his execution. His passivity almost made Kirk hesitate. He'd wanted to savor this death, but Pike was throwing himself on his sword. There was no satisfaction in this. Only the thought of what it would earn him at the end convinced Kirk that he had to go through with it.

He poured Pike a drink from the bottle of Saurian brandy on the desk at his elbow, then poured one for himself.

"I'll take good care of her," he promised. Pike showed no curiosity as Kirk turned to leave. "It won't be long now."

Pike merely nodded, resigned, and Kirk had the courtesy to dim the lights again on his way out. The Tantalus device could find its target even in the dark.

Kirk deliberately walked through the main rec deck on his way to the transporter room. He wanted to make certain he was seen. Then he hurried back to the rooms he shared with Marlena. She stood behind him at the Tantalus device as, with the touch of a button, Christopher Pike ceased to exist.

That night, Kirk slept as soundly as he'd slept the night after Captain Garrovick died, and at first, he thought the old woman's voice was part of a dream. But it was still there in the morning as he straightened the tunic of his dress uniform in the mirror, and it had a quality half thought, half speech, but nothing at all of dream.

James . . . It is James?

"Who wants to know?" he said aloud, forcing himself not to spin around to see what he couldn't see in the mirror.

We note you with interest. Christopher was weak, unsuitable. You, on the other hand . . .

"Suitable for what?"

"Who are you talking to?" Marlena murmured muzzily from the breakfast nook, puttering with the replicator.

"No one," Kirk said quickly. "Just rehearsing what I'm going to say when I get to HQ."

. . .

An hour later, as he passed through the main gate of Starfleet Head-quarters, the tale of Pike's disappearance (kidnapping, murder?) buzzed around him. He bluffed his way past the guards outside the C-in-C's office, where he knew a weekly strategy meeting was in progress. Striding to the foot of the long table before anyone could stop him, he took something small out of a fold in his lieutenant commander's sash and tossed it onto the table so that it slid down the highly polished surface almost into the indignant C-in-C's clasped hands.

It was Pike's captain's insignia. By now, forensics would have found Kirk's fingerprints on the brandy glass, some skin cells where his fists had connected with the security guards' jaws, but he'd asked Pike for this talisman of his office so that there would be no question who had assassinated him, even if no one ever figured out how.

"I've done your job for you," he said quietly, then stood at parade rest, his face devoid of expression.

He figured they would either kill him or give him what he wanted.

They gave him what he wanted. Kirk got his promotion and his ship. His superiors were candid.

"Ships' captains have a way of meeting untimely ends whenever you're in the vicinity," the C-in-C, a crusty old admiral who was rumored to have Klingon ancestry, told him gruffly. "Apparently, the only way to put a stop to it is to promote you to captain yourself."

I will stop here, Kirk told himself. A lesser man would be greedy, use the device to eliminate anyone who irritated him or got in his path, give himself away, end up taken down like a mad dog. Other men might aspire to the admiralty, the Senate, the satrapy of a conquered world. All he wanted was *Enterprise* and the power to use her, and now he had her.

Unbeknownst to anyone, even Marlena, he also had some powerful newfound "friends" taking up residence inside his head. So the Talosians found him more "suitable" than Pike, did they? The ramifications of that would prove interesting.

He personally installed the Tantalus device in the captain's quarters, cleverly hidden behind a wall panel to be used at his discretion. He knew he would have to use it to keep what he had gained but promised himself that he would use it judiciously.

He only had cause to use it one more time before they left Earth. Easier to get rid of Number One than to explain why he was promoting Spock in her place. There were murmurs among some of the bridge crew, but they eventually subsided. Whatever had made the ship's two senior-most officers disappear, no one else wanted to be next.

Accustoming himself to the feel of the captain's chair for the first time, Kirk sensed Spock's eyes on him from the science station. The ship was at station keeping inside Spacedock, the rest of the crew still reporting in, and they were alone on the bridge except for a couple of engineers running a last-minute diagnostic on the nav station; Kirk waved them toward the turbolift before swinging his chair in Spock's direction.

"Something on your mind?"

Spock chose his words carefully. "I do not subscribe to magic, Captain Kirk. Nevertheless, Captain Pike's utter disappearance, without so much as a transporter trace, has apparently been accomplished by a technology so unfamiliar to me as to seem magical."

Kirk's smile was calculated. "Better get used to working with a magician, Spock. You never know what else I might have up my sleeve."

He had requested permission to take *Enterprise* out on a shakedown cruise before the five-year mission. As the youngest captain in Starfleet, he pointed out to his superiors, it would be good for him to "get the feel of her." When he told Marlena, she marveled at him.

"What's that old Earth expression? 'Butter wouldn't melt in

your mouth'? I know what you're up to. You're easily the most evil man I've ever known!"

"Why, thank you!" he said with his most endearing smile.

He didn't have to tell Spock where they were going, either. Nor did he have to tell him to alter the ship's logs after the fact.

And he certainly didn't have to tell his newfound friends where he was headed; they could already see it in his mind.

Is this wise, Magistrate? This Kirk is not the weakling Pike was. We have not had time to condition him as we did Pike. Our influence upon his mind may not be as powerful.

Which is why we have asked him to come to us, the Magistrate replied. *To solidify the bond that will make him ours.*

But the *Enterprise* that approached the Talos star group this time was not a ship answering what seemed to be an innocent distress call, nor was it the emissary the Talosians were expecting. It was a ship plotting the best possible trajectory to wreak havoc on an enemy world.

The Talosians weren't the first aliens to underestimate James T. Kirk. They certainly wouldn't be the last.

"Their defenses are virtually nonexistent, Captain," Spock reported, having done a long-range scan. "Apparently, they have relied on their power of mind for so many millennia that they have no satellite defense system and no weapons of any kind."

"Pike's sealed reports suggested they could knock a starship out of space with their minds alone," Kirk said. "Let's not give them the opportunity. Ready phaser sweep. Maximum spread, maximum intensity. We'll strip away the atmosphere, and bye-bye, Talos IV."

"Captain." It was Spock. "Request permission to pinpoint scan for the human female, Vina. If she is still alive . . ."

"Collateral damage," Kirk said tightly, his eyes on the forward screen. He wasn't sure how much longer he could sustain the inner rage Pike's report had indicated was the only thing that could block the Talosians from his mind. He focused on the last time Captain Garrovick had humiliated him in front of the entire crew. *Who's sneering now?* he thought. "Weapons, on my mark . . ."

The Magistrate had time for one final thought. *It appears we have miscalculated . . .*

Kirk enjoyed the light show, imagined the screams of however many Talosian minds as their fragile bodies disintegrated in the vacuum the phaser blasts left behind. Pike's death had left a bad taste in his mouth, but this washed it away.

Belowdecks, Marlena was watching from the bio lab, stopping work long enough to contemplate the ruthlessness of the man to whom she'd joined her fate.

How does Marlena fit in? she wondered, knowing it would take all her wiles to hold this complex man, but also knowing that she could. As the ruined Talosian world receded on the aft screen, she smiled. She had chosen well.

Ultimately, *Enterprise*'s shakedown cruise was cut short by a subspace message ordering Kirk to set course for a world called Gorlan, where rebel factions had foolishly staged an uprising against their Imperial overlords. En route, Kirk made a brief entry in his personal log.

"Today I did something the Empire will thank me for one day. Now that there is no Talos IV, there is no longer any need for General Order Seven. A telepathic species so powerful should never have been spared in the first place. And nothing so benefits any bureaucracy as the elimination of red tape—swiftly, efficiently, and for the greater good."

The Black Flag

James Swallow

HISTORIAN'S NOTE: *This tale is set in 2277, ten years after the events of the Star Trek episode "Mirror, Mirror" and Spock's subsequent rise to power, as chronicled in* The Sorrows of Empire *from* Star Trek Mirror Universe: Glass Empires.

James Swallow is proud to be the only British writer to have worked on a *Star Trek* television series, creating the original story concepts for the *Star Trek Voyager* episodes "One" and "Memorial." His other associations with the *Star Trek* saga include the *Terok Nor* novel *Day of the Vipers;* "Closure," "Ordinary Days," and "Seeds of Dissent" for the anthologies *Distant Shores, The Sky's the Limit,* and *Infinity's Prism;* scripting the video game *Star Trek Invasion;* and over four hundred articles in thirteen *Star Trek* magazines around the world.

Beyond the final frontier, as well as nonfiction work such as *Dark Eye: The Films of David Fincher,* James also wrote the *Sundowners* series of steampunk westerns, *Jade Dragon, The Butterfly Effect,* and fiction in the worlds of *Doctor Who* (*Peacemaker, Singularity, Old Soldiers,* and *Kingdom of Silver*), *Warhammer 40,000* (*Red Fury, The Flight of the Eisenstein, Faith & Fire, Deus Encarmine,* and *Deus Sanguinius*), *Stargate* (*Halcyon, Relativity,* and *Nightfall*), and *2000AD* (*Eclipse, Whiteout,* and *Blood Relative*). His other credits include scripts for videogames and audio dramas, including *Battlestar Galactica, Blake's 7,* and *Space 1889.*

James Swallow lives in London and is currently at work on his next book.

The deck of the *Eighth Happiness* vibrated as it was struck again, the resonance humming from one end of the freighter to the other. Griffin lost his footing and fell against the wall of the long corridor that ran the length of the ship's spine.

A sweaty hand grasped his wrist and pulled. He looked up to see the navigator's smoke-dirtied face glaring back at him, wide-eyed and afraid. "You cheapskate!" cried the Proximan. "We're gonna end up dead because of your greed!"

Griffin got to his feet and shook off the other man's grip, scowling. "Stow it, Kendrew. I don't recall any objections from you when I floated the idea of a smuggling run!" He started toward the command pod at the bow of the ship.

"How could you have thought we'd be able to cut through the Taurus Reach without being detected?" Kendrew waved his hands in the air, keeping pace. He was talking loudly to be heard over the whoop of the klaxons. "Didn't you think of that? Didn't you think we'd get caught?"

Griffin cuffed him around the head. "If you don't have anything constructive to say, shut the hell up!" The deck moaned and shuddered again, as if it had been struck by a hammer. Griffin had commanded the *Eighth* for a long time, and he could read the sounds she made; the ship had been snared by a tractor beam.

What made things worse was that Kendrew was right. Griffin *did* know better. With hindsight, the idea that this rattletrap ship could sneak through the Reach without encountering any Imperial entanglements seemed idiotic. But *she* had convinced him it could be done, and like a fool, Griffin had believed her, even let her loose on the warp engines to modify their energy signature. The woman had told him it would work.

He spat. He hadn't thought her kind was capable of lying, but there it was.

"She's on the bridge," said Kendrew, clearly thinking the same way. "I told her to leave, but she wouldn't."

They passed the docking airlock antechamber and reached the hatch to the command pod. Griffin slid the thick door open. "Status?" he called, and got a string of sulky looks from the rest of his crew. "I said, what's the bloody status?"

"Shields have collapsed." The reply was metered and cool. "Engines are offline."

Griffin turned to glare at the woman, and in turn she regarded him with an air of utter unconcern. "How did that happen?" he demanded.

His passenger raised one upswept eyebrow. "This is a light freighter." She pointed to the vessel moving to bear on the bridge's viewscreen. Griffin made out a hull formed from a disc and a collection of interconnected rods. "That is an Imperial cruiser. Do you require me to provide you with a detailed explanation of the ratio to which you are outmatched?"

Griffin's hands balled into fists. "You promised me—"

The Vulcan shook her head. "I did nothing of the sort. I merely presented you with an option."

The freighter captain growled and went to his station, pulling a pistol from a compartment in the console. "You'll pay for this!"

An indicator glyph flashed on the viewscreen, and Kendrew yelped. "Transporters! We're being boarded!"

"I would suggest you drop that weapon," said the Vulcan. "It might be considered provocative." She had barely finished speaking when the air was cut by a humming buzz, and a dozen columns of ruby-gold light coalesced around the command deck.

Men and women in blood-red tunics gained solidity and form,

and Griffin's breath caught in his throat as he saw the dagger-and-planet insignia on their chests. Griffin felt as if every detail of the intruders was impressed upon him; he recognized the sashes around their waists, the slender and lethal blades sheathed at their hips. The hallmarks of Imperial Earth's chosen. But if anything, these invaders wore an air of menace that went beyond any kind of uniform. He saw a tattooed Andorian female, tribal patterning visible down her bare arms and across her midriff, silver rings in her brow and lips; cradling a plasma shotgun lazily in his grip, an ebony-skinned man so large and muscled across the chest that the tunic upon him seemed ready to burst; a wispy, pale Edoan carrying blades in each of his three hands; and standing behind the command chair . . .

Griffin found a granite-hard gaze boring into him. Lit from behind by the blinking alarm strobes, the man was tall and imposing, his face defined by the flicker of flame from a thin cigar between his teeth. He wore the uniform of an Imperial officer, but only as an afterthought. His stature was framed by a long gray coat that hung to his ankles. Both hands lay casually on the top of a cross-belt holster, the black forms of phaser pistols beneath them.

The man cocked his head and smiled, exhaling a little smoke. He nodded at Griffin's pistol. "Do you know what happens to men who point guns at me?"

Griffin immediately tossed the weapon at Kendrew, who caught it without thinking. Something silver flashed out of the Andorian's hand, and the navigator made a choking noise before he slumped to the floor, a dagger protruding from his neck.

"Yes." The officer nodded. He drew on the cigar and then gestured at the ship around them. "You tried to get past us without halting for inspection."

Griffin sneered and nodded, remaining defiant.

The man leaned in toward him. "Do you know who I am?"

He didn't; all these Fleet types looked the same to him, either pretty boys or brigands dressed up like toy soldiers.

The Vulcan woman answered the question. "Captain Zhao Sheng," she began, as if she were reading from a report, "also known as the Yellow Hand, the Untouchable, decorated six times by the Admiralty and once by the Empress Sato herself. Master of the *I.S.S. Endeavour* under the authority of Starbase 47."

Zhao shot the woman a hard look at the last statement. He studied Griffin again. "All true. And so, why did you think that this . . ." He paused, feeling for the right term. "This *scow* was a match for my ship?" His voice dropped. "I am almost insulted."

The Andorian woman had recovered her knife, and with a nod from her commander, she spoke up. "This vessel has not paid tribute for its passage through the Taurus Reach. The penalty for such an infraction is severe." She cleaned Kendrew's blood off the blade, using the dead man's shirt.

"The penalty for such an infraction," repeated the Vulcan, "is at the discretion of the officer in command, according to Imperial diktat. Punishment may be anything from a percentage of confiscation of cargo to summary execution."

Griffin glared at her. "Will you be quiet, woman?"

Zhao nodded, amused. "She's quite right." He glanced at the Edoan and the large human. "Tupo, Mkembe? Supervise the boarding parties in the cargo bays. Take half of what you find."

"Half?" Griffin choked on the word. "You're worse than pirates!"

"What about resistance?" Tupo made lazy cuts in the air with his swords.

Zhao looked away. "Deal with it."

As they left, the Andorian indicated Griffin and the rest of the bridge crew. "Sir?" She pointed with her dagger, making it plain exactly what question she was asking.

Griffin saw his chance and broke in. "Your apes won't be able to open my cargo pods! They're ray-shielded, impregnable. Even cracking the locks would take centuries!"

"Oh?" Zhao said conversationally. He considered that for a moment, then snapped his fingers at the Andorian. "Ensign sh'Zenne?

Communicator, please." He took the woman's device and activated it, then slipped the unit into Griffin's pocket.

Leaving his other men to guard the command pod and holding the hatch open so the crew could watch what he was doing, Zhao gave Griffin a shove in the small of the back and propelled him over to the airlock. Sh'Zenne opened the inner door and put the freighter captain through, sealing him in.

Griffin tried to maintain his defiance. "What are you going to do, huh? Drain out the air? Suffocate me?"

Zhao shook his head and produced his own communicator, turning away to speak a quiet command into it.

"You can't space me!" Griffin yelled, his voice muffled through the thick armor glass. "I'm the only one who knows the unlock codes!"

"Really?" said Zhao. He nodded to the Andorian, who slapped her palm over the emergency venting control.

There was a sudden screech of air, and the outer door opened. Griffin was blown out into the void and tumbled away into the dark. Sh'Zenne closed the hatch behind him and repressurized the chamber.

Zhao made a point of looking each one of Griffin's bridge crew in the eyes; then he whispered into the communicator again.

A transporter buzzed, and Griffin rematerialized on the deck at Zhao's feet. He was covered in rimes of ice, shivering and coughing. Lines of blood from his nostrils and ears streaked his face. Sh'Zenne picked up the trembling man and put him back into the airlock.

"Go . . . t'hell . . ." Griffin managed.

"Again," said Zhao, and the exercise was repeated. The airlock opened, and Griffin shot away. Agonizing seconds passed before the man was beamed back, his body racked with pain from the freezing kiss of space.

Sh'Zenne opened the lock for a third time, and Griffin wailed. Zhao gestured for her to stop. "Yes?" he asked. "Is there something you want to share with me? The codes?" Griffin mumbled something incoherent, and Zhao kicked him toward the threshold of the airlock.

With black, frostbitten fingers, Griffin clawed at the deck, trying to hold himself back. "No. No." He wheezed. "Tell you."

"Better," said Zhao, and nodded to sh'Zenne, who bent down to recover her frost-covered communicator. "Pass on the key codes to Lieutenant Tupo."

"An expedient if ruthless form of interrogation." The Vulcan woman who had spoken earlier stood before the captain. He found himself appreciating the line and shape of her, long waves of black hair falling down over her shoulders, and a cool, serene face.

"You disapprove?"

She shook her head slightly. "On the contrary. Your method shows forethought and control. Other Imperial officers would have gunned down the entire crew as a matter of course. You appear to apply object lessons more sparingly."

He was sure he detected the smallest measure of sarcasm in the words. Zhao crossed to her and pressed a phaser against her throat. "Do not make the mistake of assuming that leniency on my part represents weakness, Vulcan. As you noted, I have the power of life and death over every person on this ship."

She remained irritatingly unruffled. "And who, I wonder, has that power over you, Captain Zhao?"

Her eyes—for a moment, he found himself searching them, and in the woman's gaze, he glimpsed something . . . fascinating. He smiled thinly and shrugged the moment off, moving away. "I am a servant of the Empire." Zhao said the words by rote, ignoring the ashen taste they left in his mouth.

"As am I," she replied. "In that capacity, I offer myself to your service."

Zhao turned back to face her. "Is that so?" He holstered the gun and reached out to stroke her cheek. The flesh was warm, as if touched by the sun. She was, it had to be said, quite alluring. "Why would you do that?"

"Because I know who you are, Zhao Sheng. I know you treat your men and women well." She nodded at the Andorian. "I know what a man like you requires." He smiled at that, and she eyed him. "And I know that I will perish if I remain aboard the *Eighth Happiness*. Once you leave, Griffin's crew will kill me. They blame me for this turn of events."

"Are they right to do so, Miss . . . ?" he asked, considering her with new eyes. "You will forgive me, but I don't know your name."

"Yes, they are," she replied, "and my name is T'Prynn."

"The tribute is secure in bay two," said Klisiewicz. Zhao's first officer delivered his report, as always, standing ramrod straight and staring at a point somewhere beyond the far bulkhead of the captain's private chambers. "We have resumed our patrol pattern as ordered, sir."

Zhao nodded, assembling the items he needed from storage cupboards in one of the alcoves. "Anything else, Stephen?"

The other man hesitated for a moment. The captain knew the small tell; Klisiewicz was a rarity among the *Endeavour*'s crew, an Imperial officer who fully embraced the letter and law of the Empire's military doctrines. He typified the mentality of "by the book," and while sometimes that generated friction with the more rebellious and relaxed attitudes of Zhao's other officers, the man played an important role aboard the ship. He was the voice of reason, the echo of what the Fleet once was; and in darker moments, the captain might have been willing to admit that Klisiewicz was a mirror for the officer that *he* had once been.

"It came to my attention that a number of junior ratings had expressed seditious opinions over your handling of this action," he explained after a moment. "I've initiated a disciplinary session in the agony booth for them."

"What did they say?"

"It was suggested that you showed weakness in allowing the freighter to continue on its way."

He chuckled dryly. "What good would another obliterated starship be to the running of the Empire?"

"Indeed, sir," agreed the officer. "The questioning of your commands. That sort of insubordination is intolerable."

Zhao glanced up and smiled thinly. "You would have preferred to execute the men, wouldn't you?"

Klisiewicz gave a curt nod. "I would, as an example to others. But your standing orders disallow it."

The captain patted the bulkhead. "This is a ship full of rogues and brigands, Lieutenant Commander. Do you know how I have kept them in line?"

"Fleet diktat demands the use of discipline and the rigid application of punishments."

Zhao nodded. "And I don't shy away from those things when I need to. But my crew follow me because I keep them alive. Because I am good at what I do." He took a swig from a bottle of Saurian brandy liberated from the *Eighth Happiness*. "Because I give them the spoils. I'm not a commander who kills his way through his crews, who climbs to the top on a pile of corpses—" He halted, catching the tone of bitterness bleeding into his voice. *I'm not a man like Reyes.* He left the words unspoken, but Klisiewicz could sense his meaning.

The junior officer nodded and went on. "The woman you took as your prize has been processed," he noted. "There was a minor fracas when Dr. Leone made an attempt to conduct an examination."

"Oh?" Zhao worked the heating element in front of him.

"Yes, sir. The woman broke his arm."

"Good. That will teach him to keep his hands to himself."

Klisiewicz produced a small data card from a pocket. "She had this on her. It's encrypted. She refused to unlock it for anyone but you."

The captain took the card from him and turned it over in his hands. "Curious. Where is she now?"

"Outside, sir."

He nodded. "You're dismissed, then. Send her in as you leave."

"Captain." Klisiewicz hesitated again. "I'm not comfortable leaving you alone with her."

"Your concern is appreciated, Stephen. But I'd rather have you on the bridge. And besides, if she murders me, you'll be promoted to the center seat."

The lieutenant did as he was told and left, allowing T'Prynn to enter. The light desert nomad robes she had been wearing aboard the freighter were gone, and in their place she was garbed in a simple crew jumpsuit. Zhao smiled slightly; even in so drab an outfit, the Vulcan appeared attractive. He made a mental note to find her something more appealing to wear from the spoils in the hold.

He continued at his task, working half concealed in the alcove. "Take a seat, if you wish." When she didn't, he continued, "You assaulted one of my officers."

She nodded. "Will I be punished in return?"

"That depends. Why did you do it?"

"Your surgeon-commandant informed me that all females aboard the ship are required to service him sexually. When I declined, he offered me recreational narcotics and then attempted to assault me. I injured him."

Zhao shrugged. "He's an excellent doctor. A poor judge of character, though." He tossed the data card, and T'Prynn caught it easily. "What's that?"

The Vulcan held it between her thumb and forefinger. "I would define this as an opportunity, Captain." She placed it on the table.

"Indeed?" His work complete, Zhao deactivated the heating elements in the console before him and moved the bowls from it to a tray. He carried the steaming containers from the cooking area. Zhao set out chopsticks and some sticky rice in front of T'Prynn. "Eat," he offered. "You must be hungry."

"You cook your own food?" The Vulcan raised an eyebrow.

"Of course," Zhao replied. "I've had run-ins with poison more times than I care to recount. It's not difficult to reprogram a fabricator to add toxins to a meal. This way, I know what I'm getting." He took a few bites, then paused. "Something wrong? You don't like my rice?"

T'Prynn heard the warning in his tone and sat, taking up the proffered bowl. They ate in silence for a while, each quietly taking the measure of the other. Zhao was mildly surprised when the Vulcan spoke first.

"I assume this chamber is secure?"

"Of course." He helped himself to more vegetables.

"I have been looking for your ship for two solar weeks." She put the rice bowl aside. "My passage on the *Eighth Happiness* was my second attempt to draw *Endeavour*'s attention."

"If you wished to speak to me, why not send a subspace message?"

"It was important that this meeting be clandestine. I convinced Captain Griffin that he would be able to cross your patrol zone without detection, when in fact I had altered his ship's warp signature so that you would find it easier to detect."

Zhao took another swallow of brandy. "Go on."

"I have been placed under deep cover in order to penetrate the Taurus Reach and contact you directly." She put a slender finger on the data card. "As I said, to present you with an opportunity." T'Prynn pushed the card toward him. "The files contained here will authenticate everything I am about to tell you."

He made little stabs in the air with his chopsticks. "I'm not open to business offers," he replied. "Whoever you're working for, Klingons or Romulans, I've no interest in them. I have . . ." His voice trailed off. "I have *obligations* in the Taurus Reach."

T'Prynn continued, "This offer is made on behalf of Admiral Spock of Starfleet. I am his operative."

"Spock?" Of all the names Zhao had expected to hear, that had not been one of them. The Vulcan renegade, the dangerous man whose reputation had extended even this far, to the Empire's distant fringes. The officer who defied all attempts to assassinate him. The man who had killed the heartless James Kirk, who some said had a terrible power at his fingertips. Spock, hated by many and admired by more. Zhao had to admit that he placed himself firmly in the latter camp, not that he would have said it openly.

If Klisiewicz had been there, his response would have been immediate, placing the woman in the brig, if not terminating her on the spot. Internecine alliances and compacts between Imperial officers, while commonplace, were tolerated only when it was to the Empire's ultimate benefit. It was widely held that Spock's intentions were not ones that favored those in the corridors of power on Imperial Earth. But the Vulcan admiral's bold stance against the machinations of the Empress's court had struck a chord with *Endeavour*'s commander, and in that moment, he decided to hear T'Prynn out.

She saw she had his attention. "In revealing my identity and intent, I have shown you a degree of trust, Captain. Will you return that confidence?"

"I will," he agreed. "Nothing said in this room will leave it."

The woman continued. "In Admiral Spock's considered opinion, there is a critical situation developing in the Taurus Reach. The existence of the Vanguard station, Imperial Starbase 47, is a threat to the stability of the Terran Empire. If left unchecked, Starfleet's operations within the Reach will soon ignite a conflict that will ruin important plans for the Empire's future."

"Whose plans?" asked Zhao. "I doubt you mean those of Empress Sato."

T'Prynn ignored his interruption. "Admiral Spock requires that the command of Commodore Diego Reyes be terminated with extreme prejudice and that Vanguard's operations be neutralized."

Zhao gave a bitter laugh and let his rice bowl clatter to the table. "And you come with this to me? Spock conjures this demand from the air and expects me to fulfill it for him, to turn against my commanding officer, throw away my life?" He snorted derisively. "And the lives of my crew?"

The woman fixed him with a steady gaze. "The admiral guarantees three rewards if you succeed."

"Only three?" Zhao sat back and folded his arms. "Let me hear them, then. If only so I can give a complete accounting of your treachery to the Office of Imperial Inquisition when I report you for this madness."

"First, you will be granted the rank currently held by Reyes, with all the power and status that entails."

Despite himself, Zhao stiffened a little at her words. Reyes had made it clear in no uncertain terms that the *Endeavour*'s commander would never advance in rank, not while the shadow of Vanguard loomed large over the Reach.

"Second," she continued, "you will have the chance to recover the life of someone very important to you."

He was on his feet in an instant, his hands balling into fists. "You don't speak of her!" Zhao snarled. "You do not speak of her in my presence!"

T'Prynn showed no alarm, no concern over his abrupt flash of fury. "And third, you will recover the honor you have lost."

His anger, potent and towering, was suddenly bled away, vanishing as quickly as it had come. Zhao felt a rush of cold run through him. *An understanding.*

"This is the admiral's offer, Captain Zhao. Do you accept?"

He found himself speaking without being conscious of it, his thoughts churning. "I . . . I will consider it."

She watched the passage of emotions across the face of the human, reading them in his eyes, the tightening of the skin around his lips and a hundred other subtle cues that Zhao was not even aware of. She had studied the man and done what she could to ensure that she would attract him on their first meeting, but it was not until now, when they were alone together, that T'Prynn felt she truly had an insight into him. Her mission was to persuade Zhao to take up Spock's flag and turn against the man whose boot was pressed against his neck; but humans were so ephemeral, as hard to predict as they were easy to read. Her eyes fell to the data card on the table; she recalled the brief touch of the admiral's hand on hers as he gave it to her.

The dry, sullen heat of her homeworld, the dust suspended in the still air of an alleyway in Vulcana Regar. Weeks ago now, but as fresh in her mind as if it had been moments.

T'Prynn offered the three figures before her the ritual gesture of an open hand, fingers split. "I am here."

The tallest of the three mirrored her actions, and she saw the lines of his face in the shadows cast by an awning overhead. "T'Prynn," he said, his words resonant. "It is agreeable to see you."

She inclined her head. "Admiral. I came as quickly as I could." There was a weariness in her words that she could not conceal, despite her best efforts. He was strange that way; something about Spock's presence disarmed her, made every element of her tradecraft seem insubstantial. T'Prynn was discomforted by her inability to hide things from him. Deep inside, the very smallest ember of resentment burned in her.

If he noticed, he made no mention of it. "We move forward," Spock explained. "The progression is slow but steady. Your contribution continues to be of great value."

Another being might have thanked him for the compliment. T'Prynn said nothing, feeling no need to acknowledge what was obvious.

"You understand my time is limited, that the Empire's future requires my full and complete attention."

"I do."

"Consider a dam holding back a lake," he said carefully. "It is old and crumbling. It is best that it be dismantled and the water allowed to find an equilibrium."

"A somewhat simplistic analogy for the Terran Empire."

"Quite so, but adequate for this discussion. The dam has cracks that will widen if left unchecked, that will result in an uncontrolled flood. These flows must be stanched before they bring the entire structure down. What you have done, T'Prynn, is to enable me to tap those flows, control them or obstruct them. I wish you to understand the value of your work."

"I do," she repeated. "Not that my understanding is required. Only my obedience."

"I regret some measure of coercion was required on your part, in order to have you prosecute certain missions." Spock's admission was unexpected. "I hope you will understand it was necessary."

Necessary? The hot ember in T'Prynn's heart throbbed. *Was it necessary to hold my secrets over me for all this time?* She applied a degree of iron self-control, reaching into herself to silence the dissention—and other, more strident voices and desires.

"The Empire's future requires a total commitment, and I have surrendered my life to that duty," he continued. "But for now, I must move with caution. I cannot tip my hand to the Empress. This is why your covert skills have such importance." He looked away to the other figures, and for the first time, T'Prynn caught a scent from one of them.

Human. A female. She peered into the depths of the figure's hood but could discern only the vague impression of a face. *Spock's concubine, the one called Moreau.*

"Many obstacles lie in the path of the Empire's deconstruction," said Spock. "Of late, I have learned of a most pressing problem." He offered her a data card, and she took it, brushing his fingers. "Vanguard station, a starbase constructed out on the edges of Imperial space, in a zone known colloquially as the Taurus Reach. It sits within range of both Klingon and Tholian territories. It is fast becoming a potential flashpoint for interstellar conflict."

She turned the data card over in her hand. "For what reason?"

He did not answer her immediately. "For my plans to succeed, it is imperative that the Taurus Reach be left to the militant Tholians. Without Fleet involvement, they will drive off any probing expeditions from the Klingons, and the area will remain stable. The Empress Sato, however, has other ideas. She has turned control of Vanguard over to one of the Empire's most brutal officers, one Commodore Diego Reyes. Do you know of him?"

She nodded. Diego "Red" Reyes, as he was called, had a reputation for butchery and arrogance that broke limits even among the ruthless men and women of the Fleet. A thief in his youth who graduated to hardened criminal status in the barrios of Earth's lunar complexes, after being pressed into Starfleet service, he had risen to high rank through callous cunning and sheer violence. It was said that among his record of atrocities, Reyes had personally obliterated the colony governed by his wife in retaliation for her divorce, killing thousands of innocents and turning the world's surface to glass. T'Prynn had encountered the fringes of the man's influence in missions within Orion space, where the commodore had connections with the crime syndicates.

"The Empress has given the Reach to Reyes. In return for keeping the colonies there in line, the commodore has a free hand to do as he wishes." Spock paused. "His governance of the zone resembles that of a feudal bandit warlord more than an Imperial officer."

"You have a source inside his command?" Given the admiral's breadth of information, it seemed a logical deduction.

Spock confirmed her conclusion with a nod. "I have cultivated an agent within the staff involved on 'Operation Vanguard' and learned the true purpose of Starbase 47's presence in the Reach. Vanguard station is the nexus for a series of scientific missions across the zone, gathering and conducting research into relics of alien technology from a highly advanced precursor civilization. These ongoing intrusions are antagonizing the Tholian Assembly and drawing the attention of the Klingons."

"And that is why you wish to move now?"

He nodded. "My source has fallen silent. I am concerned that Reyes's staff have discovered something that will radically alter the balance of power in the quadrant. This cannot be allowed to occur, but I cannot openly oppose the commodore at this time."

She looked at the data card again. "You want me to eliminate Reyes?" She had killed many for Spock, men and women, from range and from close enough to taste their last breaths. She remembered them all.

"I require you to cultivate a cat's paw in order to eradicate the threat that Reyes and Vanguard present to my plans. All of the information you will require is in your hand."

When T'Prynn looked up at him again, she could not keep the weariness from her expression. She had come there today hoping, as she did each time, that he would free her from this servitude. The endless cycle of lies and subterfuge, the duplicity of being Spock's spy piled on top of the everyday deceit of life in the Imperial Fleet, dragged her down like iron chains. She wanted nothing more than to end it. To be free to be who she was, unfettered by her secrets.

"This will be the last," she said, the words tumbling from her lips. "After this, I will walk away." T'Prynn met Spock's gaze. "I believe in your vision, Admiral, and I will do all I can to serve that. But I have reached my limit with the Empire and the blood I must wade through as a Fleet officer, the mendacity of it. This far and no further." She held up the disc. "I do this, and I leave Starfleet behind, forever."

Spock answered without hesitation. "Agreed."

The corridors of the station became real around her, and Commander Lurqal stiffened. It was force of habit; every other time she had been transported aboard an Imperial craft, it had been with disruptor and *mek'leth* in hand, ready to strike out and kill everything she saw. It felt peculiar to be under different, almost cordial, circumstances. She eyed the walls of the complex and took in the troop of Imperial security officers arrayed around the reception area. They stood at parade-ground ready, clearly meant as a gesture of respect for the new arrivals; but she had no doubts that they would draw their phasers if any Klingon in the delegation made the slightest aggressive move. She heard a grunt from Turag at her side; the envoy from Qo'noS was no more impressed than Lurqal was.

The commander took a moment to gauge the scope of the chamber. The walls were adorned with rich hangings and battle pennants, flags lined with brocade drooping down to the deck, and here and there what appeared to be trophy items. The skulls of aliens, pieces of shredded hull metal recovered from dead enemies. Lurqal recognized what was certainly part of a hatch from a Romulan troopship.

She sniffed. Such displays were beneath the notice of a true warrior. Lurqal preferred to have her deeds speak for themselves, instead of constructing a museum to aggrandize them; but then the profligate display was certainly in character for the man who commanded this station, if Turag's intelligence reports were to be believed.

And now that man approached them, with a heavy-set Orion a step behind him and a bowed bond-slave following. His uniform tunic was heavy with showy decorations and rank insignia, and at his hip rested a long-barreled energy weapon. The human's face was craggy and lined, with old scars upon a shorn skull. His right eye was an augmetic replacement, a bulbous thing of polished steel. It stared back at her with an unblinking red lens. He had a mocking grin playing about his lips.

"At last," he began. "Here you are. Welcome to my castle keep, Envoy. Welcome to Vanguard."

"Thank you, Commodore Reyes," Turag said silkily. "I must confess, my agents were quite surprised by your overtures to us." He gave a little laugh. "We thought this might be some attempt at subterfuge on your part. Perhaps a ham-fisted attempt at assassination?"

"Really?" Reyes mimicked Turag's tone and manner. "That would have been a silly thing to do, don't you agree?" He glanced at Lurqal for a split second, and she felt the man's gaze rake over her. "And you are?"

"Commander Lurqal is my military counterpart," Turag explained. "If what you have to offer us appears legitimate, she will make an evaluation for the Klingon warfleet."

She took her cue. "We have come as you requested, Reyes. I suggest you show us why we should waste our time with you as soon as possible. My people are not known for their patience."

The commodore grinned. "I do like a woman who knows her own mind. Don't you agree, Ganz?" He addressed the comment to the Orion, who nodded slightly, maintaining an air of watchful menace at Reyes's side. "You're right. Why waste time? Let's cut to the chase." He beckoned them to follow. "C'mon. Let me show you why you ought to get into bed with me."

Lurqal grimaced at the ugly metaphor but said nothing and fell in line with Turag and his bodyguards.

Reyes threw a look over his shoulder as they walked. "Let's put our cards on the table. I know you ridge-heads know about Erilon and all the other places we've been digging up inside the Reach." He winked. "You know something's out here, something big, but you don't know what, and you still want it anyway, right?" He eyed Lurqal.

"Whatever has value to an enemy has value to us," she retorted. "We can take it or destroy it."

"If you can actually *get* it, yeah," replied Reyes.

Turag's manner cooled. "Did you bring us here to insult us, Commodore?"

Lurqal answered before Reyes could speak. "He brought us here to impress us." She gestured around at the walls of the starbase. "The commodore is showing off his space fortress."

"I am, at that," Reyes admitted, turning the red eye on her. "But that's just the curtain raiser. See, we've found a few things out here, Commander. Leftovers, of a sort. Relics from a species that at first we thought were dead and gone. Technology that makes our starships look like rowboats. But I'm getting ahead of myself." He patted the Orion on the shoulder, a gesture of familiarity that drew a cold glower from the emerald-skinned alien. "Ganz here, he and

I have come to an understanding about a lot of things. We've both had a . . . I suppose you could say it was an epiphany. I've come to realize my own worth, if you follow."

"I don't," Lurqal replied.

Reyes's grin widened, and he flicked at the Imperial insignia on his tunic. "One thing I've learned is that out here in the dark, the Earth is a long, long way away. A man has to be his own emperor as captain of a ship or starbase. And after a while, the size of that small kingdom . . ." He chuckled, amused by himself. "Well, it gets a little tight around the britches, you know what I mean?"

"You want more power."

"And I'm going to get it. Matter of fact, you're going to help me."

"You presume much, Commodore," said Turag. "You bring us here on vague promises and offers of servitude, but now you talk as if we are in alliance."

"Yeah, the whole servitude thing, that was just a lie." He shrugged. "Just to get you here." Reyes didn't react as Lurqal's men reached for their weapons. His calmness intrigued her, and she waved them off, allowing him to continue. She found herself wanting to hear what he had to say. "I'm not real big on kowtowing, y'see. I have larger ambitions. Namely, carving out an empire of my own. Right here."

Turag blinked. "The Reach?"

"Dead on." The Terran nodded at the Orion. "Thanks to Ganz and his associates, I already have in place what you might call the infrastructure of a secession. I just need a little muscle and someone to watch my back. Someone with an aggressive, proactive mindset."

Lurqal smiled thinly at the audacity of the man. "You intend to secede from the Terran Empire and turn the Taurus Reach into your own private fiefdom."

She got a nod in return. "It's practically that already. This'll make it nice and legal."

The commander gestured at the walls. "This is a large base, with more than a thousand loyal Imperial subjects aboard. Will they all follow you into this? What is to prevent your grand plan from being derailed by one of your fellow officers of the Empire? I'm sure anyone who exposed your intentions would be richly rewarded by that witch Sato."

For a moment, Reyes's expression turned cold. "You shouldn't question my commitment, woman. I end the people who do that. Fact is, most of the rank-and-file crew on Vanguard don't give a damn who's in command, as long as they get their bread and circuses. Me, Sato, it doesn't matter to them."

"What about the ships stationed here?" she pressed. "What about their commanders?"

The callous grin returned. "Oh, I admit I did have some issues with one of them. Sadly, shortly after that, the I.S.S. *Sagittarius* suffered a freak accident, didn't it?" He glanced at Ganz.

"Warp-core malfunction," rumbled the Orion. *"Boom."*

"The other captains saw it my way thereafter. And I've taken steps to ensure their continued obedience." He crossed to the bond-slave and dragged it forward; Lurqal saw for the first time that it was a human woman, olive-skinned and sallow. "It's important to have leverage, isn't that right, Atish?"

The woman gave a shaky nod, and Lurqal saw the flash of hate in her eyes.

"What is this?" asked Turag.

"Khatami here has a special value to one of my captains, don't you?" He sniffed at her hair, leering. "Mmm. Zhao's got good taste." Reyes pushed her away toward Ganz. "I'm keeping her as my 'guest,' so to speak."

"A hostage," Lurqal said with distaste.

"That's such an unpleasant word. But yeah, you're pretty much on the money." He puffed out his chest. "So, there's no need to fret. There's nothing to stop me taking the Reach, and in return for support from my good neighbors in the Klingon sphere, I'll be willing to offer up a generous number of worlds ripe for exploitation."

Turag folded his arms and halted. "Ah, Commodore. You're

only offering us what we can already take. And why would we wish to antagonize Empress Sato? Why would we draw the Tholians into a protracted fight? They're swarming around the fringes of this zone like angry glob-flies." He snorted. "I fail to see any incentive for my people."

"That's gonna change, real soon," Reyes replied. "Trust me on that. But to answer your question, well, as I said, Sato's a long way from here, and she's got problems of her own. And truth be told, she might gripe and moan when things go down, but in the long run, she'll deal, especially when I have you guys at my back. I'm already a king out here. She should know, she made it happen." He leaned closer. "The Tholians, well, they'll have to be put down, and hard—there's no argument about that—but I have the means. Empress Sato will deal, Turag, because she'll have no choice. Now it's time for me to show the same is true for you folks." Reyes nodded to Ganz, who crossed to a secure door and worked a code lock. "Come look at this," he said, smiling. "We call it the Vault."

The Klingons walked around the lab interior with their heads on swivels, and it was all Reyes could do not to laugh. Not a one of them had ever been this close to an Imperial secure facility on the scale of the Vault, and they didn't know where to look first. He pointed out the tall cylinders of the stasis tanks, where bodies drifted in a null-space field, preserving perfectly the manner in which they had died. "Take a gander at these poor fools. Have you ever seen wounds like that?"

Lurqal bent close to examine the bifurcated body of a Chelon. "There is matter accreted around the edges of the cut. It seems to be some kind of crystal. The flesh . . . it's been changed."

"Petrification." He threw her a nod; she was quite a looker, when you got past the tire-print forehead. "The cut goes down to the molecular level. The edge that did that can go through anything." Reyes led them on, amused as the lab staff scuttled to get out of his way. He showed them pieces of blackened matter. From a distance, they looked like melted stone, but up close, they glistened with fragments of mica. "These are remnants of a civilization that used to run this whole quadrant, back when your ancestors were still up in the trees, whacking each other with sticks. The Shedai, they called themselves." Turag's eyes narrowed, and the commodore knew immediately that the Klingons had heard the name before.

"I fail to be impressed," said Lurqal. "Is this all you have to show us? Corpses and blackened pebbles?"

Reyes felt his ire rising again, and he glared at the woman. Okay, so she was pretty, but now that he thought about it, Diego realized that she had to be little more than a kid by ridge-head standards. *The damned Klingons, they're mocking me. They sent me a slip of a girl instead of a real warrior. This is an insult!* He felt the optic implant grow hot against the scarred flesh of his face. "Don't try to play me," he growled. "I know you tried to screw around with Shedai tech you found in the Ravanar system. But while you monkeys have been hitting it with hammers and getting nowhere, we got ourselves something better." He loomed over her.

"Much better," offered Ganz.

His insouciant manner resurfaced. "I'm just building the drama, y'see? Saving the best until last." He snapped his fingers, beckoning over two men in blue sciences tunics. "Zeke. Mr. Ming. Would you be so kind as to bring out the cage? I want our new friends here to meet the star of the show."

Lieutenant Ming Xiong hesitated, shooting a look at Surgeon-Commandant Fisher's ever-cold expression. "Commodore," he began, "is that wise?"

"Didn't ask you for advice," Reyes growled. "Gave you an order."

"Aye, sir," came the reply, and the lieutenant moved to a control console to work alongside Fisher.

"Stand back," ordered the doctor. A hatch in the floor began to iris open.

Reyes glanced at Turag. "Palgrenax. You got a scout ship near there, don't you? You people been thinking about establishing an outpost on the planet."

Turag stiffened. "How are you aware of that?"

"These things come to me." He threw a nod in Ganz's direction. "Call your vessel. Get them to send a message to that ship, tell them to light outta there."

"And why would we do that?" Lurqal demanded.

The hatch was open now, and a cube of glowing metal tubes was rising up from the space below. In between the bars, something moved, flowing like smoke.

"Just do as I say," Reyes told her. "Or you'll regret it."

The Klingon commander glared at him and then spoke a string of guttural orders into her communicator.

The cage locked into place, and Turag backed off a step. He couldn't look away from the writhing, formless shape inside the structure. Reyes nodded to himself. The thing was a sight, all right. It was gas, and then it was water; it was stone, and then it was fire; it tried, as it always did, to thrash its way out of the confinement, banging against the phase-destabilized bars.

"It's quite safe," Fisher reported, in his usual flat monotone. "The Shedai cannot escape."

"You captured one of those . . . beings?" Turag blinked.

"More by blind luck than judgment," admitted Ming. "We managed to—"

Reyes silenced him with a sharp cut of the hand. "The envoy doesn't need to know how. He just needs to know that we got Smokey here on a leash."

"Smoh-kee?"

The commodore's smile flashed. "A pet name."

Energy lashed at the junctions of the crackling bars, and a wave of pressure flooded the room. *Telinaruul!* The psychic cry beat at their thoughts. *Release me! Release me or perish!*

Reyes swore. "Oh, she's peppery today, ain't she?" He nodded to Fisher. "Give her a jolt. Make sure she knows who's boss."

The doctor worked the console and gave a dial there a savage twist. Power flashed through the cage, and the Shedai wailed, the unearthly noise grating around them.

Strange colors glistened inside the bars. "Conduit is opening," reported Ming.

"Just a fraction now, we don't want her running," Reyes ordered. "Your people had your warning," he said to Lurqal, before turning away. "Fisher? Make the bitch do her trick."

The doctor nodded again and sent another powerful surge of energy through the Shedai's enclosure; in reply, it screamed and flashed blue-white. Reyes had the impression of brilliant fires streaking away, vanishing down a pinhole tunnel of warp light, then gone. Abruptly, the alien moaned and recoiled into itself, becoming dark and sullen.

After a long moment, Lurqal's expression shifted to incredulity as a tinny voice snapped out of her communicator in terse, urgent Klingon. Paling slightly, she looked first to Reyes and then to the envoy. "Our scout ship reports . . . the planet Palgrenax is breaking apart. Massive energy distortions all across the surface."

"You like that?" Reyes spread his hands. "Maybe now you'd be willing to talk some business."

A slow smile crept across Turag's lips. "With the master of the Taurus Reach? Of course."

Zhao Sheng studied the Vulcan woman before him at the table, poised and silent. Her offer hung in the air between them, the charged lethality of what she had demanded of him in Spock's stead as deadly as a poisoned dagger. The way the light in the cabin crossed her hair reminded him of Atish, and the sudden flash of recall brought a small gasp from him. Khatami had been much more than just the captain's woman aboard *Endeavour;* she had been his confidante, his sounding board, his comrade in battle as well as his lover. Not for the first time, he cursed himself for his attachment to the tawny-skinned woman. If only he had cared less, then he would not have forced himself and his crew into the bloody service of Red Reyes.

Zhao shook his head, feeling the moment fall away. Perhaps once there had been a time when he might have defied the commodore, but not now. The proud, ruthless soldier of the Empire he once was had vanished, and in his place was the dissolute man he was now. Little more than a pirate, just a bandit with a fancy starship operating under letters of marque and reprisal. A slave with a longer leash but still a slave nonetheless.

The sensible choice would be to throw her into the brig and turn her over to Leone's tender mercies for interrogation. I'm certain he would relish the opportunity. Reyes would reward him if he brought T'Prynn back to Vanguard, broken and begging. *He might let me see Atish again . . . perhaps for a little while.*

T'Prynn watched him carefully. "I require an answer, Captain Zhao."

Was she reading his thoughts? He had heard stories of the psychic powers that some Vulcans were alleged to possess. *They say Admiral Spock can make a man vanish with just a thought. What tricks might he have taught this one?* "Vanguard is too well protected," he told her. "*Endeavour* would be destroyed trying to attack it."

"We have a spy in place in the command crew, ready to sabotage the starbase's systems," she countered. "And your trusted status will allow you to close to point-blank distance before opening fire."

He sighed, shaking his head. "I have great admiration for Spock, and in any other circumstance, I would put my colors to his mast. But what you ask of me I cannot do. I . . . I am a defeated man." Zhao looked away, grabbing the brandy bottle and taking a long pull from it. "The captain your admiral sent you to find is gone. Go back and tell him that."

T'Prynn was silent for a long moment before she spoke again. "Tell me, Zhao Sheng. How did you rise to the captaincy of this vessel?"

He snorted. "The usual method. I terminated my commander."

She cocked her head. "Why?"

"Does it matter?" He took another swig of brandy. "He was in my way. I murdered him. End of story."

"That is not an explanation. Tell me what made you want to kill a man in cold blood. Tell me why you murdered an officer your oath of allegiance bound you to obey."

"Because he *deserved* it!" The Vulcan's words lit a sudden fire inside him, and he threw the bottle aside. "He had appetites that sickened me! He did not deserve to wear the uniform of a soldier of the Empire! He . . . he was . . ."

"Dishonorable?"

"Yes." Zhao sat heavily. "And now I am no better."

When he looked up again, T'Prynn was holding the data card in her hand, offering it to him. "Are you certain? Has your honor truly fled, or have you only misplaced it?"

He saw her without really seeing, his thoughts far away. *Atish. Does she think I have abandoned her? Is she even still alive? Do I have anything left to lose?*

The whistle of the intercom broke through his thoughts, and he tapped the panel. "What?"

"Sir, something odd on long-range sensors," said Klisiewicz. *"We're reading a massive energy spike in the Palgrenax system. It looks . . . well, like a planet there just exploded."*

"It's starting," said T'Prynn. "You must make your choice."

He did. "Yellow alert," Zhao ordered. "Set course for Vanguard, maximum warp, and prep the weapons. We have a fight ahead of us."

T'Prynn had been prepared for dissent; she had a small phaser hidden in the bracelet around her wrist, powerful enough for a single disintegration blast. She had been quite ready to use it, standing carefully at Zhao's shoulder, so that any member of his crew who objected to their new orders could be dispatched if the need arose.

The fact that it did not was a source of mild surprise for the

Vulcan. For all the level of open debauchery and disorder shown by *Endeavour*'s rabble of a crew, when the man spoke, all of them listened. And none of them complained; in fact, many of them took the commands to attack Vanguard with rough humor, as if it was something they had been waiting for.

Zhao glanced up at her from his command throne. "You're wondering why no one is trying to oppose me?"

She nodded.

He smiled. "Well. Ask yourself this, then. What does it tell you about Diego Reyes when every member of my crew would happily see the bastard and his comrades dead?"

"Rather," she replied, "I am considering what that tells me about *you*."

He shrugged. "My crew trust me."

"A rare commodity in the Empire."

On the main viewscreen, the massive clamshell doors of docking bay 3 were retracting into Vanguard's saucerlike upper hull. T'Prynn saw a ship moored there, a yacht of Orion design.

"Ganz's boat," Klisiewicz noted, reading a display. "I see his pennant on the hull. He's aboard."

"Distance?"

"Point-blank range in ten seconds." He frowned. "I'm also detecting a Klingon ship docked at one of the lower pylons."

Zhao threw a nod at his weapons officer, a younger man with a savage smirk on his lips. "Pen? You assured me this would work?"

"It will, boss," said the officer. "We'll fire without using sensors, so they won't detect a thing until it's too late. I've removed the safety interlocks from the torpedoes. They'll arm the moment they leave the tubes." He gave a giggle.

"The weapons will be unguided," noted T'Prynn.

"Oh, yeah," he told her, "but at this range, it won't matter at all—"

A chime from Klisiewicz's console cut him off. "We're being hailed," said the science officer. "It's Reyes."

Zhao stiffened. "Onscreen."

The view of the docking bay became the dark expression of Vanguard's commander. *"Zhao. You'd better have a good reason for ending your patrol early. I'm right in the middle of some business here."*

The captain folded his arms. "I brought you something, Commodore." He nodded at T'Prynn.

Reyes leered. *"Oh. Pretty. But if you think I'm going to trade her for Khatami, you're a million miles wrong."*

Zhao snorted. "Ah, Diego. For all your cunning, you will live and die a thug."

"In range," said Klisiewicz.

"What the hell did you just say to me?"

The captain ignored him. "And today's the day."

The rapid-sequence firing carousels in *Endeavour*'s weapons bay ejected four photon torpedoes, sending the munitions running even as the starship pivoted into a turn from the open hangar. This close, inside the starbase's deflector envelope, there was nothing to stop them. The first shots struck the Orion yacht amidships, tearing off its port warp nacelle, starting a chain reaction of concussive detonations. The second pair flew the length of the bay and struck the core spindle of Vanguard station, gouging out huge pieces of hull metal.

Endeavour surged away, keeping tight across the starbase's surface as static defense turrets began to return fire. The starship gave no quarter, releasing beams of collimated energy to cut great slashes through the station's hull. Vanguard's torpedo launchers misfired, their targeting software refusing to shoot something so close for fear of backwash damage. The *Endeavour*'s crew had no such qualms. Zhao's helmsman pushed the vessel, flying it more like a fighter than a capital ship.

Starbase 47 trembled as it was hit again and again.

Reyes punched down the man who helped him to his feet, blinded with rage. He pressed one hand to his optic implant; his skull was ringing from the impact it had taken when the torpedo blast threw him to the floor. The operations-room status board had an ugly red smear across the middle of Vanguard's systems display, right through the docking bay. He could distantly feel the rumble of secondary explosions through the deck.

"Serious structural damage in the main bay," called Commander Cooper, his voice tense. "Ganz is gone . . . reading explosive decompression in sections of the terrestrial enclosure. Emergency reports coming in from all over!"

"What is the meaning of this?" spat Turag. "We are attacked by your own ship?" He lurched forward, bleeding from a gash on his cheek. "Human *petaQ!* You make all these grandiose claims, and then this—"

He never got a chance to finish. Reyes grabbed a handful of Turag's sash and yanked the envoy forward, almost into an embrace. The high-intensity laser inside the commodore's implant buzzed, and a dart of red light flashed into the Klingon's head, burning clean through it. Reyes threw the smoking corpse at Lurqal and stalked to the primary console. "Zhao!" he bellowed. "You hear me? I'll kill that whore of yours by inches for this!"

"He's coming around for another pass," Cooper snarled.

Reyes stabbed at a control on the console. "Time to show off the Orion Syndicate's little gifts. Pop the turrets. Give that traitor a surprise."

The standard armament of a Watchtower-class space platform was twelve phaser and photon torpedo launcher units. The nonstandard armament of Vanguard was eight more Orion disruptor cannons, concealed under retractable hull plates, fitted under Reyes's personal orders and without the knowledge of any but his most senior staff. The spindly guns were lethal, capable of independently targeting or firing in concert for maximum effect. The *Endeavour* was quite unprepared for the onslaught.

"Multiple sensors targeting us!" Klisiewicz snapped. "Power surges!"

"Brace for impact!" Zhao barely spoke before the first beams of coruscating green lightning reached out to slam into the shields.

Lights flickered and dimmed across the bridge. T'Prynn ducked away as the panel behind her fractured and blew out, spitting gas and flames. She saw Tupo, the Edoan security guard, fall lifeless to the deck.

Endeavour rocked as it was raked a second and then a third time.

"Orion weapons." The first officer coughed out the words. "Damn him."

"We'll all be damned unless we survive this," Zhao retorted. He glared at T'Prynn. "Where's this spy of yours?"

The Vulcan glanced up at the view of the station turning beneath them.

Surgeon-Commandant Fisher's face twisted in a grimace as the lab's lights dimmed momentarily. Ming Xiong heard the caged Shedai make a low moan.

"Careful!" Fisher snapped. "Keep the power steady. If the flow is interrupted, the confinement field could be compromised!"

Ming looked up at the deck over their heads. "What do you think is going on up there?" Red-alert strobes were flashing on every console.

Fisher turned away. "That's not your concern, Lieutenant," he retorted. "The commodore has everything in hand."

"You really believe that?"

"He is a great man," Fisher said, bending over a power regulator. "You should remember that."

Ming saw the moment and took it. "Yes, I will." In a single swift motion, the lieutenant grabbed the older man's arms and caught him in a neck lock. Fisher cried out, but Ming had taken his balance. With a hard shove, he pushed the surgeon-commandant's torso against the throbbing energy nimbus of the open power conduit.

Fisher's body stiffened, and he screamed. Flesh blackened and crisped, spitting sweet-smelling smoke into the air. In a moment, it was done, and the man was dead.

Ming let him drop. *Only one scream, at the end.* With the number of times Xiong had seen Fisher elicit cries of agony from others, it didn't seem right that he had perished so quickly. *I should have made it last.*

He stepped away and recovered his tricorder. To a cursory inspection, the device resembled a normal Imperial-issue unit; but Vulcan technicians had secretly enhanced it with a number of capabilities, one of which was a tight-beam encrypted subspace transmitter. Ever since Reyes had upgraded the sensor capacity of Vanguard's multispectrum array, Ming had been afraid to use it— but now it seemed like a moot point. "Attention," he spoke into the device. "Asset five-four-three-Gamma reporting. I authenticate: nine-nine-five-Delta-nine. Please respond."

He wasn't surprised to hear the tight, clipped diction of a Vulcan in reply. *"Responding. You are to initiate exit strategy immediately."*

The deck vibrated beneath his feet, and once again, the Shedai howled against the bars of its cage. Ming nodded. "You don't have to tell me twice."

Pennington threw the captain a look. "Confirmed, boss. Small detonations along the main conduit. The transport-inhibitor field protecting the station is failing."

"The lieutenant was successful," said T'Prynn from the communications panel. "His orders required him to conceal explosive devices in several key power nodes. These are now being triggered."

The *Endeavour* listed as another disruptor charge splashed across the forward shields. Zhao came up out of his chair. "We won't be able to keep dancing around them like this forever. Reyes is a bloodthirsty barbarian, but he's not an idiot. It's only a matter of time until he gets another ship out here." He snapped his fingers at sh'Zenne and Mkembe. "With me. We're boarding."

"Sir?" Klisiewicz gasped. "Captain . . . I know that your lover is aboard that station, but if you go over there, there's no certainty you'll make it back alive."

Zhao turned to T'Prynn. "You will assist Mr. Klisiewicz. Keep my ship in one piece until I return."

"Klisiewicz is correct," said the Vulcan. "And Khatami may already be dead."

"Admiral Spock's offer grants three rewards." Zhao spoke over his shoulder as he made for the turbolift. "The first I have taken in defying Reyes, and the last I will accept if I survive. But she . . . she is the most important to me."

The red warning strobes had turned the lab into a vision of some arcane hell, the smoke from fried components streaming through the air. Flashes of bright blue light sparkled through the bars of the phase cage; the Shedai was beating itself against the walls of its prison, screaming and hooting in mad agony.

She knows what's going on, Ming realized. *She can smell death.*

He felt his skin crawl as the alien turned its attention on him, as eyes that were not eyes glared in his direction. Psychic pressure tightened about his skull, and he felt blood trickle from his nostrils.

Telinaruul! It was a silent roar. ***Release me! Release me!***

Through the mind touch of the Shedai, he could sense the very edges of the being's consciousness; he could see the scars across its mentality, where Fisher had brutally tortured her during her captivity. Any remnant of rationality was gone now; the creature was insane with rage, filled with a hate so powerful it could have smothered suns. It threatened to engulf him, pull him under.

"One," he called into his communicator, trying to keep himself focused. "One to beam up . . ."

RELEASE ME!

Of their own accord, Ming Xiong's fingers reached for the cage controls.

Vanguard's internal communications had gone offline in the first moments of the attack, leaving Desai isolated in the interrogation chamber. Down there, in the place the crew had nicknamed the dungeon decks, she was usually free to conduct her work as Reyes's chief inquisitor; but the power failures and alert klaxons were a most unwelcome interruption. She cursed and stalked back across the room, to where her current subject hung suspended over the drain in the floor.

The naked man was panting, barely awake after the shock of blood loss from the shallow cuts over his body. He tried to raise his head and mumbled.

"It's not a rescue, if that's what you're thinking," she spat. Desai shot a look at her slave. Normally, the woman would cower under such a glare, but Atish had a peculiar look on her face. Almost like . . . *hope.*

Desai backhanded her to the deck, and Khatami flailed, knocking over a trolley of medical instruments. "The same goes for you," she told her. "You belong to us now, body and soul. Never forget that."

For the first time in months, Atish's eyes flashed with defiance. "Body, perhaps. But never my soul. Never that."

The other woman laughed harshly, picking out a scalpel from the confusion of instruments. "Do you require another demonstration?" She crossed to the man in restraints and cooed to him. "Quinn. Quinn, can you hear me?"

He gave a gasp, bloody spittle trickling from his lips.

Desai glanced at Khatami as she spoke. "I have all I need from you. I'm going to free you."

"No," said Atish, getting to her feet.

The blade of the instrument cut through the soft flesh of Quinn's neck, and he choked and writhed, dying there before them. Desai tossed the scalpel away and sneered. "This is Vanguard, Atish. Life is cheap here."

Khatami bowed her head. "Yes. Yes, you're right."

Satisfied that she had made her point, Desai beckoned her slave toward the hatch. "Come. We must find out what is going on."

She was two steps away when the duranium door blew off its mounting and broke apart. Parts of the body of the Orion guard outside spattered on the deck. Figures stepped through coils of smoke, and Desai flinched as a towering ebony-skinned human advanced toward her. Behind him came a man in a long coat with a phaser in either hand.

"Sheng?" Khatami whispered.

Zhao holstered a pistol and touched her cheek. "I promised I would come for you. Forgive me that it took so long."

"You came," she said. "That's all that matters." Atish straightened and tore the slave hood from her shoulders.

"You're a fool!" Desai's voice was a snarl. "Whatever you think you've accomplished, you have no comprehension of the power we have at our command!"

Khatami embraced her lover and they kissed, passion burning in both of them. Her hand snaked down to his belt as they broke off. "I'm going to free you, Rana." Atish's fingers grasped the butt of a phaser. "The same freedom you gave Quinn and a thousand others."

Desai cried out, holding up her hands. Khatami spun and fired a pulse of light into her. The inquisitor's screech faded away as the blast flashed her into free atoms.

"Time to go," said Zhao. He nodded to Mkembe, who raised a communicator to his lips.

T'Prynn looked up from the console. "Transporter room confirms. Landing party and asset recovered."

Klisiewicz nodded, waving a wisp of smoke from in front of him. "Then we're done. Helm, get us out of here, power to shields and drives . . ." His voice trailed off as something huge and sharp and silver-gray exploded out of the starbase's hull on the screen before him, ripping the docked Klingon ship in two. "What the hell is that?"

The Vulcan raised an eyebrow. "It would appear to be . . . a blade."

The human was gone, but the Wanderer did not care; she had only the burning, screaming need to murder and destroy.

One moment, the cage, the horrible, tiny cage, was surrounding her; the next, it was nothing but crude matter once again. Matter that she could assimilate, that she could discorporate and make part of herself.

The Shedai screamed and exploded, in nanoseconds sucking energy and mass from the structure of the crude Telinaruul construct. She altered molecules by thought to replenish herself and spread across the Vanguard thing like a cancer, annihilating and absorbing.

The crude flickers of life panicked and died beneath her onslaught. In blinks of energy, she glimpsed little puffs of memory and thought, flashes so transient she barely registered them. She was dimly aware that she was killing these humanoids by the hundreds, trampling them beneath great blades of glittering crystal. In those moments, her rage found brief focus.

There. At the apex of the construct. One Telinaruul. The one. The pain giver. The one who would dare to name himself master of our space.

She swallowed up the chamber surrounding the Reyes flicker, slowing her advance to give it time to understand the utter hopelessness of its situation. It fired hot light into her mass, unaware that each pulse fed her a little more.

She registered sound-wave perturbations through the surface of her body; the humanoid was calling out, trying to communicate with the Wanderer. For a brief instant, she wondered what it might have to say to her; but then she dismissed the idea and killed it.

Zhao pushed his way past fallen stanchions and injured men to enter the bridge, as Klisiewicz rose from his command throne. On the screen, Vanguard diminished as the starship pulled away, but with impulse engines damaged, the retreat was agonizingly slow.

Starbase 47 was mutating. The human-made spindle shape was still visible, but now it looked like a strange, abstract rendering carved from planes of shimmering, writhing crystal. Streams of glowing matter issued from its surface, weblike filaments that turned toward *Endeavour,* seeking to snare it.

"What's happening?" said Khatami, following him.

"Molecular conversion." Ming paled. "All of the organic and inorganic matter . . . it's the alien that Reyes captured, the Shedai. It's free, it's consuming it."

"Alien?" Zhao shot T'Prynn a hard look. "You were aware of this?"

She nodded. "It was need-to-know information."

"Damn you!" snarled the captain. "You knew something of that magnitude was aboard Vanguard, and you said nothing?"

"Sir," Klisiewicz warned. "Those . . . tendrils are going to reach us. We don't have the speed to escape."

T'Prynn touched her communicator earpiece. "Do not be concerned. I have initiated a contingency plan."

"Incoming vessels!" Pennington called out. "Multiple warp signatures, dozens of them."

"Identify!" snapped Klisiewicz.

Zhao saw the distinctive arrowhead shapes flicker out of warp to surround the remains of Vanguard. "Tholians. A warfleet."

As one, the Tholian ships opened fire, a single pulse of light hammering into the faceted crystal monstrosity. For one terrible moment, Zhao thought the Shedai would absorb the attack and expand to engulf them all; but then some critical mass was exceeded, and the glittering shape became a tiny supernova, shattering, burning, and dying. *This isn't an attack,* he realized, *it's an execution.*

All that was left of the Shedai and Vanguard station cohered into a dead, smoldering mass, surrounded by broken mirror-bright pieces of itself. They watched as the Tholian craft, some severely damaged by the shockwave, disengaged and turned to face the *Endeavour.*

"Signal," said Klisiewicz.

Zhao nodded to him, and the grating synthetic tones of a Tholian voice filled the smoke-dirtied bridge. *"Attention, Terran Empire vessel. Your message was received and acted upon."*

"Our message?" Khatami glanced at Zhao.

T'Prynn gave a nod. "I contacted them. Admiral Spock suspected that events would unfold toward this conclusion and gave me the means. I offered the Tholian Assembly the chance to assist us."

The voice continued. *"Be advised. The zone of space you designate as the Taurus Reach is under our jurisdiction. The presence of alien intruders will not be tolerated. Carry this message to your government. You are never to return here."*

The signal ceased, and on the screen the Tholian ships began to move into a new formation. Zhao watched as they began to etch a web around the fragments of the lifeless Shedai.

"They're taking the dead home with them," said Ming.

Zhao nodded. "And we will do the same." He glanced at Klisiewicz. "Set course for the nearest Imperial Spacedock."

His first officer saluted, fist to chest. "As you order, *Commodore* Zhao."

Atish draped herself around his shoulders. "Commodore? You know, I never liked that rank. Not until now." She smiled. "It makes you sound like a warrior."

"And not a pirate?" He settled back in his chair, folding his arms across his gun belt. "I think it will fit me well. And when we bring the Empress Sato news of Reyes's duplicity, there will be spoils for us all."

. . .

They met on one of the lower decks where *Endeavour*'s internal security coverage was less than total.

"Show me," said T'Prynn.

Ming opened the modified tricorder and offered her a data card. "I didn't get it all," he explained. "Ninety-five percent of Operation Vanguard's research database is in here."

She took it from him. "It will be enough. And the sample?"

Gingerly, Ming produced a glass tube from a hidden compartment in the tricorder. He held it as if he were afraid of it. "Here. After what we saw it do, the sooner this is far away from me, the better."

T'Prynn held the tube up to the light. Inside was a sliver of metallic crystal, shifting between solidity and a shimmering liquid form.

"What are you going to do with that?" he asked.

"Preserve it." She glanced at him. "For the future."

The Traitor

Michael Jan Friedman

HISTORIAN'S NOTE: *"The Traitor" takes place during the 2340s (ACE), while the resistance to the Klingon-Cardassian Alliance ("Crossover," Star Trek: Deep Space Nine) is ill organized and easily stamped out. This is prior to Jean-Luc Picard working for Gul Madred, in 2366 (Star Trek Mirror Universe: Glass Empires—The Worst of Both Worlds).*

Michael Jan Friedman has written or co-written sixty-five science fiction, fantasy, and young adult books, a great many of them in the *Star Trek* universe. In an unguarded moment, he will admit to being the creator of the *Stargazer* crew, if not the *Stargazer* herself (which was first seen in the *Star Trek: The Next Generation* episode "The Battle" back in 1987). Ben Zoma and Pug Joseph, who figure prominently in "The Traitor," first saw the light of day in Friedman's novel *Reunion,* the first *Next Generation* hardcover, which came out in 1992. Gerda Idun, Wu, and some of the others originated in the *Stargazer* series that debuted a decade later.

Friedman became a full-time freelance writer in 1985 following the publication of his first novel, *The Hammer and the Horn.* Since then, he has written for television, radio, magazines, and comic books. His television credits include "Resistance," a first-season episode of *Star Trek: Voyager.*

A native New Yorker, he lives with his wife and two sons on Long Island, where he spends his free time (what little he can find of it) running, kayaking, and playing single-wall handball.

The captain had just swiveled ninety degrees in her hard, plastic command chair to call up another series of engine-efficiency reports—hoping they would help her wring a little more speed out of the *Lakul*—when Gerda Idun called her name.

There was a distinct undercurrent of urgency in the helm officer's voice, an unmistakable note of concern. And the steely-eyed Gerda Idun was not the type to show much emotion, even at the most perilous times.

"Yes?" the captain responded.

"We've got a vessel off the starboard bow," said Gerda Idun, tucking a stray lock of pale blond hair behind her ear. "Four thousand kilometers."

The captain's throat constricted. *Of all the times*— "Show me," she said, swiveling her chair back the other way to face the large, eyelike oval of the bridge's forward viewscreen.

For a moment, the image on the screen lingered, displaying the fifth planet in the sprawling star system they had entered only minutes earlier. The midsized sphere was swaddled in blankets of cloud that made it difficult to see the land and water beneath them, though the captain was quite sure they were there.

Then the scene jumped several levels of magnification, and a vessel appeared on the viewer. It filled less than a tenth of the screen, but it wasn't difficult to tell that it was a transport—a Terran model.

What *was* difficult was figuring out what it was doing there. The Alliance had a nasty habit of destroying vessels of Terran origin out of hand, without so much as a comm warning. That persuaded most human crews to steer clear of restricted space.

But not *this* crew. *Why not?* the captain wondered, leaning forward in her chair.

Then Gerda Idun supplied the explanation.

Turning to face the captain's chair, she said—with a burr of undisguised distaste in her voice—"It's the *Stargazer.*"

The captain frowned deeply. She might have said a great many things at that moment, none of them the least bit pleasant, but all she uttered was one word: "*Picard.*"

"Seems that way," said Ben Zoma, who had predictably appeared at her side.

Jean-Luc Picard was a traitor to his kind, a treasure-hunting profiteer who regularly planted kisses on the Klingons' backsides so he could relieve the quadrant of its most ancient curiosities without interruption. Other Terrans suffered hideously under the yoke of Alliance oppression, paying for their survival with their dignity and sometimes a good deal more. Of all of them, only Picard had turned the situation to personal advantage.

As far as the captain was concerned, that translated into "scum" in *any* language.

The muscles in Ben Zoma's jaw rippled beneath two days' growth of dark, gold-flecked beard. "I wonder," he said, "what he's doing in this part of the—"

"Captain!" snapped Pug Joseph from his position at the tactical console. "Picard's not alone." He swore under his breath as he consulted his monitors one after the other, his fingers flying over his keyboard like a swarm of Vobilite darter worms. "I'm picking up a Klingon cruiser—*D'tag*-class!"

The captain tamped down her anger and disappointment. After all the trouble they had gone to . . . "How far?"

"Ten minutes," Joseph spat. "Maybe a little less."

Their sensors weren't as discerning as the Klingons' or even the Cardassians'. But then, the *Lakul* was just an old cargo transport, and cargo transports didn't carry such finely tuned instruments. Not even when they needed them.

The Klingons were known to board ships at random, hoping to find evidence of some resistance against the Alliance. A sophisticated sensor system would have been exactly the type of thing they were looking for. It would have given the *Lakul* and her crew away as dissidents and insurrectionists.

Likewise a discernible weapons array—which was why they weren't a match for even a Klingon scout ship, much less a fully armed battle cruiser. They had to get out of there. But they weren't going to be leaving the system alone, not if the captain had anything to say about it.

"Gerda Idun," she said as evenly as she could, "head for the *Stargazer* at full impulse." Next, she turned to Joseph and gave him his own set of instructions. "When that's done," she said, turning back to Gerda Idun, "resume course."

The captain turned to Ben Zoma. "You've got the bridge."

"Acknowledged," he replied.

Sliding out of her command chair, the captain made her way aft to the turbolift doors. They parted at her approach—albeit a little too slowly, as usual—and gave her access to the compartment beyond. Punching a quick sequence into the control pad on the wall ahead of her, she instructed the lift to take her two decks down to the primary cargo bay.

After all, that's where the transporter was.

When the captain entered the humming gloom of the cargo bay through its open doorway, Krollage was already standing there, his phaser planted in his fist. He nodded to her.

She nodded back. Then she turned to the transporter platform, folded her arms across her chest, and waited for Joseph to finish his work up on the bridge.

Had the captain been in Picard's place, she would have amped

up the power of her vessel's token shield generators a long time
ago. That would have made it harder for people to do what Joseph
was doing. But with the Klingons on his side, Picard probably
hadn't felt the need for extra protection.

That's about to change, the captain mused.

The first thing that appeared on the slightly raised disc of the
transporter platform was a column of golden light. It would have
been bright under any circumstances, but the lack of ambient light
in the room made it look even brighter. So bright, in fact, that the
captain had to squint to discern the appearance of a shape in the
column—something that started out vague and spindly but, over
the span of several seconds, became increasingly manlike.

She had heard that Cardassian teleporters took only a few seconds to effect a transport. But she and her crew weren't Cardassians. They had to make do with the equipment they had.

Finally, the shape in the light column solidified into a recognizable individual. Only then did the light fade away, leaving an angry-
looking Jean-Luc Picard in its wake.

"What in blazes do you think you're doing?" he demanded,
taking a step down from the platform.

Krollage intervened, checking the newcomer's progress.
Picard's nostrils flared, but he remained where he was.

"I ask you again," he said, no less imperiously, "what do you
think you're doing?"

"Taking you off your ship," the captain told him, her tone flat
and controlled.

"Under whose authority?"

She chuckled to herself. "You've been sucking up to the Klingons too long, Picard. They're the ones who go on about things
like jurisdiction and authority. They and the Cardassians and the
damned Bajorans."

"They're the ones who have all the weapons," Picard reminded her.

"Not *all* of them," said the captain, tilting her head to indicate
the phaser in Krollage's hand.

Picard's eyes narrowed beneath his tousled thatch of dark hair. "What do you want with me?"

"That all depends," said the captain, "on what you're doing here."

"What do you *think* I'm doing here?"

The captain eyed him. "Didn't anyone ever tell you it's rude to answer a question with a question?"

"You know what I do," Picard told her. "Archaeologists keep the details of their research to themselves."

"Oh," she said, "you're an *archaeologist,* are you? My apologies. I thought you were a grave robber. And a traitorous grave robber at that."

Picard's mouth became a straight, taut line. "Look," he said, "this is a rather substantial treasure I have discovered. If you are looking for a piece of the action, say eighty-twenty . . ."

The captain shook her head.

"Seventy-thirty, then," he told her. "That seems fair, considering I will be doing all the work."

"I'm not looking for a cut of your ill-gotten gains," said the captain. "What I want is an explanation. Tell me how you wound up in this particular star system at this particular time—minutes after my ship showed up here—with a *D'tag*-class cruiser firmly in tow."

"A *D'tag*—?" Picard's brow furrowed. "If there's a Klingon cruiser in the vicinity, it has nothing to do with me."

"Right," said the captain. "Because you've had nothing to do with the Klingons. *Ever.*"

Picard scowled. "The Klingons tolerate me, look the other way sometimes in exchange for my help with certain matters. But I did not bring them to this system. I swear it."

As far as the captain was concerned, he was lying through his teeth. She said as much. "So you're going to remain here on my ship until we finish what we came here for."

"You can't do that!" he told her.

"Watch me," she said, and turned to go.

"Damn you," he said, his voice rising to a bellow that echoed in the confines of the bay. "This is kidnapping! Do you hear me? Come back here! *Guinan!*"

There was something about the way he said her name that set the captain's teeth on edge. "Go screw yourself," she muttered beneath her breath, and left the cargo bay.

In her most honest and forthright moments, Guinan had to admit to herself that she valued Gilaad Ben Zoma for more than his experience as a rebel.

True, the man had been trying to undermine the Alliance for the last decade or so. Also true, he knew his way around the quadrant as few others did. In fact, he had commanded a vessel of his own at one time, until the Alliance crippled it beyond repair.

But as much as all that, it was the way his eyes changed color as he went from light to shadow that she loved most about him. Just the way they were changing now from olive green to a deep, soft brown.

Ben Zoma was a handsome man, even if he wasn't a member of her species.

"We've got to move quickly," he told her, taking a seat beside her in the *Lakul*'s cramped little conference room.

The captain sat back in her chair and nodded. "It's only a matter of time before the Klingons find Morgen on the fifth planet. And when they do, they're not going to look kindly on his being there."

Morgen was a prince of the Daa'Vit, a warrior species that had made a blood alliance with the Klingons several decades earlier. However, not all Daa'Vit were altogether pleased with the arrangement. Some of them had come to sympathize with the plight of the Terrans.

Morgen was the leader of that faction. He had reached Guinan through an intricate chain of contacts, not knowing her name but aware of her reputation. Just a couple of weeks earlier, they had agreed on a rendezvous—on the fifth planet in what Terrans called the Proteus system.

Morgen was down there now. And in another few minutes, the Klingons would be there as well. Unfortunately, Morgen didn't know what kind of danger he was in.

"We can't just fly by and beam him up," said Ben Zoma, looking past her at one of the ship's few undamaged observation ports. "It would take too long to establish a transporter lock."

The captain thought about it. "True. But we can do the next best thing: drop off some of *our* people to apprise Morgen of the situation."

Ben Zoma nodded. "Make it more difficult for the Klingons to find him, even with their advanced scanning systems."

"Exactly."

"I'll put a team together."

"Make sure I'm on it," said the captain.

Ben Zoma looked at her askance. "That's a bad idea. You're too valuable to us."

"And what good is a chess piece," she asked, "if you never use it?"

If he was going to voice another objection, he reconsidered. "Don't forget to check the charge on your phaser," he told her as he left the room.

One moment, the captain was on the *Lakul*'s transporter pad, surrounded by five of her fellow conspirators. The next, she was standing on the rocky brown slope of an immense, barren valley, watching tiny lavender-colored fuzz balls waft past her on a hot, acrid-smelling wind.

Somewhere beyond the cloud-ridden, vermilion expanse of sky, the *Lakul* was speeding off at full impulse, the highest velocity to which it could aspire within the labyrinthine gravity well of a solar system. With luck, Ben Zoma would tuck the ship into the asteroid belt they had identified near the system's outskirts sometime before the Klingons arrived.

The captain looked around the expanse of the valley. So did Joseph, Paris, Wu, Pernell, and Ulelo. None of them saw anything except the fuzz balls.

"He should *be* here," the captain said, her voice snatched by the wind.

"Maybe he had some trouble beaming down," Joseph suggested. "Or maybe he plotted the wrong coordinates."

Either was a possibility. But Morgen had known the seriousness of what he was doing and the penalty he would face if he were discovered. In his place, the captain would have made damned sure to eliminate the slightest chance of a slip-up—technical or otherwise.

"We've got to find him," she said, removing her tricorder from her belt.

But she couldn't find any life signs within the device's effective radius. Judging by her colleagues' expressions, they weren't faring any better.

And they couldn't use their communicators. Not when the Klingons could monitor their signals and trace them to their points of origin.

"What now?" asked Paris.

"It's a big planet," Wu reminded them.

"If he's even *on* it," said Joseph.

The wind whistled above them, spawning dust devils along the slopes. The captain swore beneath her breath. What if Joseph was right? What if Morgen hadn't made it to the rendezvous point for one reason or another?

"We can't assume that," she decided. "Not until we've done a lot more looking."

Morgen had risked his life to help them when no one else in the quadrant would do so. They couldn't just write him off.

The captain turned to Ulelo, who knew more about sensor tech than the rest of them. "Ideas?" she said.

Ulelo bit his lip. "We can increase the range of our tricorders by linking them together. But that will take a while." He glanced at the high, lurid sky. "And if we don't find cover soon—"

"We'll be of little use to Morgen or anyone else," said the captain, finishing his sentence for him.

She scanned the slope on which they had materialized. There was an exposed shelf of light gray rock jutting out from it maybe thirty meters below them. If they could get underneath it, dig themselves in with their phasers . . .

She gave the others their orders. A few moments later, they were lying beneath the outcropping, gouging a hiding place for themselves with four converging phaser beams. Dust billowed from the point of pulverizing impact.

Not knowing how deeply the outcropping was anchored, they didn't want to go *too* far. Just far enough to shield themselves from the Klingons' sensors.

"All right," said the captain when she thought they had dug in far enough. "Let's get comfortable."

Coughing in the debris cloud they had created, the landing party wriggled into the space beneath the rock. Then, closely packed, they waited for Ulelo to link their tricorders. With every second that passed, the likelihood of the Klingons' discovering Morgen's party increased.

But Ulelo could work only so quickly. As the captain watched him, she reminded herself of that. *No point in rushing him. He knows how much is at stake.*

Finally, Ulelo completed his labors. With all five of their tricorders working together via a wireless link, he crawled out from cover and scanned the valley.

"Anything?" the captain whispered, doing her best not to cough too loudly.

"Nothing yet," Ulelo reported.

Unfortunately, the Klingons' sensor technology was more powerful than the landing party's tricorders, link or no link. If anyone were going to find Morgen, it would be the marauder that had followed Picard into the star system.

"Wait a minute," said Ulelo. He fine-tuned the controls on his tricorder. "I've got something."

Melekh, second in command on the Klingon Imperial Cruiser *Tlhab,* took out his disruptor pistol and aimed it at the transport's metallic, slightly convex control console. With a squeeze of his finger, he speared the console with a narrow blue beam of destructive force, which ripped through the metallic surface and elicited a geyser of white-hot sparks.

It was just a token gesture, a release of the smallest part of the frustration the Klingon felt.

Of course, the two warriors who had teleported with him to the transport didn't know that. They jumped at the crimson flash of disruptor fire, their lips pulling back from their teeth, their hands darting to the weapons on their hips.

Seeing that there was no danger, they appeared to relax again. But their eyes remained narrowed as they resumed their inspection of the craft's navigation logs.

Melekh smiled to himself. A warrior needed to be alert. It was good that he had shaken the others up a little, even if that hadn't necessarily been his intention.

But his good humor didn't last long. He had been sent there to find either the pilot of the transport or some indication of what had happened to him. He had found neither.

Melekh watched a thin, black twist of smoke ascend from the ruined console and collect under the low ceiling, and considered the facts as he knew them. The *Tlhab* had picked up the Terran transport's presence on long-range sensors and, in accordance with standing orders, had moved to intercept. When the transport ducked into this star system, the *Tlhab* had slowed to sublight speed and maintained pursuit.

That was when the second transport showed up on the Klingon cruiser's sensor screens, making Melekh's captain glad that he had followed the vessel. It was one thing to discover an unauthorized Terran transport in this sector and quite another to find *two* such transports. Clearly, there was something going on.

But the second transport had vanished almost as quickly as it appeared, no doubt taking refuge somewhere in the system. While the *Tlhab* tried to pinpoint its location, a scan of the first transport identified it as the *Stargazer,* a vessel registered to one Jean-Luc Picard and known to the Empire.

But what was it doing there? Why was it meeting the second transport? Attempts to establish communication with the *Stargazer* had been unsuccessful, raising further questions. Hence Melekh's mission.

Unfortunately, he had nothing to report. Nonetheless, he took out his communicator and opened a link to the *Tlhab,* knowing that his captain would want to know what had transpired.

The communications officer, a gray-bearded fellow named Pejor, responded instantly.

"Give me the captain," said Melekh.

"He is occupied with the High Command," came the response.

Melekh was surprised. Had he been the captain of the *Tlhab,* he would have waited for some positive developments before he communicated anything to his superiors. However, it was too curious an incident not to mention it at some point.

"The captain was fortunate to obtain an audience so quickly," Melekh observed, knowing how difficult it could be to get through to the High Command.

"Actually," said Pejor, *"the High Command contacted* him.*"*

Melekh absorbed the information, chewing it over like a stick of dried *targh* meat. "Interesting timing," he replied.

"I thought so, too," said Pejor.

. . .

As Ben Zoma deposited himself in the captain's chair of the *Lakul*, he took quick note of the image on the viewscreen. As before, it displayed only a thickly packed field of copper-and-blue asteroids.

No sign of the Klingon cruiser, he thought. *At least, not yet.*

"How are our shields holding up?" he asked Gerda Idun.

She glanced back at him from the pilot's seat. "They're at eighty-eight percent. But with all this radioactivity . . ."

"I know," Ben Zoma replied.

"How's our guest?" she asked in return.

He smiled to himself. "Settling in. He still claims he's innocent of any wrongdoing."

Gerda Idun turned back to her control panel. "Of course he does."

"Sounds unlikely," said Ben Zoma, "I know."

And yet he found himself starting to believe Picard's protests. What if the poor bastard really *was* innocent?

It doesn't matter, he insisted inwardly. *He's still a Klingon collaborator. If he's not guilty of this, he's guilty of something else.*

Ben Zoma couldn't afford to trust anyone beyond his crewmates. None of them could. They had too little margin for error.

And without them, the Alliance would continue to inflict one cruelty after another on the human species without fear of reprisal. If he doubted that, all he had to do was recall the events of a few weeks earlier.

They had stopped at a cold, barren place called Bering's World, where some much-needed repairs to the *Lakul* could be carried out by people they trusted—insurrectionists who hadn't yet gathered the resources they needed to join the fray. Unfortunately, the *Lakul*'s visit coincided with a Cardassian inspection.

The Cardassians made a few arrests, just to remind everyone of who was in charge in the sector. And, of course, the ones arrested weren't the ones who should have been. The inspection was almost over when one of the Cardassians was hit by a rock.

The perpetrator was a little girl, but no one knew that until after the Cardassian had fired his disruptor in retaliation. The child was dead before she hit the ground.

In the riot that followed, Guinan got to the offending spoon-head and put a phaser bolt in his ear. But before she could get away, she was busted up by the Cardassian's comrades.

Or so it seemed to Ben Zoma, who wasn't all that far away from her. And in fact, she disappeared for a while. But hardly an hour after the melee, as her crew was canvassing the capital for her, she turned up in pretty good shape.

Just a few bruises were all. Ben Zoma was grateful. He could have captained the ship without her, but not as well as she would have.

After all, he wasn't of her species. He couldn't read people the way she did.

Melekh had hardly materialized on the *Tlhab*'s transporter platform when he was summoned by the captain to the ship's council chamber.

He found Captain Druja sitting in his customary seat at the head of the chamber's heavy wooden table. As Melekh entered, the captain gestured for him to take a seat at the table's opposite end.

Druja of the House of Ajaq was short for a Klingon but very broad and muscular, with a neck like the trunk of a century-old *s'naiah* tree. In his youth, he had been a wrestler, in which capacity he had cracked the ribs of more than one overconfident opponent— or so he was quick to claim.

However, it took more than a talent for rib cracking to command a battle cruiser. After all, Klingons were political creatures. They seldom said exactly what they meant. Those who thrived in the Empire and all its institutions, the Imperial Fleet in particular, were those who could discern the grain of truth in a pile of chaff.

It was this quality that the captain occasionally lacked.

Nor was it a secret in the Fleet. In fact, Melekh had requested to serve on the *Tlhab* for that very reason—that Druja had his failings and that an ambitious officer, eager for the captain's chair, could at some point take advantage of them.

"As you know," said Druja even before Melekh was seated, "I was contacted by the High Command. It was not a coincidence that they chose to speak with me at this particular juncture."

"They were aware of the transports?" asked Melekh.

"*One* of them," said the captain. "The one we have yet to locate. It was here to conduct a secret rendezvous with a party of Daa'Vit, led by none other than the son of the Daa'Vit leader."

"Morgen?" asked Melekh.

The captain scowled, then said, "I forgot that you were on the Daa'Vit homeworld for a time."

Melekh's first assignment, on the *HeghmoH,* was to participate in war games with the Daa'Vit. Afterward there were ceremonies, renewed pledges of allegiance, a crimson liqueur with the kick of an enraged *s'tarahk.*

"I was," he confirmed.

Since that time, he had held the Daa'Vit in high esteem. They were not Klingons, but they were fierce and combative in their own way. However, if Morgen had come to talk with humans in secret . . .

"Then the information I received from the High Command may not surprise you," said the captain.

He spoke of what he had learned. Melekh listened intently, hearing each word not only for itself but also for its ramifications, which were manifold.

"The High Command," said Druja, "has apparently been tracking this meeting for some time. Our interference, while well intended, has complicated matters. However, the High Command still foresees the possibility of a positive outcome. As a result, it has devised a new plan—one it has entrusted us to carry out."

He went on to reveal what it was.

"It will be my pleasure," said Melekh, "to be instrumental in the success of this effort."

Druja nodded. "You are dismissed."

As Melekh departed from the council chamber, he turned the possibilities over in his mind. Just as he had guessed, this was not a trivial matter. *Far from it.*

His captain had blundered. The best Druja could hope for was to regain his stature in the fleet by capturing some of the conspirators. But there were many ways for the conspirators to be apprehended.

And at least some of them would allow Melekh to shine more brightly than his superior.

Ben Zoma was still sitting in the captain's chair of the *Lakul,* wondering if Guinan and the others were still alive, when he noticed something on the viewscreen.

The asteroids there seemed to be moving to starboard. But that would only be the case if the *Lakul* was changing position—and he hadn't seen any reason for Gerda Idun to make a change.

"What are you doing?" he asked her.

"I'm not doing *anything,*" she told him, her hands starting to crawl over her console.

Ben Zoma leaned forward. "What's the matter?"

"My controls aren't responding," said Gerda Idun.

"Run a diagnostic."

But she was way ahead of him. "The controls have been bypassed." She shot a glance back over her shoulder. "All helm functions have been rerouted to the auxiliary control panel in the cargo bay."

"It's not just the helm," said Kochman, who had taken Joseph's place at the tactical station. "It's everything. Engine core, life support, shields . . ."

Ben Zoma tapped the intercom button in his armrest. "Krollage, what's going on down there?"

No reply.

"Krollage?" he said again.

Still nothing.

Swearing under his breath, Ben Zoma got up and headed for the lift. Removing his phaser from his belt, he said, "Refsland, Garner, arm yourselves and meet me in the cargo bay. I think Picard is on the loose."

"Which way?" asked the captain of the *Lakul,* watching Ulelo's expression in the soft light of his tricorder screen.

Ulelo answered by pointing to the opposite slope. "*That* way. And they're not that far from here."

The captain nodded. "Good." But she couldn't let the Daa'Vit remain exposed—not with the Klingons searching for them with all the scanner power they could bring to bear. She glanced back over her shoulder and said, "Let's find them."

But before they could leave their hiding place, the need to do so was abruptly eliminated.

"It's the Daa'Vit," said Wu, gazing across the valley.

There were four of them, all tall and broad-shouldered, dressed in loose-fitting brown garb that allowed them to blend in with their surroundings. If they had been much farther away, they would have been difficult for the captain to spot, even if she were looking right at them.

"I don't think they see us," Joseph observed.

The captain didn't think so, either. As far as she could tell, the Daa'Vit were merely making their way to the rendezvous site, albeit about ten minutes late.

Moving out from concealment, she waved her arms. It took a couple of seconds, but the Daa'Vit finally seemed to catch sight of her. She was certain of it when they adjusted their angle of descent to correspond with the rebels' position.

The captain was just beginning to breathe easier when the sky opened and started dropping lightning bolts into the valley.

Not the kind she was used to, either. These were pale violet in color and straight as an arrow, and they dug a pit six feet deep wherever they struck.

At first, the Daa'Vit froze in their tracks, uncertain how to help themselves. Then they struck out across the valley, seeking the only cover they could find.

The rain of disruptor fire continued, savaging the landscape. But somehow it missed the Daa'Vit. It didn't hurt that they were so fast, their long legs eating distance at a furious pace.

Finally, the first of them reached the shelf of rock and dove for cover beneath it. In quick succession, the other three followed. But the barrage didn't stop. It kept going, gouging deep holes in both sides of the valley.

"Glad you could make it," said the captain.

The Daa'Vit all glanced at her, but none of them responded. They were too busy catching their breath.

Finally, one of them removed the brown cowl wrapped around his head and said, in a voice exceedingly deep and melodious, "So am I."

Morgen was big, green-skinned, angular. His cheekbones looked as if they could cut plastisteel.

"My transporter operator put us down in the wrong place," he explained. "We've been walking for the last ten—"

The captain cut him off. "Tell me later."

"What is it?" asked Morgen.

She scanned what she could see of the valley. The energy bolts were gone. "They've stopped."

Morgen's eyes narrowed as he sized up the situation. "They will be coming for us."

The captain nodded. "Any second now."

Ben Zoma took less than thirty seconds to reach the cargo bay. His expectation was that Refsland and Garner would be there when he arrived, since they had been closer to the bay when he contacted them.

He got there just in time to see Refsland go flying backward into a bulkhead, then slide to the deck and lie still, joining a sprawled

and unconscious Garner. Somewhere around the corner, Krollage
was probably laid out as well.

Ben Zoma frowned and placed his back against a bulkhead,
keeping himself hidden from Picard, and vice versa. "This isn't going
to get you anywhere," he said, his voice echoing in the enclosure.

"You don't understand," said Picard over the hum of the engines. "We need to get moving if we are to save your friends."

"Why would you want to do *that*?" asked Ben Zoma.

"We can go into it some other time," said Picard. "For now, you
will just have to trust me."

Right, thought Ben Zoma. *Like that's going to happen.* "You just
want to turn us over to the Klingons. Obviously, I can't allow that."

"Even if that were my objective—which, I assure you, it is
not—how do you think you could stop me? I have rerouted control
of all your systems through the auxiliary station, and I have taken
care to ensure that you will not get them back."

Ben Zoma didn't doubt it. To regain control of the *Lakul,* he
would have to incapacitate Picard—and, considering that Picard
held the high ground, that would take some luck.

Ben Zoma gathered himself. Then he took a couple of steps,
sprang, and launched himself past the corner of the bulkhead, seeking his target as he flew through the air.

He had just enough time to catch a glimpse of it, and realize it
wasn't what he thought it would be, before he was blasted into
unconsciousness.

Melekh happened to be standing behind the *Tlhab*'s tactical officer,
checking his scanner screen, when the transport registered on it.

"Captain!" the tactical officer cried out, and put the cargo vessel on the forward viewer.

Druja made a sound of triumph deep in his throat, his eyes
glittering beneath his jutting brow. "Disable it," he said.

But whoever was piloting the transport knew what he was
doing. As the *Tlhab* fired its disruptor spread, the smaller vessel

undertook evasive maneuvers and somehow managed to come out of them unscathed. Before the cruiser could retarget, the transport dipped into the thick white atmosphere of the planet below.

At first, Melekh thought the transport's captain meant to take refuge below the cloud cover. But a few seconds later, the vessel erupted from the planet's atmosphere and headed for the star at the center of the system.

But it hadn't had enough time to rescue its people, Melekh thought. Not by half, if he knew anything about the efficiency of human transporters.

Druja cursed and snapped off a series of orders. He would be leading a party down to the planet's surface, he advised them. It would be up to Melekh to catch and cripple the transport.

Melekh assured his captain that he would hold up his end of the bargain. After all, it would be harder for the transport to conceal itself near the center of the system.

The question in his mind, as Druja left the bridge and Melekh took over the captain's chair, was why the transport had shown itself at all.

Ben Zoma came to with Garner and Refsland hovering over him. His first impulse was to sit up, but it was thwarted by a terrible ache in the side of his head.

"What happened?" he groaned.

Even before the words came out, the memory started flooding back. He wrestled with it, tried to come to grips with it. But he couldn't make any sense of it.

"Picard?" he asked, though it felt funny to call the man that after what Ben Zoma had seen.

"He's left the ship," said Refsland. "Transported down to the planet's surface, as far as we can tell."

The landing party, thought Ben Zoma, fearing for their lives.

A shudder ran through the deck plates. Then another, more noticeable than the first.

"We're under attack," Garner explained, relieving Ben Zoma of the need to ask.

"Gerda Idun's trying to keep them off our tail," said Refsland. "But every now and then . . ."

Obviously, they had restored systems control to the bridge already, or Gerda Idun couldn't have been piloting the transport. But if not for Picard, they would still have been in the asteroid belt, secure and undetected.

"Got to get up to the bridge," said Ben Zoma, propping himself up on one elbow. "Before—"

His words were interrupted by an impact that sent them all tumbling to the port side of the vessel. It emphasized the urgency of their situation, as if that were at all necessary.

Dragging himself to his feet, Ben Zoma lurched into the corridor and headed for the turbolift. He didn't know what good he would be to Gerda Idun up on the bridge, but he was determined to get there.

The captain of the *Lakul* checked the charge on her phaser.

The Klingon barrage had stopped several minutes earlier, but that didn't mean the cruiser was done with them. It wasn't the Klingons' way to destroy their enemies from afar.

The energy strike had been a distraction. The real threat would be arriving soon in the form of a fully armed Klingon landing party.

From which direction? the captain wondered, looking for the first sign of trouble.

Then she got her answer. The attack came from *all* directions, Klingon warriors firing down at them from ten or twelve different positions along the perimeter of the valley.

What's more, the Klingons enjoyed a significantly better angle than their ship, as evidenced by the way their beams snuck under the rebels' ledge.

If the captain and her people stayed there, the Klingons would dig them out one by one. Certain of that, she gave the order to disperse. They would be better off seeking cover from the assorted boulders protruding from the long brown slopes and trying to return the Klingons' barrage.

It worked—for a little while, anyway. Then Wu cried out and went spinning to the ground, raising a cloud of dust, and Joseph followed her a moment later. And they couldn't find out if their comrades were alive, not unless they wanted to expose someone else to the same fate.

Not good, the captain thought. *Not good at all.*

Peering out from behind her boulder, she squeezed off a couple of phaser bursts. But neither of them found its mark. The Klingons were moving around the edge of the valley, making it difficult for the captain and her allies to draw a bead on them.

We're going to have to find another way, she told herself. *Otherwise, we're screwed.*

As if her thoughts were prophetic, Pernell caught a stream of disruptor fire. It sent him tumbling backward down the slope, his weapon flying out of his hand, his body limp.

Finally, he came to a halt, his neck craned at an impossible angle, his eyes fixed on infinity. If there was a question about Wu and Joseph, there was none about Pernell. The captain took note of the sight long enough to stamp it into her mind. Then she turned to the Klingon who had shot her colleague and fired back at him.

He went to the ground, but she couldn't tell if it was because she had hit him or because he had stumbled. She was about to fire again when she heard another Klingon's cry.

It came from behind her. She could hear it ring long and loud across the intervening distance. But it wasn't a cry of pain, the kind someone might make if he had been clipped with a phaser beam. It was a cry of surprise.

No, she realized, more than that. Of *terror.*

Glancing back over her shoulder, the captain saw a black, kraken-like creature as big as a Cardassian scout ship, a pair of Klingon warriors clutched in two of its several tentacles. As she looked on, it flung one of the warriors through the air, head over bootheels.

He landed awkwardly, bounced a couple of times, and lay still. Just like Pernell.

But how was it possible that a tentacled life-form was intervening on their behalf? She and her people had checked out the planet long before they suggested it as the site of their rendezvous with Morgen. It didn't have any life-forms big enough to get in their way, much less pick up a Klingon warrior and throw him around like a doll.

And yet there it was.

It held the remaining Klingon aloft, shook him, spun him. He bellowed with rage and tried to pry himself free, but to no avail. The tentacle was too tight about him, too unyielding.

Without warning, it slammed him into the ground, and the captain heard a distinct *crack*. When the tentacle loomed again against the sky, it was distinctly unencumbered.

Abruptly, the Klingons turned their fire on the monster, leaving the captain's party free to do as it wished. She didn't have to give any orders, didn't have to say anything at all. As one, they made their way up the slope, weapons blazing.

A second later, one of her bursts found a target, flattening one of the Klingons. Then another warrior went down under an energy volley, and another. And the tentacled creature sent two more of them flying over the captain's head.

Seeing a chance to end the battle, she pressed her attack. Yet another Klingon was sent sprawling by the force of her phaser beam, and the others were on the run. Then, just as she was about to claim victory in her mind, something happened.

The kraken screamed.

Turning to find out why, the captain saw the beast caught in a crossfire of blue energy bolts. It twisted, trying to get away from them, but it was no use. The beams were relentless.

For a moment, the creature just stood there, shuddering under the barrage. Then it toppled to one side, raising a cloud of dust as it hit the ground.

The captain looked about, hoping to locate the source of the barrage. She expected to find a Klingon, someone she could punish with a beam of her own. But it wasn't the Klingons who had brought the creature down.

It was the Daa'Vit.

It took her a moment to process the information, to accept it. And in that moment, her window of opportunity slammed shut. As she raised her phaser to fire at the nearest Daa'Vit, she saw something bright and blinding—and felt it hit her hand with bone-breaking force.

Her fingers numb, the captain couldn't hang on to her phaser any longer. It fell from her grasp and struck the ground. She knelt to pick it up, but another blast sent it skipping away from her.

At the top of the slope, someone got to his feet. A man, clutching his arm as if it were broken. *Picard,* she thought. *But what's he doing here?*

Then she put it all together.

Picard was the creature. Or, rather, the creature had taken the shape of Picard. *A shapechanger,* she thought.

It wasn't the first time she had run into one.

"Are you all right?" she called to him.

"I'm fine," he called back.

But it was clear from the way he said the words that he had been hurt rather severely. He wasn't going to turn into a form as difficult as that of the tentacled creature again any time soon, or he would have done so already.

Suddenly, a disruptor beam skewered him from the side, causing him to collapse. Instinctively, the captain started toward him.

But Morgen cut her off, making his way across the slope. "Keep your hands where I can see them," he said, his disruptor pistol pointed at the captain's chest.

Ben Zoma made his way out of the turbolift just in time to see the bridge's tactical console explode, sending Kochman flying backward. Reaching for the fire extinguisher, he played a stream of fire-retardant foam over the sparks and the smoke.

While Refsland saw to Kochman, who had been burned but not as badly as he might have been, Garner sat down at an empty console to reroute the ship's tactical functions, and Ben Zoma swung himself into the captain's chair. The viewscreen showed him a rear view of the Klingon cruiser, its weapons ports flaring as they released volley after volley.

None of which, thanks to Gerda Idun's skill at the helm, managed to score a decisive hit. But she couldn't keep it up indefinitely. No one could.

Sooner or later, Ben Zoma noted, she would zig instead of zag, and the Klingons would have them where they wanted them.

"Tactical is back online," Garner reported. "But weapons are down."

Not that it mattered. The *Lakul*'s weapons weren't powerful enough to do any real damage.

The Klingons released another barrage. This one grazed the transport's hull. Again, Ben Zoma felt a shudder make its way through the deck plates.

He tried to think of a way to shake the Klingons. *Try to make it back to the asteroid belt, maybe? Find some shelter on the planet's surface?*

Then it came to him.

"Gerda Idun," he said, "get us in close to them!"

"What?" she snapped, without looking back at him.

"Under their starboard weapons port! Do it!"

On the face of it, it sounded like a crazy idea. But it might be their only shot at survival.

Heeding his command, Gerda Idun flew them in under the cruiser's weapons port. As Ben Zoma had hoped, the tactic took the Klingons by surprise. Too late, the weapons port blazed with a barrage of disruptor beams, all of which passed over the transport without leaving a scratch.

"Now, stay here as long as you can," he told Gerda Idun.

It wouldn't be easy, as it would require her anticipating the Klingons' moves. But it would be easier than trying to shake the cruiser off their tail.

"Acknowledged," said Gerda Idun.

Now it was the Klingons' turn to execute evasive maneuvers. *Let's see how good they are,* Ben Zoma thought.

It wasn't a scheme that would keep them safe forever. Eventually, the Klingons would find a way to separate themselves from the transport.

But if the rebels were lucky, it would buy them some time.

The captain of the *Lakul* watched as Morgen's Daa'Vit companions surrounded Ulelo, the only other member of the rebel party still standing. Ulelo looked at her helplessly.

Morgen smiled. "Thank you," he said, "for your cooperation."

The captain glared at him. "You had me fooled," she had to admit.

The Daa'Vit shrugged his angular shoulders. "It wasn't difficult. You wanted allies so badly that you were willing to accept them without a second thought. Had you bothered to learn anything about my people, you would have known that we do not betray our allies. Especially not for a species as pitiful as your own."

Actually, the captain only *looked* human. However, she didn't bother to correct him.

"Now," said Morgen, "we end this little rebellion of yours before it gets started." He raised his disruptor until the captain was looking down its barrel. "Starting with *you.*"

She didn't believe he would kill her—just stun her, so his Klingon friends could interrogate her. And from what she had heard, they were *good* at interrogation, skilled at obtaining even the most closely guarded answers.

The kind that could cut out the legs from under a rebellion before it even got started.

The captain had to do something—and quickly. Fortunately, she still had a single card up her sleeve, a single option that might work. But would it be enough?

• • •

Melekh leaned forward in the captain's chair of the *Tlhab,* a place in which he felt increasingly comfortable with each passing moment.

"Fire!" he told his weapons officer.

Once again, a series of pale red beams stabbed at the fleeing form of the transport. And once again, the transport managed to elude them.

But it hadn't fired back in some time. More than likely, its weapons array was down, and its shields couldn't be far behind. Still, it would be wise to obtain confirmation.

"Report," he told his tactical officer.

"The enemy's engines are intact," came the response. "However, her weapons have been disabled, and her shield capacity is down to eleven percent."

Melekh smiled to himself. The transport had led them on an interesting chase considering the vast disparity in their tactical capabilities. *An interesting chase, indeed.*

But it was over.

Savoring the moment, as might a hunter who had come in sight of his prey, he watched the transport weave through space. Then he gave the order.

"Destroy her," he snarled.

Dutifully, his tactical officer established a fresh disruptor lock. He was about to stab the "fire" stud with his forefinger when the bridge was flooded with a gravelly and all too familiar voice, that of their commanding officer.

"Stand down!" it demanded.

Melekh made a face. He didn't understand.

The commander didn't offer an explanation. All he said was, "Let the cargo vessel go!"

There was a bitter taste in Melekh's mouth, like that of meat that had gone bad. But he couldn't disobey his commanding officer. After all, the penalty for disobedience was death.

Unless, of course, he wished to challenge his superior's fitness to command. But he wasn't ready to fight that battle at this time, especially over such a trivial matter.

"Aye," he said reluctantly. Eyeing his tactical officer, he echoed the commander's words: "Stand down."

On the screen, the cargo transport began to diminish with distance. It wasn't nearly as fast as the *Tlhab*. They could give it a head start of several minutes and still manage to catch up with it.

But that would only happen if the captain changed his mind. And judging by the tone of his order, Melekh didn't consider that likely.

He pounded his fist against his armrest. Then he sat back in his seat and wondered what had prompted the captain's change of heart.

Ben Zoma was still wondering why the Klingons had discontinued their pursuit when Garner announced that the captain was trying to raise them.

"Put her through," said Ben Zoma.

"Come get us," said the captain, her voice taut with urgency. *"We've got a window of maybe five minutes before the Klingons come back."*

"Picard's gone," Ben Zoma told her. "He—"

"I know. He's down here with me."

Ben Zoma didn't get it. But then, he didn't have to. The captain would fill him in once she was back onboard.

"Are we beaming up the Daa'Vit as well?" he asked.

"No. Just our people and Picard. And bring a med unit down to the cargo bay—Ulelo will need it for sure. Wu and Joseph as well, maybe."

She hadn't mentioned Pernell. Ben Zoma had a bad feeling that he knew why.

"We're on our way," he told the captain, gesturing to Gerda Idun to bring the ship about.

• • •

Melekh stood on the barren brown slope amid the remains of what had once been Klingon and Daa'Vit warriors and shook his head. He had heard his captain give him an order to withdraw. He could not have imagined it.

And yet, quite clearly, Druja could have used his help.

"Survey the area," he told his men. "See if the enemy is still present." But he didn't think they would find anyone.

Kneeling beside his captain, he surveyed the damage that had been done. Druja's head was twisted halfway around, but there were no other signs of violence. Clearly, it wasn't a directed energy weapon that had killed him.

It was something else.

Melekh swore beneath his breath. Something stank worse than the corpses on the slope. Snapping open his communication device, he barked into it the name of his tactical officer.

"Aye, Commander," came Ruunek's response.

"Access your files. Find Captain Druja's command to us to withdraw. Then analyze it for—" He didn't know what to say. "Anything unusual."

"Why?" asked the tactical officer. "Is there something—"

"Do it!" growled Mehlek.

"Aye," said Ruunek, and cut the link.

Rising to his feet, the commander brushed himself off and looked around again. He would allow the bodies to remain where they had fallen. With their spirits gone, they were no more than refuse.

"Commander Melekh!" called one of his men.

He turned and saw a warrior gesturing from farther down the slope. He was standing over one of the Daa'Vit.

"What is it?" bellowed Melekh.

"This one is *alive!*" the warrior called back.

Melekh made his way down the incline, raising a cloud of dust. When he reached the surviving Daa'Vit, he hunkered down beside him.

"What happened?" demanded the commander.

The Daa'Vit had broken his leg, probably ribs as well, and Melekh wouldn't have been surprised if there were a skull fracture, too. But, being a warrior, the Daa'Vit found the strength to speak.

"It was a creature," he groaned. "Like nothing I have ever seen before." And he went on to describe it.

A creature, Melekh thought. But their survey had shown no animal life. And if it had been there wreaking havoc so recently, what had become of it?

Just then, his comm device beeped.

"Melekh," he replied.

"Commander," said Ruunek, *"I have analyzed Captain Druja's communication, as you asked—and it was not he who gave the order."*

Melekh felt the blood rush to his face. "Then who was it?"

"I don't know. It sounded like Druja. But it doesn't match the record of his voice in his security file."

Melekh felt a chill crawl up the rungs of his redundant spine. *Not Druja? Who, then?*

And why had he not bothered to check the authenticity of the captain's voice? *Why?* His hands clenched into fists. *By the blood of Kahless,* why?

Without another word, Melekh left the Daa'Vit behind and walked back up the slope. To be alone. To *think.*

After all, the High Command would be expecting a report on the matter. It would want to know how Morgen and his comrades had lost their lives, how the *Tlhab* had lost its captain, and how its first officer had lost his prey. Of course, Melekh was the one who would have to provide the answers.

And take responsibility for what had happened.

The captain of the *Lakul* entered her briefing room, where the shapechanger who had taken Picard's identity was waiting for her.

"Tea?" she asked.

He shook his head. "Don't like it. Thanks anyway."

"I appreciate your helping us," she said. "If you hadn't, we would have been on our way to the Klingon homeworld by now."

"I'm glad it worked out."

"So . . . who are you? Not Picard, evidently, unless he has talents none of us knew about."

"My name is Sestro," he said. "I am an Iyaaran. My home system is beyond the area of space you have explored, but not by much."

"And you gave us a hand because . . . ?"

"My people have been monitoring your space rather closely of late, following the growth of what you call the Alliance. We have concluded that it presents a danger to our civilization and that it would be in our best interest to destabilize it. Hence my involvement here."

"What about the real Picard?"

He shrugged. "Somewhere else, in the real *Stargazer.* It is a big galaxy, after all."

The captain nodded. "That's true."

The Iyaaran frowned. "I still don't understand how you and your comrade overcame the Daa'Vit. It seemed to me they had you dead to rights."

She smiled. "Apparently, I've got more tricks up my sleeve than you give me credit for."

He looked at her archly. "In other words, you would rather not say. I can accept that—for now. But if your people and mine are to work together, it would be best to have as few secrets between us as possible."

"That sounds like an offer of help," said the captain.

"It is. And from what I have observed, you need all the help you can get."

She couldn't argue with that. "Sorry about your ship."

The Iyaaran shrugged. "A necessary casualty. Don't be concerned. My people have access to others."

That offer of help was sounding better and better. "You should rest. You took quite a beating down there."

"I did," he conceded. "Thank you."

"Thank *you,*" said the captain.

She watched the Iyaaran leave the room, remembering the way he had deceived her. In fact, she had been deceived twice in one day, if she counted the way the Daa'Vit had pulled the wool over her eyes.

And she admired deception.

After all, she wasn't the real Guinan any more than Sestro was the real Picard.

Alone in the conference room, she relaxed her powers of concentration and allowed herself to regain some of her natural features. A long reptilian tail emerged from beneath the hem of her robe. *Ah,* she thought, *that feels good.*

She would have given up her humanoid guise entirely except for the fact that her crew didn't stand on ceremony. Any one of them might walk in unannounced.

If they did, she didn't want them seeing her for what she was: a shapechanger, just like the Iyaaran, except from a different part of the quadrant.

A denizen of Daled IV, she possessed the ability to transform herself from her original form into a host of other guises, some of them capable of crushing a handful of Daa'Vit—or merely to transform her vocal cords so as to mimic a Klingon voice. And *her* people, too, wished to "destabilize" the Alliance, though she wished she had thought of the word before Sestro's people did.

It had a certain elegance.

The real Guinan, whom she had temporarily replaced on the *Lakul,* was recuperating from a serious injury back on Bering's World. When she returned to her ship and her crew, Werreth—for that was the Daledian's real name—would slip away. The exchange would leave a slew of questions, no doubt, and perhaps in time Werreth would answer them.

After her people decided to establish contact with the rebels.

Considering the antipathy between the real Guinan and the real Picard, it was ironic that the beings impersonating them might end up working together. But then, Werreth mused, revolutions—even incipient ones—made strange bedfellows.

The Sacred Chalice

Rudy Josephs

HISTORIAN'S NOTE: *"The Sacred Chalice" takes place in 2371 (ACE) as the human rebellion against the Klingon-Cardassian Alliance is on the rise ("Through the Looking Glass,"* Star Trek: Deep Space Nine), *just after Jean-Luc Picard decides to join the rebellion (*Star Trek Mirror Universe: Glass Empires— The Worst of Both Worlds*).*

Rudy Josephs was first exposed to *Star Trek* at a young, impressionable age, but it wasn't until the launch of *Star Trek: The Next Generation* that he truly got hooked. He suspects that it was mainly because he was the same age as Wesley Crusher and he figured if *that* kid could do all that he did, there was no telling what Rudy would achieve. Sadly, Rudy is still waiting for an interstellar traveler to come whisk him away from his boring life.

Betazed.

The most desolate hellhole of a planet Andrul Taqut had ever visited. Dead shrubs had overrun the landing area where his father had set down the family's private shuttle, a long walk from their mysterious destination. Andrul was not accustomed to traveling by foot for any distance. On Cardassia, he'd had a personal vehicle and driver assigned to him since birth. He still didn't understand why they couldn't simply beam down to the planet that wasn't even listed as M Class on star charts. His father had muttered some nonsense about planetary quarantine buoys, which only caused him more confusion over the purpose behind this impromptu trip.

Had his father learned of his massive losses betting on the underground slave fights or one of his many other secret endeavors? It seemed unlikely. If his father were going to kill him, it would have been done in public and with all the bells and whistles accorded such family conflicts. That was the best way to keep face in the Klingon-Cardassian Alliance. Children secretly disappearing only led to gossip and scandal that could affect Gul Taqut's position. Open filicide was the preferred method of dealing with a disappointing child.

Surely, the excuse of Andrul's entering into the Noran Tuk, the time of a youth's transition into manhood, was not the actual reason for the trip. That was a more formal gala filled with all the pomp and revelry traditional to the most archaic rituals. It was something that would be overseen by his mother. Certainly not something to be partaken on some long-abandoned world.

Empty husks of buildings lined the street of the once city. Andrul's history lessons had never mentioned any ancient civilizations in this corner of the universe. Not that the Alliance-approved texts weren't heavily edited, particularly regarding the former Terran Empire. If he'd known where his father was taking him, he would have done more research, but this mystery excursion didn't allow for any preparation, a fact, Andrul was certain, his father had intentionally planned.

A set of rusted metal doors stood at the end of a minor thoroughfare. The doors seemed neither particularly welcoming nor formidable, but Andrul's father proceeded directly toward them without hesitation. As they approached, Andrul watched as his father slid back a stone in the crumbling wall beside the door, revealing a modern keypad that clearly was installed after the planet was discarded. His father pressed a sequence of commands on the device.

"State your business." A static-filled, curt voice came out of the panel.

"We are an envoy of the Klingon-Cardassian Alliance seeking refuge from our travels," Andrul's father answered, confusing his son even further. How long was this planetary journey going to be if they were seeking refuge so soon? What was their ultimate destination?

"Greetings, Gul Taqut," the voice—now considerably friendlier and static-free—replied. *"Welcome to the Sacred Chalice."*

The huge metal doors swung open with a swooshing sound that was nothing like the grinding of rust or straining of metal Andrul had expected. Even more surprising was the lush garden waiting on the other side. Rows of exotic flower beds bursting with color lined the walkways. Flowing fountains and wooden benches dotted the greenery. Dark green vines climbed the interior walls, which looked much more heavy-duty inside than out. It was an oasis in the middle of a hellhole.

The landing party stepped hastily inside as the doors swooshed shut. An older woman in bright purple robes came hurrying toward them. She appeared Terran, but when she reached them,

Andrul saw that her eyes were completely black. His experience with Terrans was limited to their household servants, so he did not know if this was a unique trait. But he was far more intrigued by the kind of business his father could have with some planetary squatters.

"Gul Taqut," the woman said, taking Andrul's father into her arms in a highly inappropriate manner for a servant of the Alliance. "How lovely to see you again. And so soon after your last visit. I suspect that this strapping young man can only be that son of yours you've so often spoken about." Andrul doubted his father had ever said anything more than a passing reference, but the woman was clearly adept at masking true appearances, as the gardens around them indicated.

"Ambassador Troi," his father replied. "This is, indeed, my wastrel of a firstborn."

"Ambassador?" Andrul openly scoffed. The idea of this woman being the ambassador to a dead planet was the most amusing comment his taciturn father had ever made. Which was why it was surprising when his father smacked him across the face.

"Do not be disrespectful, worthless wretch," his father scolded. "Ambassador Troi serves the Alliance more honorably than you ever will."

"Now, now, dear," the woman said as she dared to take Andrul by the arm, leading him through the lush flora. "To be sure, Ambassador is more a ceremonial title. But we discourage acts of violence on the grounds of the Sacred Chalice."

Another set of doors with woven metalworks far more elegant than the first stood on the far end of the gardens. The ancient building they opened into was in far better shape than any they had passed out in the streets. It was likely the one structure on the entire planet that had been kept up.

The clouded glass and metal doors swung inward as they approached, revealing a grand entry hall with a winding staircase. At the foot of the staircase stood a row of scantily clad women. Andrul realized immediately the purpose of this place and why his father had brought him under the precepts of becoming a man.

If he only knew, Andrul thought as their party approached the collection of women. Like the *ambassador,* each woman appeared Terran, though with the same dark eyes. The sneer on Andrul's face must have been evident, as his father admonished him once again in front of the security officers and the ambassador. "Look down your nose all you want now, boy," he said. "But I assure you, no other house of pleasure in the universe has the uncanny ability to anticipate your most powerful needs and secret desires."

"It is our claim to fame," the woman said, looking uncomfortably into Andrul's eyes.

He did not believe this woman knew what he desired at all. Each of the concubines looked to be more delicate than the next. Certainly, they met his father's tastes for submissive females. Andrul had stumbled across his father's many mistresses on several occasions growing up. They could not have been further from his true desire.

"Something exotic," the woman said, walking past the row of painted women and settling on a mousy, timid little being many years older than Andrul and dressed far more conservatively than the other whores. With her thin frame, he could likely snap her in two with his breath.

The frail creature's eyes went wide in surprise. "Mother?" she asked.

Only more surprised was Andrul's own father. "I was under the impression your daughter did not entertain," he said, a note of anger in his tone. "That is what you have always told me."

"She never has," the ambassador assured him. "But I can think of no other person more fitting for the son of the great Gul Taqut than my Deanna."

That answer seemed to satisfy Taqut, but it didn't relax the woman any. "But, Mother, I—"

"Andrul," the ambassador said, cutting off her own child. "Deanna will show you the pleasures of the Room of Rixx."

Deanna stepped forward, resigned to protest no more. Andrul wanted to reject the frail female, but he knew he was committed to the task. His father would never let him turn down the honor of bedding the child of the proprietress. Though he had no desire for what lay ahead, he did take some pleasure in the idea that he was to receive services that his father had been denied.

"Don't worry," the young woman said softly as they ascended the stairs. "We provide only what the customer desires. As our parents both indicated, it is our specialty here at the Sacred Chalice."

This time, Andrul laughed out loud, knowing that his father, who was out of earshot, would assume he was getting into the spirit of things. His father was a fool if he really believed that these women could anticipate all that their guests truly wanted.

After a short walk through the upper level, Deanna announced that they had reached the Room of Rixx. She opened the door and hurried him inside. He was about to protest being manhandled by the waif, but the words caught on his tongue when he saw what awaited him. Splayed out on the enormous bed were two huge, muscular Terran men barely covered by thin sheets that left little to the imagination.

Andrul was both enticed by the men and in fear of them. How had these women known? And, more pressingly, would they share this information with his father?

"Beyond desires, it is *discretion* that we most pride ourselves on providing at the Sacred Chalice," the woman said before crossing the room and slipping out through a second exit.

Deanna Troi let out a frustrated sigh as she made her way through the back corridors of the Sacred Chalice. She found solace in the Spartan decor of the unadorned walls and simple designs of the "employees only" areas. These were her favorite rooms and pathways in the compound of a half-dozen buildings that made up her mother's domain. The grand halls and suites that were open to the visitors to the Chalice had always struck Deanna as cold and impersonal. They were designed to entice, not to comfort. Perfectly fitting for the realm created by her mother.

Lwaxana Troi could be maddening most of the time, but her actions today had been unprecedented. Serving her own daughter up like one of the poor Betazoids who had come to the Chalice in search of sanctuary. The few members of a once-proud race now serving as common—or uncommon—whores. Good thing the clients never really questioned how their pleasure givers knew how to anticipate their most intimate fantasies.

For a moment, Deanna had actually believed that her mother had finally crossed the line. It wasn't until Lwaxana had directed Deanna to take the young Cardie to the Room of Rixx that the younger Troi had clued into the plan. Deanna berated herself for not catching on sooner. The mere fact that Gul Taqut had been directed to touch down at one of the most distant of the landing pads indicated just how low he was in the Cardassian hierarchy. The day Deanna's mother lent her out, it would be for nothing less than the leaders of the regime.

"A fact you should have realized immediately." Her mother's voice entered her thoughts. *"I expect you to be more on top of your game in the future. You could have offended our guests by your reluctance to play along."*

"I'm sorry, Mother," Deanna thought. She hated that she could not even be alone in her own mind. *"I should have figured out your plan."*

"You should have," Lwaxana agreed. *"The Sacred Chalice is the last refuge of the Betazoid race. It will be yours someday, but I first need to know that you are able to handle the responsibility."*

"Yes, Mother," Deanna replied, trying to close her mind to her mother. She'd been practicing the technique for years but had never been able to make much headway.

"Don't you dare shut me out!" Lwaxana's voice screamed in Deanna's head.

"You know I feel this is a violation—"

"Our people have communicated this way for centuries," Lwaxana interrupted her thoughts. *"Even the near-extinction of our race could not stop us from being who we are."*

"Your race," Deanna reminded her mother. *"I am part Terran."*

"Now, now, no need to be snippy," her mother replied with a condescending tone. *"Just because you do not share in my abilities does not mean I am not a part of you. Now, keep to the off-limits areas. We can't have Gul Taqut stumbling across you while you are supposed to be entertaining his son."*

"Yes, Mother, I know my role," Deanna reminded her. *"I have to audition the new musician anyway."*

"See to it," her mother replied.

"Good-bye, Mother," Deanna replied, shutting her mother out of her mind as best she could. Deanna hated that Lwaxana could access her innermost thoughts at will. It was particularly annoying that Deanna hadn't inherited that particular Betazoid trait. Like her father, Deanna was purely Terran in that respect. She could not tap into any minds. She could not feel others' emotions. It was what had kept her from knowing her mother's plan for the young Cardassian earlier. It was also what probably kept her mother from selling her as she had all the other Betazoids who had come to the Sacred Chalice in search of a safe place to live. Like every other world that fell under Alliance dominion, even a hint of sanctuary came with a price. Deanna's price was to help her mother run her own miniature Betazoid Empire.

Over the years, Deanna had tried to convince herself that their people's lives were better lived in servitude at the Chalice than in hiding in the caves of Betazed. Even those who attempted to pass as Terran only did so as slaves. Life at the Chalice consisted of luxury accommodations, fabulous gifts from the patrons, and culinary delights not experienced in most of the quadrant. All that was asked in exchange was to rent out their bodies in one-hour increments.

But they were safe. Nowhere else in the galaxy could a servant anticipate your most secret dreams the way the women and men at the Sacred Chalice could. Even the highest-ranking officials of the Klingon-Cardassian Alliance never bothered to question the way they were able to guess even the most intimate fantasies. Likewise, Deanna had been able to ignore her own questions about whether or not this was the life she wanted to lead. She'd seen what making waves had done to the rest of her family. Her mother had ensured that she and Deanna would be safe. That was all that mattered.

Deanna entered her office, where she found an attractive older man waiting for her. Though she had known to expect the Terran, she was still caught short by the sight of him. He looked nothing like her own father, but there was something about him—about the way he regarded her when she entered—that brought back a flood of memories of the man who had abandoned her many years ago. The memories were so overwhelming that she threw a hand out to the wall to steady herself.

The man was out of his seat in a shot, coming to her side. "Are you okay, Miss?" he asked, with a slight accent that was unfamiliar to her. No surprise, as she'd met only a handful of Terrans in her lifetime.

"Sorry," she said, taking his hand as he led her to the chair. "I don't know what . . ." She trailed off, still overwhelmed by thoughts of her father.

"Would you like some water?" he asked. Without waiting for an answer, he poured her a glass from the filled pitcher she kept in her office. She accepted it gratefully and took a sip of the cool water while allowing her mind to clear.

"Thank you," she said as he sat in the chair facing her. "That was . . . unusual."

"Not really," the man said lightly. "Women typically swoon when they see me. Jean-Luc Picard. Most people call me Luc."

She smiled at his comment about the swooning and took the calloused hand that he offered her. The man had a firm grip and was a bit more weathered overall than the musicians they'd hired in the past. "Deanna," she said as they shook. "The Sacred Chalice is my mother's enterprise."

"Yes, the indomitable Lwaxana Troi," Luc replied. "My former patron, Gul Madred, visited your fine establishment on occasion."

"Spoke highly of us?" Deanna asked. She did not recall any Cardassians named Madred on the guest list, but that didn't mean anything. They saw so many clients. And her mother dealt with the bulk of them.

"Madred never spoke highly of anyone but himself," Luc replied. "May he rest in peace."

Deanna caught no small amount of sarcasm in that statement and decided to move off the subject. "And you're Terran?"

"Is that a problem?" Luc asked. His expression conveyed that he was worried about his human status being an issue, but something in his eyes suggested that he was not truly concerned. In truth, he seemed surprisingly calm for the interview, considering the work options that awaited a Terran man outside the Chalice. Deanna felt a surprising amount of confidence radiating from the man. She chalked it up to his charm, since she did not share any of her mother's empathic abilities.

"Not at all," Deanna said. "We've always kept a few Terrans working in various maintenance and landscaping positions." Lwaxana liked to have these people around to help with the façade that all of her employees were Terran rather than members of a supposedly dead race. Being that Luc was from Earth and did not possess any extrasensory abilities, her mother wouldn't consider him as a pleasure provider at the Chalice. Lwaxana Troi didn't believe that those with average mental acuity served much purpose in that area of her organization.

"Unfortunately, the grand piano in the salon is unavailable to us at the moment," Deanna continued. "But we have a slightly battered upright in the staff area." There was no need to clarify that the grand piano wasn't off limits as much as it was the salon itself where she was unwelcome. Gul Taqut was likely occupied at the moment, but one of his men was probably stationed in the entrance hall to keep watch. Not that Taqut was a high-profile target, but most of their guests liked to believe they were. For some reason, she felt that she could be honest with Luc about this, though she knew her mother would be angry if she explained the inner workings of the Chalice to a total stranger.

"No worries," Luc said, reaching into his satchel. He withdrew a carved stone box that looked to be quite ancient. "I wouldn't really know what to do with a piano, anyway. My talents lie elsewhere." He carefully placed the box on her desk and raised the lid. Inside was a copper-colored flute with silver accents. It was wrapped with a string that had a tassel on the end and altogether appeared rather delicate in its padded container. To say that this was not the type of music her mother was expecting would be an understatement, but Deanna saw no reason to stop Luc as he raised the instrument to his lips.

"I'll start with a favorite selection of my former patron," Luc said as he launched into a mournful tune. Like all Cardassian music, the song was precise and strong, if a little maudlin. It lacked any of the subtle qualities that would elicit an emotional response, preferring complicated runs and shows of dexterity over musicality. It was more like a mathematical equation brought to life than a piece of artistic interpretation. Luc's playing was technically adept, but there seemed very little feeling behind the performance, and the instrument did not really fit the tune. It was at times like this that Deanna wished she had her mother's empathic powers to help her understand the artist and comment on what was missing.

She gave a slight nod when the music ended. The music was accurate, if unemotional. Not that the Chalice received many music critics. Their clients only needed something in the background while they made their selections and went off with their temporary companions. "We also have a number of Klingon clientele," she said. "I don't suppose there are many Klingon concertos written for flute."

"You'd be surprised," Luc said. Deanna thought she caught the slightest roll of his eyes at the request. "My patron often entertained." He launched into an intensive tune that certainly evoked emotion, though technically it was little more than shrill squeals. Luc continued to abuse the delicate flute for another minute before Deanna placed a hand out to stop him.

"That's good enough," she said, formulating the nicest way to let him down easily. She hated turning away applicants, knowing their options outside the Chalice were quite limited. Then again, she could try to find a position for him in the landscaping department. Something about the man suggested that he would not have an aversion to digging in the dirt.

"I have another selection," Luc said. "Something that better showcases my abilities."

"I think I've heard all I need," Deanna said. She'd already decided that landscaping would be an acceptable offer. Her mother wouldn't be too upset with her.

"Just one more," he gently insisted. "Something a little different. From an ancient civilization, long forgotten, called Kataan."

"Kataan?" Deanna asked, enjoying the sound of the name. She knew so little of the universe outside the Chalice as it was. The idea of a forgotten civilization besides her own was exciting to hear.

"This flute is all that is left of them," Luc said with sadness in his eyes. "How I came across it . . . well, it's an interesting story for another time." He raised the flute to his lips again. "If I may?"

Deanna shrugged. She couldn't go anywhere until Gul Taqut's party left the establishment. "Why not?"

This brought a smile to Luc's face and a light to his eyes. It was as if her comment had breathed life into the man. He took a deep breath and began.

This time, Luc didn't launch into the music as he had the others. He slowly built the intensity, allowing the music to carry him into the piece. Closing his eyes as he played, it looked as if he were falling into the sound as it repeated and evolved. The music had a calm, pleasant tone unlike anything Deanna had heard before. It lulled her in as well.

When Luc opened his eyes again, there was a passion in them that matched the intensity of his playing. She saw how the music moved him. And she felt it in her heart.

Deanna's chair jumped back with her when she was hit by an unprecedented wave of Luc's emotions. They flooded into her, mingling with her own as the music ebbed and flowed. The screech of the metal chair produced a dissonant tone that brought Luc out of his musical trance, stopping him.

"Is something wrong?" he asked, clearly afraid that he had offended her somehow with his music.

"No," she said, feeling nothing but her own surprise now. "It's just . . . it was very moving."

"Thank you," he said, though he stayed on alert, clearly trying to figure out what had gone wrong.

He wasn't the only one.

The Betazoid telepathic and empathic powers were nothing more than a myth to the rest of the galaxy, known by a rare few who had truly studied their histories. It was certainly not something to be discussed with a stranger. But still. Deanna wondered what it was about this man that allowed her finally to tap into what she never before thought she possessed, had been told, on many occasions by her mother, that she never *would* possess. It had come and gone so quickly that Deanna was already wondering if it had even happened. Looking at Luc now, she could feel nothing but her own confused emotions roiling inside her.

Deanna barely had a moment to give the matter any thought when her mother blew into the office unexpectedly. Deanna and Luc both jumped to their feet, as if Lwaxana had walked in on them in the midst of an intimate moment. Though this was the one person she could talk to about her new experience, Deanna was not ready to share it. Her mind again went through the mental exercises she'd learned as a child. The lessons her big sister, Kestra, had tried to drill into her head so many times. *To protect us from Mom,* Kestra had often told her, though Deanna had no idea back then what they needed protecting from.

She experienced another first as she felt the invisible walls around her mind go up immediately when she called on them. The sudden look of frustration that briefly flashed across her mother's face confirmed that she'd been successful.

"Did I interrupt?" Lwaxana asked, sounding as if she hoped that she had.

"We were just finishing up, Mother," Deanna said. "This is Luc . . . um, Jean-Luc Picard."

"The new pianist?" she asked.

"Flutist, actually," Deanna said.

A sneer crossed her mother's face as she looked over the man. "What would we possibly need a flute player for here?"

"Hard to go from room to room with a piano strapped to my chest," Luc said in a joke that fell flat.

Lwaxana gave him the once-over. "He's not much to look at," she said, causing Deanna to blush in embarrassment. "But since you've come all this way, I should at least interview you properly."

Luc made a move to return to their seats, but Lwaxana did not budge. Instead, she threw on her hostess persona, breaking into a huge smile and taking Luc's hands into her own. The pleasant greeting she exchanged with him carefully hid the fact that she was reaching into his mind to explore his true motivations for seeking employment. Deanna recognized the subtle traces of expression on her mother's face that revealed she was not getting all that she wanted to know. It was like this sometimes with Terrans accustomed to a life serving the Alliance. They were inherently practiced at hiding their emotions from their masters. They didn't even realize how deep they were able to keep those secrets from even the most adept telepaths. Deanna took some pleasure from the thought that she could touch Luc's emotions in a way that her mother could not.

But Deanna had more pressing concerns at the moment as she listened to her mother run through her list of standard follow-up questions. Even though Luc answered each inquiry perfectly, she could tell that her mother was not impressed. Unless Deanna stepped in, Luc would be gone before she had the chance to understand if her newly emerging ability was related to the man in front of her.

"Well, we do have some other candidates to see," Lwaxana said, wrapping up her part of the interview. Deanna knew that it was now or never.

"Actually, Mother," Deanna said, shocking both Troi women in the room, "I was about to extend an offer for Mr. Picard to join us. With a standard contract, of course."

"You were?" Lwaxana asked, looking Luc up and down again, clearly trying to get more of a read off him.

"Yes," Deanna said firmly. "He plays beautifully."

"I am certain that he does," Lwaxana said. Deanna could feel her mother trying to break down the mental barriers to see inside her daughter's mind. Deanna had never before in her life been allowed to make a substantive decision about the running of the Sacred Chalice. Lwaxana was sure to have questions about this unexpected development.

Deanna knew she had to take a chance and let down her guard, allowing her mother inside. Remembering back to her lessons, Deanna sectioned off the surprising discovery she had made earlier and let her mother access the areas of her mind she considered safe.

The moment those invisible walls came down, Lwaxana's familiar voice filled her head. *"What are you doing, Deanna?"*

"You keep insisting that I take on more of a role in day-to-day operations." Deanna allowed her mother to take those words from her mind. *"I thought I would start with some tasks of lesser importance."*

"But I cannot get a full read on this one," Lwaxana said. *"I feel as if he is hiding something."*

"Isn't that true of everyone under the current regime?" Deanna silently asked in response as Luc looked on. He merely saw a mother and daughter staring each other down.

"Fine," Lwaxana replied aloud. "Mr. Picard, welcome to the Sacred Chalice. You will be directly under my daughter's supervision. We'll put you on a probationary period for the month. If it doesn't work out, I have some Klingon friends always looking for help in their mines. Please don't do anything to make me regret this."

"Thank you," Luc said as he took Lwaxana's hand again in a friendly gesture, not realizing that it only reminded Deanna of how close he'd come to losing the job.

Deanna looked on with the thrill of anticipation, mixed with some concern. Though it wouldn't have seemed so to an outside observer, she had just made a notable change in the nature of the relationship between herself and her mother. Lwaxana had already reacted with a thinly veiled threat. Deanna hoped that she wasn't making a mistake.

It had been three days since the hiring of Luc Picard, and Deanna had barely seen him since. Her mother kept finding tasks that would keep her away from the salon, as if Lwaxana suspected something was going on between them. Not that Deanna had any romantic inclinations toward the man. Her feelings for him fell squarely into a fatherly role—a relationship that had been missing from her life since her mother had chased away Ian Andrew Troi long ago.

Deanna hadn't been exposed to any more of Luc's thoughts or emotions since the interview. She was practicing every day at sending out her own thoughts to tap into his, or to anyone else's in the Chalice, but with no success. At the same time, she was building up her own mental strength for keeping her mother out of her mind. Lwaxana kept making attempts at sudden invasions with ever-increasing frequency. Deanna was getting stronger at blocking her mother out, but the mental exertions were exhausting her. Several staff members had commented on how tired Deanna had looked of late, each quietly blaming Lwaxana for the cause. They were only partially correct.

It was the dream music that had woken Deanna so early in the morning. Another tune, different from the one Luc had played for her, had seeped into her sleeping mind until her eyes flitted open in the dark room. The morning silence greeted her, causing her to wonder what part of her subconscious had created the song.

Deanna got out of bed and threw on a dressing gown for a morning stroll through the compound. She liked the early hours at the Chalice, as they were usually the most serene. The prior evening's guests had gone, and the overnight visitors had usually fallen asleep or passed out by now. She only greeted a few staff members on her walk. They were all dressed far less conservatively than she was in her nightclothes.

As she walked through the public areas of the Chalice, Deanna was startled by the sounds of the flute from her dream floating out from the garden. Her waking mind now recognized it as a lullaby that her father had sung to her as a child. It was impossible for her to have heard the music all the way in her private chambers but far too much of a coincidence not to explore. Besides, the tune could only be coming from one person.

Deanna paused at the entryway to the garden. Luc's back was to her. She didn't want to disturb him while he played. Music was never scheduled for this time of the day. And Terran music was never on the schedule at all, which is why she assumed he had risen so early to play. Lwaxana was safely in her bed in the house farthest back in the compound.

Deanna stood silently with eyes closed, allowing the music to flow into her on the gentle breeze. It shared the serene quality of the other piece that Luc had performed, but this one was faster and more playful. The notes seemed to skip over one another, racing around the garden and out to her. Deanna found herself swaying along with the tune, remembering her father—no, her entire *family*—sitting together in their private chambers. Her mother lying back on the divan. She and her sister on the floor, mimicking their father's song. She lost herself to the memory, until the wave of emotion overwhelmed even her own deep feelings, nearly knocking her off her feet.

Her eyes popped open as she grasped a trellis for support. The contentment that she now felt was not her own. It was a kind of peace she had never had in her own life. It washed over her, subduing her feelings of loss for her family and calming her momentary shock. But in that peacefulness, there was something else. Something darker, just underneath. If her mother were there, she would have immediately identified it. She would have forced her way into Luc's mind to explain all of this away. But the feelings were shut off as quickly as they had come. And Deanna was, once again, restricted to her own emotions.

Luc stopped playing abruptly, as if he had felt something as well. He turned to see Deanna watching him and jumped up from the bench he'd been sitting on.

"I'm sorry," he said. "I thought I'd be alone at this hour."

"It's hard to be alone anywhere in Mother's compound," Deanna said, not bothering to explain on how many levels that statement was true. "But you don't have to apologize. I rather enjoyed it. It was a song my father used to sing to me."

"I'm sorry," Luc said, seeing the sadness in hey eyes. "May I ask how he . . . ?"

"Oh, he's not dead," Deanna clarified. "Just gone. He wanted to do more than this." She waved back to the Chalice and all it represented. "He wanted to work with the Terran rebels. Make a difference."

"That doesn't seem like something your mother would have liked," Luc said. He sat back on the bench, motioning for Deanna to join him.

"It made her furious," Deanna said, taking a seat. The early morning air smelled sweet in the garden. Part of that was the flowers. Part of it was the synthesized scents her mother had pumped in to add to the illusion of this Shangri-la. "But not because she's complacent. She was afraid any contact with the rebels would jeopardize what we are doing here."

"Running a pleasure palace?"

"Is that all you see?"

"Is there more?"

"The Sacred Chalice *is* known for the joys of the flesh," Deanna admitted, knowing she was about to reveal a carefully guarded secret. But if Luc was going to stay at the Chalice beyond his probationary month, the truth was bound to come out. He seemed rather perceptive. Maybe he had figured it out already.

"This flute you play," she said, taking the instrument from him to examine it more closely. "You said that it's from a forgotten race."

"The Kataan," he said. "It's known as a Ressikan flute."

She held it to her lips but did not play it. "The Chalice is a similar relic," she said, handing the flute back to Luc. "As are its residents. Most people assume that Mother's family found this desolate planet and claimed it as their own. But that's not exactly true. In reality, we never left. You see, we are the last of the dying race of Betazoids who once called this planet home. We've been scattered throughout the galaxy for the past century, after the Terran Empire killed any race that exhibited powers they deemed dangerous."

"I had heard legends," Luc said, "about a race of telepaths."

She did not respond.

"So . . . you can read my mind? I can see how that would help the Chalice earn its reputation."

"Yes," Deanna said as her eyes dropped to the floor. "And no. Our telepathic abilities are dying out as well. According to Mother, the more diluted our lineage becomes through marrying other races, the less we can tap into that power. I cannot access it at all. Which, I think, is the only thing that keeps her from making me take on more personal responsibilities with the Chalice guests. Until the ability is extinct, Mother has found what she believes is the best way to put it to use. To keep us all safe."

"You don't agree?" Luc asked, reading the look on her face.

Deanna considered the question. It was one that had popped up in her mind numerous times over the years. Every time it had, she'd managed to focus on other, more trivial matters. It was easier than coping with the reality. "My father didn't," she said. "He wanted us all to be more active in the resistance against the Alliance. Not that things were much better when the Terran race was in charge. But still, there's a chance for improvement when people like my father are involved. I'm sure you can imagine how knowing what the leaders were thinking could be very useful."

Luc nodded.

"My mother refused," she continued. "She didn't want to put her family at any more risk than she had to."

"What side did you come down on?" Luc pressed.

"I didn't have a side," she explained. "I was too young. My sister—"

"Sister?"

"Kestra." Deanna wasn't sure why she was opening up to this stranger, but it felt right. It was always hard to think of her father, but Deanna rarely let her big sister into her memories. That pain was too intense. "She was old enough to notice the distance growing between my parents. She often joined in their fights, taking my father's side. Like me, she didn't have any telepathic powers, but she was willing to use whatever she could to help in the fight against the Alliance."

"But she was only a child, too?" Luc guessed.

"When my father left, yes," Deanna said.

"Left?" Luc asked. "He just abandoned his family?"

Deanna shrugged. "Abandoned. Forced out. We never knew. One day he was just . . . gone. Kestra and I didn't know what to believe. Kestra stopped trusting our mother that day. I was just confused. Of course, Mother thought the fight died in Kestra with Father's disappearance. But my sister was simply being silent. Waiting for an opportunity. Once she was old enough, Kestra stowed away on one of our guests' ships. To search for our father."

"Do you know if she found him?" Luc asked.

Deanna shook her head, fighting back the tears. She had never shared this story with anyone. Her mother had forbidden it. "Kestra was discovered as soon as they broke orbit. My mother told me she was executed immediately. Her body was dumped into space. I never had a chance to say good-bye." Deanna pushed past the sadness, forcing a fake smile. "I know. It's the kind of story you hear a lot these days."

"That doesn't make it any less painful," Luc acknowledged. "Thank you for sharing it with me."

Deanna straightened herself up, wiping away her tears in an attempt to be more professional. Or as professional as she could be while wearing a dressing gown. "I'm going to speak to Mother," she said, rising from the bench. "I see no reason we can't sprinkle in music from worlds other than Cardassia and Qo'noS during your musical sets. Every once in a while couldn't hurt."

"I don't know that your mother would agree," Luc said.

Deanna allowed a genuine smile. Luc had only been in residence for a couple of days, and he already had a handle on Lwaxana Troi. Deanna bid him good morning, as they both started down the opposite paths that led to their chambers. Deanna paused to watch him walk off, wondering why she hadn't mentioned anything about tapping into his feelings. She'd been so open about everything else.

In the moment Luc turned the corner, Deanna was struck by another mental link. This one was more powerful than all of the others. It was not an emotion. It was a memory, a picture, really. Jean-Luc Picard had an image of Deanna's sister, Kestra, in his mind.

The sight of the image in Deanna's mind knocked the wind out of her. Her sister looked familiar yet different. She looked much older, her features care-worn. But that was impossible, since she lived only a few hours longer than Deanna's last image of her.

Deanna tried to explain it away as her imagination. A fleeting daydream brought about by her thoughts of her sister. The picture was there and gone so quickly that Deanna hardly had time for it to register. But this felt different from a memory. Even a powerful one. It had come to her through an external force, as when her mother entered her mind for private conversation. Certainly, having lived with a number of Betazoids over the years, Deanna was used to unwanted images coming into her head. But that was different. Those images assaulted her mind. This was something that she had pulled from Luc without him knowing. If asked to explain the difference, Deanna knew that she could not, but it was definitely a unique experience.

Once she recovered from the unexpected image, Deanna decided that she had to talk to Luc about her emerging talent. If she was ever going to learn why she could tap into his mind in ways she could not with any other person, she was going to have to share the full truth with him. It was the only way she could determine what these thoughts of Kestra could mean.

She considered talking to her mother first. That would be the logical course of action, since Lwaxana knew more about the Betazoid race than anyone else Deanna knew. But Deanna wasn't functioning logically at the moment. She was running on pure emotion when she decided to follow Luc through the Chalice. It was logic, though, that stopped her from calling out to him when she saw him enter through a door that did not lead to the staff dormitory.

Much of the grounds of the Sacred Chalice was off limits to the patrons, but only a few areas were forbidden to the staff. It was possible that Luc had made a wrong turn, being so new. But there was something suspicious about him making this particular wrong turn at a time when most of the staff were still in bed. Any doubts about it being a mistake were wiped away when Deanna watched him enter the small communications chamber. Only she and her mother knew the pass code required to gain access to the room.

Deanna hurried to the door that had closed behind Luc. She leaned in, listening as she and her sister had done when they were children. Though the guest rooms and private suites in the Chalice were soundproofed for more discreet reasons, the same was not true of this room. It was an unfortunate design flaw of which her mother was still unaware. A viewscreen capable of long-range communications was set just inside the door. It linked with the computers in her mother's office and private suite. Those were the only areas in the Chalice where one could communicate offworld.

Within moments, Deanna was able to hear two voices on the other side of the door. It was always easier to hear her mother in there, as Lwaxana's voice tended to carry. Whomever Luc was contacting understood the need to speak softly, though Deanna could hear the vocal tones of both voices. It was a woman. A very familiar woman.

Paying no heed to the need for concealment, Deanna pounded the code into the keypad, opening the door. Even though she'd had her suspicions of what she would find, the image on the viewscreen caught her entirely off guard.

"Kestra!" Deanna said with a gasp as she came into the room, making sure that the door shut behind her. Even in the shock of seeing her sister alive, Deanna knew that whatever was going on was something her mother could not know about. At least, not yet.

"Hello, Deanna," Kestra said from the viewscreen. She looked exactly like the flash of an image Deanna had seen earlier. Kestra's blond hair was streaked with premature strands of gray. Her face was far more weathered than the youthful skin of the teen she was when they were last together. A scar ran along her cheek, suggesting that she had seen some hard times since her alleged death. While Deanna took in the appearance of her sister, Kestra seemed to be doing the same to her.

After what seemed like an eternity, Kestra was the first to break the silence. *"I know seeing me is . . . unexpected."*

"Unexpected?" Deanna said, louder than she'd intended. "I was told that you were dead."

"I suspected as much," Kestra said, with a nod in Luc's direction. *"That was Mother's lie, not mine. I always intended to come back for you. It just took me a bit longer than I'd expected."*

"Years," Deanna pointed out to her sister. "It's been years. You couldn't have gotten a message through? Couldn't have let me know you were alive? Kestra, what is going on?"

"Deanna," Luc said, laying a calming hand on her shoulder. "Your sister had some good reasons—"

Deanna turned on him, slapping his hand away. Now she understood what was buried under the emotions she had felt from him earlier. She knew why her mother had been suspicious of him.

What he'd been hiding from them since he first came to their doorstep. "She abandoned me," Deanna said to Luc while pointing back to the viewscreen. "Left me alone with Mother. I want an explanation. I'd prefer to hear it from my sister."

"It's okay, Jean-Luc," Kestra said. *"Let me talk to her."*

Luc stepped off to the side, but he did not leave the room.

"I know this seems crazy," Kestra said, *"but I can explain all of it. I thought it best to send Jean-Luc to make contact with you first. To get to know you. Because we need your help."*

"You couldn't come yourself?" Deanna asked.

"Mother wouldn't allow it," Kestra said. *"I've tried to contact her before, but she refuses to acknowledge that I'm alive. The one time we spoke after I left, she made her position clear. She thinks I put all of you in danger. And that is unforgivable."*

"And Father?" Deanna asked. "Have you found him?"

Kestra shook her head. *"It's a big universe."*

There was a pause in the conversation. Clearly, both sisters had so much they wanted to say. And so much that they knew they couldn't.

"What do you want from me?" Deanna asked, breaking the silence. "I'm assuming you're not here for a simple reunion, or you wouldn't have Luc sneaking around for days before contacting me. No, wait. You didn't contact me. You let me stumble across you." She looked at Luc. "What did you do to me? How did you lead me here? Are you Betazoid, too?"

Luc laughed, throwing up his hands in an exaggerated manner, as if defending himself from her. "Don't look at me," he said. "Talk to your sister."

Kestra shook her head in resignation. *"We don't have time for this. The longer we're in contact, the greater jeopardy we're all in."*

For the first time, Deanna noticed that her sister was standing on the bridge of a small ship. Shadows of movement behind Kestra suggested she was not alone, but the screen was cut in tight on her, so as not to reveal too much of her surroundings. "Where are you?" Deanna asked.

"Orbiting the planet," Kestra said. *"In Jean-Luc's ship. Believe me, I wouldn't have come back here if it wasn't important. You know about Mother's secret files."*

"The recordings she keeps as leverage on our guests," Deanna said. Those data streams had always been the worst-kept secret in their family. It was the thing her parents had fought over the most when their father was still alive. Recordings of the most powerful people in the universe in less than powerful positions.

"Not those," Kestra said, shaking her head and allowing a wry smile. *"Same ol' Deanna. Never questioning anything more than you need to know."*

Deanna couldn't help but think that if her sister was trying to come to her for some kind of help, there were better ways to do it. Putting Deanna down as she did when they were kids wasn't the best way to convince her. Then again, the questions Kestra was providing for Deanna's mind to roll over were certainly making her curious to learn more.

Kestra let out a sigh that could be heard through subspace. *"Mother taps into the deepest recesses of the mind of every guest of the Chalice. She's kept a file of all of their secrets since the first day of operations. Assassination attempts. Secret battle plans. Weaknesses to exploit. Strengths to avoid. Years' worth of information on everything she would need to protect herself if anyone started looking into the weird powers these people possessed who seemed to know their guests' innermost desires."*

"That sounds like Mother," Deanna allowed.

"Too much like her," Kestra said. *"Dad always wanted to get Mother to use that information to help the resistance. She probably has enough stored up to take the Alliance down ten times over. But she would never consider it. Never wanted to risk her people getting hurt."*

Deanna didn't see how that was a bad thing. Her mother wanted to protect what was left of the Betazoid race. If anything, it was a noble goal. Several hundred people called the Chalice home. Why should her mother risk all of those lives to go against a government that largely left them alone? If the history Deanna had been taught was correct, it wasn't as if anyone had rushed to the aid of the Betazoids when they were victims of genocide.

"All we're asking is for you to access those files, make copies, and give them to Jean-Luc," Kestra said. *"That's it. We'll go off, and you'll never hear from us again. Unless you want to. You know you're welcome to join us."*

"That's all, betray Mother?" Deanna said.

"Mother betrayed us!" Kestra said bitterly.

"What are you talking about?" Deanna asked. She could see that her sister was trying to calm herself.

"Mother has been lying to us since birth," Kestra said. *"The Betazoid telepathic powers aren't dying out. We both inherited some of her abilities. Or, at least, I know that I have. I'm empathic. With some flashes of telepathic images from time to time. But mostly, I can just read other people's emotions. Jean-Luc thinks you can, too."*

"Luc . . . Jean-Luc . . . doesn't even know me," Deanna said, with a glance back at the relative stranger.

"But you know Jean-Luc, don't you?" Kestra asked. *"At least, you've had a few glimpses into his mind, haven't you?"*

Deanna should have been surprised, but her ability to tap into Luc's mind was too much of a coincidence. They had to have set this up in some way. "You've been planting emotions and images in my mind? How?"

"Not planting them," Luc said. His calm tone was almost a whisper compared with Deanna and Kestra's heated dialogue. "Allowing you to experience them." He raised his foot and slipped a small metal device out of the heel of his shoe. "With this." He pressed down on the device, and Deanna was hit by the full force of Luc's uncensored thoughts. .

It was the worst sensation she'd ever felt in her life. Luc's conscious and subconscious were entirely open to her. As was the mind of every other person in the Chalice. Love. Hate. Passion. Fear. She felt it all, jumbled together with an orgy of images that she did not want and could not make sense of. It was as if everyone in the compound were screaming into her mind. Even Kestra was coming through over the viewscreen, and Deanna couldn't begin to imagine the distance those feelings were traveling. It was all a blur of colors and moods. The only clear messages came from the person physically nearest her. Everything else was a cacophony.

Deanna's legs collapsed beneath her, and she fell to the floor. She may have passed out, because the next thing she saw was Luc squatting beside her as her mind started to clear the din.

"You never told me that would happen," Luc admonished Kestra with a level of anger the previously serene man had never revealed before.

"*I didn't know for sure,*" Kestra said with a shrug. "*It was a possibility. Deanna was never taught how to focus her powers. She couldn't even manage to keep Mother out of her thoughts. It took me years of practice to hone my abilities.*"

"What is that thing?" Deanna asked. Her eyes were locked on the slender device that Luc was slipping back into hiding. "Something that plants images and emotions in my mind?"

"*Just the opposite,*" Kestra said. "*It allows you to tap into what has always been there.*"

Deanna didn't respond.

"*After I escaped on that Romulan shuttle,*" Kestra said, "*I slipped off at the next port, where I had arranged to meet one of Dad's old friends. He'd lost contact with our father, but he was able to tell me what he knew about us. That Mother had been suppressing our powers since birth. As soon as we'd shown a predisposition to the Betazoid gift, she had a neural suppressor implanted in each of us to conceal those abilities.*"

"Why?"

"*To protect us? To control us? Who knows?*" Kestra said. "*The point is, she's been lying to us our entire lives. I had the device removed and taught myself how to tap into my abilities. How to use them. It took years, because I'd started so late. After I got the hang of it, I started using my powers to help out where I could. During one of my missions, I stumbled across Jean-Luc. He'd recently turned against the Alliance himself.*"

Deanna looked to Luc, who merely shrugged. Even with the

neural suppressor functioning again, she knew that there was deep sadness behind his controlled response.

"We teamed up," Kestra said. *"And found a scientist who possessed the technology to tap into the neural suppressor. It was then that I knew it was time to reestablish contact. To see if you'd be willing to help us."*

"You're asking a lot, considering most of it is based on lies," Deanna said.

"I know," Kestra said. *"But all I'm truly asking is for you to look into Mother's files. Then you can make your decision based on what you find."*

Before Deanna could respond, a klaxon sounded on the bridge of the ship. Kestra maintained her cool, but Deanna could see concern in her sister's eyes.

"Looks like we've got company," she said as the shadows behind her moved more frantically. *"Jean-Luc, talk to her. I've got to go."*

"What's happening?" Deanna asked.

"I love you, Deanna," Kestra said as she cut off communication.

The viewscreen went suddenly blank, leaving Deanna in silence. Her sister was alive. Her sister was alive, and her mother had been lying to her since birth, if Kestra was to be believed. And now Deanna was expected to help this virtual stranger betray their mother. All in all, it was not the morning she had expected.

"It's a lot to take in," Luc said. "But you can trust your sister. And you can trust me."

"I know," Deanna said. "I saw it in the flood of information. I could make out a few things. Kestra has grown very fond of you."

"We make a good team," he said.

"It's more than that," Deanna said. "The emotions . . . they're similar to how she feels when she thinks of our father. I suspect I was feeling some of that myself."

"I never did have any children of my own," Luc said. "Though I've often wondered what became of my nephew. It might be nice to have a family again."

"I'm not so sure that you'd want to be a part of this one." Deanna surprised herself with the joke, considering all that was going on inside her own head at the moment. She had felt something else in the rush of emotions. Something much darker that she couldn't quite access yet. Luc's emotions were still there, in the back of her mind, along with another secret he never intended to reveal.

"Deanna, I know this must be difficult," Luc said. "But I also know a thing or two about going along with the status quo simply because it is the easier way. I allowed myself to be oppressed by my Cardassian patron so long that I convinced myself that I was actually a free man. Is that really so different from your relationship with your mother?"

"How is it you're keeping your thoughts from her?" Deanna asked.

"Your mother's not the only one who knows how to whip up a neural suppressor," Luc said. "The one I've got just works in reverse."

Deanna nodded, wanting to keep him engaged while her mind worked through the confusion to remember what it was she had seen. She was so focused on both tasks that she almost failed to notice the door opening.

"Now, this is an interesting surprise," Lwaxana said coldly, as she entered the communications chamber.

For once in her life, Deanna was not cowed by the woman's attitude. "Mother, we need to talk."

"Yes," Lwaxana said, eyeing both her and Luc suspiciously. "Yes, we do. But now is not the time. We have some very high-profile guests on their descent. We must prepare."

Deanna was about to protest, but when she caught the eager look in Luc's eyes, everything fell into place. Her mind had finally pieced together his true mission. This kind, fatherly figure had somehow become an assassin.

Tension filled the salon of the Sacred Chalice along with the Klingon music Luc provided with his Ressikan flute. Had there been time to find a replacement musician, he would surely have been exiled from the planet, simply for being in a room where he was not permitted. That, coupled with his mind still being closed to Lwaxana, was more than enough for Deanna to worry for his very life. But that was not the main concern at the moment. Deanna was certain of Luc's plan to assassinate their approaching guests.

Half of the staff were lined up in the main hall to receive their special guests. It was like this every time they visited. Their tastes changed on a whim, which only the varied talents of the Chalice pleasure providers could quench. Lwaxana had even abruptly shown several of the overnight guests of lesser position the door to avoid any unpleasantness. This was one of the few arrivals that could have pushed back the discussion Deanna and her mother were destined to have.

When Lwaxana finished addressing the staff in the hall, she came into the salon, where Deanna was sure to keep as much room between herself and Luc as physically possible. A wave of Lwaxana's hand silenced Luc's playing. "I assume you know some Terran music?" she asked.

"I may have picked up a song or two," Luc said, throwing a smile in Deanna's direction. She looked away quickly. If he got the idea that it would be funny to play her father's lullaby, it was likely that her mother would kill him on the spot.

"Do not trifle with me this morning. It will not improve your situation any," Lwaxana said. "When they heard we had a Terran musician, they requested music from your homeworld. Something slow and mournful is more to their tastes."

Luc made a show of thinking about the request. "I guess I could try—"

"I do not *care* what you play," Lwaxana said. "Just play."

As Luc began the first notes of a suitably morose tune, Lwaxana returned to the main hall to greet the new arrivals. He tried to make light of the situation by screwing up his face and throwing a glance in Deanna's direction. She was in even less of a mood for that than her mother and ignored him. She was too busy trying to figure out a way to stop the inevitable. It would not be the first assassination attempt to take place at the Chalice, but it would be unique in that it involved an employee. That would not be good for business.

Deanna silently cursed her sister for setting this situation in motion and then hovering in orbit while it played itself out. Now that she and Luc were alone, Deanna considered speaking to him about it, but voices from the grand hall put that plan to a halt. Their guests had arrived.

After an initial review of the selection of pleasure providers, Lwaxana led her guests into the salon to rest from their travels and settle on their tastes for the visit. The Klingon women of the House of Duras, Lursa and B'Etor, were known for being difficult to satisfy. They put much thought into their pleasure and rarely chose their partners without due consideration. The debate between the two women was considered part of the foreplay. Many times, Deanna had been torn between embarrassment and horror as she listened to the women plan their activities for the day. Having some musical accompaniment to drown them out was much appreciated.

"Do tell me that this fine specimen is available to us as well," Lursa said as she entered the room and set her eyes upon Luc.

"Sadly, no," Lwaxana said, quickly adding a lie to keep them from being offended. "All musicians at the Chalice are eunuchs. It ensures that they focus on their jobs and not the guests."

"A grand idea," Lursa said, with a pointed look to her guard as if she were considering adapting the concept for her own needs. "But it is a pity," she added, with a lingering glance at Luc.

Deanna watched Luc watch the women as they settled onto the couch to discuss their options. She couldn't help but notice that he was positioned with his back against the wall, standing equidistant from the two exit points of the room. Lwaxana was hovering over their guests the entire time. If only Deanna had seen what Luc was planning, she might be able to stop it. But the abilities that revealed themselves were more empathic than telepathic. She was just glad that she'd gotten a glimpse into his intentions. All she could do was be vigilant.

"We are in need of something special," B'Etor said to Lwaxana, "as this may be our last visit to your establishment."

Lwaxana looked horrified by the suggestion. "Is there something here that displeases you?"

"Security issues," Lursa explained. "A known rebellion ship was orbiting your planet. A ship flying under the name *Stargazer*. Naturally, we blew it out of orbit, but who knows what might come in its place?"

Deanna's mind went immediately to her sister. She refused to think it possible that she could have lost Kestra again, so soon after being reunited. These two Klingons were so blasé about it that it would be easy to let herself believe it didn't happen. Luc, however, did not seem to have any doubt. His body tensed, visibly, which did not go unnoticed by Lwaxana.

Before Deanna could take control of the situation, she lost control of herself entirely. Maybe it was an unintentional shifting of Luc's foot or the movement of his heel, but the technology that tapped into Deanna's neural suppressor suddenly powered up at the worst time. Once again, she felt the onslaught of mixed emotions, none more powerful than the rage Luc felt toward the Klingon women. It was now mixing with her own.

The murderous intent took over Deanna's body, and she flew across the salon, attacking the source of her pain. Deanna tore at Luc's clothes, pummeling him, fueled by his own rage. He raised his arms to defend himself but refused to fight back. The Klingon guards snapped to attention, watching the bizarre scene. Lwaxana was screaming at her daughter to calm herself.

In the melee, Luc's pocket ripped away, and a small round device rolled out onto the floor. Seeing things more clearly than she had before, Deanna lunged for the device, scooping it into her hands.

She stood and faced the women who had killed her sister. Her father. No. Not her father. He was not dead. Just her sister. The sister who raised her when her mother failed to. The sister who came back to her. Who found her a new father to protect her. To use her.

The Klingon women stood across the room in a state of shock and confusion. Their guards' pistols were raised. Her mother was trying to calm them.

Her mother. Who had abandoned her own child. Suppressed Deanna.

Before she realized what she was doing, Deanna pressed a button on the round device and flung it at the trio of women. The guards fired on Deanna, but Luc threw her to the ground a split second before the shots hit their target.

A split second before the explosion struck.

Deanna took what she assumed was to be the last look at her home planet from the emergency escape shuttle she shared with Luc Picard. It was the first time she'd ever seen Betazed from space. Oddly, it looked smaller than she'd always imagined it. Her entire life had been contained in the Sacred Chalice, which led her to dream that the world outside its walls was so much larger than it actually was.

The universe, however, was a different matter. As they headed off to meet with Luc's contacts, Deanna wondered what her future held. The Klingons would see to it that the path her mother had laid out for her since birth was no longer possible.

The explosion had killed her mother instantly. Deanna hadn't even had a farewell moment with Lwaxana. The woman's motivations remained a mystery to Deanna, who apparently had a chip in her brain as her legacy.

Luc had apologized repeatedly, to the point that it was becoming rote. He claimed that he hadn't meant to press down on the heel of his shoe and activate the device when he learned of his crew's death. His body had simply reacted without heed of the consequences. She wasn't so sure that she believed him. Her breakdown would have made for an aptly timed distraction. As it was, she had fulfilled his mission on her own, by killing the Duras sisters.

Deanna found it hard to forgive Luc, but she knew that she had to for her own good. He was her only connection to the universe at large. She needed him now that they'd abandoned the Chalice.

Lursa and B'Etor's ship hung in orbit on the other side of Betazed. Knowing it could take out the Chalice in a single shot, Deanna was forced to follow Lwaxana's emergency escape plan and have her people flee the planet in the ships hidden for just such an emergency. Once it was discovered that the Duras sisters were dead, there would be a price on the head of everyone associated with the Chalice.

Once again, the Betazoid race was going to be hunted for something over which they had no control. Deanna wanted nothing more than to pawn off this problem on Jean-Luc Picard and his friends, who had successfully destroyed her life and the lives of all of the people in the shuttles that were following hers. She couldn't even mourn for her sister. Deanna was on her own for the first time in her life. At the same time, she held the lives of the last of the Betazoid race in her hands, just as Lwaxana had always promised she would.

The only saving grace came from the files Deanna had taken from her mother's computer. It was all there, as Kestra said it would be, the secret thoughts of some of the most powerful minds in the Alliance. It was a commodity she would use to find her people a new sanctuary. And maybe her father as well.

As Deanna flew off into the unknown with Picard, she felt the despair of those people wash over her as they were being forced, once again, to abandon their home. It was an emotion that she feared was going to become familiar.

Bitter Fruit

Susan Wright

HISTORIAN'S NOTE: *This tale is set in late 2371,*
several months after the events of The Mirror-Scaled Serpent
from Star Trek Mirror Universe: Obsidian Alliances.

Susan Wright's latest fantasy novels were published by Penguin/ Roc: *To Serve and Submit* (2007) and *A Pound of Flesh* (2008). Her forthcoming novels, urban fantasies set in New York City, are called *Confessions of a Demon* and *Demon Revelation,* with *Confessions* scheduled to be published in November 2009 by Penguin Group. Susan has written nine *Star Trek* novels: *Dark Passions* (Vols. 1 & 2), *Gateways: One Small Step, Sins of Commission, The Best and the Brightest, The Badlands* (Vols. 1 & 2), *The Tempest,* and *Violations.* Susan has also written a number of nonfiction books on art and popular culture, as well as *Slave Trade,* her first science fiction trilogy, published by Pocket Books (2003–2005). The uncut version of *Slave Trade* book 1 is now available in free chapter downloads on Book View Café at www.bookviewcafe.com. Susan founded the National Coalition for Sexual Freedom in 1997, and currently serves as spokesperson. Her website and a link to her blog are at www.susanwright.info.

Kes perched on a rock, slippery from mist at the base of the waterfall. The droplets fell on her face and uplifted hands, filling her with hope. In the Alpha Quadrant, water was like space itself—there was more than enough for everyone. This waterfall was even more remarkable because it had been created along with the underground oasis by the Genesis Project nearly a hundred years ago as part of the far-reaching plan of a man long dead.

Despite her delight, Kes couldn't stop tracing the contours of the rock wall that indicated where cracks might exist. It was silly, because the lift could take her from the Memory Omega base to the surface of Regula. But the Vulcans here said it was too dangerous to risk exposing herself while the Alliance might still be looking for her, and feeling confined had brought out old habits. Back home with the Ocampa, she had spent most of her time searching for a way out of their underground city. Eventually, she had discovered a gap in the security field and a crevice that led to the surface, where she had found love in the person of Neelix and horror at the hands of the Kazon-Olga, who had tortured her to reveal the secret entrance to the Ocampa's home.

Those Kazons were the first men I murdered.

She shuddered at the memory. From behind her, a measured voice asked, "Are you cold, Kes? Perhaps you should sit in a different location."

"Tuvok!" Kes scrambled down over the boulders to greet the first friend she had made in the Alpha Quadrant. "Your wife didn't tell me you were coming. How's Neelix?"

Tuvok, like the other Vulcans, didn't smile. "Mr. Neelix is doing well. He now serves as a pilot for the Terran rebellion."

"He must like that." Kes gave Tuvok an impulsive hug, even though she'd learned that Vulcans didn't like displays of affection, and uninvited physical contact even less. But since she couldn't hug Neelix, he would have to put up with it.

Tuvok waited until she was done. "Kes, would you like to help, too? It would mean leaving Memory Omega for a short while."

"*Yes!*" Tuvok raised one brow in question, and she added, "Everyone here has been good to me, Tuvok. I'm learning very fast—T'Pel told you, didn't she? But I've never liked being shut up in one place."

Tuvok held out a padd. "You should see this before you agree. It will not be an easy assignment."

Kes activated the stored message on the padd. The face of a Cardassian woman she had never seen before appeared on the small screen. Bright body paint was smeared across her lips and cheeks, with delicate chains draping over her head. At first, Kes thought she was pretty, but the woman twisted her lips in a disdainful way that destroyed the pleasing effect.

"*We have a problem. My target just told me that he's perfected his gene-resequencing technique. He's been trying to seduce me, and he thought I would be impressed by his success.*" The Cardassian smirked. "*He claims to have augmented a half-Klingon test subject—and now she can read minds. It's got to be B'Elanna! My target is irate, because he wants to present the findings to the Alliance, but for some reason, she's stalling. The best we could do is tail them when they leave. Request instruction. Seska out.*"

Kes handed back the device. "Is it really B'Elanna?"

"We believe so, but Harry has been unable to obtain visual confirmation. Seska's target is Crell Moset, a Cardassian scientist who was one of the project managers on Monor Base, the place you were being held when we rescued you. The Alliance listed him as 'suspected dead' along with B'Elanna after the base was destroyed."

Kes suppressed a shudder. B'Elanna had ordered another one of her scientists, Dr. Louis Zimmerman, to experiment on Kes soon after she and Neelix had arrived in the Alpha Quadrant. This time, her torturers sought to unlock the secret of her telepathic talent, instead of the secret entrance to the Ocampa's home.

"Since it appears that B'Elanna may now be able to read minds," Tuvok continued, "I called off Harry's planned attempt to infiltrate their safe house. They are in the underground city of Archanis, living in the tunnel complex of a wealthy Ferengi businesswoman named Ishka. We have discovered at least one instance in which Ishka completed a business deal with B'Elanna's mother, Miral."

"So Ishka's sheltering them. Does she know about the telepaths?" The Vulcans had explained how vital it was to protect their underground network of telepaths until the time was right to overthrow the Alliance. Their long-term predictions of how events would play out had been correct until now, so Kes was inclined to believe them.

"Perhaps," said Tuvok. "It is not enough to stop B'Elanna and Crell Moset if Ishka has gained access to their research. We also need to recover the tissue samples they took from you."

Kes rubbed her hands over her damp arms, chilled to her core. Since gaining her telepathic abilities, she had been nothing but a danger to others. Her mind was so powerful that she could destroy people with a thought. As panic rose within, she took slow, deep breaths as the Vulcans had taught her.

She got herself under control and met his steady gaze. "Do you want me to kill them?"

"I deeply regret asking you this, Kes. If there is any other option, I intend to take it. But as a last resort, where ordinary weapons cannot reach, your powerful mind may penetrate."

"I've been learning how *not* to kill people with my mind."

"I understand." His compassionate eyes said he knew the struggles she had been through. For someone so unemotional, he had a distinctly sympathetic way about him.

"You have to keep the Alliance from creating telepathic operatives," Kes agreed. She owed him; Tuvok had saved her life, first by rescuing her from Monor Base and then by bringing her here so she could learn how to control her formidable abilities. "I'll do what it takes. You'll be with me, won't you?"

"Yes. We shall leave immediately."

Kes felt a twinge of empathy for T'Pel, Tuvok's wife. For decades, she had seen him only a few times a year. These Vulcans sacrificed everything for their cause. It made Kes feel selfish about pining for Neelix, but at least T'Pel knew Tuvok was alive. Neelix thought Kes had been transformed into pure energy—that's what Tuvok had told him during their escape from Monor Base.

Kes stopped short on the trail back to the quarters. "I can tell Neelix now! If it's safe for me to go outside, then the Alliance isn't looking for me."

Tuvok hesitated. "Mr. Neelix's ability to maintain your cover is uncertain."

"He can do it, I'm sure of it. Especially since he knows it would mean life or death for me."

"It means life or death for all of us," Tuvok corrected.

Kes stared at him. "You said Neelix could be told when the time was right. I think we've waited long enough."

Tuvok urged her forward. "You are cold and wet, Kes. We will discuss this on the ship. There are many aspects to consider."

Kes dug in her heels. She was still that obstinate girl who had defied her elders' warnings about seeking a way to the surface of Ocampa. She wouldn't deny her love for Neelix. When the Kazon-Olga nearly killed her, he had returned to rescue her in spite of the danger. He had persuaded the rebellion to save her from B'Elanna's scientists on Monor Base. It was no ordinary love they shared. She would be true to Neelix—she had found her partner, the man for her. And he had proven himself; she would never doubt his love.

"I'm not going anywhere until you agree that I can see Neelix."

Tuvok's brow rose. "Is it that important to you? You would risk allowing B'Elanna to become more of a threat rather than give up Mr. Neelix?"

"Yes." If Tuvok was going to ask her to violate her most cherished beliefs about the sanctity of life, then she was going to hold Neelix close to her heart again.

"Agreed, then," Tuvok said. "Mr. Neelix can visit you here. Since I doubt he will be able to keep the secret unless you convince him, he will be summoned, and you can tell him yourself that you are alive."

Relief flowed through her. "You'll see, Tuvok, everything will work out fine."

Kes flicked her fingers nervously through her dyed black hair. She had straightened it on the journey to Archanis and wasn't used to the bangs hanging against her forehead, but the layers concealed her distinctive Ocampa ears. Tuvok had added dark spots on her face and down her neck so she looked like a Trill. Tuvok was posing as her Vulcan slave, though she wasn't doing a very good job of ordering him around.

It was also her task to negotiate with the elderly owner of the Archanis complex for access to the tunnels closest to Ishka's home, where B'Elanna was assumed to be hiding. "We would greatly appreciate it if you agreed," she finished, after she had outlined their offer.

They were seated in the reception tunnel of the Archani's ornate complex. The tunnel walls arched into the ceiling and were polished to a satiny texture that revealed the red and orange layers in the rock, swirling and rippling like frozen water. The floors were springy and absorbed sounds well. Passing through the many levels of tunnels in the city, Kes had been forced to pull her cap over her ears to muffle the echoing noises. But here it was serene, with chimes playing in the background and sweet scents in the air. Graceful violet fish with lacy fins circled in a pillar of cloudy gas in the center of the reception room. With the brightly embroidered cushions and glowing glass ornaments, it was luxury like she'd never seen before.

No, Kes, you must insist, Tuvok urged silently. *Make him agree to let us stay. I know you can do it.*

She had practiced on a few people at Memory Omega, but this was real. She mentally pressed her desire on the Archani as she had been taught.

"We shall only stay a short time," Kes repeated more firmly as she compelled the old man to agree. "The two rooms in that tunnel will be for our exclusive use. In exchange, you'll accept our latinum and won't say a word to anyone. You'll also order your servant not to speak to anyone about us."

The Archani's reluctance evaporated. "Agreed," he said pleasantly. "My servant will escort you there now."

Tuvok nodded slightly as he spoke directly to her mind. *Well done, Kes.*

It was easier than she expected. Her pangs of guilt were reassuring; she refused to be complacent about manipulating people. She was doing this for the good of people who were trying to overthrow an oppressive regime, not for her own gain.

Kes did everything Tuvok silently directed as they took possession of two rooms in the tunnel adjacent to Ishka's complex. They were finely decorated, though not nearly as grand as the reception room. Despite the flowery incense, she could detect a faint, dank odor that was all too familiar.

"Stuck in another cave." Kes sighed. "I was looking forward to being above ground so I could see the sun again."

"Rock is a formidable protection. Let us see if you can penetrate it."

Kes sat down on a hassock and prepared herself. If she couldn't reach through the rock, their options were going to be limited. Everyone was relying on her.

"Relax," Tuvok told her. "You can do this."

She smiled up at him. Other than Neelix, nobody had ever had such faith in her. It helped calm her excitement caused by their journey to Archanis in his ship. The rhythm of her heart slowed as she relaxed. Nodding to Tuvok, she closed her eyes and reached out . . .

Inside the rock, the only sounds were the distant tremors of the planet vibrating in basso echoes; it was like being in the womb. She had spent her life underground, and nothing was more familiar. Where there was rock, there were cracks and chinks from the movement of the earth. Tendrils of her mind found passage through those cracks, until suddenly she was questing in a vast open space. There were people nearby, their thoughts like birdsong, with too many notes to distinguish between them.

Kes gasped, as if straining to hear through a heavy door. She forced her fingers to unclench. One had to work with the flow of the mind, not fight it, in order to gain access. Soon snatches of coherent thought began to reverberate inside her head.

. . . to get that replicator back online before . . .

. . . she'll love it. Maybe she'll be so happy she'll . . .

. . . no, no, no, NO, NO!

Her eyes flew open, but Kes managed to cling to the mind link she had formed. She couldn't sink in further because of the pain, the excruciating pain.

"Stop it!" B'Elanna screamed, putting her hands to her head. "Shut up! Shut up!"

Kes was looking through B'Elanna's eyes down at a Terran slave tied naked to the table in front of her. The young man's protests weren't uttered out loud, but they filled B'Elanna's head until she couldn't get away, as if she herself were crying out, *"No!"*

B'Elanna bent over, clutching her hair while still holding the pick she had been using to torment the slave. Small beads of blood decorated his smooth belly and chest like a broken necklace.

"I can't stand it!" B'Elanna gasped.

Kes realized that B'Elanna couldn't shield her mind. Here was proof that Crell Moset had successfully resequenced her DNA using Kes's genetic material. But unlike Kes, B'Elanna couldn't yet control her ability; she was always hearing the thoughts of others. They played even through her dreams at night.

Kes could see it all: B'Elanna had been triumphant at first when she realized she could sense what everyone around her was thinking. She trusted Crell Moset because he longed for nothing more than elevating his own status, which he would achieve through his breakthrough with B'Elanna. Kes sensed that he was more than ready to leave, but their return had to be handled carefully. They would have the advantage if B'Elanna could master her new abilities. Rather than dwell on the potential negative consequences of his scientific greed, Moset was distracting himself nicely with a Cardassian bath girl.

Mercifully, Ishka was a blank, as were other Ferengi B'Elanna had encountered. Ishka had funded Moset's research in the hopes that both it and B'Elanna's telepathic power would benefit her financially. Unfortunately, B'Elanna couldn't bear to go into the city because of the barrage of thoughts she encountered, so she could only be helpful when Ishka had brought home non-Ferengi business associates.

Frenzied was Kes's overriding impression. B'Elanna did nothing but wrestle with her telepathy, practicing with every person in the complex, hating the constant babble. The effort was slightly more bearable when she got to indulge her sexual appetites.

Splayed out on the table for her amusement, the slave whimpered, his dusky skin glistening with sweat. She had once reveled in the sight of the lovers secured for her use, making them endure whatever she did to them. *The power of holding a life in your hand, of feeling that ultimate pleasure flow through your body . . .*

"*tlhomaS,*" B'Elanna said out loud. Thomas had belonged to her in every way, and he had never protested at her touch, crying out wordlessly when the pain was too much for him to bear. She had pushed him as hard as she could without killing him. For a while after Monor Base was destroyed, she had created a hologram of Thomas to satisfy herself, but that was too pathetic, and she had returned to using Ishka's slaves.

B'Elanna wondered if Thomas had begged in his mind as this slave was doing. *Make it stop!* he silently pleaded. All of the slaves bargained for their lives, even the ones who didn't believe in supreme beings. He strained his neck to see the blood seeping from the wounds in his stomach and chest, as his wrists jerked against the restraints that bound his limbs to each leg of the table. *Make it stop! Please, make it stop! I'll give you anything, do anything, if only you make it stop!*

B'Elanna glared at him. They all begged for help, unable to accept what was happening to them. She found herself mouthing the words along with the slave's thoughts until they became her own. *Make it stop . . . Please, make it stop!*

Her hand tightened on the pick. The grip was cast from her own hand, fitting her like a glove, with a hand span of silver plasteel sharpened to a razor point. "Make it stop!" B'Elanna shouted. She lifted the pick over the slave's heart.

Kes realized that B'Elanna was going to silence him for good. In that horrifying moment, Kes wanted to blast B'Elanna with her mind, but she didn't have the strength to penetrate the thick rock wall between them.

Desperate to do something, anything, Kes tugged on B'Elanna's thoughts, like teasing fiber into a thread and drawing it closer. The point of the pick wavered, and Kes tugged harder. B'Elanna's wrist turned until the pick was aimed at her own face. Kes encouraged B'Elanna, *Yes, make it stop. This is how to make the terrible noise stop. Blessed silence at last . . .*

Looking through B'Elanna's eyes as the point neared her face, Kes felt a spike of fear. It felt as if she were about to kill herself. Her fear seeped into B'Elanna, and she began to struggle.

With a last gasping effort, Kes jerked the pick toward her face. But B'Elanna turned her wrist, slashing it down. It pierced the slave's eye. B'Elanna screamed along with the Terran, as his death cries vibrated between them. The slave had a gory red pit where his eye once was, with the handle of the pick protruding from it. His body jerked convulsively against his restraints, then settled heavily as his last breath escaped.

Kes broke her mind link, screaming. Tuvok supported her to

keep her from falling to the floor. "She killed him!" She gasped. "She killed a helpless man! I tried, but I couldn't stop her, Tuvok. I couldn't!"

Tuvok put his arm around her stiffly, unaccustomed to such things. It seemed that he truly cared about her. She was comforted by that, and by his assurances. She gave him confirmation that B'Elanna was indeed now a telepath, but her failure to prevent the man's death made her weep. "You can't expect to succeed in your first try, Kes. At least, now we know you can reach her."

Relaxing in his arms, she wished for a moment that Tuvok was Neelix. She felt bad, because Tuvok was trying to give her what she needed. But she couldn't stop thinking about the slave whose name she didn't know.

B'Elanna let go of the pick that was still in the slave's eye and took a step back. "What the *chay'!*" She looked down at her own hand, suddenly alien to her, remembering how it had brought the tip of the pick closer to her eye. She had been mesmerized by the shiny point, with a tiny drop of the slave's blood hanging from the tip.

"Have I lost my mind?" she cried out loud.

The slave was dead, the pick in his left eye. That was exactly how she had killed Thomas—by throwing her *d'k tahg* into his left eye, after he had betrayed her.

She bent over, clutching her stomach, feeling the loss again like a physical blow. She'd had no feelings after she had killed Thomas, but the unfathomable, infuriating pain that filled her in the days that followed betrayed the true depth of her feelings for him, however she might deny them. She hated herself for it.

In revulsion, she stared down at the slave. She, who had once playfully dabbled in her victims' blood, couldn't bear to pull the pick from his brain. The blood was too alive with memories. She could still feel him in her own mind, thinking his thoughts as if they were her own.

"I killed myself," B'Elanna murmured, not sure what she meant. But she did know with a sinking certainty that he would be the last Terran she ever tortured. She couldn't bear to have their fear and pain become part of her. It made her feel . . . weak. Like *them*.

Because the rock walls of the tunnel prevented Kes from attacking B'Elanna with lethal psionic force, manipulation was her only option. Kes could take it for only so long, and she had to retreat to recover between each attempt. At dinner, she tried to make B'Elanna slice her own wrist with her eating knife but succeeded only in enraging her. Then, as B'Elanna dreamed, Kes planted a compulsion to shoot herself with her disruptor. On waking, B'Elanna went so far as to turn the emitter around to herself, but her finger jerked spasmodically before Kes could make her press down on the trigger. Instead, B'Elanna threw the disruptor away with a snarl, her thoughts of destruction turning to other victims both dead and alive—on Cestus III, Monor Base, even her own mother, whom she had unsuccessfully attempted to poison.

Kes fled her mind in horror.

"You are identifying too closely with your target," Tuvok patiently reminded her. "Your instinctive fear of death is preventing you from completing your mission."

"How can I not identify with her? The reason B'Elanna is telepathic is that my own DNA was spliced with hers."

"Center yourself properly, Kes, as you have been taught. Do not lose yourself."

But it was impossible to distance herself from the vicious swirl of B'Elanna's thoughts. The Klingon hybrid's failure to master her telepathy had ignited the old wounds of her dual heritage. B'Elanna couldn't face her greatest fear—she wanted to kill herself for the same reason she hurt her Terran lovers, because she herself was part Terran. Her mother had always declared that B'Elanna had the heart of a Klingon. But perhaps that wasn't true. She had failed in command twice now and had shown a weakness that was disturbingly Terran.

Kes couldn't understand how B'Elanna could despise Terrans yet be so obsessed with them. But B'Elanna's memories of Thomas were filled with a deep craving even as she sliced his flesh and breathed deep of his burnt skin. She dwelt on how his eyelashes had quivered, beaded with teardrops during their sessions, and the way his raspy voice after too many screams made her long to have his hands on her body. She had gazed into his brilliant blue eyes for hours, it seemed, soaking in every nuance of his reactions.

It made Kes feel soiled. Her only comfort was the true love she shared with Neelix, sustaining her even while they were apart.

Kes began avoiding B'Elanna's mind and instead tried to push one of the others in the complex into killing her. When a Terran slave passed B'Elanna carrying a propellant tank for a personal pod, Kes tried to make him bash B'Elanna over the head with it. But the slave crumpled against a wall, so cowed by fear that his body shut down at the very idea.

Ishka was useless, because she was head-blind. Crell Moset wasn't swayed by Kes's prodding, because he fervently wanted to present B'Elanna to the Alliance to prove his research. Now that his work was completed, he mostly thought about Seska's naked body. The rebel spy had not yet indulged his desire, but she had come close, and Moset's elaborate fantasies needed no more assistance. Kes came out of her immersion with his mind grateful that he didn't mix violence with pleasure and amused by how sincerely the old, respected scientist wished to abase himself before the lowly bath girl.

From the other room, she heard, "*. . . I thought we could deploy the remote probe through the ventilation system, but Seska suggested she plant it on Moset tonight. We should target B'Elanna first to make it easier to infiltrate the complex and destroy their research.*"

Tuvok replied, "What are the chances of the security system detecting your device?"

Kes went to the arched doorway. Tuvok was standing in front of the screen mounted on the wall with his back to her. A young man with a round, boyish face was using a lot of technical words in his answer. Despite his enthusiasm, he never smiled, and his narrow eyes remained oddly flat.

When he finished, Tuvok agreed, "I will allow you to attempt it, Harry."

"I'll have to come to your location to operate the remote probe." When Tuvok hesitated, Harry added impatiently, *"I can't set up outside their ventilation grill, Tuvok. The rock wall should be thin enough there that my equipment can penetrate."*

Tuvok nodded. "Very well."

Kes cleared her throat to let Tuvok know she was there. As he turned, the image on the screen was replaced by a different man with a crown of wispy hair and arcs of yellow, red, and orange spots across his head. *Neelix.*

But Neelix's usual cheery expression was gone. The bones of his skull protruded too sharply, as if he hadn't eaten in months, making hollows of his cheeks and dulling the once-iridescent colors of his skin. At first, she thought he was sick. Then she realized he was in pain.

"Neelix!" she cried out.

He apparently couldn't see or hear her, because he was reporting to Tuvok. *"All secure here in the crater. I had to recharge the alpha battery because of—"*

"Understood. Tuvok out," Tuvok interrupted.

Kes ran up to him, seeing Neelix's puzzlement at his abrupt dismissal as his image winked out. "Neelix is here? You didn't tell me! Call him back, Tuvok, so I can talk to him."

"That is not acceptable at this time. In his surprise, Mr. Neelix could reveal that you are alive to Harry or Seska."

Her heart was pounding from the shock of seeing Neelix. Tuvok had deliberately concealed his presence from her.

"Tuvok! Neelix wouldn't do anything to hurt me. If you're that worried, he can come live with me. Even trapped underground would be better for him than *that*." She gestured to the screen, where she could still almost see his skeletal image.

"Too many questions would be raised by his disappearance."

"I have to tell him, Tuvok. I never should have let you claim I was dead. It was wrong. Look at how he's been suffering! I'm as bad as B'Elanna, torturing the man I love."

"It was necessary."

"Was it? I was so desperate to learn how to control my powers, and scared by how easy it was to murder those people, that I let you take care of me. I gave up everything so I could pretend it wasn't my fault. I wanted to feel safe and innocent again. But that was wrong."

"Kes, if the Alliance discovers you are alive, they will stop at nothing to get to you. And if they succeed, that will end the rebellion. Your supposed death is the only thing that has saved us all."

A cold spike of fear went through her at his words. It was hard to believe, but it was true. "You never intended to tell Neelix that I'm alive. You lied to me."

There was no trace of shame in Tuvok's reply. "You are correct, we cannot tell Mr. Neelix. His current state is the surest indication that you are indeed dead and not hidden away somewhere. Alliance moles in the rebellion may be watching him, and they would see the change in his demeanor."

"I can't keep torturing him!"

"The needs of the many outweigh the needs of the few. Or the one, Kes."

With a wordless cry, Kes slipped the leash on her mind, the fragile cord that held back her killing power. She lashed out at the man who had lied to and manipulated her. She wanted nothing more than to destroy him to get to Neelix.

As the killing burst swelled inside her head, with white-hot spears of pain exploding from within, Tuvok grabbed the side of her face with one hand. His fingertips pressed in as his other arm circled her back, keeping her from twisting away.

Kes struggled, glaring into his eyes. He had been her friend only to control her. He would shut her away forever in that underground base with his people as her watchdogs.

She would never see the sky again, never see her beloved Neelix again.

She fought for her life, trying to escape his grasp, trying to resist the intrusive waves of his thoughts. If she could break free, she would have the advantage, but under his hand, she couldn't resist. Her raw talent couldn't beat his lifetime of training.

His thoughts became her thoughts. She swam in his reasoning for making Neelix believe she was dead and felt his regret and responsibility for Neelix's suffering. Someday Kes might see Neelix, but not soon, not this year, at least, an eternity for a short-lived creature like herself. She could sense through Tuvok the millions of lives that hung in the balance and knew that she could be the cause of their deaths if the Alliance acquired her powers.

Kes felt herself calming down, breathing in rhythm with Tuvok, becoming as emotionless as he was. His detachment was soothing. She didn't have to feel bad for endangering so many people simply by being alive. Her pain lifted away, and she no longer wanted to kill him. She understood why he had lied to her, though she still thought Neelix should be told.

In that last moment before Tuvok released her, shame flooded through her. She had sworn she would never kill in rage again. She had betrayed herself even more than Tuvok had betrayed her.

"You could not have killed me." Tuvok let go of her and stepped back. "Everyone from Memory Omega has developed a technique for shielding ourselves against the particular psionic frequency you emit to kill."

She swallowed her resentment, carefully controlling her expression. "Good to know."

Tuvok gazed down at her, exactly the same as always. As if Kes weren't flushed and her blackened hair weren't ruffled up from wrestling against him a moment ago. She touched the tender spots on her cheek and jaw. She would have bruises there tomorrow, five oval marks where his fingertips had dug in.

"I sincerely regret hurting you, Kes. I consider you to be one of my friends, despite how this appears."

She wanted to throw his words back in his face, but she was at his mercy. Even worse, Neelix was at his mercy. To protect the rebellion, Tuvok would kill Neelix if he had to. He would also kill her, she was sure of it. He had not meant to reveal that much in his mind-meld, but she was stronger than he knew.

She had managed to hide her true thoughts within that genuine burst of shame she had felt at the end. She never should have lashed out at him like that. It was a deplorable loss of control. No, she would have to lay her plans carefully if she was going to get out of this alive with Neelix.

"I know you mean well—you've taken responsibility for the welfare of your people," she forced herself to say. "I'll work on this mission with you because I understand what you're fighting for. But don't expect me ever to trust you again, Tuvok."

When Harry came to their tunnel to commence the remote probe attack on B'Elanna, Kes did as Tuvok requested and hid behind a mosaic screen that blocked the archway to the other room. Kes didn't need to see Harry; she sank slowly into his mind.

Harry was nearly as bloodthirsty as B'Elanna, but he kept his rage contained. He wouldn't be satisfied until every Klingon in the galaxy was ripped to pieces, and then he'd gladly go back and rip those into smaller pieces. *Funny how much space the need for revenge takes up in a man's mind,* Kes mused. She resolved to remember this lesson.

Seska's voice came from the wall screen, announcing that she had planted the remote probe. *"Moset just went into Ishka's complex. Do I get to kill him next time I see him? I'm sick of fawning over that pompous idiot."*

"Await further orders." Tuvok signed off. "Harry, you may proceed."

Kes felt Harry's rising anticipation as he checked his equipment. "I have a signal. Activating the passive sensors."

A shadowy representation of a wall and a curved ceiling appeared on the upper screen. A dark patch filled the lower two-thirds. The image blurred for a moment, then stabilized, only to blur again. Harry analyzed it instantly; the probe was caught in Crell Moset's boot cuff.

Tuvok leaned over Harry's shoulder, making Kes twitch self-consciously. But Tuvok had no way of knowing that she was along for the ride in Harry's mind.

"Activating antigrav," Harry said.

The view shifted as the probe lifted. Kes's fingers twitched as if she were operating the probe along with Harry. It felt as if her brain were stretching too hard to try to understand the technical terms he was thinking, but the gist was that he had succeeded in evading Ishka's security system.

The probe floated up to the ceiling of the tunnel, where it wouldn't be noticed in the shadows. Harry carefully passed through the corridors, checking each room. They found plenty of house slaves, but there was no sign of B'Elanna. Then Kes nudged Harry into following a slave with a tray of food, and the probe trailed him straight into B'Elanna's quarters.

Kes mouthed the words along with Harry. "Target sighted."

The slave deposited the covered tray on the table nearest the door, practically running back out as B'Elanna winced and irritably gestured for him to leave. The rooms looked as if they hadn't been tended in some time. B'Elanna didn't seem interested in the food and continued pacing back and forth like a caged animal.

A wash of cool, clean energy seemed to flow through Harry. He focused on his prey with an intensity that heightened his senses and sped his reaction time. The probe circled to approach B'Elanna from behind and suddenly darted in. In the targeting screen was a swath of vulnerable skin at the back of her neck.

It happened so quickly; there was no hesitation, only ruthless intent in Harry's mind. But Kes couldn't let him kill B'Elanna, not yet. Tuvok would take her back to Memory Omega as soon as their mission was complete, and first she needed to find a way to make everyone leave her and Neelix alone.

She pushed hard on Harry's desire to kill the Klingon. It was far easier to make someone do something he already wanted, rather than fight against him. She pressed her thumb down, wanting B'Elanna dead, willing Harry to make it so.

Harry pressed the button even as he realized it was too soon to activate the laser pulse. The tiny probe wasn't in position yet. A beam of blue light deflected off B'Elanna's leather vest, burning a deep scar across the brown hide. Klaxons sounded along with lurid flashing lights.

"Security alert!" Harry scrambled to activate the self-destruct. The image on the screen went up in a puff of smoke.

"What happened?" Tuvok demanded.

Harry was astonished at himself. It was a novice mistake to let his emotions interfere in his work. His sense of professional pride was stung. "I rushed my shot."

If Tuvok was disappointed, it didn't show. "How long before you can assemble another probe?"

"I'll have to collect some of the components. It could take a few days."

"No matter, I have another plan. Did you bring the holocube I requested?"

"Yes." Harry handed over the device, shutting his emotions down tight. He had needed that kill; he had been tracking B'Elanna for months, and having her within his sights, then losing her, was too much. He almost hoped she would panic and run. Even if he didn't personally get to finish the job, he could take a measure of satisfaction in flushing her out of hiding so someone else could.

. . .

B'Elanna waved at the smoke, trying to clear it so she could see if there were any remains of the device that had imploded. The particle beam had gotten her attention, to say the least. It had punched her in the back, and the blue light had blinded her for a moment. She had her reinforced leather vest to thank for her life.

The device had been reduced to ash. Her gaze darted around the room, expecting another attack. She almost ran to the transporter room to get to the safety of the ship. But what then? Crell Moset would have to come with her, and he was probably the one behind this. He had been increasingly impatient with her delays, and he had just returned to the complex. Was he trying to drive her out?

She wasn't ready to face the Regent. She would be mentally overwhelmed, and she wouldn't be able to defend her decision to verify Moset's theories instead of returning at once to Qo'noS. After Monor Base had fallen from the sky on her watch, nothing less than a proven success would resurrect her life. And she almost had it.

I'm not ready yet!

When Tuvok shifted the screen aside, he found Kes deep in a mind-meld with B'Elanna. Kes eased out, truthfully reporting everything she had discovered. "B'Elanna confronted Crell Moset, but he denied knowing anything about it, naturally. He thinks that they've been discovered, and he's really shaken. He just left the complex again. Ishka thinks a business associate is behind the attack, and she's ordered upgrades on her security system. B'Elanna is holed up in her room again."

"Frightening her out will not be easy," Tuvok said. "Klingons typically become aggressive when cornered, but she is reacting in quite the opposite manner."

"It's the telepathy. She feels other people's thoughts as her own, so she's confused about herself."

Tuvok came closer, trying to bridge the formal distance that had sprung up between them. "Kes, this is very important. You must discover what B'Elanna wants above all else. Something that will make her leave the complex to get it. Press on that. Make her think that she cannot live without it."

"She needs to find out how to control her telepathy. If she knew I was here, she'd probably claw through the rock to get to me."

"Anything but that, Kes. Make her use the transporter to go someplace outside the tunnels, to her ship or anywhere else on Archanis."

"Why?"

"Because you can push her into inputting coordinates that will transport her into this." Tuvok held up a palm-sized cube. Tiny silver conduits snaked over the surface. "The rebellion obtained this device during the raid of an Alliance research facility. It is a self-powered quantum storage unit, capable of converting a subject's transporter pattern to a holographic matrix and encoding that matrix in its memory core."

"So, B'Elanna will still be alive?"

"Yes, along with Crell Moset, who will also be placed inside."

"B'Elanna won't like that."

"That is not my concern." Tuvok gestured. "Rest now, and later you may be able to reach out to B'Elanna again."

When Kes woke from a short nap late that night, she searched mentally for B'Elanna and found she was also awake and on her way to Moset's laboratory. He had left again, shortly after the probe attack, and had not yet returned. B'Elanna ordered the lights on and sat down at his terminal. The data on the telepathy research were in neatly organized files.

B'Elanna copied the entire set of files into a capsule carrier. She shoved the capsule into a hypospray and injected it into her upper arm with a grunt. It was a lot larger than the standard pharmaceutical dose and left a bump under her skin. Now B'Elanna had everything that the Regent would need to create his own telepaths.

As she went back down the corridor, Moset returned moist and fragrant from the baths. B'Elanna's nose wrinkled at the sexual fog clouding his mind. His bath girl had been imperious with him tonight. He had kissed her toes as he had dreamed of for so long, and the sight of her smug face leaning over him had satisfied him as no other woman ever had. His memory of her was miraculously perfect, obviously idealized past any resemblance to the real bath girl. B'Elanna was sorely tempted to smack him across the head.

Kes was deep inside B'Elanna's mind, and her own hands clenched with desire to strike the blissful old man. She had suggested to Tuvok that Seska assume a more assertive role with Moset. Apparently, it was working.

"Ha'DlbaH!" B'Elanna sneered.

Moset trembled, but he held his ground. "We must return to the Alliance. I could lose everything I built for myself, my decades of hard work and my home on Chin'toka II. What if they declare us dead? If we wait any longer, it may be too late."

She shook her head. "I need more time."

"Then I'll go alone," Moset insisted. "I'll explain that you're working on mastering your skills. I'll explain everything."

"I know what you'll say! You'll tell them that it's my fault we came to Archanis, that I made you work on the telepathy research. You'll make sure you get the rewards, while I get all the suspicion and punishment!"

B'Elanna closed with him threateningly. She had to intimidate him into agreeing with her; she would be stronger if they stood together.

But the stirring in his groin was an altogether different response. Her display of dominance excited him. He had seen her fight before and had been terrified and aroused. Now that she was swaggering over him, he wanted to creep at her feet like a worm.

"I'll do whatever you say," he promised, holding up his hands clasped together.

Snarling, she almost vented her frustration on his ugly gray face. More than his misplaced lust, she hated the fact that he was so utterly sure of himself. No matter what he felt or did, he knew exactly where he stood with his people. He knew his discovery would bring him fame and fortune, benefiting his large extended family as well as himself. He was eager for their gratitude; they had supported him, aiding him with official appointments and serving as a buffer against the excesses of the Alliance.

B'Elanna was alone.

"I'll tell you when it's time to go," she ordered through gritted teeth. His spasm of delight disgusted her, but it would serve her purpose. For now.

She whirled and stalked away from Moset. Kes leaned hard on B'Elanna's feelings of loss and failure, suffering her own shame. Kes knew exactly what it felt like to make every mistake along the way.

B'Elanna caught sight of herself in the mirror as she returned to her quarters. She had donned her full body armor, and the crest on her chest mocked her. Miral had never added the symbol to her crest to indicate that she had borne a daughter.

Why not?

B'Elanna fought under this very crest. It was a deliberate insult every time she wore it.

As if I don't really exist.

Miral had helped her all she could, but that had been for her own benefit. Certainly, her mother had been disgraced by B'Elanna's first failed command, or she wouldn't have been "promoted" to Intendant of Earth. Was Miral mourning her daughter's death, or was she glad to be rid of her? Was she glad to be finally rid of the shame of having borne a half-Terran child?

Kes wallowed in B'Elanna's pain, encouraging her self-pity and her self-righteous need to know the truth. Perhaps Miral had lied to her. Perhaps B'Elanna was truly Terran, loathed by all Klingons including her own mother. Loathed even by herself—

"Tuvok! I've done it," came from the other room, breaking into Kes's concentration.

Kes knew she had found the key to B'Elanna, but that was Seska reporting in. She withdrew from the mind-meld and crept to the archway.

"I've convinced my target that we should return to Cardassia now. I made up a story about my boss pressuring me for sexual favors. He turned puce, you should have seen it." Seska's manic grin was frightening in the midst of the body paint that streaked down her cheeks as if she had been crying. She looked like the kind of woman who could turn on a loved one in an instant and rip out their throat. *"He should be back in the complex by now. He said he would meet me at the ship within the hour."*

Tuvok signed off and appeared in the doorway just as Kes resettled herself. "Quickly, Kes. Crell Moset is leaving."

Kes sank into the required frame of mind. She found Moset peeking from his room into the corridor to be sure B'Elanna was no longer there. He had nothing in his hands to show that he was leaving; data rods were secured in his pocket along with the tissue samples, everything he needed to ensure his glorious future. As a bonus, he would get his bed warmed every night. He fantasized about taking his little bath girl to his fine home high on the hill overlooking the lights of the city, where he could lift her above everyone, serving her in every way possible.

He entered the transporter room and ordered the lights on. Kes leaned on him as he input the coordinates. He was so excited he didn't realize that he had keyed very different numbers from the ones he had intended. The coordinates he input would transport him inside the holocube sitting on Tuvok's desk.

Moset took his place on the transporter disc, patting his pocket one last time to be sure he had his research materials. He had wiped the copies from Ishka's computer and hadn't noticed that B'Elanna had copied them before him.

Kes mentally willed him to go, feeling the first tendrils of thoughts of someone else approaching.

"*Energize,*" he ordered.

Through his eyes, she saw the hanging panels of brocade that decorated the transporter room begin to shimmer as the beam took hold of him. Suddenly, sparks shot out of the console reaching nearly to the ceiling. She flinched as Moset wanted to, but he was too deep in the dematerialization process to move. The last thing she saw was an even bigger burst of sparks.

Kes gasped as their link was severed. "S-something happened," she stammered. "The console exploded."

Tuvok moved too deliberately for her taste as he checked the holocube. "Empty."

"He's not there? What happened?"

"You tell me, Kes."

She didn't want to say it, but the way the link had been snipped was too stark to ignore. She had felt Crell Moset disappear, painless though it was, snuffed out.

She sat cross-legged directly on the floor, seeking her meditation position to help calm herself. After a few moments, she found B'Elanna in Ishka's transporter room.

B'Elanna was infuriated that Moset had forced her to kill him this way; she had laid her transporter trap as a fail-safe right before she had copied his files. *I should have beaten in his face for even considering abandoning me. It would have been more satisfying.*

She opened the underpanel of the console and, using a sonic wrench, began removing the restrictor circuit she had placed there. The only place Moset would transport to was the ship, so B'Elanna had programmed her trap to trigger automatically if a Cardassian used the transporter. The circuit blew the redactor coil at the critical moment. She had a spare redactor coil in her bag that she intended to install.

Kes broke the mind link and returned to Tuvok. "It was B'Elanna! She killed him using the transporter. Because he was leaving without her."

"That is unfortunate." Tuvok positioned the holocube in exactly the same spot on the desk. "Please continue your surveillance, Kes."

That was too much. "She killed him, Tuvok! How can you be so blasé?"

He frowned, looking distinctly pained. "Kes, I will mourn each and every death that happens here for the rest of my life. I am complicit in their demise, and I will have to atone for each one. Believe me, I do not take this lightly. I have surrendered my very being to our cause. I have done things I deeply regret—deceiving you is just one of them. I do these things only because I know it will prevent suffering as this part of the galaxy has never seen before. I would do it for no less."

Sincerity rang through his words. She didn't need to meld with his mind to see that he was an honorable man making his way as best he could under a regime of terrible oppression. He had pledged to protect a secret that could destroy his people, and he would die keeping that pledge.

But she hated what he had forced her to become. She didn't want to lie or hurt people, but she couldn't sit back and be a good girl when that meant Neelix was dying of a broken heart.

"I don't have to like it," she finally said.

Tuvok gave a slight nod, acquiescing. "I understand that I have sacrificed our friendship, and for that I am truly sorry."

Kes didn't want to accept his apology, but she had to. "Thank you for that, Tuvok."

It took longer than usual to calm herself, as she reached out again to B'Elanna. The Klingon hybrid was completing the repairs and closing the panel back up, even more agitated than before, dwelling on the betrayals she had suffered. B'Elanna tapped the console, cycling the transporter through a self-diagnostic.

Ishka appeared in the doorway. "What's going on here?" Her silk robe hung loosely on her, but it couldn't hide the saggy flesh under her chin and around her ankles. Her drooping ears were puckered, as was her ridged nose.

B'Elanna was repulsed, but at least the Ferengi was wearing something. Ishka preferred nudity when at home, but neither Moset nor B'Elanna appreciated the elderly Ferengi form.

"If you must know, I caught Crell Moset sneaking off without me. He was going to claim all the credit for our accomplishment."

"It's about time someone did. Why are *you* still here, hiding away in my home? When are you going to profit from what you've discovered? More important, when am *I* going to profit?"

Kes whispered into B'Elanna's mind, *She knows your mother despises you, or she wouldn't speak to you this way.*

"This isn't about you!" B'Elanna sneered. "I had to defend myself."

"So you killed him? In my home? Using my transporter? It wasn't enough that you've killed two of my slaves—two of them! Who do you think you are?"

She knows what your mother thinks, Kes taunted. *Ask her what your mother thinks of you.*

B'Elanna pounded her fist against her chest. "I'm Miral's daughter! Why didn't she change our crest? Why has she denied me?"

Ishka drew back. "Have you lost your latinum? You've been acting odd ever since you started the treatments. Your mother wouldn't stand for your behavior, I can tell you that."

She knows! Kes goaded. *Your mother hates you. When she finds out you're alive, will she be happy or mad? If you could read your mother's mind, would you find love or contempt?*

"I can't stand it!" B'Elanna screamed, clasping her hands over her ears, as if she could somehow stop Kes's voice in her head.

"I'm calling Miral," Ishka declared. "You need help."

"No!" B'Elanna lunged at Ishka, grabbing her sticklike arm.

Ishka's knees buckled, and she let out a high-pitched squeal as if she were being murdered. "Let me go!"

"I have to be there when she finds out. I have to know the truth." B'Elanna gave Ishka a final shake, releasing her.

Ishka collapsed onto the floor. Her gnarled hands covered her

face as she moaned and rocked. "This is the thanks I get for helping you?"

"*Tam!*" B'Elanna ordered. "If you send a message to my mother,
I'll come back and *kill* you, I swear! Do you understand?"

B'Elanna nudged Ishka with her toe, and the Ferengi let off
another panicked squeal. "I won't! I swear! Don't hurt me . . ."

B'Elanna longed to shake her until she shut up, until her head
flapped back and forth like a broken bird. But her mother wouldn't
like it if she killed one of her business associates without a good
reason. "Don't you forget it—not a word to my mother or anyone
else that I'm alive, or you'll regret it. I'm going to Earth to see her,
and I'll know if she's surprised."

Trembling from rage, B'Elanna activated the transporter to take
her verbal command. There was a red haze hanging before her as
she stepped onto the disc. She had only one thought: to see her
mother and find out the truth behind those fierce eyes. To find out
if Miral despised her as much as B'Elanna hated Miral.

B'Elanna prepared to order the transporter to take her to the
ship, but as she spoke, Kes pushed her into tapping out altogether
different transporter coordinates. B'Elanna realized too late that
something was terribly wrong, because she was already saying,
"Energize."

B'Elanna materialized in a black room with a yellow grid on the
walls. A holodeck. It was definitely not her ship.

"Computer, what is my location?" she demanded, but there
was no response. "Transporter, return me to Ishka's complex."

She didn't dematerialize; the black walls dissolved into the
arched red rock of her quarters on Archanis. But these tidy rooms
lacked the dense layer of discarded clothing that had somehow accumulated over the weeks.

With a catch in her voice, she ordered, "Take me to Monor Base."
The cavernous white space of her old office appeared with the

window wall in front of her. She went forward and pressed her face against the cold plasteel, looking through the clouds at the planet turning below, exactly like it was before the floating city crashed to the surface. She wondered if she would find her old torture chambers down on the seventh level and if Thomas would be waiting inside.

B'Elanna demanded in every way she could, in every language she knew—*Get me out of here!* But the walls simply melted into new rooms, in both the past and the present. The only time a disembodied voice spoke was when she summoned up a *d'k tahg* and in pure desperation tried to stab it into her own chest.

"*Safety protocols prohibit injury,*" a computer stated in a pleasant female voice.

"Who are you?" B'Elanna screamed, beating her fists against the window. But the voice didn't speak again. Was it a trap laid by Crell Moset? Had Ishka somehow forced her to say those coordinates? Who had caught her like a rat in a cage?

She flailed against the window until she finally sank to the floor, gasping. With a whimper, she whispered, "I want my mother."

Miral appeared before her, wearing full armor and carrying a *bat-leth*. From her sharply defined forehead ridges to her strong, square hands, she was the embodiment of her people. But B'Elanna knew there was a flaw at her core, a weakness inside that made her desire fragile Terrans in her bed. If she hadn't had that weakness, then B'Elanna wouldn't have been born a half-breed. Then B'Elanna wouldn't have tried to kill her.

"You were supposed to die!" she cried. "Why did that doctor save you?"

Miral sneered at B'Elanna lying on the floor. "*WejpuH!* Show them you have the heart of a Klingon!"

B'Elanna moaned and put her hands over her face, remembering how Ishka had done the same. She was nothing better than a doddering old woman. "End program!" she cried. She couldn't stand to see her mother and not read her mind. Not know the truth about who she was.

Huddled in the black holodeck, she beat on the yellow grid on the floor until her fists were bloody.

Tuvok held up the holocube. "B'Elanna is contained. Well done, Kes."

Queasy, Kes could almost feel B'Elanna's enraged misery radiating from the cube. "She deserves it. She's a perverted excuse for a humanoid."

Tuvok gave her a look. "I did not expect vindictiveness from you, Kes."

"It's not because of what she did to me, Tuvok. You haven't been inside her mind for days like I have. She's consumed by herself, by her own desires." *I'm not like her, I'll never be like her . . .*

"Are you all right, Kes?"

Kes forced herself to meet his eyes. "I'm glad I could help you stop them."

"As am I." Tuvok seemed ready to say more, but he thought better of it. "Gather your belongings. It is time to leave."

While she was in the other room, she heard Tuvok contact his ship. Kes went to the archway to see Neelix appear on the screen. His sad expression lifted somewhat when Tuvok reported, "Our mission is complete, Mr. Neelix. Once Harry and Seska wipe Ishka's computer, you may all depart."

Kes clasped her hands to her heart at the sound of Neelix's raspy voice. *"So, you caught them? I'm sure a lot of people will be glad to hear that, very glad to hear that."*

"We caught B'Elanna," Tuvok corrected. "Crell Moset is regrettably deceased."

"I'm sure you did your best, Mr. Vulcan. You can't blame yourself when things go wrong in a complicated task such as this."

It was typical of Neelix to worry about others and try to cheer them up even when he was feeling bad. But Tuvok normally didn't engage in small talk. Why was he speaking to Neelix in front of her?

It's a test. Tuvok needs to know if he can trust me.

Kes let herself imagine what it would be like to trust Tuvok again, to feel protected and cared for once again. But it was too late for that. She forced herself to stand there and not call out to Neelix. She stared at his face, searching every new hollow and line that she had given him, and hoped he could forgive her.

Several days later, Tuvok dropped Kes off at the entrance to the Memory Omega base deep inside Regula. She paused in the doorway to the lift that would take her down inside the cavern. "I'm sorry everything has gone badly between us, Tuvok."

"As am I," Tuvok said.

As Kes walked into the lift, she patted her bag, where she had secreted the holocube with B'Elanna inside. She had switched it for a duplicate holocube that she had replicated on the ship while Tuvok was sleeping. It was a surface facsimile only, but it had a readout exactly like the original, as if B'Elanna's energy was contained inside. He wouldn't discover that it was fake until he tried to beam her back out, assuming he ever did.

Kes wasn't going to let them stop her from rejoining Neelix. She would leave soon enough with the holocube in her possession, giving her the leverage she needed to keep the rebellion from interfering with her.

Then . . . then they'll find out they messed with the wrong telepath.

Family Matters

Keith R.A. DeCandido

HISTORIAN'S NOTE: *This tale is set in 2372 (Old Calendar), several months after the events of the* Star Trek: Deep Space Nine *episode "Shattered Mirror."*

Keith R.A. DeCandido has chronicled the adventures of Klag, son of M'Raq, in the mainline *Star Trek* universe in numerous places: the novels *Diplomatic Implausibility, The Brave and the Bold* Book 2, *A Good Day to Die, Honor Bound, Enemy Territory,* and *A Burning House* and the short story *"loDnI'pu' vavpu' je"* in *Tales from the Captain's Table.* He's also worked in the Mirror Universe before, having provided the short novel *The Mirror-Scaled Serpent* in *Obsidian Alliances,* telling the tale of the MU equivalents to *Star Trek: Voyager*'s characters. His other *Trek* work includes novels (*Q&A, Articles of the Federation, The Art of the Impossible, Demons of Air and Darkness,* and the *USA Today* bestselling *A Time for War, a Time for Peace*), short stories (in the anthologies *Prophecy and Change, No Limits, Tales of the Dominion War, Distant Shores, The Sky's the Limit,* and the forthcoming *Seven Deadly Sins*), eBooks (ten installments of the *Starfleet Corps of Engineers* series, which he also co-developed, and the final part of the *Slings and Arrows* miniseries), and comic books (*Perchance to Dream,* the forthcoming *Alien Spotlight II: Klingons: Four Thousand Throats . . .*). He's also written fiction in plenty of other universes. Find out more at his official Web site at decandido.net, or read his inane ramblings at kradical.livejournal.com.

**Transcript from Obsidian Order listening device placed
in the offices of Supreme Legate Skrain Dukat**

SUPREME LEGATE SKRAIN DUKAT: Ah, cousin! Come in.

GUL AKELLEN MACET: Thank you, Legate.

DUKAT: Please, Akellen, let us not stand on ceremony. We are
family. We need not speak so formally.

MACET: Perhaps, but I am not here as your cousin, but rather as
a gul in your service.

DUKAT: Very well. Some *kanar*?

MACET: Please. [*sound of drink being poured and Macet sitting down*]
Thank you.

DUKAT: So, tell me, Akellen, what duty brings you back to the
homeworld?

MACET: The weapons-manufacturing facility on Mempa VI—
convoys from that facility have been raided with alarming
regularity.

DUKAT: I seem to recall a security briefing on the subject—it
was Terran rebels, I thought.

MACET: I don't believe it is the rebels, cousin. Whoever planned
these raids knew the best locations to attack the freighters,
knew when they'd be farthest from any assistance, and also
knew precisely where to hit them to cause maximum damage.
I don't think the rebels are *that* well informed. Do you?

DUKAT: Then who do you believe *is* responsible, Akellen?

MACET: Someone with access to high-level Alliance intelligence.

DUKAT: You accuse a citizen of the Alliance?

MACET: Not just any citizen. It has to be someone powerful or rich.

DUKAT: The one tends to go hand in hand with the other.

MACET: True. It is also likely a Klingon.

DUKAT: Really? Why is that?

MACET: Because the weapons used against the freighters were *all* Klingon disruptors. The Terrans take weapons wherever they can get them—same for their ships. But all of the raids have used Klingon weaponry.

DUKAT: You make a compelling case. But if I recall correctly, Mempa VI falls under Captain Kurn's purview.

MACET: I know. That is why I am coming to see you.

DUKAT: [*laughs*] You claim to come as gul to legate, but in truth, you wish to ask a favor of your cousin.

MACET: [*pause*] Yes. I have attempted to alert Kurn, but he has not responded to any of my attempts to communicate with him, nor has he acknowledged my reports.

DUKAT: And his snubs offend you?

MACET: My offense is of little concern—I simply wish to preserve the safety of the Alliance.

DUKAT: Kurn is a difficult case. He is the brother to the Regent and therefore feels he is entitled to be more than the captain of a Bird of Prey. In fact, rumor has it that he's angling for one of the new Regent-class vessels.

MACET: I thought all of the shipmasters for those ships were assigned.

DUKAT: The *Gorkon* still remains captainless.

MACET: Didn't the Regent give that one to General Martok's whelp?

DUKAT: [*chuckles*] Almost. Drex was made first officer, thus simultaneously doing a favor to Martok and offering him insult.

MACET: [*sighs*] I care little for the politics, cousin—I am more than happy to leave such matters to you. I simply wish to find out who is raiding our weapons deliveries.

DUKAT: As do I. I will look into the matter. Have the *Trager* standing by. With luck, I will be able to send you to Mempa VI soon.

MACET: Thank you, cousin.

DUKAT: No, thank *you*, Akellan. Your devotion to duty will not go unnoticed, I assure you.

Transcript from the official record of the Klingon High Council

COUNCIL HERALD: Kurn, son of Mogh, step forward!

REGENT WORF: It is good to see you, brother.

CAPTAIN KURN: And you as well, my Regent.

REGENT: I assume you come here for reasons of duty, since family matters would not require a formal audience with the High Council.

KURN: Indeed, my Regent. I believe that there is a plot to stockpile weapons, possibly by the Terran rebellion.

REGENT: Rebels! *Pfagh!* I spit on the rebellion!

KURN: As do we all, my Regent. That is why these raids must be stopped. Several shipments from Mempa VI have been hijacked.

REGENT: Terrans. They haunt my every step. They must be destroyed!

KURN: Of course, my Regent. With your permission, I will use the *Hegh'ta* and two other vessels to protect the next convoy. We will expose the Terran cowards and destroy them!

REGENT: I expect no less from you, brother—you *will* bring the rebels to me!

KURN: It is my honor to serve you, my Regent.

LEGATE CORAT DAMAR: My Regent, if I may, these attacks are known to me. I believe that one of our guls—a fine officer named Macet—has, independently of Captain Kurn, detected a pattern to these attacks. I hereby request that the *Trager*, Macet's vessel, be part of the captain's convoy.

REGENT: It will be done! *Qapla',* brother!

KURN: *Qapla',* my Regent.

Message from Captain Kurn, son of Mogh,
on the *I.K.S. Hegh'ta*, to Commander Drex, son of Martok,
the House Martok estate, Qo'noS

Our hour is at hand, my friend. I have been alerted by a Cardassian gul to a series of attacks on weapons convoys from Mempa VI. It may well be Terrans, but even if it is not, I have alerted my brother to the attacks, and let him know that I shall be at the forefront of the effort to stop them. I believe that a successful blow to the Terran rebellion will be what it takes to allow my brother to give me command of the *Gorkon*.

I grow weary of the political games. The Cardassians claim to be offended by nepotism, so Worf keeps me off the High Council and leaves me to command only a Bird of Prey to appease the Cardassians. Yet the gul who alerted me to the raids was a man named Macet. That *petaQ* that Dukat sent to represent Cardassia on Qo'noS, Damar, forced Macet's ship, the *Trager*, to be part of the convoy. Damar doesn't use the commode without consulting with Dukat first, so Damar's request had to come straight from him—and Macet is Dukat's cousin. I will need to keep an eye on Macet, make sure he does not attempt to suborn my own ambitions. Whether these are Terrans or not, I will make sure that my brother *thinks* it's the Terrans. His obsession with them since the defeat at Terok Nor will someday prove his undoing. For now, I will use it for my own ends. And for yours.

The third vessel will be the *I.K.S. Pagh*. Her captain is a fat fool named Kargan, but he is of the same House as Councillor K'Tal—and the councillor will be a useful ally. Unlike Macet, I doubt Kargan will have the ability to take credit for this victory from me.

Once we both serve on the *Gorkon,* my friend—oh, that will be a *great* day . . .

**Message from Commander Klag, son of M'Raq, on the *I.K.S. Pagh*,
to Commander Dorrek, son of M'Raq, on the *I.K.S. Slivin***

Greetings, brother! It is good to hear that you played such a critical role in the battle against the Tholians. Well done! I only wish Father were still alive to see your victory. At this rate, you will win our wager and become the first son of M'Raq to command his own ship.

For my part, I am content to serve under Captain Kargan. He is a great man from a noble House, and it is an honor to serve with him.

We have been assigned to a duty far less glorious than the front lines against the Tholians. We are to aid Captain Kurn and Gul Macet in their defense of a weapons convoy from Mempa VI.

I must confess, brother, I find this duty unsettling. Kurn is the brother to the Regent, and he has proven a difficult commander to follow. Kargan assigned me to be the liaison with Gul Macet—which was a surprise, as Kargan generally assumes such duties himself—and Macet informed me that he believes a highly placed Klingon is responsible for these attacks. Based on the available evidence, I was compelled to agree with the Cardassian's conclusion.

Kurn took offense at that notion, and questioned my honor. I defended myself with the truth, but I honestly have no idea if that placated him or not. I must be on my guard with Kurn.

**Transcript of communications logs of the *I.K.S. Pagh*, while
communicating with the *I.K.S. Hegh'ta*, the Central Command
vessel *Trager*, and the freighter *Kamich***

CAPTAIN KURN (*Hegh'ta*): Captain, I believe that—
LIEUTENANT KEGREN (*Pagh*): Captain, I am detecting a warp imbalance in the *Kamich*.
GLINN TAROC (*Kamich*): Captain Kurn, this is Glinn Taroc. Something has happened to our warp engines. We must drop out of warp *now*.

KURN: Report!

TAROC: I told you, Captain, something happened.

KURN: And I told you to report, Glinn!

COMMANDER KLAG (*Pagh*): What happened?

KEGREN: I'm not certain of the cause, sir, but the freighter's warp core will breach in two minutes if it isn't shut down.

TAROC: Captain, I'm shutting down my warp engines now. If you want to kill me, do it later when I've saved your precious cargo. Taroc out.

KURN: All vessels, slow to impulse power. Take up formation around the freighter, pattern *vagh*.

CAPTAIN KARGAN (*Pagh*): Follow the captain's instructions, pilot. Take up position to protect the freighter.

LIEUTENANT VIGH (*Pagh*): Yes, sir.

KLAG: Captain, recommend we move both Klingon ships ten thousand *qell'qam*s closer to the freighter. That will improve our sensor efficiency.

KARGAN: Your recommendation has been noted, Commander.

GUL MACET (*Trager*): Kurn, I will be transporting to the *Kamich*.

KURN: For what purpose?

MACET: That freighter was inspected four times prior to launch. And Glinn Taroc is one of our finest engineers. I think the engines were sabotaged, and I want to investigate personally.

KURN: If that is what is required to assuage your pride at flying a faulty freighter, Gul, feel free. But in case you are correct, Commander Klag, you will accompany Gul Macet to the *Kamich*. I would know exactly what happened to slow this convoy down.

KLAG: Yes, sir. Permission to leave the ship, Captain.

KARGAN: Granted. Kegren, take command of the bridge. I will accompany my first officer to the transporter room.

Message from Commander Klag, son of M'Raq, on the *I.K.S. Pagh,*
to Commander Dorrek, son of M'Raq, on the *I.K.S. Slivin*

A warrior does not admit to fear, my brother, but I must confess that I am concerned with the way this mission has developed.

The freighter we are protecting, the *Kamich,* suffered a catastrophic warp-core breach. Macet and I were quickly able to determine that the vessel was sabotaged, thanks to a security layer that Central Command has put on all of its vessels but is known only to those ranked gul or higher. The *Kamich* is commanded by a glinn.

But even before that, I grew concerned. Prior to beaming over to the *Kamich* to aid Gul Macet in his investigation of the *Kamich*'s sabotage, Kargan accompanied me to the transporter room—something he has *never* done. He told me that I had served the *Pagh* well and that he trusted me to do what was best for the Alliance. I have no idea what prompted such a talk, and I am not ashamed to admit that it worried me, brother. Kargan is one of our finest warriors, and I have spoken for his crew for many turns. Why now does he test my loyalty this way?

Worse, after we came out of warp, I suggested a variation on the pattern of defense. Kurn had called for pattern *vagh,* which only makes sense with three Birds of Prey. But the *Trager*'s sensor efficiency is less than ours, and pattern *vagh* left us with many holes in our sensor net. I recommended a shift in pattern to Kargan, which he dismissed out of hand—something else he has *never* done before.

This proved problematic, as before Macet and I could find the saboteur, the convoy was attacked by a vessel that flew in through one of the gaps in our sensors. Macet is correct. The Terran rebellion simply could not be this well informed. The *Hegh'ta* and the *Trager* have been badly damaged, the cargo has been stolen, and the *Pagh*—the only ship to be left unscathed by the thieves—lost them while trying to pursue.

Still, Macet and I were able to learn the saboteur's identity by rather simple methods. One engineer on the *Kamich* suddenly had more money than he'd ever had before. For a low-paid freighter engineer, it was a huge sum, but it was only a small fraction of the value of the stolen weapons. We are about to interrogate the engineer, but I wished to send this message to you. There are treacherous waters ahead, brother, and I wish to make sure that there is a record of the truth *somewhere,* even if it is only in messages between brothers.

Qapla', Dorrek. If this mission should take my life from me, I ask only that you avenge me should I not die well.

Transcript of the interrogation of Engineer Pol Straken by Gul Akellen Macet and Commander Klag, son of M'Raq

CAPTAIN KLAG: We should use the mind sifter.

GUL MACET: You do not trust Cardassian interrogation methods? I can assure you, they're quite brutal.

KLAG: I am sure that they are, my friend, but it is efficiency that I am concerned with. The mind sifter will leave little doubt about the veracity of Straken's information, coming as it will straight from his own memory without filtering.

MACET: Only if the highest setting is used. If we do that, Straken will be little more than a vegetable.

KLAG: I realize that you prefer a defendant in your trial who won't be insensate, but—

MACET: No. We shall use the mind sifter. If there is a trial to come from this incident, this fool will not be a part of it. Straken is hardly the mastermind behind these thefts. He wasn't even assigned to the other freighters that were attacked. All we need from him is who paid him those two thousand *leks.* Your mind sifter should give us that information. As for Straken himself, he is of no use to the Alliance, so I'm quite happy to dispose of him and replace him with an engineer who would not betray us for mere coin.

KLAG: Very well. *Bekk,* bring in the prisoner—and also the mind sifter.

BEKK GRIK: Yes, Commander!

KLAG: I must confess, I am not overly fond of the mind sifter.

MACET: Oh?

KLAG: I prefer to face my foes in battle. Torture is often the refuge of cowards, a battle where only one of the participants has a chance.

MACET: And yet our government uses it quite often.

KLAG: I merely stated a preference, my friend. I also prefer *gagh* to *taknar* gizzards, but I will eat the gizzards if that is what the chef has prepared.

MACET: [*laughs*] Indeed.

GRIK: Here is the prisoner, Commander, Gul.

POL STRAKEN. I don't understand! I haven't done anything! What is that?

KLAG: It is a mind sifter. We will use it—

STRAKEN: No! Please, don't! I know what those things do to you! I'll tell you anything, just *please,* not the mind sifter!

KLAG: Do you believe him, Gul?

MACET: Not particularly, Commander. He's obviously going to lie to us while pretending to give in, so he can avoid becoming a drooling vegetable.

KLAG: I agree. It allows him to be both a coward and a hero to his cause.

STRAKEN: I have no cause! Believe me! I just needed the money!

MACET: Really? For what? You carry no debts, have no expensive hobbies. Your collection of the works of Tor Yakros is impressive but hardly something that is in danger of bankrupting you.

STRAKEN: It's—it's my brother. He lent me money years ago, and now he needs me to pay him back so he can pay his gambling debts. He lost a lot of money on *tongo* on Elvok Nor, and these two Nausicaans were going to break his legs if he didn't—

KLAG: Enough! Your mewling offends me, Straken.

STRAKEN: So, I took the two thousand *lek*s. That paid it all off!

MACET: Who paid you?

STRAKEN: I don't—I don't know.

KLAG: You lie!

STRAKEN: I swear! He hid his face!

MACET: Who did?

STRAKEN: I don't know his name!

KLAG: You know it was a male?

STRAKEN: Yes! I mean, I think he was a male Klingon. He—

MACET: A Klingon? You're sure!

STRAKEN: Yes, but he never showed his face!

KLAG: Then how did you know it was a Klingon?

STRAKEN: He—he had a crest! And he wore one of those long jacket things that they wear!

KLAG: We must use the mind sifter.

STRAKEN: What? Why? I've told you everything that I know!

KLAG: You've admitted only that a high-ranking Klingon paid you to sabotage the *Kamich,* yet you do not provide his name!

STRAKEN: I swear it is true! *Please,* not the mind sifter!

KLAG: Your wishes are no concern of ours. Attach him to the mind sifter!

GRIK: Yes, Commander.

STRAKEN: Noooooooooooooo! Please, *no!* [*incoherent screams*]

MACET: Is there no way to sort the images?

KLAG: No. It is why the mind sifter is not always the most ideal tool. While memories are more reliable than speech, they are also not sorted in any meaningful fashion.

STRAKEN: [*more incoherent screams*]

MACET: His fascination with Vulcan women seems to be quite prominent.

KLAG: My father had a female Vulcan slave once. She had impressive stamina.

MACET: I imagine so.

KLAG: You do not approve?

MACET: I dislike women with such smooth skin. I also prefer my wife.

KLAG: [*laughs*] No doubt. Wait! See there!

MACET: The image is not clear.

KLAG: But that is the cassock of a member of the High Council.

MACET: Or the cassock of someone pretending to be a member of the High Council. I'm surprised he even bothered to include visual with the transmission.

KLAG: I am not. It is not honorable to deal with others without showing one's face.

MACET: But he didn't show his face, he obscured it.

KLAG: Yes, but no doubt he was able to assuage his dishonor by at least putting up the appearance of behaving honorably. I have found, my friend, that it is hypocrisy, rather than hydrogen, that is the most common element in the galaxy.

STRAKEN: [*screams break off*]

GRIK: The prisoner is nonresponsive.

MACET: He's told us enough. Such a waste.

KLAG: We must report this to Captain Kurn immediately.

Personal message from Gul Akellen Macet to Supreme Legate Skrain Dukat

Greetings, cousin. I hope your wife and children are in good health.

As you have no doubt heard by now, there was yet another raid, as depredators were able to make off with the entirety of the *Kamich*'s cargo. After a saboteur onboard the *Kamich* forced us all to come out of warp, the thieves disabled both the *Hegh'ta* and the *Trager* with a single shot to each, and they came into the system using a trajectory that we were sensor-blind to in our configuration.

To make matters worse, Commander Klag and I interrogated the *Kamich*'s saboteur, and he revealed that the person who paid him to perform the sabotage was apparently a member of the Klingon High Council.

I don't need to tell you what this might mean.

Kurn, of course, is as giddy as a child. I suspect that he now is setting his sights higher than the *Gorkon*. He may be angling for the High Council seat of whoever it is who is plotting against the Regent.

We are working hard to repair our vessels. The only ship that was left undamaged was Captain Kargan's ship, the *Pagh,* but they then lost the thieves.

My concern is this: Commander Klag, Kargan's first officer— and a good man, I might add; he aided me in the interrogation of the saboteur—suggested a different alignment to defend the *Ka-mich,* which Kargan then ignored. Had he listened to his first officer, the thieves would have been detected. Furthermore, the *Pagh* was never fired upon, and then they lost the thieves when pursuing them.

Kargan is a member of the House of K'Tal. I don't need to tell you where my suspicions are leading me.

I have not shared this suspicion with Kurn. It's possible—likely, even—that he has come to a similar conclusion, but if he has not, I do not wish to give him the opportunity to use my conclusions once again for his own purposes.

However, I suggest that you alert Legate Damar to keep an eye on K'Tal. I, meanwhile, will do the same for Kurn and Kargan both.

Message from Commander Klag, son of M'Raq, on the *I.K.S. Pagh,* to Commander Dorrek, son of M'Raq, on the *I.K.S. Slivin*

Something has happened, brother, and once again I am forced to confide in you so that I can be assured that somewhere there will be a record of what has truly happened.

The *Pagh* has been searching for the thieves who stole the weaponry from the *Kamich* while that ship, as well as the *Trager* and the *Hegh'ta,* effect repairs. Tonight, when my duty time ended, I found a padd in my cabin. It contained navigational data regarding the thieves' course.

To my shock, they spelled out the precise course the vessel was on when the *Pagh* lost them, from which it is quite simple to determine their destination. There is also an access code on the padd, though I know not what it provides access *to.*

I do not know who has provided this intelligence to me. Obviously, I must make use of it. But someone has granted me this without showing his face.

And I have other suspicions as well. The *Pagh* is a fine ship and Kargan a great captain. I find it difficult to believe that they could lose a vessel of thieves. (I was offship with Macet, interrogating the saboteur of the *Kamich,* when the pursuit took place.) That saboteur revealed that he was hired by a member of the Klingon High Council—or, at least, someone pretending to be a councillor. The head of Kargan's House also serves on the council. And Kargan did not accept my recommendations for the realignment of our defenses, which left us vulnerable.

I have served Kargan loyally for many turns now. I do not wish to believe this of him. But if he *has* betrayed the Regent, then I will be forced to kill him.

The only question is whether or not the House of K'Tal's paid *qutluch* would then repay me in kind.

I will wait until I know Kargan is not on the bridge and then call Kurn and Macet simultaneously while summoning Kargan. This way, I know that it will be brought to all three at once. We will see where it leads us.

Transcript of communications logs of the *I.K.S. Pagh*, while communicating with the *I.K.S. Hegh'ta* and the Central Command vessel *Trager*

COMMANDER KLAG (*Pagh*): Kegren, open a channel to the *Hegh'ta and the Trager* both, and summon Captain Kargan to the bridge.

LIEUTENANT KEGREN (*Pagh*): Yes, Commander. Captain Kargan, to the bridge.

CAPTAIN KURN (*Hegh'ta*): What do you want, Commander?

GUL MACET (*Trager*): Have you learned something, Klag?

CAPTAIN KARGAN (*Pagh*): Why have you summoned me, Commander?

KLAG: I have determined the course that the thieves took.

KURN: What? How?

KLAG: I spent much of the night studying the navigation logs from the *Pagh*'s pursuit. The thieves took an evasive course, but I was eventually able to determine its pattern. They could only have had one destination: the Marcan system. There is one habitable planet in that system.

KURN: Yes, the fifth one. I know that world. It is on the outskirts of the Allicar sector. *Quvatlh!* We have lost *hours* to these *petaQpu'*!

MACET: We must proceed there immediately. The *Trager*'s repairs are not complete, but we once again have warp drive, and the weapons will be ready by the time we arrive at Marcan.

KURN: Our warp drive is still not repaired. We will remain here and join you when we are able. In the meantime, Macet, you and Kargan will proceed to Marcan and find these thieves. Screen off!

Message from Captain Kurn, son of Mogh, on the *I.K.S. Hegh'ta,* to Commander Drex, son of Martok, the House Martok estate, Qo'noS

Our plans may have changed, my friend. I believe that the House of K'Tal may be the ones who plot against the Alliance. If that is so, then Kargan is the one who betrays us—and K'Tal's request that the *Pagh* be part of our convoy makes more sense. We only know this much because of the interrogation performed by Macet and Klag. I still do not trust Macet, but Klag may be a useful ally, especially if he may be turned against his captain.

If all goes according to plan, then I may well be rewarded with a seat on the Council, rather than simply be given my own ship. If that is the case, then I will do all in my power to make sure that you receive command of the *Gorkon*. If he continues to be useful, I will recommend that Klag be your first officer. Also, General Talak is part of that house—if he is indeed a traitor, then your father's position will improve also.

Unfortunately, the *Hegh'ta* is still under repairs, so I have been forced to send the *Trager* and the *Pagh* to Marcan V ahead of me. I need you to find a way to alert your father and have him send a ship that we know is loyal to take control of the situation if the *Hegh'ta*'s repairs are not complete in time.

This will be a great day for both of us, my friend. For too long, we have lived in the shadow of our family members. Soon, we will remind the Alliance that there are others in the House of Worf and the House of Martok . . .

264 Keith R.A. DeCandido

while communicating with the landing party on Marcan V
and the Central Command vessel *Trager*

COMMANDER KLAG (Marcan V): We have transported down safely, Captain.

CAPTAIN KARGAN (*Pagh*): Move quickly, Commander. We have detected other ships approaching the system.

GUL MACET (*Trager*): Confirmed. One of them matches the configuration of the ship that attacked the convoy.

LEADER VEKMA (Marcan V): No life signs, Commander.

KLAG: Very well. Secure the rest of— [*sound of disruptor fire*] [*screams*]

MACET: Klag, what is happening?

KARGAN: Report, Commander! [*more sounds of disruptor fire*]

KLAG: Lower your weapon, Leader!

VEKMA: I'm sorry, Commander, but I cannot do that.

LIEUTENANT KEGREN (*Pagh*): Captain, enemy vessels on attack vector! They're arming disruptors.

MACET: Klag, what's happening?

[*more sounds of disruptor fire*]

BEKK WOL (Marcan V): Commander, are you all right?

KLAG: Well enough, *Bekk*. Thank you for—for your loyalty. Captain, Leader Vekma and three of her squad took arms against me. My—my right arm has been lost. *Bekk* Wol has—has saved my life. I—I will now carry out—out my mission.

MACET: Klag, wait, there may be—

KARGAN: Be silent, Macet! Commander Klag will continue his mission.

MACET: Why, Kargan, because your assassins failed?

KARGAN: Not exactly.

KEGREN: Enemy vessels firing on the *Trager*.

MACET: Open fire! Damn you, Kargan, *help* us!

KLAG: Captain, I am standing before a computer screen. I have just entered a code that allows me access to encrypted files on this computer.

KARGAN: Have you, now?

KEGREN: *Trager* taking heavy damage, Captain.

MACET: Kargan, you're responsible for this!

KARGAN: I am responsible for any number of things, Macet. Including what is about to happen.

KLAG: Macet, hear me! These files were encrypted by the House of K'Tal, and they contain a great deal of sensitive information, including full details of the security of Mempa VI!

MACET: Then my suspicions were correct. We will destroy your cohorts, Kargan, and then we will destroy you.

KARGAN: You are outnumbered, Macet. You will not survive without assistance.

KLAG: Captain, do not do this!

KARGAN: I have already done too much, Commander, and my honor and that of my House have suffered greatly for it. I hope that with my final act, I may redeem the House of K'Tal. Pilot, set course for the nearest vessel attacking the *Trager*— ramming speed!

**Message from Commander Klag, son of M'Raq,
on the Central Command vessel *Trager*,
to Commander Dorrek, son of M'Raq, on the *I.K.S. Slivin***

I have always said that Kargan was an honorable man, but until today, I did not know how fine a warrior he truly was.

It was Kargan who provided the information that sent us to Marcan V and Kargan who gave me the access code that allowed us to read the files on the computers on that world. And Kargan ordered the *Pagh* to make a suicide run on the vessels attacking the *Trager*. His sacrifice allowed Macet to achieve victory in orbit of that world while *Bekk* Wol and I gleaned all we could from Marcan V's computers.

We are now en route to the Homeworld. There will be a *meqba'*, and the fate of the House of K'Tal will hang in the balance.

As for myself, I have lost my right arm. The Cardassian doctor tried to persuade me to have a prosthetic machine placed on my shoulder, which I, of course, refused. And I have lost my ship. Only Wol and I survive, and I have promised that she will be rewarded on her next assignment.

What that assignment will be, I do not know. But I do know that I will mourn the loss of Captain Kargan deeply. A great warrior is in *Sto-Vo-Kor* today, even if the others of his ignoble House will ride the Barge of the Dead to *Gre'thor.*

Macet came to me after I was released from his ship's infirmary. He also was suspicious of Kargan after we interrogated Straken. I asked him why he didn't share that with me. He asked me why I didn't share the true source of my information about Marcan V.

Gul Macet is a good man. The Alliance will need people like him if we are to survive the Terrans getting above themselves and the Romulans, Tholians, and others who try to nip away at our empire like *ramjep* birds. In the future, we will know to trust each other.

Transcript from the official record of the Klingon High Council

REGENT WORF: The *meqba'* has ended. I have heard all of the evidence. It is clear that the House of K'Tal must be dissolved, its principals killed, its lands seized.

COUNCIL HERALD: K'Tal, son of K'Dan, step forward!

REGENT: Do you have anything to say for yourself before you are put to death, traitor?

COUNCILLOR K'TAL: Only that the Klingon peoples will be led to ruin as long as *you* sit in Kahless's chair—and as long as we remain allied with spoonheaded filth!

REGENT: You are a fool. It is the alliance with Cardassia that has made us strong, that enabled us to conquer the Terrans, that made us the greatest power the galaxy has ever known. It is *you* who would have led us to ruin, K'Tal. But now you will lead only the others of your House to the Barge of the Dead. Bring them forward!

[*The* Yan-Isleth *bring the members of the House of K'Tal forward*]

REGENT: You have betrayed the Alliance. You have no honor. You shall not leave this chamber alive. [*sound of* d'k tahg *blades unfurling*]

[*Regent and councillors slash the throats of the members of the House of K'Tal*]

REGENT: Take the bodies away!

COUNCIL HERALD: Kurn, son of Mogh; Klag, son of M'Raq; Akellen Macet, step forward!

REGENT: You have done well, all of you. A cancer has been removed from our alliance. Gul Macet, I leave whatever reward you might gain from this campaign to your superiors at Central Command, but know that you have the gratitude of the Regent.

GUL AKELLEN MACET: That is high praise, indeed, my Regent. Thank you.

REGENT: Klag, son of M'Raq, a true warrior knows to act for what is honorable, and you have done that, at the cost of your good right arm. There is an opening for a captain on the *I.K.S. Gorkon,* and I can think of no one better suited to take command of that vessel than you, *Captain* Klag.

CAPTAIN KLAG: My Regent?

REGENT: Do my words displease you, son of M'Raq?

KLAG: No, my Regent, they *do* surprise me. Kargan is the true hero here, not I. I simply followed the path he laid out for me.

REGENT: Perhaps. But Kargan is dead, and of all those in his misbegotten House, he is the only one who will be enshrined in the Hall of Warriors, for he has put the Alliance before all. But your role is not inconsequential. Because of you, I have

removed a threat to the High Council and to our very way of
life. For that, you have earned a captaincy.

KLAG: Yes, my Regent! Thank you!

REGENT: Kurn—my brother.

CAPTAIN KURN: Yes, my Regent?

REGENT: Do not think that I have forgotten your role in this.
You, too, will receive a new ship to command—the *Ya'Vang* is
in orbit and awaiting your arrival. You have all served the Alliance with honor. *Qapla'!*

KURN, KLAG, AND MACET: *Qapla'!*

Message from Captain Kurn, son of Mogh, on the *I.K.S. Ya'Vang*, to Commander Drex, son of Martok, on the *I.K.S. Gorkon*

Curse that *yIntagh* of a warrior! Curse that spoonheaded legate's
cousin! They have conspired to ruin *everything*!

The *Ya'Vang* is a fine ship, it is true, and a far greater trophy than
the *Hegh'ta*. But the *Gorkon* should have been mine!

It was Macet. It *had* to be. He and Klag were like lovers on that
mission, they were together so much, and that *petaQ* likely peti-
tioned his cousin to put pressure on my brother to reward Klag.

The son of M'Raq has made an enemy today. And you, my
friend, will be the *d'k tahg* I use to bring him down. Not right
away—we cannot move against one my brother has rewarded immediately. But soon, my friend, very, very soon. Observe the son of
M'Raq carefully for any opening, and then strike like a *wam* serpent. You are Martok's son; you will be protected.

Our plans will come to fruition one day, Drex, of that you can
be assured.

Message from Captain Klag, son of M'Raq, on the *I.K.S. Gorkon*, to Commander Dorrek, son of M'Raq, on the *I.K.S. Slivin*

So, it seems I win our wager, brother. I have become the first son of M'Raq to command his own vessel. The bloodwine is on you when next we meet, Dorrek.

The *meqba'* was shocking, for all that I knew the evidence ahead of time. To see a noble House so awash in betrayal and dishonor was staggering. Apparently, K'Tal felt that we did not need the Cardassians—as if we would be able to maintain so great an empire alone—and that we should be rid of them. K'Tal, Talak, and the others of their House intended to use the weapons they had stolen to take up arms against the High Council and also against any in the Defense Force or Central Command who did not agree with them.

It was glorious to see their throats cut by the council. In his observer's chair, I could see Legate Damar leaning forward, almost as if he, too, wished to take a blade to K'Tal's throat. For his part, Macet was not pleased. He said he prefers capital punishment to be cleaner. But death is death—to prettify it is pointless.

The Regent seemed pleased with my own performance, but I suspect that there is more to his appointment of me to the *Gorkon*. Macet confided in me that his sources had told him that Kurn was hoping for the *Gorkon*. But Kurn also promised to bring Terran rebels to the Regent's feet, and he failed to do so. That was not Kurn's fault, of course, but the Regent is obsessed with the Terran rebellion, and he would not tolerate any failure to bring them closer to defeat.

Macet and I shared a drink in the tavern across from the Great Hall, where we drank to Kargan and the noble crew of the *Pagh*, who were sacrificed in order to expose the traitors.

And now I report to you from my very own command. My first officer is Drex, son of General Martok. With Talak's death, Martok's position has improved, and that means Drex's has as well. I will likely need to keep an eye on him. I have, however, been able to reward Wol, who saved my life at Marcan V, by making her *QaS DevwI'* of First Company.

I must go now, brother. The *Gorkon* is one of the finest vessels in the fleet, and she will be used to crush the Alliance's enemies. We head now to the Bajoran system.

Qapla', my brother.

Homecoming

Peter David

HISTORIAN'S NOTE: *"Homecoming" takes place during the late 2370s (ACE) as the rebellion is gaining a foothold against the Klingon-Cardassian Alliance ("Shattered Mirror,"* Star Trek: Deep Space Nine*) and after the Romulan slave known at M'k'nzy of Calhoun (*Star Trek: New Frontier*) takes command of the ship now called* Excalibur *and vows to make the Alliance pay (*Star Trek Mirror Universe: Obsidian Alliance—Cutting Ties*).*

Peter David is the *New York Times* bestselling author of numerous *Star Trek* novels, including the incredibly popular *Star Trek: New Frontier* series. He has also written dozens of other books, including his acclaimed original novel, *Sir Apropos of Nothing,* and its sequels, *The Woad to Wuin* and *Tong Lashing.*

David is also well known for his comic book work, particularly his award-winning run on *The Incredible Hulk.* He recently authored the novelizations of *Spider-Man, Spider-Man 2, Spider-Man 3, Fantastic Four, The Hulk,* and *Iron Man.*

He lives on Long Island with his wife and daughters.

*M**ac. I need you to disengage from Soleta and focus on what I'm saying for a moment.*

"Dammit, McHenry!"

The frustrated shout came from Soleta and Mac simultaneously. Mac complied, although it was less a response to McHenry's request than it was a reflex action. He nearly tumbled off the far side of the bed, but caught himself at the last moment. Soleta grabbed a sheet and pulled it up, as she said furiously, "You cannot be doing that, McHenry! You cannot just rummage around inside our minds when we are . . . otherwise occupied!"

How would I know that you were otherwise occupied if I weren't inside your mind?

It was a reasonable question and one for which neither of them had an easy answer. Mac looked at Soleta and said reasonably, "Why are you covering up? He's not in the room. He's still floating in the null sphere that powers this vessel, down in engineering, same as always."

Soleta growled at him. She hated it when he pointed out things that she should have realized. She kept the sheet over herself, probably just to spite him.

Rolling his eyes and wisely choosing not to pursue the matter, Mac said, "What's the problem, McHenry?"

He knew that technically, he didn't even have to talk; all he had to do was think his responses. Soleta could converse with McHenry without opening her mouth, but Mac felt the need to speak aloud. It helped him frame his thoughts.

"All right, McHenry," he said. "You have my attention. What is it?"

I'm receiving a distress beacon. The source appears to be a single emergency life pod. At full speed, we can be there in ten minutes.

"Fine," said Mac.

But Soleta spoke practically right on top of him. "Not fine. Hold on, McHenry. Don't do anything."

Mac turned to her, puzzled. "Why not?"

"It could be a trap."

"What makes you think that?"

"What makes me . . . ?" She looked at him in disbelief. "Mac, do you have any idea how many problems we've been giving the Alliance? Going from colony world to colony world in the *Excalibur,* breaking the Alliance's control. Gathering a small army of people into the ship . . . and by the way, we're starting to reach capacity."

"I'll be certain to place 'Get us more ships' at the top of my priority list," he said dryly. "Soleta, I don't see the problem. Harassing the Alliance, letting them know that we're not simply going to roll over for them, that's our goal. That's what we want to be doing. To be fighting back, to be a symbol . . ."

"I know all that, Mac. What I'm saying is that there is no way that we can embark upon such a course of action and not get the attention of the Alliance."

"And if we get their attention, what of it?" His face was grim. "If they wish for a fight . . ."

"If they wish for a fight, they will do exactly this: try to lure us into some sort of trap. A trap such as someone sending a distress beacon calling for our aid. We've no way of knowing it's legitimate."

"And we likewise have no way of knowing it isn't."

She blew air impatiently between her lips. "Do you have any concept of how frustrating you can be at times?"

"If I did not before, certainly I have you to tell me." Mac was already in the process of pulling on his loose gray trousers. Then he drew back his shoulder-length black hair and tied it to keep it out of his face. "Bring us there, McHenry. And," he said with a deferential nod to Soleta, "be certain to sweep the area carefully before we approach. Make certain that no Alliance forces are anywhere in the vicinity."

Very well, Mac. Soleta, is that acceptable to you?

"How kind of you to ask, McHenry. It is nice to know that someone around here values my opinion," she said pointedly.

There was a pause, and then McHenry said, *You two are not going to be having sex anytime soon again, are you?*

"That is none of your business, McHenry," said Soleta at about the same time that Mac said, "Probably not." When Mac of Calhoun said that, Soleta emitted a final, extremely annoyed grunt and headed for the bathroom. The door slid shut behind her.

I do not understand women.

"I find it comforting, McHenry, that even you—who can actually go inside women's heads—can still find them incomprehensible."

You actually don't find that comforting at all.

"No, I really don't," admitted Mac.

The vessel dubbed *Excalibur* had originally been called the *Stinger.* That was back when it was piloted by Si Cwan of the house of Cwan, a Thallonian prince. But Cwan and his crew had since been thrown out of the ship by the actions of M'k'n'zy of Calhoun, along with his lover, Soleta, and the bio-entity known as McHenry whose endless life force powered the vessel. It had been felt that a new crew required a new name. Robin Lefler, formerly a human slave and now a valued crew member of the ship, had suggested "Excalibur." The name meant nothing to Soleta or Mac. According to Robin, however, it was the name of a famous weapon, a sword, wielded by a mighty ruler. A ruler, she went on to say, who had held great fascination for the late Elizabeth Shelby. The mere mention of Elizabeth's name was typically enough to sadden Mac, for her demise had been abrupt and violent and, he felt, premature, as if she were meant for great things and never had the opportunity to achieve them. Besides, the prospect of naming the ship after a powerful sword was attractive to Mac. Thus did the ship become renamed the *Excalibur,* and it had been that name that had been stabbing at the perimeter of the Alliance's interests.

On one of the outlying worlds, they had freed the members of a small colony that had been under the Alliance's yoke. Most of the colonists had chosen to flee, hoping to find a stretch of space that was beyond the Alliance's reach. A few had remained with the *Excalibur,* however, and one of them was an older, haggard human named Jellico. He was lean and muscular, with thinning blond hair and a beard that had been scraggly when he first came to the ship but which he had since started trimming meticulously, even obsessively. He had a great deal of knowledge about vessels and strategy, and his advice had served Mac well on more than one occasion.

Jellico now paced the bridge of the *Excalibur* while Mac sat in his command chair, watching the screen intently. Robin and Soleta were there as well, along with Kalinda, sister of Si Cwan and the only survivor of the previous command crew. Mac had considered tossing Kalinda out the airlock on more than one occasion on principle alone, but Robin had implored him not to, as had McHenry. Kalinda had developed a rapport with McHenry that even Soleta felt transcended whatever bond he had with them. Furthermore, Kalinda and Robin had likewise developed a relationship. Mac had not been sanguine about that, since he still didn't entirely trust Kalinda, but finally he had shrugged it off and decided that one simply could not dictate the directions in which one's heart took one.

"Soleta's right," Jellico said, leaning in toward Mac.

"My two favorite words," Soleta said.

Jellico ignored her. Mac knew it was because he and Soleta did not get on particularly well. He distrusted Romulans, if for no other reason than that they were allies of the Alliance, albeit reluctant ones. But he knew about Mac and Soleta's history and, being a latecomer to the *Excalibur,* knew that he was in no position to gainsay Mac's faith in her. "It could be a trap."

"Yes, that's been made abundantly clear. McHenry? Have we got it yet?"

Coming up on it now, Mac.

"It's just ahead," said Soleta.

Jellico looked around and then frowned in frustration. "You know, it's damned inconvenient that you and Soleta and Kalinda can hear him, but I can't. Doesn't it make you nervous that he runs the entire ship?"

"What do I know about running ships?" Mac said reasonably. "There's nothing I could do in running the controls that McHenry couldn't do better and faster."

"And do you think I enjoy it, Jellico?" said Soleta. "I repeat what McHenry says for your benefit, mostly to forestall your complaining, and you complain anyway. Do you think it remotely entertaining, having my primary job be to repeat what the ship is saying? Especially when McHenry can tend to go on and on, providing all manner of unasked-for details that I couldn't possibly want or need to know? Do you think that is fun for me? Do you?"

"Fine, forget I said anything," said Jellico, raising his hands in surrender.

"I already have."

"There!" Mac said, pointing at the screen. "There it is."

A small pod was floating against the darkness of space. A single light was mounted dead center, flickering on and off.

"Scan it, McHenry," said Soleta. "If we're going to bring it onto the ship, we don't need to have it blow up once it is aboard."

It is nothing more than what it seems to be, Soleta. Sensors indicate one life-form aboard.

"What sort of life-form?"

It appears to be Romulan.

"A Romulan?"

Jellico moaned softly. Soleta fired him an annoyed look but said nothing.

"McHenry, can you beam the occupant directly into the bridge?"

Yes, Mac.

"Do it."

There was a pause, and then the air filled with the familiar shimmering of transporter beams. Seconds later, they coalesced into a female shape. She had been partly curled up and lying on her side in the pod and, as a result, fell over the moment she finished materializing. She lay on the floor for a moment, blinking against the comparatively bright light of the bridge, and then looked around in confusion.

"Welcome to the *Excalibur,*" said Mac, extending his hand. She took it, looking no less bewildered, as he helped her to her feet. "I'm the captain, M'k'n'zy of Calhoun. Everyone calls me Mac."

"Hello," she said uncertainly. "I . . . am Thue."

"Are you all right?"

"I am . . . dehydrated. I could use—" She stopped and arched an eyebrow in surprise when she saw Soleta. "Oh. Is this a Romulan vessel? No . . . obviously not," she said. "I do not understand. Romulans . . . humans . . ."

"I'm Xenexian, actually. It's a common mistake."

She inclined her head slightly, acknowledging the error. "But then . . . with whom are you affiliated?"

"We're independent operators," said Robin. "We should get you down to the medical bay and—"

"That can wait," said Jellico sharply. He came around the bridge and faced her, adopting a pose that was both defensive and belligerent. "How did you wind up in the middle of nowhere?"

"I was dumped here. I was a crewmember aboard a transport ship that was making a cargo run headed for Romulus."

"What sort of cargo?" said Mac.

"I do not know. It was loaded on, unlabeled, and there was no record of its specifics in our database."

"Meaning," said Soleta, "that you checked."

Thue shrugged. "Even a simple crewmember can be . . . curious. But I learned nothing definitive."

"What did you learn?" said Jellico.

"That it was intended to create some manner of weapon. That much I discerned from overhearing casual conversation by the ship's captain. The late captain," she amended.

"Why late?"

"We were attacked by Alliance forces."

Everyone exchanged looks. The mood on the bridge instantly became charged with tension. "The Alliance?" said Mac.

She nodded. "They boarded the ship, claiming they were looking for contraband. But the moment they were aboard, they just started shooting everyone. I barely managed to escape."

"Miraculous," said Soleta, her eyes narrowed, "that they didn't blow your escape pod out of space."

"Not so miraculous, really. They were interested in what was on the ship. They probably didn't even notice my departure."

"Possibly."

Thue stared at her. "Are you insinuating," she said, "that my presence here is suspicious? I am a single, unarmed woman. If you believe I pose a threat to your vessel, feel free to beam me back into my escape pod, and I will take my chances elsewhere."

"Might I point out," Robin Lefler spoke up, "that while you are all arguing about this, a vessel carrying material that could be transformed into weaponry is currently in the hands of the Alliance and is heading God knows where?"

The current course of the vessel has it continuing toward Romulus.

"It's continuing toward Romulus?" said Soleta.

"How do you—?" began Robin, and then she sighed. "Oh. Right. Of course."

"Are you certain?" said Mac.

Absolutely. I can detect its ion trail. The Alliance vessel continued alongside the smaller ship, presumably acting as an escort. The course remains straight and true for Romulus.

"But none of this makes any sense," said Soleta, slowly pacing the bridge. "Why would the Alliance grab a ship bound for Romulus and then keep heading toward that same destination? What's the point of that?"

"So they could be in control of it," said Jellico. "Power is all about possession, and the Alliance is all about power."

"But they're not going to Romulus simply to say, 'Look, we have this,'" said Mac. "It has to be more than that."

"Maybe there's something going on on Romulus," said Robin. "Maybe . . ." Her voice trailed off.

"Maybe what?" said Mac.

"Maybe, if this thing is part of a weapon, then the weapon is being assembled on Romulus."

"Meaning," said Jellico, "that the Alliance would want to have control of the last piece of the puzzle. The Romulans are constructing some sort of weapon, and the Alliance doesn't trust them."

"Imagine that," said Soleta pointedly. "Someone not trusting Romulans. It must give you a great deal of comfort, Jellico, knowing you have something in common with the Alliance."

Jellico ignored the barb. "If the Alliance is going to this much trouble, then whatever it is, this weapon, it must be fairly significant."

"I have a question," Kalinda said slowly.

This prompted a reaction of mild surprise from the others. Kalinda was usually the last person to involve herself in any discussions on the bridge. Typically, she sat quietly and appeared to listen to whatever everyone else had to say. Sometimes she would say something softly to Robin, who might then follow up on it, but that was about it.

"What do you want to ask, Kalinda?" said Mac.

"Well . . ." She shrugged. "How is this any of our business?"

"What do you mean?"

"I mean, how is it? Don't you see? The Romulans don't trust the Alliance, and the Alliance doesn't trust the Romulans. From what my brother . . ." She paused. Mentioning Si Cwan was obviously still a problem for her. She lowered her gaze from Mac's, because she knew she was looking into the face of the man who had ordered her brother's death, and that could not be an easy thing for her to deal with. "From what my brother said," she continued, although not without effort, "the Romulans and the Alliance have an uneasy truce at best. The Romulans avoided being subsumed by the Alliance only by promising to develop weapons technology for them."

"This could well be it, then," said Mac. "In fact, it probably is."

"Perhaps. But I very much doubt it's going to be something as simple as that the Romulans produce the weapon for the Alliance, which then takes it, says farewell, and goes on about its business. There may very well be some sort of double-cross in place, on the part of both sides."

"That would not surprise me," said Soleta. "Praetor Hiren is incredibly paranoid as it is. He may very well be planning to double-cross the Alliance . . ."

"Which, of course, the Alliance would know and plan something right back," said Jellico. "So, if we stay the hell out of the way, they could wind up doing serious damage to each other while we sit back and laugh."

"Let them," said Soleta with decided heat in her voice. "Let them obliterate each other. I would rejoice in seeing the demise of Hiren the Praetor."

"Then you are a fool," said Thue.

There was no trace of anger in her voice; she had spoken very matter-of-factly. That did not deter Soleta from rounding on her and saying, "You're rather free with the insults, considering you've been onboard for ten minutes and we just saved your ass from deep space."

"Neither my gratitude for your saving me nor my length of time aboard should have any impact on the simple truth. The Praetor, for all his quirks . . ."

"*Quirks?*" said Soleta. Her fists clenched and unclenched in anger. "That bastard was responsible for my father's death. And when this man"—she pointed at Mac—"was but a youth and in Hiren's power, Hiren banished him to the mines of Remus. There are scores to be settled, and if the Alliance is going to settle them for me, then I have no problem with that."

As if Soleta hadn't said a word, Thue said, ". . . could be a valuable ally. The Romulan fleet is formidable. Perhaps not formidable enough to stand up to that of the Alliance, but it would be a start. He could help you."

"We don't need help," said Mac.

"Oh?"

"What's that supposed to mean?"

Thue hesitated and then said, "Look, your activities are not unknown to me."

"Aha!" said Robin.

They looked at her. "Aha what?" said Thue.

Robin shrugged. "I . . . don't know. It just seemed like an 'aha' moment, that's all."

Thue shook her head as if dealing with an idiot and continued, "They are not unknown to many of us. Believe it or not, you have your admirers, even among Romulans. But the colony worlds you have helped have been of marginal interest to the Alliance at best. You are, thus far, merely an irritant. If you wish to accomplish more than that, then you will have to start thinking in grander terms. If, on the other hand, you are satisfied with the status quo, then you need do nothing different from what you already are doing. However, sooner or later, it is my suspicion that the Alliance will grow weary of your insect-sized bites and will decide to swat you—perhaps with whatever is being built for them on Romulus or perhaps with something else. It does not matter which. What matters is that you are one ship, and it does not matter how many strays, outcasts, or would-be warriors you've amassed on this vessel. If you fall into the Alliance's sights, as matters currently stand, you will be annihilated. I believe you know this on some level. So why not . . ."

"Why not what?" said Soleta. "Toss aside personal enmity? A sense of justice? If the Praetor gets what is sorely coming to him, we should intervene, because he might, or might not, be of use to us in a full-scale conflict with the Alliance?"

"Essentially, yes."

"That is the most ridiculous notion I have ever heard. Don't you agree, Mac?" said Soleta.

M'k'n'zy did not answer immediately.

His lack of response drew immediate curiosity from everyone on the bridge. Mac simply stood there, staring into the depths of space.

"Mac?"

He didn't reply to Soleta. Instead, he said, "McHenry. Set course for Romulus. Best possible speed."

Very well, Mac.

"Are you out of your mind?" Soleta shouted.

Everyone else began talking at the same time. M'k'n'zy of Calhoun silenced them all with a glance.

"If any of you," he said softly, "disagrees with me, that is acceptable. But I have made my decision. I will kill anyone who endeavors to interfere. Is that understood?" When no response was forthcoming, he repeated the question with a bit more force. This time, heads nodded in unison.

He stalked off the bridge then. He walked through the corridors, and various Xenexians and others whom the *Excalibur* had rescued smiled to him or saluted him, and a couple of the more fervent ones dropped to their knees and bowed their heads in submission. Those he merely patted on the backs of their heads and nodded.

Why do you say things like that?

"Like what, McHenry?"

Like that you'll kill anyone who tries to interfere. You know you would never do that.

"Yes, but they don't."

Considering what you are rebelling against, do you really think it wise to try to command the loyalty of others through fear and intimidation? How does that distinguish you from the Alliance?

Mac didn't respond to that immediately.

Mac?

"I'll get back to you on that."

All right. I'll wait.

And Mac knew that he would do exactly that, no matter how long it took.

Soleta finally heard what she was waiting for: slow, steady breathing that indicated Thue was sleeping.

McHenry, override the door lock.

Yes, Soleta.

The door to Thue's quarters slid open, and Soleta eased herself in. Just as her sensitive ears had informed her, Thue was on the bed that her stark quarters provided. Most of the quarters on the *Excalibur* had two or three occupants because of the considerable number of crewmembers the vessel had acquired, but they had cleared out space for Thue while she was recovering from her ordeal.

She lay stiffly, like one dead, her arms at her sides. It seemed an odd posture, but Soleta didn't devote much thought to it. She had other things on her mind: specifically, to discover just what it was that Thue was hiding. She didn't know what it was, nor did she have any concrete reason to believe that Thue had been less than candid. But she was positive that there was something, and was determined to discover precisely what it was.

There was a very easy way to go about it.

Soleta had never used her abilities to probe a sleeping mind or manipulate it in any way. How hard could it be, though? After all, if she'd been able to ease her way into the conscious minds of various Romulans, certainly she wouldn't have any difficulties penetrating an unconscious one.

She approached the sleeping Thue. Her hand hovered over the woman's head for a few moments as she composed herself, and then she touched either side of Thue's head. She felt the steady pulse in Thue's temples against her fingers and then slowly, carefully, eased her thoughts into Thue's mind.

To her shock, she encountered resistance.

What the hell? Soleta thought, as even as she did, she endeavored to push through the mental block.

Thue's eyes snapped open and bored straight into her. Soleta's instinct was to pull back, but she was too deeply committed. Tossing aside the subtlety of a scalpel, she went for the force of a bludgeon as she tried to push her way past the mental blocks that Thue was inexplicably producing.

Get . . . out . . . of my head!

The voice was irresistible and yet oddly emotionless—more of a cold order than an impassioned outburst. Soleta tried to resist the impulse and made one final determined thrust.

And she found something just before she was jolted out of the woman's head.

Soleta fell back and hit the floor, landing hard on her rump. Thue was upright in the bed, and there was a fearsome glare in her eyes. "How dare you? You had no right—"

"*No right!*" An infuriated Soleta cut her off. She got to her feet, and there was pure venom in her voice. "*You* would dare lecture *me?* You, who came aboard this ship hiding her name? Her very race?" Then, silently, she called out, *McHenry!*

Yes, Soleta? McHenry's voice came to her in response to her summons.

Why the hell couldn't you determine she was a Vulcan?

I knew she was a Vulcan.

You said she was a Romulan!

No. I said she appeared *to be a Romulan. The surface genetic manipulation she had done created that appearance.*

And you didn't see fit to mention that?

You had just finished complaining about my tendency to provide unasked-for details and how you found it irritating. So I waited for you to ask. You never did.

She closed her eyes a moment in irritation and then composed herself. Then she turned her attention back to the woman standing before her. "Selar. Your name is Selar. And you're a Vulcan."

"There is no logical reason to deny that which you have already, and rudely, discerned."

"But why? Why hide what you are?"

Selar hesitated but then clearly decided that there was no point in prevaricating. "I am part of an underground group," she said. "Spies, for lack of a better word. Since Romulans are nominally allies of the Alliance, I have more latitude for movement within the Alliance, and on Romulus, as one of . . . you."

"Vulcans spying on the Alliance? Why?"

"I see no reason to give you the full particulars of my endeavors. This should, however, prompt you to put aside any paranoia you may have that there is some manner of trap involved. There is no love lost between my people and the Alliance."

"If you're asking me to completely trust someone who came aboard this ship under false name and hidden race, then you're requesting more than I have to offer." She looked at her askance. "You blocked my mental probe. How did you do it?"

"How do *you* have such abilities?" countered Selar.

Soleta realized that her secret was already in the hands of this woman. "My mother," she said slowly, "was a Vulcan. I never knew her. Never had the opportunity to ask her. But I always wondered if . . ." Her voice trailed off.

"If you received your abilities from her?"

There was a deathly silence for a long moment.

"My God," said Soleta.

"You must tell no one . . ."

"My God, you all have . . ."

Selar took a step toward her, and when she spoke, her voice was low and intense and not at all dispassionate. "You hold the future of my people in your hand, halfbreed. If the Alliance knew what we were capable of, we would be rounded up, experimented on, or perhaps simply annihilated outright because of the threat we would present. Do you want genocide on your conscience?"

"You acknowledge I even have a conscience? I know what Vulcans say about Romulans and in what low regard you hold us."

"This is no time for racial division. The stakes are too high."

"If that is the case, then the first thing I suggest you do is never call me 'halfbreed' again."

Selar inclined her head slightly. "Very well . . . Soleta. But I need to emphasize—"

"No. What you need to do is shut up." She sat in the nearest chair, staring dazed into space. "So many questions I've had, for so long, and never anyone to ask, until now. Rest assured that I've no more interest in having my secrets exposed than you do with yours. I need time to—"

"Take all the time you require, but I need your word now."

"Or what?"

Selar's face was unreadable, but there was a look in her eyes that suggested the level of the stakes and the lengths to which Selar would go to protect her race.

"You have my word," Soleta said. "But in exchange, you will immediately tell the others your true nature and real name. Protecting the fate of the Vulcan race is a sufficient show of good faith on my part. I don't need to be worrying that I'll slip and call you by your true name, calling my own loyalties into question. I'm not interested in keeping secrets from Mac."

Selar hesitated and then nodded. "Your terms are acceptable. I simply hope that your M'k'n'zy of Calhoun doesn't overreact and kill me."

Soleta rolled her eyes. "You can't take him seriously when he says things like that."

"Would you bet your life on that?" When Soleta didn't respond, Selar simply inclined her head slightly and said, "I thought as much."

It was two hours later when McHenry reported that the ion trails had diverged. The larger vessel, the one from the Alliance, had broken off, leaving the smaller transport ship to continue to Romulus on its own. Without hesitation, Mac ordered McHenry to keep the ship on the trail of the transport ship. He ignored Soleta's protests that it could be another form of trap, nor did he particularly care why the larger ship had veered off. "Perhaps they had some other mission they had to undertake," he said, and that was sufficient for him. It was less than inspiring for the others, but they didn't see the point of going up against Mac. Not when he was in this sort of mood.

Forty-seven minutes later, they overtook the transport ship.

The battle was short. The transport was armed, but the *Excalibur* deftly outmaneuvered it, and pinpoint assaults from the *Excalibur*'s big guns managed to disable the transport's offensive capabilities while leaving the rest of the ship intact. They then steadily battered the shields, punching a hole through them sufficient for a strike team, composed entirely of Xenexians, to beam aboard.

Mac, naturally, was at the head of the strike team. He wouldn't have it any other way, despite Soleta and Jellico both asserting that he had a responsibility to the ship to keep himself as safe as possible. "How would my people respect me," he had said, "if they thought that I was afraid to face the perils to which I would subject them?"

Now Soleta, Selar, and Jellico made their way through the corridors of the captured transport. Any Xenexians they encountered bowed deeply upon seeing them, as was their custom. The three of them also had to step carefully over fallen bodies—Cardassian, for the most part. It had been a ferocious battle, and Jellico almost slipped more than once in pools of blood that had not yet been cleaned up.

They met up with Mac in the cargo hold. Soleta noticed that his long hair was flecked with blood. He either didn't notice or else didn't seem to care. "All right, *Selar*," he said sarcastically. He had not been at all pleased when she had confessed her deception to him, although he hadn't seemed inclined to kill her. At least, Soleta didn't think he had been; it wasn't always easy to tell. "What are we dealing with?"

Selar entered the cargo hold and cracked open one of the crates.

She studied the contents and then nodded. "It appears to be canisters of C-170."

Mac exchanged confused looks with the others. "What is that?"

"It's a radioactive isotope," Jellico said promptly. "Used in the manufacture of weapons."

"What sort of weapon?" said Soleta.

It was Selar who responded. "Weapons involving Thalaron radiation."

"So you're a spy and a scientist?" said Jellico. If he had been suspicious of her when she was "Thue" and a Romulan, he was even more so now that he knew she had been less than candid from the very beginning.

"A scientist by training; a spy by necessity," said Selar, and then went on, "To be specific, C-170 is a triggering agent required to instigate a cascading biogenic pulse."

"How significant a pulse?" said Mac.

Selar fixed him with a look. "It could generate a pulse sufficient to destroy an entire world."

"My God," said Jellico. Mac let out a low whistle. Soleta said nothing.

"The Romulans likely have the rest of the materials already in place or are receiving delivery from other sources," said Selar. "But there is no substitute for C-170. Without it, whatever device they've created would be useless. Obviously, the Alliance wanted to have possession of the C-170 so that the device—"

"Bomb," said Jellico. "Let's call it what it is."

"So that the bomb," said Selar without hesitation, "would be created on the Alliance's timetable. They wanted to hold the final piece."

"And now we hold it," said Mac.

"Let's go."

"Go?" said Mac to Jellico, who had just spoken. "Go where?"

"Back to the *Excalibur,* obviously. So we can blow this damned ship to bits and its cargo along with it."

"Why would we want to do that?"

Jellico looked astounded. "Because it's a doomsday weapon, Mac," he said, gesturing toward the crates and clearly amazed that he needed to explain it. "If we destroy this shipment, we can—"

"We can what? Prevent the doomsday weapon from being made? When this vessel goes missing, they'll just arrange another shipment from somewhere else, sooner or later."

"Then what are you suggesting? That we deliver it?"

"That's exactly right."

Jellico paled. "You can't be serious."

"It makes sense," said Soleta.

He turned to her as if she had just stabbed him in the back. "How can you say that?"

"My mouth forms the words; it's not all that difficult."

"Consider, Jellico," said Mac. "If a doomsday weapon is going to exist, why shouldn't we be the ones in control of it?"

"Because we'll be tempted to use it!"

"If the Alliance has it, they'll be far more than tempted."

"He is quite correct," said Selar. "We have every reason to believe that the Alliance has allowed the Romulans to exist unmolested—or relatively so—because they have been waiting precisely for the creation of this sort of weapon. At present, even the Alliance does not possess weaponry capable of annihilating an entire world. A Thalaron bomb will provide them with exactly that. They would not desire such a device unless they fully intended to use it."

"Even if we manage to acquire this bomb," said Jellico, "that won't necessarily prevent the Alliance from doing so."

"Maybe. But maybe it will persuade them not to use it," said Soleta. "After all, if they know we have it and can retaliate in kind should they employ it, that knowledge might serve to prevent them from utilizing it in the first place."

Jellico looked as if he were about to reply, but Mac was already turning to Selar. "The techniques used to create your . . . appearance," he said. "Can you replicate them? Disguise others to look like Romulans?"

Slowly, she nodded. "I could cannibalize some of the equipment in this vessel's medlab. The transformation would be far more painful for the subject than the technique used on me. It might even kill a human . . ."

"I'm not considering using it on a human."

She eyed him. "You mean yourself." He nodded slowly. "Very well. Come with me. We will get started."

Selar and Mac walked out. Jellico, meanwhile, was still staring at the crates and slowly shaking his head. "Problem, Jellico?" said Soleta.

He turned to her and said, "All this talk about using our own weapon to deter the Alliance from using it first. But what's to stop *us* from using it in the first place?"

"That's easy," said Soleta. "We're the good guys."

"Are we? Are you sure?"

Soleta didn't reply.

Hiren, Praetor of the Romulan Alliance, was not one typically to stand on ceremony. So it was that he literally sprinted down the corridor leading to his private study upon learning that the final element for Project Parity had finally arrived. A team of scientists had beamed down with it and were prepared to assemble the device that would finally put them on equal footing with the Alliance.

Hiren knew what they said about him. He knew that they claimed he was swallowed in paranoia to the point of near insanity. He knew that they claimed he was unfit to rule and should be forced out of office at the earliest opportunity. He knew that they claimed he was the Alliance's puppet, kowtowing to their every whim in exchange for questionable promises of safety.

They know nothing of me. Nothing.

He turned the corner and saw that guards were standing to either side of the study doors. He remembered that he had posted them there, but abruptly he began to second-guess himself. The eyes and ears of the Alliance were everywhere, and he didn't need random guards listening in on his plans. "Has everything been brought in?" he said. The guards nodded. "Very well. You may leave."

The guards exchanged confused looks. That was acceptable to Hiren. Let them be confused. There was no need for them to be aware of what was happening. The assorted parts for Project Parity had been brought from half a dozen different points around the city, each prepared independently so that no individuals save Hiren and the chief designer would know what the nature of the final device would be. And what with the chief designer having met with a tragic accident just two days earlier—having thrown himself off a cliff after stabbing himself repeatedly—Hiren only had to worry about his own trustworthiness. Of that, as always, he was fully confident.

Of course, there was the matter of the scientists themselves. They were the ones who were going to be working from the chief designer's plans and constructing the device. Naturally, they were going to figure out what it was they were assembling. But that was acceptable. After all, once the device was assembled, there was nothing that could be done to disassemble it. Hiren would have his weapon, parity would be achieved with the Alliance, and all would be well. And if the scientists proved to be a problem down the road, well . . .

. . . there were plenty of cliffs out there.

The guards had obediently departed, and Hiren walked into his private study. He looked with approval at the assorted containers stacked neatly. Standing at the far end were three Romulan scientists, two female and one male.

"Greetings," he said. "I am Hiren, Praetor of the Romulan Alliance."

"Yes. We know," said one of the females. There was an edge to her voice, a harshness that seemed wholly inappropriate to the occasion. Typically, people groveled upon meeting Hiren, which was the way he preferred it.

Plus, there was something vaguely familiar in her voice. He

tilted his head thoughtfully and said, "Have we met, young woman?"

"On several occasions, yes." She walked slowly toward him. The far end of the study had been cast in shadow since the sun was setting, and even in the best of light, Hiren's eyes were not what they once were. "I was usually in the company of my father."

"Your father?"

"Yes." She was close enough now that her features were clearer to him. "Perhaps you remember him? His name was Rojan. You had him killed."

Hiren's mouth moved, but no words came out at first. Then he found his breath and started to cry out for help. Even as he did so, however, the male Romulan—who had not moved a muscle until that moment—was across the room, covering the distance in one leap like some sort of beast. He drove a knee into Hiren's chest, knocking him to the ground, and a face both familiar and unfamiliar snarled down at Hiren.

"Remember me?" said the male Romulan. "You condemned me to die in the mines of Remus because I committed the unpardonable crime of refusing to murder my father."

The ears, the brow, were Romulan, but the eyes burned with an intensity that Hiren would never forget, even though they had been in a much younger face when he'd last seen them. "Muck," he whispered.

"So you called me. Now I am Mac. And perhaps I should make up for that uncommitted murder right now."

The other woman now stepped forward and said firmly, "Is this what you intended with this mission, Mac? To kill the Praetor?"

"Are you going to stop me?"

"No. I simply wish to know."

"If he doesn't," said Soleta, moving toward him, "then I will."

"And is that," said the other woman sharply, "how you are going to prove that you are 'the good guys'? By murdering someone in the name of vengeance?"

"In the name of justice," Mac said.

"Never confuse the two. I never do." She came over to him and said, "We have everything we desire. The entire weapon is right here. One assumes that Hiren has the plans to assemble it. Once he provides us with those . . ."

"Then you kill me," Hiren said, mentally upbraiding himself for dismissing the guards. There was no one to whom he could call for help, thanks to his own stupidity. "Hardly an incentive for me to tell you how to complete the . . ." He hesitated.

"Weapon, you idiot," said Mac. "The word you're hesitating to speak is 'weapon,' as if we didn't know what—"

Suddenly there were shouts from outside the Praetor's study, shots fired, orders issued, and more shots.

The former Muck hauled the Praetor to his feet. "Expecting company?"

The doors to the Praetor's private study burst open. A Klingon strode in. His face was narrow, and his beard and temples were tinged with gray, but he looked as formidable as any Klingon Hiren had ever seen. Right behind him came a Cardassian. His skin was deathly pale, his black hair slicked back, and—curiously—several pieces of bone were missing from the characteristic ridges on his face. Backing them up was a squadron of Alliance guards, a mix of Cardassian and Klingon troops.

"I am Krone," said the Klingon and, indicating the Cardassian just behind him, continued, "And this is Tome Ari. We were told you would be expecting us."

Not this soon, damn you. Not for days yet.

"Of course," said Hiren, forcing a smile.

Tome Ari looked suspiciously at the three other figures in the room. "Who are they?" he demanded.

Everything froze as Hiren realized he was holding the fate of three people in his hands, and at least two of those people would like to see him dead.

. . .

On the bridge of the *Excalibur,* Kalinda suddenly sat bolt upright in her seat and said, "Change course. Now."

The abrupt pronouncement caught Jellico off guard. Robin Lefler turned to Kalinda and said, "What?"

Kalinda ignored both of them. She was on her feet and saying, "You heard me, McHenry. *Now!*"

As you wish, Kalinda.

The *Excalibur* had been en route to Romulus. Mac, Soleta, and Selar had taken the transport vessel and had by that point arrived at their destination. There were any number of Romulan vessels orbiting the Romulan homeworld, so the transport was the logical means for Mac and his crew to penetrate Romulan security. The *Excalibur* had been approaching slowly to serve as backup, moving into communication range but not sensor range.

But there had been an abrupt change of plan as Romulan space receded on the viewscreen. "What the hell is going on? What are you doing!?" said Jellico.

Kalinda was undeterred by his anger. "Remember the Alliance ship that broke off from the science transport? McHenry said a vessel matching its ion trail is coming in from warp space. It's heavily armed, and we are no match for it. He's operating on the assumption that they have a description of this vessel and will attack on sight. So it makes sense for us to keep out of sight."

"And they're heading for Romulus?"

"Yes, Edward," said Kalinda. "So it would seem."

Jellico and Robin exchanged worried looks. "If they're planning to meet with the Praetor . . ." said Robin.

"Who else would they be meeting with?"

"Then this could pose a serious problem for Mac and the others. What should we do, Jellico?"

"We wait," said Jellico, "and we hope that Mac can lie his way out of whatever situation he finds himself in."

. . .

Mac feigned confusion to the best of his ability and said, "Noble Krone, honored Tome Ari, my associates and I have absolutely no idea why you should be surprised that we're here. What reason would you have to think that something unusual transpired in our voyage here?"

He folded his arms and waited. His hand rested comfortably on the palm-sized blaster that was secreted just inside his tunic. If Krone, Tome Ari, or any of their men made any sort of abrupt move, Mac would open fire and hope for the best.

Krone exchanged a glance with Tome Ari and then growled. "We were informed that representatives of the Alliance had boarded your vessel to provide . . . protection. Commandeered it, actually. Took command. Or so we were told."

"Who made that allegation?" Selar spoke up.

"The commander of the *Warship Blackmorn,* the ship that transported us here," said Tome Ari. "He broke off from your vessel to rendezvous with us at Terok Nor so that we could come here and see for ourselves this masterful weapon you're about to create for us." That last was directed more to Hiren than it was to Selar.

"Well," Selar said carefully, looking as if she were immensely concerned for Tome Ari's and Krone's feelings, "I would never wish to imply that your commander was less than candid with you. Never for all the world. Yet on the other hand, you are faced with the irrefutable proof of your own eyes. We are here, and there is no sign of your representatives, and if they were in charge, certainly they would have come down here instead of us, would they not?"

"That would have been my assumption," said Tome Ari.

"Well, then," said Selar, "it appears we have a miscommunication here."

"Yes, and fortunately, there has been no harm done," said Hiren. He brought his hands together and rubbed them briskly. "And my team of scientists here are prepared to assemble the Thalaron bomb, just as I have long promised."

"Yes, very long promised," rumbled Krone. "There are some who believed that promises were all we would see."

"And there were others," said Tome Ari, looking suspiciously at Mac, as if trying to determine where he should know him from, "who believed that you were planning to make it secretly and use it against us, or at least threaten to do so."

The Praetor harrumphed. "Nonsense. Nonsense and calumnies. I have given my word as Praetor, and the Praetor's word is his bond. Now, if you wouldn't mind giving my scientists a bit of space."

"Space?"

"This is a delicate procedure," said Soleta. "Having you watching over our shoulders would add stress that, frankly, we do not need. Plus, if something were to go wrong and either of you were injured as a result, the recriminations would be severe. None of us needs that."

There was a long pause, and Mac prepared to yank out his blaster and begin shooting.

"Very well," said Tome Ari. He smiled, which, on his face, gave him the appearance of a death's head skull. "I'm quite sure that Hiren can provide us with suitable accommodations while you assemble the device. By all means, be careful, and take your time—but not too much time." He started to turn away and made a bit too much of a show of turning back and saying, "Oh, and we will be monitoring your vessel's energy emissions. If we see even the slightest attempt to beam you and the bomb's components off the planet's surface, we will blow it to atoms."

"That sounds fair," said Mac evenly. He noticed that Krone was staring at him. "Is there a problem, honored one?"

"You seem familiar to me," said Krone. "Why would that be?"

Mac shrugged. "I've no idea, honored one. To the best of my knowledge, we have never met."

Krone continued to study him for a moment and then turned away with a dissatisfied grunt.

Moments later, the room was filled only with Romulans or pseudo-Romulans. It was only at that point that Mac eased his hand out of his tunic, away from his blaster, and he said to Hiren, "Why didn't you turn us in?"

"What a superb idea," said Hiren sarcastically. "Inform representatives of the Alliance that the notorious commander of the *Excalibur* and two of his crew are standing right here. It would convince them that I'm allied with you, and my life wouldn't be worth spit. And if by some miracle I managed to persuade them that I didn't know who you were . . ."

"It makes you appear incompetent and easily fooled," said Soleta. Hiren nodded. Soleta turned to Selar and said, "You spoke quickly and well. Good job."

"Thank you," said Selar. "I only wish I knew what we do now."

"Now?" said Mac. "That's obvious: We build a bomb."

McHenry . . .

Yes, Soleta?

Are you within the area?

No, Soleta. When the Alliance ship showed up, Kalinda had me put some distance between us and them.

Yet I can still communicate with you?

We're not having a conversation via subspace, Soleta. Distances have no relevance. Our minds are linked. You can summon me wherever you are. Pause. *You've almost completed work on the bomb, haven't you?*

Yes, McHenry, that's correct. And I've been considering all the ways that this could possibly turn out, and keep coming around to the same conclusion: We're going to wind up fighting, and we're going to need you here when it happens. How quickly can you get here if we need you?

Minutes. Less. Even Kalinda doesn't realize how quickly I can move if I have to.

Good. And McHenry . . . don't let me down.

I would never let you down, Soleta. Not ever. I will fight for you. I would die for you.

Pause.

McHenry . . . what are you saying?

I believe you know what I am saying. Call me, and I will come, and your enemies will die, or I will in their place.

Let's . . . aspire to the former, okay?

Pause.

As you wish, Soleta. As you wish.

Hiren rubbed the sleep from his eyes as he approached his private study. He could have had Mac and his people moved to a lab, but he decided that was too public for the nature of the weapon they were assembling. So he had them remain exactly where they had been and working on Project Parity.

Parity. Well, that was a joke now, wasn't it? The Alliance had outmaneuvered him. They'd shown up earlier than expected, and their presence now hung over the entire business. He had lost the advantage of surprise, lost the advantage of everything.

Damn them and their timing.

Hiren had provided M'k'n'zy of Calhoun and his people the detailed plans for the assembling of the bomb, and had spent many hours watching them meticulously and laboriously putting the damned thing together. But Hiren was not young anymore, and eventually, he had run up against a wall of exhaustion. Mac's people seemed tireless, but Hiren eventually retired with explicit instructions that he was to be informed as soon as the project was completed.

The summons had now come.

When he arrived at the door to the private study, Tome Ari and Krone, along with their omnipresent guards, were arriving from the other direction. He cursed inwardly. Who the hell had told them? He had a leak among his own people. That was precisely the sort of aggravation that he didn't need. Now he was going to have to go through his personal staff one at a time, root out who had informed the Alliance representatives, and kill whoever it was. Some days the job of Praetor was simply not all it was cracked up to be.

"After you, Praetor," Tome Ari said, bowing deeply and mockingly. Krone just glared at him.

The Praetor nodded in response, while picturing his hands around Tome Ari's neck and squeezing very, very hard until the Cardassian's eyes popped and his throat collapsed beneath Hiren's fingers like a brittle bouquet of flowers. He entered the study, the others following close behind.

Project Parity was completed.

The bomb stood two meters high. It was triangular in shape but wasn't a solid pyramid; instead, it was a series of interlocking tubes, with a sphere in the middle that contained the C-170. Hiren had long known the design, could envision it in his head, but seeing it now, here, completed and gleaming in the dim light . . . it was beautiful.

"Well?" said Krone. "Will it work?"

Soleta wiped sweat from her brow. She looked exhausted. She had been the primary driving force in constructing the bomb, although Mac and the woman introduced to him as Thue had done as much as they could to help. "Yes," she said. "It will."

"It will release Thalaron radiation in a single burst?" Krone looked skeptical. "And how will that destroy a planet? It makes no sense."

"That's because you're thinking too small," said Soleta. "Everyone in the vicinity of the bomb will die immediately, yes. But that's just the beginning. Once detonated, the device will transform all natural ambient gamma radiation currently existing on the selected planet into Thalaron radiation. Within a week, anyone who survived the initial detonation will be dead."

There was silence for a moment, and then Tome Ari nodded approvingly. "Praetor Hiren," he said, "I owe you an apology, on behalf of both myself and my associate . . . and also on behalf of the Alliance. Many among us had doubts that you would come through on your promises. But this achievement is monumental enough to still the wagging tongues of any critics. We thank you for your endeavors. Now that the bomb has been assembled, we will return with it to our vessel, run scans on it so that we will have all the details of its construction, and then, of course, test it."

"Really. And where are you planning to do that?"

"Here on Romulus."

The Praetor blinked in confusion and then laughed.

"Praetor," Soleta said, "I don't think he's joking."

Tome Ari said gravely, "Of course not. Why would I joke about impending genocide? That would be in exceptionally poor taste."

Abruptly, the squadron of guards had their weapons up and leveled at the Praetor. It was at that point that the Praetor realized the gravity of the situation.

"Young woman," said Tome Ari to Soleta, "bring the device out here, please. We have a schedule to keep to and a planet to destroy. We can't just stand around, now, can we?"

At which time Hiren laughed.

His reaction was not at all what the Alliance representatives expected. The Klingon, Krone, scowled even more fiercely. Tome Ari merely looked politely puzzled. The rest of the troops exchanged confused looks.

Then the Praetor walked straight up to Tome Ari and practically snarled in his face. "Do you truly believe that I would not have foreseen this possibility and allowed for it?"

"Really. And how, precisely, would you have allowed for it, Praetor?" said Tome Ari with his exceeding politeness. "Considering that I see no armed troops around to present any sort of—"

The Romulan soldiers appeared from everywhere.

Walls that had appeared solid in the great hall outside the study suddenly swiveled, and Romulan troops stepped out, heavily armed and encircling the Alliance forces.

The Alliance forces didn't hesitate. They aimed every weapon they had at the Praetor.

"Tell them to lower their weapons," said Krone, "or you will be the first to die, Praetor."

The Praetor's eyes narrowed. "As opposed to what? Should you detonate the device here, I will die regardless."

"We've no intention of detonating it here," said Tome Ari easily. "We'll be bringing it to another part of the planet, far enough away that you, Praetor, and those close to you will be able to escape before the full potency of the weapon is reached. Think of it as a gesture of consideration."

"And I can think of several gestures to offer in return," said the Praetor.

"How dare you—!" snarled Krone.

Tome Ari didn't appear the least insulted. He actually seemed amused. "I appreciate your fiery resolve, Praetor. Just as I'm sure that you appreciate the Alliance's technology and resources. For instance, there's Maneuver Ten."

"Maneuver Ten?" said Hiren. "What would that be?"

The answer came immediately as the Romulan troops promptly shimmered out of sight and the whine of transporter rays filled the great hall.

Hiren made a distinct choking sound as he witnessed his men disappear, and Tome Ari chuckled at his reaction. "That, dear Praetor, was Maneuver Ten. I've had an open channel to the *Blackmorn* the entire time." He tapped his right ear. "A handy implant. I can hear communications from my ship, and they can hear my voice. It's a bit more subtle than open comm devices, don't you think?"

"Return my men this instant!"

"That would be a problem," said Tome Ari with mock sadness, "since their molecules were already given the widest possible dispersement in space. Reassembling them would be beyond even our prowess. And that fate awaits you and your associates unless you cooperate every step of the way. Now," he said, turning to Soleta, "bring the device out here. We will beam up with it to the *Blackmorn* and—"

"No," said Soleta. "I don't believe you will."

She glanced toward Mac, and he nodded with what appeared to be approval. It was as if they were reading each other's mind.

Tome Ari seemed as amused by Soleta as he had been by the Praetor. "Oh? And on what do you base your opinion?"

"You're going to find out in about five seconds."

"My dear woman," said Tome Ari, "that sounds like a threat. And you shouldn't be doing such things unless you—"

Then he stopped talking. From the way he was reacting, Hiren could see that he was being told something by his ship that wasn't meeting with his approval.

"Can back it up?" inquired Soleta. "Is that what you were going to say?"

Tome Ari turned and said with mounting fury to Krone, "They can't beam us out! They have their shields up because they're under attack!"

"From whom? Who would dare!"

"The *Excalibur*!"

"Calhoun's ship! That son of a whore! That—"

And suddenly, something appeared to click in Krone's mind. He spun on the balls of his feet to face Mac and bellowed, *"You! It's you!* That's where I knew you from! I've seen images of you, taken during your assaults on our interests! You're M'k'n'zy of Calhoun!"

"Pleasure to meet you," said Mac, and he yanked his blaster from concealment and fired at Krone.

The blast struck the Klingon squarely in the chest, lifting him off his feet and sending him crashing into several of his men. They went down in a heap.

The sane, rational thing for Mac to have done at that point would have been to fall back.

Mac did the exact opposite. He charged forward as if he outnumbered them, firing his blaster furiously in a sweeping arc that took down half a dozen men before any of them knew what was happening.

The troops quickly rallied, swinging their weapons around

and bringing them to bear on the fast-moving Mac. As one, they opened fire.

Mac leaped high and backward, clear of the assault, and his attackers' blasts slammed into each other. The semicircle cut itself to pieces as Alliance troops went down under the withering assault of their own compatriots.

The others fell back, regrouping, and Mac was ready to attack once more when Soleta suddenly grabbed him by the arm and shouted, *"No! Come on!"* He tried to pull away, furious. This was the sort of situation that he lived for, thrived on. The heat of battle was the only time he was able to shed the veneer of civilization he wore in order to command the *Excalibur* and become the person he truly believed himself to be. But Soleta's grip was firm, and she pulled him into the study. Hiren was next to her, and the moment Soleta had Mac inside, Hiren secured the door.

"You've trapped us!" said Mac angrily.

"She did as I told her to," said Hiren. "You may not wish to accord me any respect, Muck, but being the Praetor of the Romulans still counts for something." He pulled aside a hidden panel and touched a flat panel within. Immediately, a far wall slid aside, revealing a passageway. "Grab the device. Let's go," he said.

Seconds later, the door to the study exploded inward. A livid Krone, followed by an equally fuming Tome Ari and the remainder of their troops poured into the study, only to find it empty.

"A hidden escape route!" shouted Krone. "That has to be it! Tear the place apart until you find it! You," and he pointed at the nearest Cardassian. "Grab your tricorder, and come with me! You, too, Tome Ari!"

Mac, Soleta, and Selar, meanwhile, were making their way through the narrow passage within the walls of the palace. It was designed to be used by one person at a time, so it was slow going as they made their way in single file. Nor was it easy maneuvering with the bomb, which Soleta was carrying as carefully as she could. Suddenly, she stopped, so abruptly that Selar banged into her.

"*Excalibur* is in trouble," she said. "McHenry says the *Blackmorn* is pounding them. We're doing some damage but not enough."

"You heard her. My ship is strong and maneuverable," Mac told Hiren, "but it's not going to be able to stand up to the *Blackmorn*. You have an entire fleet up there in orbit."

"Yes, and they are most certainly doing nothing at the moment. Their standing orders are to remain neutral should they witness an Alliance ship under assault."

"This is no time for them to remain neutral. If they aid the *Excalibur* . . ."

"Then we'll have crossed a line we can never uncross. You're asking me to take the Romulans and put them against the Alliance, the exact thing I've been trying to avoid."

"You can't, Praetor," said Mac. "Not anymore." His voice became more fervent, more insistent. "I don't know what happened to you over the years, but the man I first met years ago—the man who took me away from the father who despised me, the man who first exposed me to philosophy and strategic thought and everything that made me what I am—that man wouldn't back down from the Alliance."

"But I did," said Hiren. "Even then I did, all for the good of my people."

Soleta stepped forward and said angrily, "It wasn't for the good of the people, you selfish bastard. It was for your good. That's all you cared about. What was right for you in terms of being able to hold on to whatever power the Alliance let you have. The only question left now is whether you're too stupid to realize that power that others let you have is worthless. If you want power, you have to seize it and hold on to it with both hands and never, ever let go until someone pries it away from you."

Mac waited for the Praetor to scream at her or bellow at her or tell her she didn't know what she was talking about and how dare she say such things.

Instead, the Praetor stared at her for a long moment and said, "How much like your father you are. I think I did our people a disservice by suspecting him of treasonous thoughts."

"Is that what you think? Should I feel gratitude for that?"

"No. You should feel gratitude for this."

The Praetor reached into his belt buckle and removed a communications device. He activated it and spoke slowly and gravely. "Attention to all fleet commanders within the sound of my voice. This is the Praetor, priority identification code zero three zero five. As you are doubtless aware, there is an Alliance vessel currently locked in combat with a rebel vessel, the *Excalibur.*" He took a deep breath and let it out slowly, as if he were preparing to jump off a very great height. "It is my order that you join forces with the rebel ship and attack the Alliance vessel. Blow them to hell. Repeat, blow them to—"

The wall next to them blew open.

The impact knocked them back, and debris from the crumbling wall came raining down on them. It was all Mac could do to avoid a concussion. As the smoke cleared, he saw the snarling face of Krone glaring in at him. His disruptor, which he had doubtless used to blow apart the wall, was pointed straight at Mac.

"This time," Krone said, obviously unable to resist extending his moment of triumph, "you die."

It turned out to be a calamitous indulgence, as far as Krone was concerned.

As he said "this," Mac's fingers were wrapping around a piece of debris. When he said "time," Mac was cocking his arm. By the time he got to the word "die," Mac was whipping his arm around and flinging the chunk of debris as hard as he could.

It smashed squarely into Krone's face. Blood sprayed from his nose, shattered by the impact, and Krone stumbled back. His shot went wide, exploding harmlessly overhead.

The world seemed to slow down for Mac as he clambered free of the debris. He didn't bother with his blaster. Instead, he yanked out a knife that was secreted inside the top of his boot. The blood was pumping hot through his veins, driving him to throw himself recklessly into combat where just shooting down his opponent wouldn't suffice. There were two soldiers, a Cardassian and a Klingon, and they had their weapons out. They fired at him. He threw himself forward, ducking under the blasts. He hit the ground, and his knife lashed out. It sliced through the tendons just above the Klingon's heels, hamstringing him. The Klingon let out a scream of fury as he collapsed. The world slowed further as the Cardassian turned to bring his disruptor to bear. Mac thrust upward with the blade, gutting him just under the ribcage. Blood exploded from the Cardassian's midsection, splashing onto Mac's face. Mac smiled and yanked out the blade.

"Behind you!" shouted Hiren, and Mac turned and threw the knife all in one motion. Tome Ari had been about to open fire with his disruptor. Instead, the knife that Mac had thrown buried itself in Tome Ari's chest, up to the hilt. Tome Ari staggered back, waving his arms wildly.

He landed atop the Thalaron bomb.

Soleta had lost her grip on it, being tossed to one side when the wall exploded. Tome Ari wrapped his arms around it even as Soleta cried out a warning. Selar tried to scramble over her to get to it.

A dreamlike smile played across Tome Ari's face, and his fingers caressed the controls as one would the body of a lover.

The lights on the bomb flared to life, and it began to emit a high-pitched whine.

"Aw, *grozit*," said Mac.

Soleta! The Romulan fleet has joined us in attacking the Alliance ship. It doesn't know where to look first. Isn't that marvel—

McHenry! The Thalaron bomb has been activated!

Oh. Well . . . that's not good.

Get us out of here! Drop your shields, and beam us out now!

Why don't I just beam out the bomb?

Because with the radiation signatures in random flux, you won't have time to get a lock on it! Beam us out now! Now, dammit, now!

• • •

The last thing M'k'n'zy of Calhoun saw before he dematerialized was the furious face of Krone. Then the Klingon's eyes widened in shock as he realized what was about to happen, and suddenly, the world in front of Mac went white as the sound of the transporter filled his ears.

The next thing he knew, he was tumbling off the transporter deck of the *Excalibur.* Soleta and Selar were on either side of him, and Hiren . . .

Hiren was sobbing pitifully.

"My people," he was howling. "My people, what have I done, what have I—"

Soleta had no patience for it. None at all. She was upon him in an instant, like a wild animal, and she slammed his head against the floor and snarled in his face, "Your people are dead right now! A goodly number of them, anyway. Dead thanks to a weapon that you engineered and I built! There's blood enough for everybody's hands, but you don't see me crying about it! There's still time to save a portion of the populace before the Thalaron radiation makes the planet uninhabitable! Organize the fleet! Do what a Praetor should do! Don't just whine over—"

Hiren boxed her ears.

Soleta let out a startled howl of fury and pain as she rolled off him, clutching the sides of her head. Hiren got to his feet and looked down at her with smoldering rage.

"You," he said, "have not earned the privilege of addressing me so. And just so you know: You never will." He glanced over at Mac. "You might, someday. Now, let's finish blowing those bastards out of the sky and then get busy with saving as many of my people as we can."

Mac strode toward him and stopped inches away. "I give the orders here," he said in a low, angry voice. "And my next order will be to beam you back down to the planet unless you apologize to Soleta and help her to her feet."

"You wouldn't dare."

Mac waited a moment and then said, "Don't worry, Praetor. We'll tell your fleet that you died in noble combat with the enemy, your teeth sunk deeply into a Cardassian throat." He grabbed Hiren and started to push him toward the transporter.

"A thousand pardons, Soleta!" shouted Hiren.

Mac released his grip on Hiren and watched with clear satisfaction as Hiren helped Soleta to stand. She glared at Hiren and said to Mac, "Can I kill him now?"

"Later," said Mac, "when he's no longer of any use to us."

"I believe," said Hiren, "that I may have taught you too well, Mac of Calhoun. At least too well for my own good."

By the time Alliance vessels arrived at Romulus, they found a dead planet laden with the remains of charred corpses. Floating in space nearby was debris that constituted the only remains of the ship *Blackmorn*. The planet was uninhabitable and would be for the next 950 years. Since so many of the bodies had been reduced to pure ash, it was impossible to determine the total number of casualties.

The fact that the fleet was missing prompted much attention from the Alliance. It was determined that the Romulans had turned against the Alliance, and word was spread to all points of the Alliance: Romulan vessels were to be destroyed on sight.

The word even managed to reach the Romulan vessels themselves. Standing in Mac's quarters in the *Excalibur*, gazing out the observation port, Hiren and Mac looked on the fleet of ships that contained the last remnants of the Romulan race. Only 49,998 had survived and were now residing on the Romulan ships.

"I've been giving it a good deal of thought, Calhoun," said Hiren, who had taken to addressing Mac by his place of origin, the closest thing to a family name that Xenexians had. "I believe that we are stronger together than separate."

"As do I," said Mac. "Except I have no interest in constantly struggling for power with you."

Hiren gazed at the survivors of his race. "I've begun to think," he said, "that power may be overrated. I think I have lost my taste for it of late. I am perfectly willing to defer to your judgment in all matters having to do with the safety and survival of our fleet."

"Our fleet?"

"Yours . . . Commodore Calhoun."

Mac raised an eyebrow. "*Commodore* Calhoun?"

"That would be the title appropriate to one commanding a fleet."

"Perhaps," said Mac slowly, "but for some reason, I find that I prefer the title of captain. I think it suits me better."

"Whatever you say." Hiren bowed. "Captain Calhoun."

A Terrible Beauty

Jim Johnson

HISTORIAN'S NOTE: *The present-day portions of this tale are set in early 2376, two weeks after the events of* Saturn's Children *from* Star Trek Mirror Universe: Obsidian Alliances.

Jim Johnson offers profuse thanks to Marco Palmieri for the opportunity to contribute to this anthology and to the ongoing Mirror Universe saga, and to fellow authors Dave Mack and Sarah Shaw for setting the Mirror U. literary bar so very high. Jim would also like to thank Rosalind Chao, Colm Meaney, Jeffrey Combs, and Kenneth Marshall for their outstanding performances on *Star Trek: Deep Space Nine,* all of which were significant inspirations during the crafting of this story.

Jim has also contributed to the *Star Trek* literary universe through three short stories published in various *Star Trek: Strange New Worlds* anthologies ("Solemn Duty" in SNW VII; "Home Soil" in SNW 09; and his personal favorite, "Signal to Noise," in SNW10).

Jim's other published works include a novella titled "Lifting the Gingham Veil" in the *Tales of the Seven Dogs Society* anthology published by Abstract Nova and a big chunk of wordage contributed to the forthcoming *EVE Storytelling Game* by White Wolf Publishing. He has a number of original fiction works completed or in progress as well, including several novels and dozens of short stories.

Jim is a proud member of SFWA (www.sfwa.org) and IAMTW (www.iamtw.org), and is a founding member of the Paneranormal Society, a small group of writers living in and around the D.C. Metro area. When he's not writing, Jim works with local community theater groups (usually as an actor or a playwright) and bleeds burgundy and gold following his beloved Washington Redskins. He lives in Virginia with his wife, Andi, several cats, and a chestnut mare that thrives on cookies, carrots, and starlight mints.

For the latest news and even more randomness, visit Jim's official webstite at www.popcornfalls.com. It might even be updated by the time you get there.

"The important thing is this: To be able at any moment to sacrifice what we are for what we could become." —Charles DuBois

2358

Keiko Ishikawa ducked under a slave's lazy swing and drove her elbow into his stomach. Before she had a chance to follow up her attack, she was grabbed from behind and pushed to the ground.

Heavy boots swarmed all around her. Disruptor fire crashed into the mining shaft's ceiling. Dirt and pebbles showered her and the others around her. Fine dust got into her nose, and she stifled a sneeze.

A gruff voice yelled out, "That's enough!"

The noise all around her, reverberating off the narrow corridor, abated as the handful of slaves were corraled. A Cardassian guard she knew by sight but not by name reached down to grab her arm. He pulled her to her feet. Keiko got her legs underneath her and used the Cardassian's arm to help steady herself.

The Cardassian pushed her against the wall. "Explain yourself."

Keiko wiped the dirt and blood from her face and pointed at the slave she had been fighting. A fat Klingon held him facedown against the hard stone floor. "That one threatened me if I didn't do what he wanted."

The Cardassian glanced at the slave in question. "What did he ask you to do?"

"Submit to him, sexually. I told him I preferred Cardassians." She offered him a lascivious wink.

He laughed, then, without warning, backhanded her across the face. Surprised, she pressed her hands against her stinging cheek.

He glared at her, then moved toward the slave on the ground. He gestured to the Klingon to pull him to his feet.

Once upright, the slave spat into the Cardassian's face. "You don't care how we slaves live. As long as we meet our ore quotas."

The Cardassian drove the butt of his disruptor into the slave's stomach, doubling him over. "Of course we care. We're here to look out for your best interests."

The guards around him traded rough laughter. The Cardassian pulled the slave's head up and glanced at the designation on his chest. "Eight-seven-Gamma. You've been a problem ever since you got here."

The slave shook his head and pointed at Keiko. "She's the problem, not me!"

The Cardassian shook his head and leveled his disruptor at the slave. "She's much more attractive than you." He pulled the trigger and shot the man in the chest.

As the slave crumpled to the ground, the Cardassian said, "If you people have all this time to go after each other, we'll increase your workloads. Consider all of your quotas doubled for the rest of the week. Any of you who fail to meet them will end up like this one." He gestured at the writhing slave with the barrel of his disruptor.

Groans and sighs met his statement, but the remainder of the slaves went back to work, heads bowed and backs bent in reluctant obedience. They all carefully avoided looking at the wounded slave. Keiko retrieved her mining gear and started to head back to her place in line, but the Cardassian grabbed her arm and pulled her down the corridor, out of sight of the others.

He pushed her against the wall and kissed her. She responded by dropping her tools and wrapping her arms around his neck. She leaned into his kiss.

Finally, he broke off the embrace. "I don't like shooting slaves. It's bad for morale."

Keiko nuzzled the ridges of his neck. "The one you shot has been sowing dissent. He did it on the transport when we arrived a month ago, too. I imagine what you did will send him a warning to stop."

The Cardassian stepped back and dusted off his armor. "Why would you turn in one of your own?"

Keiko shrugged and brushed what dirt she could off her miner's overalls. "Our life is hard enough without someone giving us false hope. I don't want to be here, but I'll make the best of it if I can. If we were to listen to what he said, we'd all end up in worse shape. Maybe even dead."

The Cardassian nodded. "You keep pointing out the dissenters like that, and you might make your life here a little more bearable."

Keiko offered a tentative smile. "Really?"

The Cardassian shrugged. "Possibly. Who knows? Maybe I'm the one giving you false hope now." He gestured toward the mining tunnel. "Go on, get back to work. Expect me tonight."

She nodded in deference. She picked up her mining tools and left him without looking back. She schooled her features to keep a smile from spreading across her face. She'd been on the Korvat mining colony for less than a month, and she had already made inroads with one of the guards, the first step in her larger plan. Some had questioned whether her skills were complete, and now she was well on her way to proving just how complete they were.

2376

Keiko stared out the viewport of Terok Nor's wardroom and tried
to tune out the argument volleying back and forth between Miles
O'Brien and Michael Eddington. The two of them had been going
at it for fifteen minutes, and the constant barrage pounded on the
remnants of her overextended nerves.

She crossed her arms and gazed past the station's docking ring,
focusing on the green-blue planet of Bajor the station orbited.
Keiko wondered if anyone on the planet would detect what was
about to happen, but suspected they would not. The last thing anyone in the Alliance would be looking for would be . . .

"Keiko!"

She started, not enough to move but sufficient to derail her
train of thought. She turned to face Miles, the man she loved and,
perhaps more important, the leader of the Terran rebellion. He
stared at her with poorly disguised frustration, an expression she'd
grown accustomed to seeing on his face in recent days.

She said, "I'm sorry, Miles."

Miles braced his arms against the wardroom table. "Did you
hear anything I just said?"

Keiko uncrossed her arms and moved next to her chair. She
actually hadn't heard what he had said, but she guessed at the
gist of it.

"Of course. You're concerned about the Alliance movements
in this sector, and you believe that our hidden forces in the Badlands won't be sufficient to counter their advances."

Miles, who looked as if he were going to launch into one of his
tirades, blinked as if in surprise. "Right, that's right. If these dispatches are accurate"—he indicated a pile of datapads in front of
him—"our people are going to be outgunned at least four to one."

Eddington leaned back in his chair and steepled his fingers.
"Those reports were compiled by very reliable sources."

Miles slammed a hand against the table. A couple of the padds
jumped. "That's not the point. The point is, I don't know how

we're going to bolster our defenses. Thanks to Zek and Bashir." He all but spat out their names.

Keiko raised a hand. "Thanks to Zek and Bashir, we're limited in our options. That should make things easier, not more difficult."

Miles stared at her, then nodded and sat down with a sigh. "I guess so. It's just that it's been so damn hard to think straight lately."

Keiko nodded and took her own seat. "I know, Miles. We've all been running ragged these last two weeks. It's fortunate the Alliance didn't follow up their attack on Empok Nor with an assault on this station. We'd be in even worse shape than we are now."

Eddington folded his hands into his lap and nodded. "Probably true." He glanced at Miles. "Should we start again, from the top?"

A sudden explosion shook the room. The klaxons sounded, and the lighting changed to display alert status. A rough voice filtered over the comm system, calling all senior officers to ops. Keiko joined Miles and Eddington in rushing up to the station's command center.

There, Luther Sloan worked at the tactical station. Leeta was at an engineering panel, and there were a handful of others hard at work.

Sloan glanced at the three of them as they piled off the lift. "There's been an explosion in engineering. We've lost long-range sensors."

"What about the backups?" asked Eddington.

Miles said, "I had them taken offline this morning for overhaul." He glanced at Keiko—it had been her idea.

"They were long overdue," she said. "And the mains showed no signs of problems."

Miles shook his head and turned to Sloan. "Any other damage? Any casualties?"

Sloan worked his console, then shook his head. "No one was scheduled to be in the immediate area when the explosion occurred. There is minor damage to supporting systems but nothing we can't handle. The long-range sensors are the most affected system."

Miles considered that. "Any idea what caused the explosion? A power failure, something else?"

Leeta looked up from her panel. "Hard to tell. Internal sensors for that area are unavailable. We'll have to get a team down there to check it out."

Miles nodded. "Probably just a relay blowing out. Those Cardassians never could build a reliable power-transfer conduit."

Eddington cleared his throat. "There's another possibility we should consider."

Keiko turned to him. "What's that?"

Eddington stared at Miles. "This may be the prelude to an Alliance assault. We did discuss the possibility that an attack on this station might be preceded by an act of sabotage."

Miles clenched his hands on the central ops table. "I can't believe that. We may have been spinning our wheels for the past two weeks, but there's no way our screening process could have missed an Alliance operative here on the station."

Keiko rested a comforting hand on his shoulder. "While that may be true, I don't think we have the luxury to discount the possibility. If the explosion was the result of sabotage, it's likely an Alliance attack is imminent." She gave him a steady look and added, "We need to be ready for that attack."

Miles stared into her eyes, then nodded.

Keiko turned to Eddington. "Michael, let's gather up a scanning team and go see what we can find." She returned her gaze to Miles. "You can start getting the rest of the station ready for a fight."

Keiko gave Miles a quick peck on the cheek, then moved toward the lift with Eddington. Before they left, Miles said, "If this is sabotage, I want you to find out who it is and hold them until I've had a chance to have a little chat with them."

Keiko traded a look with Eddington and gave her lover a nod before the descending lift blocked him from her view.

2361

Glinn Broca pushed Keiko to her knees. She managed to flex her legs just enough to avoid the worst of the impact on the hard stone floor, but it still hurt like hell. There were plenty of thick, comfortable-looking rugs in Gul Zarale's antechamber, but they weren't for slaves—only the cold, unyielding floor for her and her kind.

Broca pressed a hand hard against the back of her neck and leaned in close. "I'm not sure how you persuaded me to do this, but if you so much as look at the gul cross-eyed, I'll hurt you in ways you haven't dreamed."

Keiko dropped her eyes to the flagstones and nodded. She folded her hands in her lap and settled her rear on her ankles, trying to take what weight she could off her knees. Having her knees and ankles driven into the cold floor was perhaps more painful than any torture Broca could devise, but she didn't vocalize the thought. Broca wasn't all that creative—she knew that much from the past three years of cultivating him—but now was not the time to test him.

Apparently satisfied, Broca stood and crossed in front of her. He knocked on the door leading to Gul Zarale's inner chambers. After a long pause, a muffled voice from within said, "Enter."

Broca glanced at Keiko, as if to remind her of his threat, then opened the door and stepped into the room beyond. He shut the heavy wooden door behind him, leaving Keiko to stare at the unexpectedly attractive bas-relief carved into it. The Cardassians may not have a lot of imagination when it came to inflicting pain, but they had an interesting artistic style.

She heard a muffled conversation through the door, but the two Cardassians talked low enough that she wasn't able to make out the specifics. The tone of the discussion suggested that Zarale was at least intrigued by what Broca had to say. Keiko would have expected yelling and a dismissed Broca otherwise.

She returned her gaze to the floor when she heard the voices move closer. The door swung open, and two pairs of heavy Cardassian boots moved into her field of vision. One pair she recognized as Broca's—they'd decorated the floor of her hovel often enough.

The other boots were immaculate, shining with an odd metallic luster. Keiko pursed her lips. Gul Zarale had a bit of vanity, then. She'd suspected it for some time, seeing as he had never bothered to enter the mines or the slave pens in at least her four years on Korvat.

Filing away that piece of data, Keiko shifted her eyes to watch Zarale's boots as they moved to her right and then out of her line of sight. Zarale was circling her, looking her over, evaluating her.

In a deep, confident voice, Zarale said, "So, this is the slave who had the temerity to request an audience?"

Keiko sensed the question wasn't for her, so she kept her hands folded in her lap and her eyes aimed at the flagstones.

Broca said, "Yes, sir. She told me she had some important information and that she'd share it only with you."

Zarale's boots entered Keiko's field of vision again and moved to stop in front of her. "Indeed? And why did you not simply beat this important information out of her?"

Broca cleared his throat. "This one has proven to be . . . useful . . . over the last few years. I thought perhaps you would wish to hear it from her personally. I can vouch for her good conduct in your presence."

Zarale grunted. "Well, slave? What information is so important that you need to tell it to me personally?"

Keiko straightened her back, sitting high on her haunches. "If it please you, Gul, it is a matter concerning Overseer Kozak and his slave gangs."

Zarale's boots moved closer to her. "Indeed? And what important information would a little slave girl have about one of my overseers?"

Keiko risked lifting her head to meet Zarale's eyes. In a steady tone, she said, "I have reason to believe that some of the slaves under his management are planning to . . . rcmove him." She held his gaze, willing herself not to look away.

Zarale pursed his lips and made a noncommittal sound. He leaned down to trail one thick finger along Keiko's jaw line. She didn't flinch back, didn't move a centimeter. She widened her eyes just so, inviting Zarale closer, slowly spinning her web.

Zarale said, "And why would I care if a few dirty slaves tried to harm my overseer? They should know better than to imagine they could ever succeed."

Keiko gave Zarale a languid blink before responding. "If this were merely a couple of slaves, of course it would not be worthy of your attention, Gul Zarale, but I can prove that the plot is much more extensive than that. There are at least a dozen slaves planning to kill Kozak."

Zarale cupped his hand under her chin and moved her head from side to side, as if he were inspecting a piece of succulent fruit or perhaps judging livestock. He glanced at Broca. "This one is lovely. How do you think she manages to stay so clean in those dark, dirty mines?"

Zarale chuckled, clearly not expecting an answer. Broca offered a laugh, but a glare from Zarale stopped him in mid-guffaw. Zarale pressed his hand against Keiko's jaw, encouraging her to rise to her feet.

She did so, slowly, letting each limb stretch and shift the folds of her clothing. She had worn a loose-fitting tunic today, anticipating that the rumors about Zarale's taste for attractive female flesh regardless of species were accurate. She had known she would be on display for Zarale and needed to give him a good show.

Judging from the subtle change in his coloration and the slight widening of his eyes, she was succeeding. He nodded at her and indicated that she should turn around. She did so, careful to adjust her position in such a way as to show off her curves. She spared a glance at Broca as she conducted the display and noted that he was as engrossed in her as Zarale was.

She finished her rotation and stared into Zarale's eyes, offering a questioning glance. Zarale's smile widened as he raked his eyes over her frame.

"Tell me, Glinn, is this one familiar with how we Cardassians prefer our women?"

Broca cleared his throat. Keiko suspected he hadn't anticipated the question. "Ah, yes, Gul Zarale. She has proven to be most capable in that respect."

Zarale lifted an eye ridge at that. "Indeed? Well, then." He clasped his hands together and addressed Keiko. "You will provide Glinn Broca with the details of this slave uprising. We must not let our dear Overseer Kozak come to harm, now, must we?" He offered her a toothy grin and turned to Broca.

"Take her information, gather up the slaves she names, and eliminate them."

Broca nodded, but Keiko cleared her throat. She offered Zarale her winningest smile. "May I dare ask a boon of you, Gul Zarale?" He seemed to like the way she said his name.

He indulged her with another smile and crossed his arms. "This should be interesting."

She took a deep breath, as if to steel herself for her request. "I am led to understand that productivity in Overseer Kozak's section has been less than sufficient for your needs." Zarale's eyes darkened, so Keiko pressed on. "I believe it would be far more effective to discipline these slaves than to kill them. Kozak has had more than thirty slaves killed in the last two months. His methods are, shall we say, less than effective."

Zarale's face dropped into a glower. "Do you presume to tell me how to run my mining colony, slave?"

Keiko shook her head slowly. "Of course not, Gul Zarale." She held his gaze a moment longer, then dropped her gaze back to the floor.

Long seconds passed, and Keiko feared that she'd be tossed out of his quarters. Instead, Zarale chuckled again. "You prove most interesting, little one. I will order Broca merely to discipline these slaves. In return for this gift, you will make yourself available to me whenever I may have cause to call upon you."

Keiko forced herself not to smile. She injected what bright-eyed innocence she could muster into her expression and raised her head to meet his gaze. "Thank you, mighty Gul."

Zarale's smile widened. He turned to Broca. "You heard me, Glinn. Gather the slaves she names, and have them disciplined. But not killed. Should I hear that one of them died under punishment, you'll be working the mines right alongside them."

Broca nodded in acquiescence, then led Keiko out of the chamber. Keiko gave Zarale one last inviting smile and followed Broca out of the room, grinning inwardly at all of the prospects ahead of her.

2376

Keiko leaned down to place a scanner in Eddington's outstretched hand. His hand disappeared under the ruined machinery that had once been one of the power relays of Terok Nor's primary long-range sensors. Keiko stood up straight to stretch out her sore back muscles. She brushed her sweat-soaked hair away from her face. The explosion had also taken out the local temperature regulators.

She glanced in the direction of the other power generator in this section and gave Shar what she hoped was an encouraging smile. The Andorian stared at her, the antennae sprouting from his short-cropped white hair flicking back and forth. She hadn't known him all that long, Shar being one of the station's newest arrivals, so she attributed the action to annoyance. She pursed her lips. Truth be told, Shar always seemed to be annoyed.

Eddington pulled himself out from under the machinery. Keiko took the scanner back from him and examined the data displayed on the small screen. Eddington rested his greasy arms on his knees and glanced up at her. "Well, I'm no expert, but the damage doesn't appear to be as severe as it could have been."

Keiko turned her attention to him. "How so?"

Eddington shrugged and pulled himself to his feet. "My guess is that whoever did this was either in a rush or just didn't know much about Cardassian power generators."

Keiko frowned as she thumbed through the data contained in the scanner. "So, you're confident we have a saboteur to thank for this?"

Eddington nodded and started to put his tools away. "No doubt about it. I found a few pieces of the detonator, and there are traces of sarium krellide all over the place." He snapped shut his toolkit. "We have a saboteur onboard, and a sloppy one at that."

Keiko shook her head and offered him the scanner. "Just what we need."

"General, you're going to want to take a look at this." Keiko and Eddington turned toward the sound of the muffled voice. A pair of boots, a pair of legs, a long torso, then two gloved hands emerged from underneath the second generator, followed by the mottled alien face and copper-red hair belonging to Tiron.

Tiron reached under the machinery and carefully pulled out a small, sinister-looking device. He handed it up to Shar, who took it gingerly, his antennae in constant motion.

Keiko moved over to the two of them. "What did you find?"

Tiron wiped the sweat from his pronounced forehead with the back of his gloved hand. "A second explosive device."

Shar's antennae flattened against his head, and he offered the thing back to Tiron, who took it with a smirk. "It's inoperative, Shar. Nothing to fret over."

Tiron rotated the bomb to show Keiko the detonator. "This has to be one of the most amateur devices I have ever seen. The saboteur used a power cell too weak to bridge the final connection."

Eddington moved over to them and took the device in order to get a closer look. "Rather fortuitous for us, I suppose." He frowned. "It's not like an Alliance operative to make such an error."

Tiron stared past Eddington, finding and holding Keiko's gaze. "Quite so, General. Perhaps the saboteur was indeed in a rush. Or"—he inclined his head toward Keiko—"perhaps the saboteur left this one to be found on purpose."

Eddington glanced in the direction of Tiron's gaze and gave Keiko a puzzled look. Shar followed Tiron's look and stared at Keiko. Keiko focused on Tiron. "You have something to say?"

The corners of Tiron's mouth quirked up. "I seem to recall you leading a repair team in this section a couple of days ago."

Keiko crossed her arms and nodded. "And? I'm afraid I'm missing your point, Tiron."

Eddington angled an eyebrow upward and glanced at Tiron. "Yes, Tiron. What's your point? You're not accusing Keiko of working for the Alliance. I thought we'd heard the last of that nonsense."

Tiron met Eddington's glance. "Have we, General?" He turned his piercing gaze over to Shar. "Isn't it convenient that most of her detractors ended up on Empok Nor just in time for the Alliance attack? And isn't it convenient that none of them has returned from that . . . abominable disaster?"

Keiko traded an amazed look with Eddington. She glanced at Shar and frowned. The Andorian's face had flushed a new shade of blue, and his antennae were at attention. Clearly, he was considering Tiron's words with great interest.

Keiko asked, "You are not suggesting that I had anything to do with that disaster?"

Tiron shot Shar a significant look. "What I'm suggesting, Miss Ishikawa, is that an Alliance collaborator shouldn't be leading this security investigation, much less be living on this station."

Shar took an aggressive step toward Keiko, but Eddington blocked his path.

Eddington said, "Just a moment, Shar!" He turned to Tiron. "Do you have any proof to back this up, or is this just more of your pointless posturing?"

Tiron sucked in his breath, as if stunned. He spread his hands in a supplicating gesture. "My dear General, this is nothing of the sort. And I'm devastated that you would think so."

Eddington shook his head. "We are not going to discuss this

here." He glanced at Keiko. "I'm confident this is a misunder-standing."

Keiko looked at Shar, who looked ready to break something, and then at Tiron, who looked rather annoyed. She said, "We're all going back to ops to discuss this with General O'Brien. In private."

Eddington nodded. "Good idea. Let's get this resolved quickly, before the speculation moves beyond the four of us." He glared at Tiron, then led the way toward ops.

As the four of them left the generators behind, Keiko glanced over her shoulder and stared hard at Tiron, who met her gaze with a wide grin.

2365

Keiko moved down Korvat's narrow mining corridors, a pair of Cardassian guards following in her wake. She gathered up the folds of her expensive, diaphanous skirt, keeping it from brushing against the worst of the dirt and grime that pervaded every crag and cranny of the mine. Zarale had bought the skirt for her, and she didn't want to damage it.

Zarale. She'd left him behind in their quarters, sated and asleep. She'd worked hard over the last four years, bending Zarale to her wiles, and only hers. All of his other comfort women had found themselves either placed back in the mines or sent off-colony, their services to the gul no longer required.

In that span of time, Keiko had also worked herself into Zarale's confidence, enough that she was able to issue orders to the guards under his command as if they were her own. The only person she had been unable to influence, the only person who had refused her particular talents, was that Klingon overseer, the drunkard Kozak.

And she was on her way now to take care of him.

Kozak had been the overseer when Keiko first arrived at Korvat and had only changed for the worse in that span of time. He drank too much bloodwine, enjoyed the benefits of his position far too much, and spent far too much time in the beds of various and sundry slaves. The result of his excesses added up to a mining colony operating at far less than peak productivity.

Keiko turned a corner, brushing past slaves dozing where they worked. Keiko had examined the most recent status reports while Zarale bathed. Korvat colony was in the mid-range percentile of delivering ore. Not enough to garner immediate interest from the Alliance command but enough to set off alarms through Keiko's mind. She had worked too hard here to see it all wiped away if the Alliance decided to remove Zarale and replace him with someone new. Keiko had invested too much time and effort to lose it all in the dregs of some Klingon's cup.

Keiko stopped in front of a slave's hovel, a thin curtain pulled across its entrance. Grunts and moans filtered through the curtain. She nodded at the two Cardassian guards. They drew their disruptors, and then one of them reached out to draw back the curtain. The reek of low-grade bloodwine wafted out of the revealed chamber, forcing Keiko back a half-step. The foul thing must bathe in it, judging from the stench. Kozak lay sprawled out on the hovel's cot, naked save for his boots. A thin young Bolian woman leaped off him and rolled into a thick fur blanket, staring toward Keiko with embarrassed surprise.

Keiko glanced at the girl. Kozak was breaking in a new slave. She recalled the latest list of arrivals, remembering that it contained a small contingent of Bolians, Andorians, and members of other assorted species. Not the most ideal welcome to Korvat, but then again, what was?

Kozak lifted his head from the thin mattress and turned glazed eyes toward Keiko. "Mwuh-uh?" He belched.

The guards gave her a questioning glance, and she nodded. The two of them aimed their disruptors at Kozak. The Klingon frowned, his ardor deflating.

Keiko said, "Overseer Kozak, you have been found derelict in your duties and are hereby relieved of your station by order of the commander of this facility, Gul Zarale."

She stepped back. Kozak managed to utter another unintelligible grunt before the two Cardassians shot him dead. Keiko imagined he'd have a hard time getting into Sto'Vo'Kor in his condition.

Their duty done, the guards holstered their weapons and dragged Kozak's corpse out of the Bolian's hovel. Keiko glanced at the Bolian, whose black eyes bulged out of her powdery blue face. Keiko shrugged and said, "Welcome to Korvat colony. Things will improve for you."

Keiko turned away from her and followed the two Cardassians toward the main slave assembly chamber. They deposited Kozak's body in the rough center of the room and then took up protective stances next to Keiko. Some two dozen slaves filtered in, shooting one another confused or speculative looks.

Keiko cleared her throat, getting their collective attention. She gestured at Kozak. "Overseer Kozak has been relieved of duty. I am your new overseer. From here on, you will answer to me. Work hard, and you will be rewarded. Slack off, and you will be punished."

She passed an even glance over them all, saw a mixture of expressions on their faces. Some bold, some compliant, some despairing, some resigned. She pointed at a handful of the more defiant-looking ones.

"You, you, and you. Dispose of that." She indicated Kozak's body. She swept a final glance over the rest of the slaves, all now her responsibility. "The rest of you, get back to work."

The three slaves she had indicated stepped out of the crowd and approached Kozak's body. One of them, easily recognizable from his shock of coppery-orange hair, met her eyes. "Madame Overseer."

She nudged her chin toward him. "What is your designation?"

He glanced at the other two slaves as they gathered up Kozak's remains. He turned back to her and, in a voice laced with anger, growled, "Tiron."

Keiko inclined her head. "Slaves don't have names. What is your designation?"

The man stood up straighter, fixed his bright blue eyes on her. "My name is Tiron."

She glanced at one of the guards and nodded. The Cardassian glared into Tiron's face and slammed a fist into the slave's stomach. Tiron doubled over with a wheeze. The Cardassian brought his clenched fists crashing down onto Tiron's back, knocking him to his knees. The other guard aimed a kick at Tiron's chest. The impact flipped Tiron onto his back. He curled up into a ball, gasping for breath.

Keiko waved off the two Cardassians. She didn't want this one dead. He had some strength in him that might prove useful someday. She leaned down close, so that only he could hear. "You may have a future here, Tiron, so I suggest you relearn your slave designation and remember it."

He cracked open one eye and gave her a myopic look of sheer hate. She gave him a brief nod and swept out of the rough-hewn chamber, her Cardassian guards falling into step behind her.

2376

"No! There's no bloody way!" Miles slammed his hands down on the large desk in his office. Everyone assembled in front of him flinched.

Miles pointed at Tiron. "There's no way Keiko is working for the Alliance."

Keiko kept her eyes forward, looking at Miles, but out of the corner of her eye, she saw Tiron glance at Eddington and then Shar, as if looking for support. She moved her head slightly to get a better look at the three of them. Shar looked as if he were ready to take a swing at someone, whether it was Keiko or someone else, she didn't think he cared. Eddington looked more thoughtful, and Tiron, of course, was attempting to make his point in the most obsequious manner possible.

Tiron spread out his hands in that infuriating supplicating gesture of his. "General O'Brien"—his voice silk over velvet—"consider, for just a moment, the facts."

O'Brien leaned toward him. "Facts? What facts?"

Tiron raised his palms toward Miles. "The facts. Miss Ishikawa led a work detail in the sabotaged area just a few days ago. Miss Ishikawa was the slave overseer at the Korvat mining colony for more than a decade. Surely, the intelligence we've appropriated from the Alliance can verify that."

Eddington said, "That's beside the point, Tiron. No matter what she may have done in the past, Keiko has proven herself time and again to our cause."

Miles stabbed a finger toward Tiron. "Do you have any proof to back up your claim, or what? You've had a poor opinion of Keiko ever since you arrived on the station. I don't need to remind you that you were a refugee on the same transport Keiko brought here from Korvat."

Tiron nodded, clasping his hands behind his back. "Yes, I was aboard that transport. However, I believe that the entire slave liberation was a carefully staged stunt."

Miles alternated a look between Keiko and Tiron. "Staged? What the hell for?"

Shar bristled. "Perhaps for just this reason. Perhaps it was staged to get Ishikawa into a position of importance."

Tiron nodded. "And here she is, right at the heart of the rebellion."

Miles furrowed his brow. Keiko knew his looks well enough to know that he wasn't convinced, but he wasn't ignoring what he was hearing, either.

She said, "I have never been, nor will I ever be, an Alliance agent. My cause is your cause: freedom from the Alliance."

Miles glanced at her and nodded. Tiron took a half-step toward the desk and Miles. "At least, allow General Eddington and Shar to ask her a few questions, in a controlled environment. Surely, there is no harm in that."

Keiko covered a flinch by crossing her arms in front of her. "I'm first officer of this station, and I will not be treated like a criminal." She turned to Miles. "You can't allow this."

Miles glanced at her, then back to Tiron. "Keiko is not an agent. I'm done with this conversation."

Tiron turned to Eddington. "General, I spent many years in Korvat colony. In that time, I saw Ishikawa manipulate more than one man. I fear that General O'Brien may be likewise influenced."

Miles launched himself over the desk toward Tiron and hit him with a powerful right hook. Tiron slammed into Shar, and the two of them crashed to the deck in a pile of flailing limbs. Eddington managed to grab hold of O'Brien to keep him off Tiron. Keiko did her best to avoid the melee.

She glanced out the windows of the office doors, down toward ops. Several faces were aimed in her general direction. The personnel at work at their stations were starting to take notice of the commotion in the general's office. Sloan yelled something at Leeta, then grabbed a disruptor from somewhere. He moved toward the stairs outside the office door.

Keiko turned back to the ongoing fight. Eddington had Miles in a lock, preventing him from going after Tiron. Miles yelled at Eddington to let him go. Tiron and Shar were struggling on the deck, fighting over something. Keiko's eyes widened when she saw that Tiron had Shar's disruptor in his hand.

Shar swatted at Tiron's hands, but Tiron managed to avoid the motion and took aim at Keiko. He cried out something about traitors and fired. Keiko saw a sudden flash of yellow energy, felt a searing pain drill into her stomach, and then she was staggering backward.

Her head hit something unyielding. The deck rushed up toward her while a variety of constellations starred her vision. The patterns spiraled around, blurred, and then winked out.

• • •

The quiet chirp of a biomonitor roused Keiko out of the cottony darkness. She cracked open one eye and found it was dim, wherever she was. Confident that she wouldn't be blinded by a bright light in her face, she opened her eyes. She shifted her weight but groaned when the movement sent a spark of pain across her shoulders.

Miles moved into her field of vision, smiling tenderly down at her. She felt him take one of her hands in his and squeeze, the warmth of the action comforting.

"There you are," he said. "The medics weren't sure how soon you'd come around." He sat down next to her, presumably on a chair out of her field of view.

She offered a weary smile. "How long was I out?"

Miles glanced at his chrono. "Maybe three hours, four at the most."

Keiko nodded, but the motion sent another stab of pain down her neck. She winced.

The expression on Miles's face dropped. "Keiko? Are you all right?" He turned toward the far end of the Infirmary. "Bowers!"

Keiko squeezed his hand. "No, Miles. I'm all right. Just a bit sore."

Sam Bowers, serving double duty as a medic, joined them at the edge of her bed. "You're awake. That's good. Try not to exert yourself." He glanced at the readings on the monitor. "Are you in any pain?"

"Headache."

"You've got a mild concussion. I'll get you something to take the edge off."

Keiko glanced up at Sam in appreciation. He moved away, leaving her and Miles alone. Miles settled himself more comfortably next to her.

"I got you here as soon as I could after Tiron shot you. Bowers thinks you were lucky. Tiron missed your heart by about a dozen centimeters."

Keiko managed another weary smile. "Then I'm glad Tiron can't shoot as well as he talks." She paused. "Where is he now?"

Miles glanced toward the entrance of the infirmary, as if he could track Tiron wherever he was on the station. His expression darkened. "Shar and Eddington have him in a cell."

Keiko frowned. "Interrogating him?" The guess was probably a good one, all things considered.

Miles nodded. "Our people don't go shooting each other for dodgy reasons. They're . . . discussing the matter with him."

Keiko squeezed his hand. "Please don't let them kill him."

Miles stared at her, surprise evident in his eyes. "Keiko, the man tried to kill you."

Keiko shook her head slowly, so as not to invite another jolt of pain. "I'd like to talk to him. Give him a chance to explain himself to my face."

His frown deepened. "I don't know if that's such a good idea."

"Please, Miles? This is important."

Miles looked away, clearly thinking about letting her near the man who had almost killed her. She squeezed his hand again, getting his attention. "Miles. I'll be all right." She tried a grin. "I'll have Michael and Shar there to protect me in case Tiron tries anything again."

Miles returned the grin, his more wolfish than hers had been. "You're damn right about that. I'll tell them that if he so much as blinks at you funny, they're to take care of him."

Keiko stared into his eyes, scared for a reason she couldn't place. How had she been so fortunate to fall in with him? A crawling sensation wended its way down her spine. She blinked, confused. Sam returned then, distracting Keiko from her conflicting thoughts.

He reached a hypospray toward Keiko. She glanced at it. "What's that?"

"Just a mild painkiller. Nothing heavy. It won't put you to sleep."

Keiko nodded, then felt him press the instrument against her skin. It was cold to the touch. A quick hiss and a sting of pain on her neck indicated that the medicine had been administered. She felt a momentary rush, and then the aches in her head and neck dissipated to a manageable blur. Sam gave the two of them a final nod and left them alone.

Miles brushed Keiko's hair off her forehead and leaned down to give her a gentle kiss. "I'll head out so you can get some rest."

Keiko stared at him. "Wait, Miles. What about the station? Are we ready for an attack?"

Miles gave her a sidelong grin. "It's been hours, and we haven't seen anything yet. Bajor's been quiet, too. My people are working on the repairs, though. I've mobilized our forces. We're about as ready as we can be."

Keiko kept hold of his hand, keeping him from leaving just yet. "Promise me they won't kill Tiron until I've had a chance to talk to him."

Miles looked into her eyes, searching for something she couldn't guess at. Again, the look in his eyes set off a feeling of something in Keiko, but she couldn't place it. She covered her confusion with a hopeful smile.

Finally, Miles relented. "All right."

Keiko gave his hand a squeeze and pulled the thin sheet up to her chin. "Thank you, Miles." She was surprised to feel warm tears well up in her eyes.

He pursed his lips but gave her an encouraging smile, then left her alone in the infirmary. Keiko watched him leave and sighed once he was out of sight. She settled her head deeper into the pillow and frowned.

What had made her hesitate? What was that feeling she got when she looked into Miles's eyes? She stared at the ceiling for an interminable time, puzzling out her feelings. Finally, she gave up and sighed deeply. She slowly rolled her head from side to side, testing her neck muscles. The drug Sam had administered seemed to be doing its job—she no longer felt so much as a twinge.

She glanced at the entrance to the infirmary and then checked to make sure Sam was nowhere nearby. Satisfied that she was alone, she rolled onto one side and reached out to the computer next to her bed.

"Computer, recognize Keiko Ishikawa, command code six-six-nine-Delta-three."

The computer uttered a few beeps, then said, "Recognized."

Keiko stared at the wall for a time, finally nodded in determination. If she didn't carry this through, everything that had happened up to now would have been a waste.

"Enable programs Keiko One through Six. On my mark." She paused. She could still back out of this, maybe talk to Miles. He'd understand, in time, she was sure of it. She frowned. Well, maybe not all that sure.

Damn it! Why was she hesitating?

She shook her head once more and said, "Computer, mark." A couple of beeps, then a confirmation flashed on the screen before it went dark. There—it was done. She was committed.

She settled back onto the bed and glanced at the entrance to the infirmary again. She hoped that Miles would understand but found that she was actually afraid he wouldn't. She didn't like how that made her feel.

2372

Slave 296-Theta bowed to Keiko and handed her a data padd. Keiko took it and waved the slave away, sending him back to his other duties. He was one of her more recent projects and was coming along nicely. In due time, he would follow her lead without question.

She glanced down at the data padd and thumbed through the information displayed on the screen. Ore quotas were up, mining accidents were down, and a new batch of slaves awaited her review before processing. A punishment detail also awaited her sign-off. She looked at the recommendations made by 296-Theta and nodded in approval. The suggested punishments weren't too harsh, but they weren't too lenient, either. He *was* coming along nicely.

Satisfied at that, she called up the list of new slaves. This batch consisted of two dozen Terrans and a handful of other species. She pursed her lips as she scanned the list. Most of them were listed as being in good health. She had been thinking of starting up a secondary tunnel off one of the more productive mineshafts before it played out, and this new influx of personnel would almost certainly allow her to do that once they were familiarized with their new life.

She thumbed off the display screen and tucked the padd under her arm. She made her way into the central assembly area, taking in the new batch of slaves. Slave 404-Theta saw her approach and cried out, "Slaves, attention! Prepare to be addressed by Madame Overseer Ishikawa."

Keiko grimaced mentally at the title. She hated the presumption of it, but Zarale insisted that it was necessary to maintain the proper level of respect and fear. As if he'd know—Zarale had never bothered to step into the mines under his command. He was so satisfied with Keiko's management that he didn't feel it necessary to see to anything personally.

Keiko allowed herself a tiny smug smile. It was just as well. If Zarale did come down there and see what she was building, he'd probably have her stripped of rank and tossed into the mines herself. Or, worse, taken outside and shot. She was confident of her hold over him, though. As long as the ore continued to flow and the quotas continued to be met, he would be happy. Keiko had turned the whole facility around after taking over for Kozak.

She returned her attention to the slaves gathered before her and realized that she was impatient to get back to work. In a loud, clear voice, she said, "Welcome to the Korvat mining facility. This is your new home. Work hard, and you will be treated well. Fail to work, or otherwise cause problems, and you will be punished. Pay attention to the Thetas in command of your work group, and you will flourish here. That is all."

Short and sweet, just how she liked it. She nodded at 404-Theta, her signal to dismiss them.

Slave 404-Theta said, "Follow me for quarters assignment and work detail."

Keiko clasped her hands behind her back and watched them shuffle past, some of them shooting her looks that alternated between frightened and defiant. She evaluated them as they went by. Some would definitely need attitude adjustments, some looked like sheep that probably wouldn't last long, and the rest looked malleable. Not a bad batch at all.

One of the new slaves, a thin Terran with close-cropped dirty-blond hair, gave Keiko a wide-eyed look as she walked by. Keiko furrowed her brow. There was something . . .

Keiko stepped forward and pointed at the blonde before she broke eye contact. "You. Step forward."

The woman shifted her eyes to either side, then broke out of line and approached Keiko, with perhaps more confidence than Keiko would have thought likely for a slave.

Keiko glanced at the woman's designation on her filthy, baggy coveralls. "Seven-oh-one-Delta." She lowered her voice slightly. "You have something to say?"

The girl nodded once and kept her eyes focused on Keiko's feet. "Yes, Madame Overseer. I had a question for you, if I may."

Intrigued, Keiko said, "Very well. Ask your question."

The blonde raised her head, daring to look Keiko in the eyes. In a breathy whisper, the girl asked, "Would you like to learn a new technique from a love slave?"

Keiko stared at the girl, the question rolling around in her head. She consciously had to keep her mouth clenched to keep it from dropping open in shock. Keiko leaned in close. "What makes you think I need to learn anything new?"

The blonde stared into her eyes. "You've been in this facility a long time. Things change. There are new techniques you've probably never dreamed of."

Keiko held the woman's eyes, matching her smile with one of her own. Keiko inclined her head, then nodded. She turned to 404-Theta, who stood near one of the tunnel exits. Keiko indicated the blonde.

"I'm going to process this one myself. See to the others."

Slave 404-Theta nodded in silence. Keiko had occasionally singled out a slave for personal attention—this was nothing new.

Keiko turned back to the blonde and indicated the tunnel that led to a row of slave quarters. "Follow me."

Keiko waved off the two guards who normally accompanied her in the mines and led the slave into the tunnels. Most of the quarters were little more than niches with curtains covering their entrances, but some of the chambers were large enough to move around in.

Keiko stopped in front of one such chamber and pulled the curtain aside. She indicated the narrow bed revealed inside. The blonde moved past her and into the chamber, unsnapping her coveralls as she did so.

Keiko stepped in behind her and pulled the curtain closed. The new slave pulled her clothing off and slipped into the bed, covering herself with the thin sheet. Keiko glanced at the curtain, aware that guards and slaves could enter or pass by at any moment.

Keiko moved to the side of the bed and undressed quickly, then slid under the sheet with the woman. The bed, little more than a thin mattress on a metal frame, was too narrow for them to lie side by side, so Keiko put her arms around her. The blonde did likewise, hugging Keiko close so that she could whisper into her ear.

"My name is Tasha. I can't tell you how relieved I am to find you alive and well."

Keiko nodded into the embrace. "It's been a long time. Why have our friends waited so long to contact me?" She was careful to keep her voice low. Keiko rubbed Tasha's back and shoulders, playing the part in case anyone should discover them.

"I don't have those details, but I do have a message to deliver. Unfortunately, I can't read it. It's for your eyes only." Tasha nuzzled her neck, following Keiko's lead to keep up appearances.

Keiko blinked in confusion, then breathed into Tasha's ear. "By what means are you to deliver the message?"

Tasha combed her fingers through Keiko's long hair. "There's a tattoo on my leg."

Keiko nodded, impressed at the ingenuity. Tattoos were common enough among many slaves. The Alliance didn't care what Terrans did to their own bodies, as long as the work got done.

Keiko glanced at the curtain covering the entrance to their chamber, sensing a presence on the other side. She suspected they were being watched—as hard as she tried, she hadn't been able to purge all the Alliance voyeurs from her command. A few still lingered, like the one outside her curtain now.

She met Tasha's eyes and quickly glanced at the curtain, indicating to Tasha that they were being monitored. Tasha nodded imperceptibly and gently pushed Keiko's head down.

Keiko kissed Tasha's neck and shoulders, then lifted the sheet to cover her movement as she switched her orientation so that her head was near Tasha's feet. She worked her way up Tasha's legs, seeking out the tattoo Tasha had mentioned.

Tasha settled herself more comfortably on the bed and uttered a low moan. Keiko grinned under the sheet. Clearly, Tasha had been trained by T'Lara, just as Keiko had been all those years ago.

Keiko found the tattoo high up on Tasha's thigh. She shifted her weight to a more comfortable position and examined the tattoo. At first, it seemed to be nothing more than an elaborate design consisting of black whorls. On closer inspection, Keiko discovered that the tattoo was actually made up of densely packed lines of Japanese calligraphy.

Keiko grinned. She doubted there were many in the Alliance who would bother to investigate Tasha's tattoo any closer than with a surface glance, and she doubted that there were any in the Alliance who could even read the writing if they recognized it for what it was. Keiko had known of only two other people who knew how to read it, let alone write it—her mother and her honored grandmother. And her grandmother had passed on years ago.

Another low moan from Tasha broke Keiko out of her reverie. She realized that Tasha was keeping up the show, which meant that their voyeur hadn't left. Keiko needed to speed things along, before that voyeur decided to get a closer look or, worse, join in.

Our efforts proceed apace. rebellion growing in Bajor sector. Proceed with training and liberation. Destination: Terok Nor.

Keiko read it twice to make sure she got it all, then worked her way back around to face Tasha. She kissed Tasha lightly on the lips.

"Thank you for your help and your service," she whispered.

Tasha nodded breathlessly, keeping up the act. "What do we do now?"

Keiko wrapped her arms around Tasha and hugged her close, finding unexpected comfort in the embrace. Tasha was the first person she'd seen from her old world in years. "Now we form an army and get off this rock."

2376

Keiko walked the short distance from the infirmary to the security office, scratching the fabric of her blouse where it covered the healing skin underneath. The wound would heal, but the process would be an itchy distraction for some time. She paused outside the security doors, noting that she didn't see anyone in the office or at the desk.

She palmed the gift she had for Tiron and stepped into the office. As the doors closed behind her, she glanced at the screen on the wall displaying the interior of the holding cell area and winced.

Eddington and Shar circled Tiron, who was kneeling on the deck with his arms bound behind him. Dark blood trickled out of his nose and the corner of his mouth. Eddington looked as if he wished he were somewhere else, but Shar . . . Keiko shuddered at the look on the Andorian's face.

Keiko entered a few quick commands into the security monitor, altering the angle of the security pickups and deactivating the audio sensors. She took a deep breath, steeling herself for the scene she was about to unfold, and entered the holding area. All three men glanced up as the warning bell sounded, announcing that someone had entered the room.

Eddington nodded at her. "I'm glad to see you're up and about. Feeling better?"

Keiko answered with a nod and crossed her arms in front of her chest, keeping a fair distance from the bound Tiron.

Shar glanced at her, then returned his attention to Tiron. "O'Brien told us to save a piece of him for you."

She nodded again. "I wanted a chance to talk to him before . . . before you finished with him."

Tiron gave her a wide-eyed look, no doubt reading the subtext of her statement.

Eddington gestured at the prisoner and said, "You're more than welcome to talk to him. There's not much he can say in his defense, though." Keiko gave him a questioning glance. Eddington explained, "He's all but confessed to doing this on his own. He's not an Alliance operative. He's simply a former slave with a vendetta against you."

Tiron started to stand in protest, but a sudden backhand from Shar sent him crashing back to the deck. Tiron looked up at her, desperation evident in his bloodshot eyes.

"Please, Keiko! What they're saying isn't true!"

Shar sneered and kicked Tiron in the stomach. "Shut up! We have all the evidence we need." He pressed his boot down on Tiron's neck.

Keiko turned to Eddington. "Evidence?"

Eddington nodded. "Sloan contacted us about a half-hour ago. He went through Tiron's quarters and found his personal files." He glanced down at Tiron. "They're sufficiently incriminating."

Keiko shook her head. "What did Miles have to say?"

Eddington shrugged. "He wasn't happy, that's for sure. But he told me to take care of this for him. He's busy reallocating the resources he gathered for the Alliance attack we thought was coming."

"Could we have pulled off an adequate defense?"

Eddington nodded. "Miles managed to move a lot of things ahead of schedule and called in some markers I didn't know he had. We could have defended the station long enough to get everyone evacuated. I don't know if you'd classify that as an adequate defense, but it's better than what we had earlier in the day."

Keiko nodded, relieved. It had worked. She looked down on Tiron. "I'd like to have a minute with him, alone."

Shar stared at her as he ground his boot against Tiron's neck. "Do you think that's such a good idea?"

Keiko nodded. "I'll be all right. You two will just be in the next room, right?"

Eddington asked, "Are you sure?"

"I just want to hear him tell me why he did all of this." Keiko moved over to Tiron, waving Shar away. She pushed Tiron over onto his back with a carefully aimed kick. "Trust me, I have this under control."

Eddington gave her a doubtful look but nodded to Shar and led him out of the holding area. Keiko watched the door close and turned to Tiron.

"You've certainly made a mess of things."

Tiron managed to roll over onto his side, blood dripping off his face and onto the deck. He offered a weak smile. "I have, at that."

Keiko walked around him in a circle, then stopped and kneeled down next to Tiron, using her body to block him from the cameras.

She leaned in and, in a low voice, said, "I can't thank you enough for all of the services you have done for me."

Tiron looked at her with hope in his eyes, an odd counterpoint to the trickles of blood on his face. In a quavering voice, he asked, "Did everything turn out the way you intended it to?"

Keiko nodded, offering Tiron a gentle smile. "You did well, Tiron."

She raised her hand and presented her gift to him, a small green capsule. "This is for you."

He glanced at it, then at her. "How long will I have?"

She held his gaze. "About an hour. Do you think you can hold out for that long?"

Tiron glanced at the door Eddington and Shar had gone though, then back to Keiko. He nodded. "I suffered worse at the hands of Kozak. I can handle this well enough."

Keiko frowned. "I wish you didn't have to, but I don't know of another way."

Tiron shook his head. "Freedom doesn't come without its price, Keiko. I'll be all right. Give me the pill."

She stared into his eyes, finally nodded. She placed the capsule in his mouth and leaned down to give him a chaste kiss. She leaned back on her haunches and watched as he dry-swallowed the pill and grimaced.

She stood and said, "Thank you again, Tiron. Good luck. I hope we can meet again someday under better circumstances."

He looked up at her and nodded in silence. A film started to crawl over his eyes—the drug was taking effect. She gave him a final nod, then joined Shar and Eddington in the security office.

Eddington stared at her as she walked in. He put a hand on Shar's shoulder and said, "Go see to the prisoner."

Shar gave Keiko an ugly grin and pushed past her. Once the door had closed behind him, Eddington turned to Keiko.

"Care to tell me why you altered the angle of the security cameras and deactivated the audio pickups?"

Keiko pursed her lips. "I needed to talk to Tiron, and I didn't want an audience."

Eddington stroked his chin as his frown deepened. "Keiko, I

didn't want to say anything in front of Shar, but something about this whole situation just doesn't feel right."

Keiko sighed. Eddington was no idiot. She gave him a tired smile. "A lot of things don't feel right, Michael." She walked past him toward the main doors, which opened as she approached. He didn't offer another comment, so she walked out onto the Promenade and didn't look back.

2375

Tiron pulled Keiko out of the line of fire and pressed her against the side of the rough-hewn mineshaft. "That way's blocked off, Keiko! Where do we go now?"

Keiko glanced past Tiron and saw a handful of guards, a mix of Cardassians and Klingons, working their way toward her group's position, firing their weapons with indiscriminate glee. "We'll have to go the other way around. At least, we know the way behind us is clear."

Tiron nodded and moved past her back down the corridor. Keiko and a couple of her freed slaves fired their weapons toward the approaching guards. Keiko didn't check to see if they'd hit anyone—she was more interested in slowing them down at this point.

Tiron led Keiko and the others through the main assembly area and into the prefab corridors that made up the facility's command and control center. Stepping over bodies of guards and slaves, Keiko moved over to the remnants of the computer consoles her people had destroyed a few minutes ago and addressed the twenty or so rebels with her.

"We can't take the easy way to the landing pads, so we'll have to work our way around to the ore loaders and get out that way."

Some of the former slaves traded groans and grimaces, but Keiko was pleased to see most of them nod with determination. She'd spent a long time training these people under the collective noses of Gul Zarale and his Alliance guards.

The large door leading deeper into the Alliance facility cycled open, and Keiko and her group took covering positions and aimed their weapons toward the door. Keiko saw who was on the other side and raised her hand. "Hold your fire!"

Tasha leaned her head in, then gave Keiko a smile when she laid eyes on her. "Oh, it's you."

Keiko stood up out from behind her cover and waved Tasha in. Tasha entered the control room, more freed slaves following behind her.

Keiko grinned. "Good work. How many do you have with you?"

"Forty-seven." She indicated the corridor from which she'd entered. "We lost some along the way, though."

Keiko nodded in sympathy. She'd lost several as well. "We need to keep moving." She pointed in the direction of the mining area. "We have guards moving in."

Tasha nodded and thumbed toward the Alliance corridors. "That way is clear. We didn't find Zarale, though. He must have slipped out."

Keiko frowned. "He's probably making a run for the transports. I should have killed him in his sleep last night."

Tasha gave her a sidelong smile. "Not much we can do about it now. Where to?"

Keiko waved Tiron over and clapped him on the shoulder. "Cover our backs, all right?"

Tiron nodded. "Go ahead."

Keiko moved back toward the mining corridors, Tasha and the others following behind. A massive Bolian fell into step with Keiko, taking point with her. She didn't recall his name.

The two paused near the opening to the central assembly area. Keiko checked the area and waved the others to follow. She turned to the Bolian.

"Go on ahead, and scout out the passage to the ore loaders. We'll be right behind you."

The Bolian nodded and trotted off in that direction, disruptor pistol in hand. He disappeared into one of the corridors leading off the assembly area. Tasha and the others joined her at the entrance.

Keiko glanced at them. "We head for the ore loaders and then on to the landing pads. We don't stop. We don't go back. Understood?"

Tasha looked into her eyes and nodded. Even if no one else understood what was at stake, at least she did. If they went back for someone who had fallen, or slowed their pace, they all might fail to get away. And they needed to get off the planet. There wouldn't be a second chance.

Keiko saw that her people were about as ready as they were ever going to be. She saw the Bolian at the entrance to the tunnel he had gone into. He waved at her to follow. She nodded.

"All right, people! Let's move!"

Keiko led the way, the other slaves charging in behind her. She followed the Bolian into the mining corridor, blasting the few remaining guards as they went, freeing what slaves were still imprisoned and adding them to their numbers. As they rushed through the mining complex, Keiko estimated that she had almost two hundred slaves with her. She and Tasha hadn't trained more than a third that number, so the remainder made for a nice bonus. The Terran rebellion on Terok Nor would no doubt appreciate the additional personnel.

In less time than Keiko would have expected, they were all rushing up the conveyor belt that carried ore to the transports. The Bolian rushed to the top of the conveyor and out onto the landing pad. A flurry of disruptor fire cut him down. Keiko paused at the entrance and looked out at the landing pad.

Two Cardassian transports sat on the pad, surrounded by a dozen or so Alliance guards, a mix of Klingons and Cardassians. Gul Zarale stood in the rough center of the group, hitching a bathrobe closed. Keiko saw that he wore only his underwear beneath the robe. For some strange reason, the image made her laugh.

Zarale yelled out. "Keiko! Surrender yourself!"

Keiko shook her head. "I don't think so!"

Zarale aimed a disruptor at Keiko, but Keiko was quicker on the draw. Zarale went down in a tangle of bathrobe and flailing limbs, an expression of surprise and betrayal evident on his face.

A moment of stunned silence followed, then Keiko's people rushed out from behind her and opened fire on the surprised guards. They cleared the landing pad in short order.

Keiko moved toward one of the transports, sidestepping Alliance bodies as she went. She glanced at Tasha and pointed toward the second transport. "Take command of that ship and get your people aboard! We're getting off this planet!"

Tasha tossed her a wave and directed her people toward the second transport. Keiko leaped aboard her own charge and moved to the cockpit. Slipping into the command chair, Keiko started up the launch sequence. She glanced out the forward viewport and saw dozens of former slaves rushing toward the transports, some firing behind them as they ran. The Alliance hadn't given up completely, even with their commanding officer dead.

Keiko continued the preflight preparation and yelled down the narrow corridor behind her. "Get those people aboard and secured! It's going to be a bumpy ride out of here."

Someone, she didn't know who, yelled an affirmative at her. Keiko finished the preflight and keyed on the comm system. "Tasha, Tasha, do you read?"

"Loud and clear, Keiko."

Keiko glanced out the side viewport at the other transport, saw Tasha at the controls. Several slaves piled into the second ship. Keiko guessed that Tasha saw much the same over there.

"Preflight is complete. I'll be ready to launch as soon as we've got everyone aboard."

She saw Tasha nod. *"I'm right with you. Preflight's complete, course set for the Badlands. I figure we can set a new course for Terok Nor from there."*

Keiko turned back to her own console and nodded. "Entering a similar course now. Once we get to orbit, we'll have to—"

A disruptor shot splashed against her fore viewport, making Keiko duck instinctively. She glanced outside. A handful of Alliance guards were firing at the two transports and the last few stragglers. A few slaves fired back, dropping a guard here and there.

Keiko keyed her transport's internal comm system. "Get the rest of our people aboard! We've got to go!"

Another affirmation was shouted out, and after a long moment, someone's voice filtered over the speaker. *"Everyone's aboard, and the hatch is sealed. Take off!"*

Keiko didn't need another request to do so, and she hit the controls to get the ship off the landing pad. She lifted off as someone piled into the seat next to her. She glanced over to see who it was.

"Bowers, right?" At the man's nod, she added, "Power up whatever sensors and shields this crate has, all right?" She remembered that he had been a shuttle pilot before the Alliance had appropriated his colony.

Bowers worked the console in front of him with long brown fingers. "Shields are negligible, but sensors are at full. We have a Klingon Bird of Prey in orbit. I suspect they know we're coming."

Keiko swore under her breath, then hailed Tasha's transport again. "Tasha, we're going to have company once we hit orbit."

Tasha's voice filtered in over the connection. *"Understood. We're airborne, but this thing handles like a chunk of ore."*

Keiko nodded, struggling with her own controls. "Don't I know it." She glanced through the viewport, seeing the cerulean skies darken as they neared the edge of the atmosphere. "Be ready. We get clear of the planet, and we hit warp as soon as possible. We're in no position to take on a Klingon warship."

Tasha acknowledged the order and signed off. Keiko glanced at Bowers. "What's the status of the Klingon?"

He glanced at her, then turned back to his controls. "Powering up weapons and shields. She's setting course to intercept us as soon as we clear the atmosphere."

Keiko shook her head and channeled more power into the transport's engines. She keyed the internal comm again. "Listen up, folks. We're about to enter orbit, but we're going to have company. This ship doesn't have any weapons, so we have to make a run for it. Make sure you're strapped in."

Keiko rolled her ship so that she could see Tasha's transport. Tasha had taken position off her port wing. Keiko saw Tasha and others in the cockpit.

"Tasha, we're going to have to do some fancy flying once the Klingon engages us."

"We've come to the same conclusion. Hope these transports are up for it."

Keiko nodded. "We don't have the means to fight back. Do your best to get clear, and then get your people to warp. This isn't a fight we can win—best to run from this one."

Tasha said, *"Not something I like to do, but you're right."*

Keiko manhandled the controls and brought her transport into low orbit. Within moments, she felt the concussive shocks from disruptor fire. The Klingon Bird of Prey swooped over her ship, rattling the cockpit.

Bowers worked his console. "Shields down to seventy-three percent. I doubt I'll be able to recharge them. This vessel wasn't built for fighting."

Keiko swore again and sent the transport into a series of evasive maneuvers. The thing responded like a brick in water. More disruptor blasts shook the sluggish ship.

Bowers said, "Minor damage to RCS system. Shields holding." He checked his readings, then added, "Keep up the evasive patterns."

The ship shook from another brace of blasts. Keiko shot him a look. He shrugged and said, "Really. They're helping."

Keiko shook her head and concentrated on the controls, continuing to use maneuvers that she hoped wouldn't tear the ship apart. The ship bucked again from another Klingon volley. Keiko caught herself on the side of the console and forced herself to keep her seat.

Bowers said, "The Klingon is veering toward the other transport. He's opening fire!"

Keiko rotated the ship to get a better look, and through the main viewport, she saw Tasha send her transport into a series of maneuvers much like the ones Keiko had so recently used. The Klingon stayed on her, bracketing her with bolts of deadly green energy.

As Keiko watched and worried, the Klingon scored a direct hit on the transport's starboard engine. It sparked and glowed, and the transport shuddered violently. Almost immediately, Tasha's voice filtered in over the comm.

"Starboard impulse engine is out!" Keiko heard her swear. Then, *"We're leaking plasma."* As the statement sank in, Tasha added, *"I don't think we're going to make warp, Keiko. Get your people out of here. I'll distract the Klingon for as long as I can."*

"Tasha, I—"

Tasha cut her off. *"No time to argue. One transport is better than none. Get out of here. Get to Terok Nor. Help the rebellion."*

Keiko stared at the console, as if she could somehow see through it to Tasha. She glanced at Bowers, saw his eyes clouded with concern. He frowned but nodded. She sighed, resigned to what she had to do.

Keiko rotated in her seat to take one last look at Tasha's transport as it staggered toward the Klingon warship. She then turned back to her console and sent her own ship into warp. She offered a silent thanks to Tasha and her crew, knowing that their sacrifice made Keiko's escape possible. She vowed to make good on that sacrifice, no matter how long it took.

The airlock door wheeled open. Keiko took a deep breath, centering herself and putting aside her sorrow for the time being. She stepped through the opening and onto Terok Nor. The barrel-chested leader of the Terran rebellion, Miles O'Brien, stood just inside the corridor attached to the airlock, along with a handful of technicians and armed guards.

She mustered up a smile as she approached and offered her hand. "Miles O'Brien?"

A momentary look of confusion crossed his face, but he soon replaced it with a sidelong smile. "Yeah, that's right." He took her hand and shook it with a firm grasp.

"Keiko Ishikawa. Thank you for allowing us to dock here. I've led a transport full of former Alliance slaves off the Korvat mining colony. Could you use our help?"

O'Brien stared at her, apparently not expecting such a windfall. He glanced over her shoulder at the dozens of former slaves making their way off the transport. He turned back to Keiko, still holding her hand. "Uh, yeah. Yes, of course."

He let go of her hand and smiled. "All the help we can get. How many of you are there?"

Keiko glanced behind her. A couple of O'Brien's men escorted her former wards into the station. Techies from the station worked their way around the transport, no doubt eager to repair it and press it into service. Keiko turned back to O'Brien.

"I took a head count just after we went to warp speed. This transport carried myself and ninety-four freedom fighters, from a variety of worlds." Keiko forced herself not to be overwhelmed by the thought that she could have delivered a second transport and as many more former slaves.

O'Brien nodded, his eyes focused on her. He started, as if forgetting something. He gestured down the corridor. "Ah, I could assign you some quarters if you want to clean up a bit?"

Keiko nodded and took his arm. "Is there someplace on this station to get something to drink? We have a lot to talk about."

O'Brien glanced at her, then grinned and led her into the station. Keiko followed, keeping a firm hold on his arm, partly for camaraderie but mainly because she was bone-tired and needed the support. Even as worn-out as she was, Keiko discovered that she had an odd warm feeling. It had been a very long time since she had been free.

2376

A quiet, consistent chirping dragged Keiko out of the soft, dark folds of sleep. She pulled the thin cover off and slipped out of bed, careful not to disturb Miles. She slipped into a thick, comfortable robe and glanced at her lover, so peaceful at rest. She walked over to the door of their bedroom, which whisked open.

She paused as the soft door chime sounded again. She glanced at Miles, but he didn't move. They had worked late into the night with Eddington, putting the last few touches on their plan for the rebellion. Miles had put in a couple of extra hours seeing to the last of the station's repairs.

Keiko padded over to their main door and opened it. A tall Vulcan stood on her doorstep, dressed in drab clothing. He had a dour look on his face and a small box in his hands. Keiko didn't recognize him.

The Vulcan looked into her eyes and said, "It is agreeable to meet you, Miss Ishikawa. Memory Omega sends its greetings."

It startled her to hear the name of the secret movement into which she'd been raised spoken aloud after so very long. Founded decades ago by Emperor Spock, Memory Omega worked for the future—awaiting the proper historical moment when its members would effect social change on an interstellar scale. *A galaxy without tyranny,* she thought, recalling Omega's lofty goal. *I wonder if I'll live to see it.* Keiko glanced behind her, toward her bedroom door, then joined the Vulcan in the corridor outside her quarters. She glanced down the corridor and offered a questioning look.

The Vulcan inclined his head. "I made all necessary precautions prior to meeting you, of course. This section of corridor is protected by sensor dampeners and force fields. We will not be disturbed."

Keiko gave the Vulcan a smile. "You have me at a disadvantage, Mr. . . . ?"

The Vulcan nodded. "I am Chu'lak."

Keiko didn't recognize the name. "Thank you, Mr. Chu'lak. I take it our friend is safe?"

Chu'lak nodded. "Indeed. Mr. Tiron is secure aboard my vessel. The soporific you provided him with was sufficient to convince his captors that he had, in fact, died at their hands. Once they disposed of his body, I beamed him aboard and made use of my modest medical abilities to revive him."

"I'm glad to know he'll be all right."

"His service will not go unrecognized."

Keiko nodded. "I'm sure. Please give Tiron my thanks. What else do you have to tell me?"

"I have monitored communications both on and off the station. It would appear that your subterfuge proved most effective. There are no dissenting opinions regarding your status in the rebellion. In fact, you seem to have cemented a remarkable yet unenviable position for yourself."

Keiko frowned. "That was not my intent. The goal was to push the rebellion into a better strategic position for the battles to come."

Chu'lak nodded. "And I believe you were successful. The rebellion is now in a far superior state of readiness than it had enjoyed a week ago. This will prove most useful in coordinating our collective efforts." He paused, then asked, "Do you intend to tell General O'Brien the details of your subterfuge?"

Keiko considered the question, taking in Chu'lak's posture. While the question was asked in the same low voice he'd used for the entire conversation, she sensed a subtle undertone of menace. She suspected that if she answered wrong, he'd take care of the problem without hesitation.

In an unwavering voice, she said, "Not at the moment. Perhaps in time, I'll be able to reveal the details to him, but for now, some things must remain secret. Particularly the existence of our organization."

Chu'lak seemed to relax upon hearing her statement. She must have passed the unspoken test. Chu'lak offered the briefest of smiles and presented the small package in his hands to her.

"This is from your mother."

She took the package, certain of its contents. He added, "It also includes a data rod containing information I have gathered on the Alliance. The rebellion should find it most useful."

Keiko cradled the gift to her body and nodded. "Thank you, Chu'lak."

Chu'lak raised his right hand in the traditional Vulcan salute. "Live long and prosper, Keiko Ishikawa."

She returned the salute. "And you."

He dropped his hand and walked away, disappearing around the curve of the corridor. Keiko heard a series of force fields snap off. She glanced down at the box in her hands and returned to her quarters.

She took a seat on the long couch and opened the small box. She gasped in pleased surprise at what she saw. She reached in and pulled out a single orange data rod of Cardassian design and a yellowed and chipped china cup, decorated with a bold green stripe around the inside rim and faded Japanese calligraphy on the exterior.

Keiko rotated the cup in her hand, fancied that she could almost hear her Obachan humming in the background. Keiko used to help her grandmother with her calligraphy by filling this same cup with water for the brushes. Keiko smiled in remembrance.

"What's that?"

Keiko started but had the presence of mind not to fling the precious cup out of surprise. Miles shuffled out of their bedroom doorway, already wearing pants and slipping on a rumpled shirt as he approached the couch.

Keiko palmed the data rod and slipped it between her leg and the couch cushion, forcing herself to keep a smile on her face. She hoped he hadn't caught the sleight of hand.

"It's a calligraphy cup. It used to be my grandmother's."

Miles sat on the couch and shifted his weight to put a comfortable arm around her. She curled up next to him, feeling the data rod sink more securely between her and the couch.

Miles took a long look at the cup, then at her. "Where'd you get it?"

She rotated the cup in her hands again, taking in the familiar shape unseen for so long. "It was passed down from my grandmother to my mother, and now it's been passed down to me."

Miles shook his head. "That's not what I meant. How did you get it here? You didn't arrive on the station with any personal belongings, and I'm sure you didn't live here before Korvat."

She gave him a playful swat on the chest. "Of course not. A friend of the family dropped it off for me." She waved toward the front door. "He just left."

Miles glanced at the door. "Oh. I didn't hear him come in."

She shrugged noncommittally at that, hoping that the explanation was enough for him. She felt him shrug, and then he pulled her into a more comfortable embrace. She placed the cup on the low table in front of them and relaxed, enjoying the comfort of his arms around her, his body pressed against hers, and the touchstone from her past sitting on the table in front of her.

They sat in companionable silence for some time, then she felt him tense up. He said, "Do you have any other surprises for me?"

She idly reached out and turned the cup halfway around. She pressed her head into his chest. "Surprises?"

"Yeah. Surprises. Like family gifts appearing from out of nowhere or perhaps a poorly placed bomb somewhere on my station?"

Alarmed, Keiko sat up and shifted away from him. She felt the data rod settle squarely under her butt. "Miles, what are you talking about?"

He offered a smile, but the expression didn't extend to his eyes. "I've learned a thing or two from you in the last several months, Keiko."

Keiko shrank back on her side of the couch, uncertain where Miles was going with this. From the set of his jaw, she suspected they were heading for an argument, and that was the last thing she wanted. She said, "I'm not sure what you mean, Miles."

"I think you had a hand in Tiron's sabotage." At her stunned look, he added, "I know you were frustrated with our lack of progress after Empok Nor was attacked. Me and Eddington and the others, we were all sort of spinning our wheels. Trust me, I know how unhappy you were."

Keiko nodded, remembering the nights full of heated discussions as Miles grasped at ideas, no matter how insane, and she had tried to shepherd the ideas into something coherent.

Miles continued. "And I know Tiron came with you on the transport from Korvat. I had him checked out, and he seemed to have acquitted himself well against the Alliance during your escape."

Keiko nodded. "He fought as well as any of us, and he helped us escape." That much was the truth, at least.

Miles sat up straight on the couch and pointed an accusing finger at her. "And you let Shar kill him. For nothing!"

Keiko crossed her arms in front of her chest. "His sacrifice wasn't for nothing, Miles. There was a reason for—"

Miles sliced the air with his hand. "It wasn't worth it, Keiko. All this. The bombs, the sabotage, the lies. We would have figured something out. You just needed to give us time."

Keiko shook her head. "Miles, there wasn't any time to waste. You know how vulnerable we were. I still can't believe the Intendant and her cronies didn't attack the station immediately after Empok Nor. I don't think they realized how close they came to wiping the rebellion out." She let that sink in, then added, "And I don't think you or Michael or anyone else realized how close we were, either."

Miles considered that, but shook his head. "I still don't think it was right, sacrificing Tiron like that."

Keiko threw up her hands in annoyance. "He volunteered, Miles! I presented the idea to him, and he asked to be part of it. He knew what he was getting into."

Miles shrugged and looked away. She sensed a full-blown pout coming on. "You still could have told me, Keiko. I am the bloody general here, damn it."

Keiko stared at him, stunned. He wasn't mad at what had happened, not the specifics. He was mad at her for lying to him, for betraying him. She was surprised to feel hot tears welling up in her eyes. She had disappointed Miles. The one man in her life who had offered her unconditional love, who had stood beside her through all of the accusations and dangerous moments, the man she had discovered she loved more than anyone else in her life. She was shocked to discover that she couldn't bear to have him leave her, that she feared her recent actions had driven an impenetrable wedge between them.

"Miles, I . . . I don't know what to say."

Miles stared at her, his features softening somewhat when he saw the tears rolling down her face. In a lower tone of voice, he said, "I just wish you had said something. I would have gone along with you, helped you. Tiron was a good man."

Right then, Keiko almost broke down, almost told Miles everything. But she dug deep and maintained her hold, the training drummed into her keeping her will strong. This wasn't the time. The greater cause had to persevere in secret for a while longer.

She tentatively raised a hand to Miles's cheek, hoping that this wouldn't drive them apart. She cleared her throat and said, "Miles, I'm sorry I didn't share the plan with you. I didn't mean to hurt you."

He nodded and took her hand in his. She felt the strength in those hands, the hands that could please her as no others could. She feared those hands striking out against her but knew that Miles would never do such a thing.

He carefully placed her hand in her lap and stood up. "I've got to get to work. We can talk about this later."

Keiko brushed her tears away in frustration. Miles was upset, and rather than take it out on her, he was going to go bust up some of the station's recalcitrant machinery.

She nodded at him, not trusting herself to talk. He took one final look at her, grabbed his boots, and stomped out of their quarters.

As the door cycled shut behind him, Keiko forced back the

sobs threatening to rush from her throat. Why did she feel this way? What was it about Miles that had her in such disarray?

She stared around the quarters, her eyes finally falling on Obachan's cup. She stared at it, letting the tears flow freely. It all came down to family. She wanted Miles in her life, in her family. And what she'd done, what she had had to do, had hurt him.

She glanced at the doorway where he had gone. This would pass in time. Miles wasn't one to hold his frustrations in for too long. The two of them would have a long talk, maybe several long talks, and they'd walk on eggshells around each other for a while, but they'd work through it.

Keiko pulled the data rod out from underneath her. Perhaps it contained the information the rebellion needed. Perhaps it would be enough. She clenched it tight and held it close to her breast, as if it were the most precious and fragile thing in the galaxy . . . next to her love for Miles.

Empathy

Christopher L. Bennett

HISTORIAN'S NOTE: *This tale takes place in late 2376, approximately one year after the events of* Saturn's Children *from* Star Trek Mirror Universe: Obsidian Alliances, *and three years before the events of* Star Trek Titan: Taking Wing *in the mainline universe.*

Christopher L. Bennett is the author of two novels in the *Star Trek Titan* series, *Orion's Hounds* and the upcoming *Over a Torrent Sea*. He has also authored such critically acclaimed novels as *Star Trek: Ex Machina*, *Star Trek: The Next Generation—The Buried Age*, and *Star Trek: The Next Generation—Greater Than the Sum*, as well as the alternate *Voyager* tale *Places of Exile* in *Myriad Universes: Infinity's Prism*. Shorter works include *Star Trek: S.C.E.—Aftermath* and *Star Trek: Mere Anarchy—The Darkness Drops Again*, as well as short stories in the anniversary anthologies *Constellations* (original series), *The Sky's the Limit* (TNG), *Prophecy and Change* (DS9), and *Distant Shores* (VGR). Beyond *Star Trek*, he has penned the novels *X-Men: Watchers on the Walls*, and *Spider-Man: Drowned in Thunder*, and is also developing original science fiction novel concepts. More information, original fiction, and novel annotations can be found at http://home.fuse.net/ChristopherLBennett/.

Dr. Jaza Najem hated his audiences with Governor Khegh. The fat, unkempt Klingon put up a boisterous front, but his jovial manner masked a ruthless manipulator, and his hedonism contained a strong sadistic streak. It was people like Khegh, in Jaza's view, who stained the reputation of the Klingon-Cardassian Alliance and enabled its enemies to rationalize their attempts to destroy it.

But Khegh was Lru-Irr's planetary governor, and Jaza had to face him if he wanted to persuade him to mitigate Dr. Ree's methods. Not that he had much hope; Ree's fondness for playing with his prey (including his Irriol research subjects, the "prey" in his hunt for knowledge) appealed to Khegh's sadism. Jaza knew he would have to speak in terms of the success of the project, striving not to appear soft on the Irriol. This wasn't about mercy; these were perilous times, with Terran insurrectionists gaining strength by the day, and Jaza understood the danger Terrans posed as well as did any Bajoran. He accepted that preventing the terrorists' victory was worth the sacrifice of a few individuals. But he knew Khegh was already inclined to dismiss him as a bleeding heart.

So he had instructed Christine to act properly deferential toward him during the audience and had attired her in something revealing enough to satisfy Khegh's expectations for a slave, even a Theta. He wondered if it was wise to bring her at all, for it would undermine him if Khegh caught a glimpse of his true feelings for her. But he was useless at organizing his notes without her help. He would just have to keep up a suitably tough façade.

He therefore tried not to grimace at the sight that presented itself when he entered the ornate main hall of Khegh's headquarters. The "entertainment" Khegh was currently laughing at involved a clear-walled tank of water in which a willowy blond slave woman was immersed totally nude, lacking even the collar and chains that were the standard and sole accouterments of the other slave women who flanked Khegh's thronelike seat. The weakly thrashing woman's delicate skeletal structure and chevron-shaped nasal-frontal ridges showed that she was not a Terran like Christine, but a more exotic breed of slave.

"Quite a sight, isn't she?" Khegh roared, noting Jaza's gaze. "Rare catch, too. An Elaysian—the Terrans destroyed their world a century ago. But some refugees finally turned up, and . . ." He gestured to the woman in the tank. "Cost me two Deltans. Hardly worth the expense, though. Low-gravity species. Too fragile to hold up to beating or bedding, so I had to find another way to get some fun out of her." He took a hefty bite from a leg of something (Jaza didn't want to know) and talked around it as he chewed. "Water's ice-cold . . . but if she climbs out on the shelf . . . her own weight crushes her, and soon enough she has to go back in the water! Clever, eh?"

Hence the lack of a collar, Jaza thought, looking at it analytically to harden himself to the sight. *She's too weak to escape, particularly in the above-normal gravity here.* Beside him, Christine shuddered, and Jaza caught a flash of anger before she caught herself and lowered her gaze, her long auburn hair tumbling over her face. He wanted to reach out and comfort her, but he restrained himself.

"Indeed, it is imaginative," came the articulate growl of Dr. Shenti Yisec Eres Ree. The Pahkwa-thanh medical researcher strode forward to study the Elaysian, his long-snouted, brown-scaled head tilting contemplatively. Jaza stepped back to dodge the sauroid's heavy tail, which tended to thrash about when he was intrigued. "Although I confess I fail to see the point in playing with a creature one does not intend to eat."

Khegh laughed. Klingons generally were not comfortable with

sentient species shaped differently from themselves, but they respected the Pahkwa-thanh's predatory nature. The Klingons had lost thousands in their failed attempt to conquer the Pahkwa-thanh homeworld, and apparently granting such honorable and songworthy deaths to so many warriors was the Klingon idea of a generous diplomatic overture, since the two species had become stalwart allies thereafter. "If you like," Khegh told the doctor, "I could give her to you when I'm done with her."

"Hrrr . . . too bony. And I prefer prey that can run."

"Good point, good point." Khegh took another huge bite and washed it down with a swig of bloodwine. Jaza reflected that it had been a long time since the governor had been in any shape to run after anything. "So what's this all about this time? And quickly, I'm a busy man!"

Christine handed Jaza a padd, and he stepped forward. "Governor, despite my earlier protests, Ree is still engaged in unnecessary and needlessly destructive research upon the Irriol subjects."

"I dispute 'unnecessary,'" Ree countered politely. "If we are to understand the Irriol mind, we must understand all of its facets. Few things engage the psyche as profoundly, as primally, as the confrontation of pain, terror, and death."

"And ingestion? Governor, I have seen Ree *eating* his subjects' organs as he vivisects them. He isn't preserving them for study. That is . . . wasteful." He strove to maintain detachment. He held out the documentation, but the governor waved it aside.

"I have many Irriol organs on file already," Ree responded, "and scans are sufficient in most cases. But there is much that a researcher's own senses can reveal. Bajorans are a visual species. My people rely more on scent . . . and taste. Additionally," Ree went on, his tail writhing more excitedly, "observing the subjects' response to their own ingestion is informative."

Khegh roared. "You can't argue with that! Nothing like the look in an enemy's eyes as you rip out his heart and bite into it."

Jaza fought to keep down his last meal. Christine gave him a surreptitious look of encouragement, hidden from Khegh by her hair. "I can't fault my colleague for . . . enthusiasm," he said, drawing a gracious nod from Ree. "But we must not lose sight of what's at stake here. We're trying to harness the power of a whole race of empaths. Imagine what a weapon that would be for the Alliance."

"I know why we're here," Khegh snarled. "Only reason we conquered these pathetic *jeghpu'wI'* in the first place." Psi-capable species were a rare prize, since the Terran Empire, fearful of their power, had done their best to wipe out every telepathic race they discovered. The Alliance was not so shortsighted or reflexively destructive; its standing policy was that any psi-capable race or individual must be secured, regulated, and analyzed, its power used to strengthen the Alliance. Ree was an expert in the field, thanks to his people's extensive study of their own empathic minority, though he himself was psi-null.

"But we need to go about it in the right way," Jaza argued. "The Irriol think in terms of the gestalt they share with the other life forms on their world. If we want to harness that gestalt, we should take advantage of their communal psychology. We should present ourselves as partners, build trust and affinity the same way they do among themselves, so they will cooperate voluntarily. Making them fear us as predators is counterproductive."

"On any other world, I might agree, Najem," said Ree. "But the Irriol have a keen understanding of their place in nature. They do not perceive their predators as enemies but accept them as players in the gestalt. They will sometimes surrender to predators voluntarily when they subconsciously sense that it serves the greater good of the ecosystem."

"But predators do not inflict unnecessary suffering, as a rule."

"Do we not? We play with our prey to wear it down, disorient it. It may feel unnecessary to the prey, but it is not. I believe the Irriol understand this through their gestalt." Ree shook his head in excitement. "It is bracing to confront a prey creature with a conscious understanding of its role in the hunt," he said. "I am learning much." Jaza knew that Pahkwa-thanh propriety precluded hunting any sapient species that did not accept its role as prey. The Irriol appeared to be one that did, or at least came close enough to satisfy Ree's definitions, and he was taking full advantage of it, not only in the lab but also out in the wilds, pursuing a far more literal hunt when the mood seized him.

Jaza didn't blame Ree for being what he was; he was only behaving according to his species' nature. But he still felt that what Ree was had no place on this expedition. He only wished he could convince Khegh of that.

But Khegh was grinning at Ree, sharing in his predatory enthusiasm. "There you are," he told Jaza. "They're used to being prey, so let us treat them as such. Any race that would lie down and let itself be eaten is *jeghpu'wI'* to the core, unworthy of being treated otherwise."

"It isn't a question of worth, Governor," Jaza objected. "It's a question of finding the most effective way to harness and augment Irriol mental powers." Christine handed him the appropriate padd, though he doubted Khegh would take any more interest in this one.

"Ree tells me you've already made progress at boosting their, what, their gestalt. Says it could be a way to communicate without subspace radio."

"Among other applications," Ree said. "Though so far, they are strictly local."

"And dangerous to the Irriol," Jaza said, holding out the padd. "Most of our test subjects have suffered crippling or fatal brain damage over time. Their brains aren't adapted to channel psionic energies at these levels."

"It is a work in progress," Ree conceded. "Normally, Najem, I would be happy to proceed more cautiously. But I need not remind you, do I, of the urgent threat we face from the insurrectionists?"

Ree had him there, though there was only sympathy in his growling voice as he brought it up. Jaza's home province still bore the scars inflicted by the Terran Empire's brutal occupation generations ago. He had been raised with tales of the horrors the Terrans had inflicted upon his family and community, so that he and other Bajorans would never forget, never let it be done to them again.

But aren't we doing the same to the Irriol? he asked himself. He strove to believe it was different, that Ree was right and the Irriol accepted the imposition. He strove to believe that his government—and he—were acting out of necessity, to defend against the far worse horror that would befall the quadrant if the Terrans were freed to resume their conquering ways.

But when he saw Khegh's Elaysian slave trembling on the shelf above the tank, her eyes pleading with him to help her before her pain forced her to plunge back into the icy water, he had to wonder how much better the Alliance was.

No, he told himself. The Alliance had freed Bajor, made it strong and safe. The things that went on in places like this were necessary so that Bajorans, Cardassians, and other enlightened peoples could live free and peaceful lives—and people like Khegh were simply part of the price that had to be paid to ensure that.

Besides—what else was there?

When Jaza and Christine returned to their quarters, he sagged into her arms. Ever responsive to his moods, she kissed him gently, sat him on the bed, removed his tunic, and began kneading his shoulders with her strong, deft hands. "I'm sorry you had to see that," he told her. "And I'm sorry you have to read about the things Ree does to his subjects. I wonder if I should've brought you here at all."

"You'd lose all your notes in a day without me," Christine teased. "Besides, if you'd left me behind, I'd think I wasn't your favorite concubine anymore." Her lips brushed his ear.

He clasped her hand upon his shoulder. "You're my only concubine, you silly Terran. And the only one I'll ever need." He lifted the hand to his lips. "I love you so much."

"Not so loud. What if someone heard you?" But as her lips brushed his ear, she breathed, "I love you too, Najem."

"Why shouldn't I be in love with my own concubine?" he asked. "You certainly deserve it. You're a Theta—you've earned a degree of respect. You're intelligent, capable, decent, kind. More so than any Terran I've ever met."

"Only through your guidance, beloved. Only because you encouraged me and touched me with your own kindness."

"Still, you deserve better than to be treated like—like a slave."

"You treat me wonderfully."

"I mean by others. By society. I feel you've earned the right to be treated like, well, a person with rights."

Christine came around to sit on his lap. "To be 'free?'" she asked. "What would I do? Join the rebellion? Be commanded by brutal strangers, risk my life on their whim? Or wander off into untamed space and scrounge for my survival? You'd call that freedom?" She shook her head. "Remember what you taught me about physics? Degrees of freedom are always finite. Everyone lives under constraints of one sort or another. And I have far more freedom as your slave, my dear, kind master, than I could ever have as a 'liberated' Terran." She took his bearded chin in her hands and kissed him again, deep and long.

She undid the clasp on her minimal top and let it fall. But Jaza grasped her wrists, still preoccupied. "As *my* slave, perhaps. But slavery . . . it's so contingent on the good intentions of the masters. It can so easily be corrupted." He felt a twinge of guilt, remembering his own feelings when he had first purchased Christine. He had relished the opportunity to debase a Terran, to avenge the evils her breed had inflicted on Bajor. He had not beaten or raped her, but he had enjoyed making her work herself to exhaustion or humiliate herself for the amusement of his friends. But she had borne it with unexpected strength and quiet dignity, defying his expectations about Terran barbarism. He had come to respect her, showing her more kindness, giving her more liberties to make amends for his earlier treatment. He had learned of her sharp intelligence and taught her literacy and science and Bajoran culture, and she had amazed him with her ability to grow into a truly civilized being despite her heritage. She had given him her body freely by then, and he was irrevocably in love with her before he even realized it.

"What if something happened to me, Christine? What if I died or had to give you up, and you ended up the property of someone like Khegh?"

Christine held his gaze. "I would die before I would live without you. Belonging to you is what gives my life meaning. I am nothing except what you made me, Najem."

Then her lips and hands went to work again, and he let himself forget his doubts and surrender to her passion. He may have owned her life, but she owned his heart. And it was immensely comforting to know that she would always stand by his side.

"Mr. Riker, Ms. Lavena, report to the bridge, please."

Will Riker didn't look up from sharpening his *mek'leth,* merely scoffing at the arbitrary formality the captain insisted on as though they were a military crew instead of a small bunch of raiders. But Aili Lavena hopped out of the bed they shared and began donning the moisture suit and hood that she wore most of the time to keep her blue-green skin and the two wispy gill crests on her head and back from drying out. Back on her homeworld, her people stayed close to the water, an option she didn't have on this crate. It wouldn't be long, in fact, before the Selkie outgrew her amphibious phase and had to spend the rest of her life underwater. Riker wouldn't miss her, though; in fact, he was benefiting from it now, for she was looking forward to the life of hedonism that came in a Selkie's aquatic, postparenting phase and was thus eager to indulge her sexuality as much as possible in order to feel more "mature." And once she entered that phase, not only would she be unable to do it on land, but her four ample breasts would flatten out for streamlining. At that point, Riker would have no more use for her.

Once Lavena had dressed, she glared at Riker. "Are you just going to sit there? The captain wants us."

"Yeah, yeah. When I'm ready."

Her glare redirected itself to the *mek'leth.* "Honestly. You love that hunk of metal more than me."

"Perceptive girl." Indeed, this blade had never let him down. It had belonged to his family's Klingon owner on Luna, where he'd grown up. He'd used it to kill the father who had beaten him constantly for fifteen years, and then to kill the Klingon and escape the Sol system. He'd shaped himself in its image—cold, sharp, ruthless, a precision instrument that killed and never asked why.

"Hasn't there ever been anyone you cared about, Riker? Anyone who taught you what it was like to feel for another person?"

"You mean love?" He scoffed. "A trick of our genes, using us to propagate themselves. Nobody uses me. I use them."

"Oh? Then how come, after five years in the resistance, you've never had your own command?"

In an eyeblink, he had her against the bulkhead, the *mek'leth* at her throat. "Do you *want* me to gut you like a salmon?"

She trembled, knowing he was capable of it, but remained defiant. "Never mind. I just got the answer to my question."

After another moment, he let the sword drop, not wanting to waste it on her. He backhanded her across the cheek instead. "What makes you think I want a command in this gang of soft-hearted fools? I just stick around for the action." He leered at her, making it a double entendre.

Lavena shook her head and stormed out. Riker wasn't bothered; he knew she'd come back to his bed, for want of other options. After wiping the blade clean of her skin oils, Riker set it down with a sigh, figuring he should get to the bridge before that gray-haired fool of a captain started pestering him. It was a short trip, since this was a small vessel for its power. In moments, he was on the bridge, seeing through the ports that they'd dropped to impulse around a planet that must be their destination, Lru-Irr. Lavena kept her eyes on the helm console, studiously ignoring him.

"This spy of yours better be on the level," Riker told the captain.

Ian Troi turned his balding head to take in his first officer. "Not to worry, Will," said the seventyish rebel commander. "Christine Vale has earned a position of trust among the researchers. Otherwise, she would never have been left alone to contact us. I think we can be confident this isn't a wild-goose chase."

"I still say it's a trap."

"You say everything's a trap," Troi said, a smile crinkling his rounded, avuncular face.

"And sometimes I'm right."

"I can vouch for her," Lavena said, not speaking directly to Riker but refuting him to the bridge in general. "Christine wouldn't betray us."

The other occupant of the bridge spoke up. "Trap or no," said Tuvok, "it is imperative that we take the risk. Even aside from our ethical obligation to protect the Irriol, we must prevent the Alliance from harnessing their psionic abilities as a weapon."

"So what if the way to do that is killing them all?" Riker shot back. "Are we here to spout platitudes or get the job done?"

"Your eagerness for bloodshed notwithstanding, Mr. Riker, it would be prohibitively difficult for the few of us to eradicate a planetary population. Our goal is to sabotage the Alliance research outpost and foment resistance among the Irriol. Remember, they would be as great an asset to us as they would be to the Alliance."

"You and the captain can worry about that," Riker told the Vulcan. "I'm here to kill Alliance scum. You want that place blown to hell, I'll take care of it. But if any of the locals go up with it, I won't shed a tear."

"That, Mr. Riker, is self-evident."

"Enough, you two," Troi said. "We shall do this my way. We protect the Irriol if at all possible . . . but if, and only if, it comes to that, we do what we must to keep the Alliance from exploiting their abilities. Understood?"

"Yes, Captain," Tuvok said. Riker just grunted, but inwardly he was seething. What kind of a leader did this man think he was, anyway? His idea of a command decision was to compromise right down the middle.

Oh, well. With any luck, the old fool would get himself killed, and Riker could take over the *Deanna.* Captain Troi had named the ship after some long-lost kid of his who'd died or been stolen or something; Riker could never be bothered to listen to the old man's sob stories about his tragic family history. But the captain nurtured and tended the ship as though it were his own child. As a result, *Deanna* was one of the most beautiful, swiftest, and smoothest-running ships in the rebel fleet. Riker had to give Troi credit for that, at least. But that wouldn't stop him from claiming this ship for his own when he got his chance. He deserved her—her speed, her power—more than the old man did. And once he could possess her, he could cut loose of this pitiful rebellion and be his own master, dependent on no one.

Riker kept this to himself, of course. Troi was not so circumspect, laying an affectionate hand on the bulkhead. "Once more unto the breach, my girl," he whispered, as though a hunk of duranium could hear him. "Ms. Lavena, do you have the vector Ms. Vale gave us?"

"Aye, sir. I'm reading a narrow gap in the sensor grid. I should just be able to squeeze her through it."

"I have no doubt you can, Aili. Take her in."

After penetrating the orbital grid, *Deanna* entered the atmosphere around the curve of the planet from the Alliance outpost and proceeded at low altitude, using a mountain range for cover from ground sensors. Upon landing, Captain Troi, Riker, Tuvok, and Lavena disembarked, leaving Olivia Bolaji and Gian Sortollo to mind the ship. Tuvok surveyed the landscape with interest as he exited the vessel. As a disciple of the late Emperor Spock, Tuvok valued scientific curiosity for its own sake as well as for its tactical benefits, though naturally the latter took primacy. And the empathically linked ecosystem of Lru-Irr was well worthy of study.

Tuvok opened his mind, taking care to do so passively, for preserving the secrecy of Vulcan telepathy was of the highest priority. But he detected little that he could be sure of, only a subliminal awareness that might be a mere projection of his own expectations.

As he scanned for life signs, however, Tuvok noticed something. When their ship had landed, the local avians and fauna had fled the area, and now more distant animals seemed to be retreating as well. This could be simply because those animals saw or heard the flight of the avians, but the overall movements of the life signs seemed more coordinated than one would expect.

As the party gained distance from the ship, they began to see various small animals following the normal pattern for this world— the four limbs typical of most vertebrates, plus a pair of extra appendages flanking the mouth. The specific forms those buccal appendages took varied from species to species, though. Tuvok knew the Irriol had two thick proboscies ending in grasping digits and were covered in rhomboidal keratinous plates. But in the avians he saw, the buccal appendages had evolved into short, somewhat beaklike pincers. A small, spiny ground mammal had short appendages ending in heavy claws for burrowing. And in the trees, he spotted an animal brachiating past using its long prehensile trunks and hind limbs, while its forelimbs hugged its babies to its chest.

While Riker dismissed these animals once he'd determined they were no threat, Captain Troi continued to observe them, suggesting that he, too, valued scientific curiosity. He seemed disappointed, though, and after a time said, "I'd expected to see more evidence of symbiotic behavior."

"The gestalt," Tuvok explained, "is not a full symbiosis but merely a subconscious awareness of large-scale patterns within the biosphere. According to the reports smuggled out by Ms. Vale, it is more an intuitive response to perceived conditions than a conscious cooperation. Superficially, it would not appear very different from the normal homeostatic processes of any planetary ecosystem."

"I see. We're looking on too small a scale to see it."

"Indeed." He showed Troi the scanner readout. "For example, our arrival has driven the animals of our landing zone into retreat. This has served to concentrate them more at the perimeter of the zone, and that, in turn, is drawing a number of predators. Holistically speaking, this could be seen as analogous to a body's immune response; the increase of predators surrounding a potential danger could serve as a defense mechanism to protect the larger biosphere."

Riker had his phaser out. "Are they about to attack?"

"No—merely present in increased numbers on the periphery."

"You heard Tuvok," Troi added. "They're not reacting to us but to the way their prey animals have moved in response to us. As long as we don't provoke a reaction by confronting them directly, we should be all right. Yes?"

"As 'all right' as one can be in the wilds of any planet." Troi nodded, taking Tuvok's point and remaining alert. Tuvok was impressed with the man's intelligence and wondered what he might have become in the free and democratic society that Spock had envisioned—and what the odds were that such a society could be created in what remained of the Terran's lifetime.

Soon they reached their rendezvous point, a crevice in a mountainside. The fistrium deposits made scanning difficult, so Tuvok listened carefully for predators or Alliance troops. His ears registered only one set of light footfalls, mere moments before an auburn-haired Terran, no doubt Christine Vale, emerged from cover. Her stealth was impressive.

But perhaps unwise, given what the captain called Riker's "itchy trigger finger." The large bearded man spun, swinging his weapon to bear. But Lavena was already rushing forward. Riker held his fire but did not lower the weapon. His fingers tensed on its grip as Lavena and Vale fell into each other's embrace and kissed passionately.

"Ohh, I've missed that," Vale said once they disengaged. "It's been too long, Aili. You don't know what it's like, having to pretend with that Bajoran scum." She shook her head. "He thinks he's so enlightened, the way he coddles and patronizes me, as if it makes up for all the humiliation—" She noticed the others and broke off. "I'm sorry," she said, turning to them. "I'm babbling, aren't I? It's just been so long since I've been able to talk openly about what I feel—"

"Quite all right, Ms. Vale," the captain said. He introduced himself and his team, then added, "But we must dispense with further pleasantries, since we have a lot of Irriol to save. Can you help us contact their leaders?"

"They don't have leaders in the usual sense," Vale told him. "It's more of a loose clan structure. But I can take you to the nearest village. At least," she added with a grimace, "the nearest one that isn't being culled for research subjects right now."

As they proceeded, Lavena and Vale held hands and conversed softly. Tuvok was aware that Lavena had recruited Vale during her months on Bajor; as a member of a neutral species, the Selkie had been able to travel freely there, providing valuable intelligence to the resistance leaders on Terok Nor. However, as he told the captain *sotto voce,* "I was not aware that the relationship between Ms. Lavena and Ms. Vale was an intimate one."

Troi gave him a wry look. "I didn't think Vulcans had much interest in gossip."

Tuvok lifted a scathing brow. "We do not. But our trust in Ms. Vale is based upon Ms. Lavena's assessment. If her objectivity is in doubt—"

"I trust Aili's judgment," Troi said. But then he softened and gave a slight shrug. "But I still look out for her. I checked up on Ms. Vale before I approved this mission. Her story checks out. Dr. Jaza is well known for his resentment of Terrans, and he's been seen humiliating her in public." He shook his head. "I can only imagine what he's done to her in private. In fact, I prefer not to."

Tuvok frowned. Ian Troi was more agreeable than many in the resistance and was looked on by many as a father figure of sorts. But that also appeared to be his weakness. He had been involuntarily separated from his family over three decades ago, and that deprivation seemed to have created a yearning in him, an eagerness for surrogate familial bonds. He trusted too easily as a result. A case in point was his willingness to bring William Riker on this mission.

Tuvok had worked with similar Terrans before and found them too driven by their own self-interest and bloodlust to be reliable. Riker in particular had a frustrated ambition for command that led him to see Troi as a rival. Tuvok was not convinced the man would protect the captain if it came to that. Which was why Tuvok considered it incumbent upon himself to stay close to Troi and see to his safety.

Tuvok realized he was reacting with excessive anxiety. While it was logical to be alert to possible threats, the emotional component of his response was distasteful. His control was no doubt weakened due to the erratic meditation schedule that life in the resistance enforced. He quashed the anxiety and focused again on logic.

Up ahead, Riker seemed to have managed his initial jealousy toward Vale and was speaking to the two women, making a lewd suggestion involving the three of them. Vale took offense and struck his cheek. Lavena, despite her initial curiosity at Riker's suggestion, spoke angrily in support of her friend. But Riker ignored her, grabbing Vale's wrist and shouting, "Nobody does that to me!" as she cried out in pain.

"Will! Stop that!" Troi was running forward before Tuvok could react. Just then, a signal from his scanner distracted him. They had just come around a large fistrium-laced outcropping, and on the other side—

"Ambush!" he cried. But it was too late. In moments, they were flanked by a pack of predators built somewhat like *le-matya* or Terran felinoids but with four long, tusklike claws on either side of the mouth. An additional predator jumped down from the outcropping, cutting off their retreat. But another was already charging Troi—perhaps recognizing the aged captain as the weakest member of the pack. It pounced before he could finish drawing his weapon, knocking him down. Tuvok was firing his own phaser before they hit the ground. But it was too late. Those razor-sharp tusk-claws had dug into Troi's neck, and the impact of the massive creature had shattered bone. The dead weight of the creature collapsing atop him in this high gravity finished the job.

Tuvok realized he had been a fool. The anxiety he had felt had been a perception of the empathic gestalt of this world, a legitimate warning of an approaching threat. On this world above all, he should have trusted his intuition.

But there was no logic in self-recrimination during a crisis. Riker and Lavena were already firing at the predators, clearing a path for their retreat. Tuvok joined them and Vale in making for the nearby trees, firing back at the pack hunters as they ran.

Then a screech came from the sky. Riker spotted a large avian swooping toward him and raised his arm to fire, but the beaklike pincers ripped his phaser from his hand, almost taking the hand with it. Tuvok shot down a second avian as it dove toward him, but a third ripped through Lavena's hood and tore her gill membranes. Luckily, that was not a serious injury in this phase of her life cycle.

Before they could reach the trees, their way was blocked as several large animals came forth. These were not unlike Terran elephants, their double trunks long and prehensile, but were lower and wider, their backs sporting bony shells with spiked fringes. They were clearly herbivores, and yet they acted aggressively against the rebel squad, grabbing at them with their trunks, seeming unconcerned about the charging felinoids.

"The animals are working together!" Tuvok called. "The Alliance has somehow amplified their empathic rapport!"

"Shut up and fight!" Riker barked. He had drawn his *mek'leth* now and was slashing at one of the herbivores, but it charged forward without regard for the damage to its probosces. Apparently, whatever the Alliance had done to these animals was subverting their survival instinct as well—or subsuming it to the needs of the whole.

Although the creature was badly injured in the process, it managed to knock the blade from Riker's hand and drove him into the clutches of another herbivore, which gripped him tightly in its trunks. Tuvok, attempting to fight off the felinoids and avians with his phaser, soon found himself in an herbivore's grip as well and deemed it wise to stop struggling, lest the powerful appendages crush him. Vale had also been captured . . .

Except that *captured* proved incorrect, for the herbivore that held her was in fact lifting her onto its back, out of harm's way. Lavena, oblivious to this detail, rushed toward her, crying her name—until she realized that Vale had a weapon pointed at her. "Drop it, Aili, if you don't want to be cat food. You know how they love fish."

Lavena was dumbstruck. "Christine, what are you doing?"

Riker scoffed. "She's betraying us, you dumb trout! I told you it was a trap!"

"Not just a trap," Vale said proudly, "but a test. A demonstration of what my master's brilliance has achieved on this world in mere weeks."

"But you hate him!" Lavena cried.

"I could never hate Jaza Najem," Vale responded. "He's given me everything. Let me rise above my pathetic birthright, become more than just another Terran savage. It's people like you, who'd set the Terrans free upon the galaxy again, that I hate." She smirked. "You were so easy. So eager for new experiences. I didn't even have to pretend I loved you, since all you cared about was the sex. That's what comes of working with Terrans, Aili. Their stupidity is contagious."

Her face contorted with fury, Lavena raised her weapon. Vale was quicker, her own face showing no expression as she fired and left the Selkie with no face at all.

"You traitor," Riker growled—although his gaze was locked on Vale and he showed no reaction to Lavena's death. "When I get out of this, I'll show you what happens to people who betray me. They die slow, and they die suffering. I'll enjoy showing you just what 'Terran savagery' means."

"And I'll enjoy watching the governor show you what happens to enemies of the Alliance. He's very creative with interrogations."

"Efforts to extract information through physical pain are ineffective on Vulcans," Tuvok pointed out.

"Maybe," Vale said. "But this one'll break. I know his type. Doesn't care about anyone but himself. He'll give up your whole rebellion if he thinks it'll save his skin."

At some unseen command, the herbivores turned and headed off with their prisoners—and passenger. Tuvok considered that Vale was probably correct about Riker and wondered if he would need to terminate the man to protect the cause. It would be a far smaller loss, he reflected, than the two the rebellion had just suffered. In his own private, Vulcan way, he allowed himself to grieve.

"Very good, all of you," the biped called Jaza said. "Just stay focused a little longer. Soon they'll be here and you can rest."

Orilly Malar barely heard his words. The clamor in her mind was too intense. The gestalt awareness that should be a comforting background presence had been amplified into a painful torrent as the outsiders' machines forced her to share the awareness of dozens of other beings. Worse, she felt their distress and confusion when she and her fellow Irriol compelled them to act in unnatural ways. She wished she could stop, but the outsiders would not let her. If she fought them, she might end up as her little sister Jerel had, eaten by that cheerful killer Ree and forced to watch as it happened.

The thought filled Orilly with anger, made her want to strike at these invaders, even at the cost of her own life. But even through the din of her amplified perceptions, she could feel the collective will of the other Irriol holding her back. They felt loss and anger as well but feared more for the safety of the community. The Jaza creature had told them that if they cooperated, they would suffer less. That sounded sensible, for it was usually when Irriol resisted the larger flow of events that they suffered most. Yet that did not explain to Orilly why submitting to the outsiders felt so wrong, or how forcing the other species of Lru-Irr to act against the natural flow could be the proper choice.

For now, ending the immediate pain was motivation enough. In moments, the captured bipeds would be here, and she could release her hold on the *monollir* that carried them. Mercifully, she and her kin had already been allowed to break their link with the *navoliro* and *gariya* birds before they had begun feasting on the bodies left behind.

The *monollir* arrived outside the large laboratory structure, hesitating as the shimmering curtain at its entrance—the "force field," the outsiders called it—stung at their skin. The field deterred animals from entering unless the Irriol pressured them to overcome the discomfort and push through, as they did to the *monollir* now. Orilly was finally able to see the captives with her own eyes—both bipeds, but one large and burly with pink flesh and black fur on its head and face, one more slender with brown skin and no facial fur. The large one was fierce, with the look of a cornered predator, but the slender one appeared amazingly calm. A third *monollir* bore the servant creature Christine on its back, though she looked far less subservient in comparison.

The Jaza creature ordered the Irriol to make the *monollir* set his servant down and place the other two in restraints, telling them they could send the animals away and rest afterward. He ran to the female and clasped her forelimbs once this had been done. "I'm so glad you're safe." It seemed to Orilly that he was holding himself back from an even more emotional display, though it was hard to tell with creatures not part of the gestalt.

"I knew you wouldn't have let me go if you couldn't keep the animals under control," the Christine creature answered.

"That control was relative," Jaza said unhappily. "I was hoping to take more of them alive."

The female winced. "Sir, I didn't know. I acted rashly, I—"

"It's all right. It was chaotic, and you're only a Terran."

She bowed her head, then threw a subdued look at the prisoners. "At least it was an easier death than these two will get."

"That depends on how cooperative they are," Jaza countered. "Maybe it doesn't have to come to that."

"We'll get nothing from Tuvok here."

The Ree creature came closer to the dark, slender captive. "Hrrr, don't be so sure. I would welcome the chance to examine a Vulcan."

"Why?" Jaza asked. "We know all there is to know about them."

"The Terran Empire was not as certain. Few study their writings today, but it is a hobby of mine. There were rumors among them that Vulcans possessed telepathic powers."

"You mean the magical powers Emperor Spock supposedly used to claim the throne? Just superstitious ramblings, fabrications to rationalize their conquest by a Vulcan, of all things. Honestly, Ree, if Vulcans had the power to destroy their enemies with a thought, why would they have been such unresisting slaves for generations?"

"Perhaps, as with my people, the abilities are only present in a minority. But it is my hope that studying the Vulcan brain and genome might offer clues to the existence of such abilities. The tales of Spock's magic may be exaggerations rather than outright fictions."

Orilly did not understand much of what they said. But even now, with the amplifying machines inactive, her senses were still heightened enough from Ree's surgical invasions that she could feel the mental presence of this "Vulcan." He did have what the invaders called "telepathy," but they did not know this. If she told them, would that spare the Vulcan from Ree's tortures? *No,* she told herself. *If this truth were known, his people would be cut into and hooked to machines as we have been. They were wise to keep it hidden.*

I am gratified that you realize that.

Orilly was startled. It was a clearly voiced thought—but not her own. The surgeries let her feel the minds of her fellow Irriol more keenly than usual, but that was more a sharing of emotion and sensation. These were words.

Then more words came. *I am Tuvok of Vulcan. Are you receiving my thoughts?*

After a moment, Orilly ventured thinking, *Yes.*

Excellent. Clearly a by-product of your amplified abilities. She sensed concepts beneath the words—the Vulcans could share thoughts but usually needed touch. *As you have discerned, I need your assistance to escape before I can be subjected to study. In return, I will help you liberate yourselves and organize resistance against the Alliance.*

Orilly was not sure if the others could hear him as clearly as she could, for she was nearest. At the very least, they sensed her reaction to his words, and she felt their resistance and distress, which she relayed to him. *We cannot! It will merely bring down more suffering. The Jaza creature tells us that if we cooperate, we will be safer.*

That is a lie.

I sense his honesty. She shared with him her impressions of the guarded compassion she sensed within Jaza, restrained by pragmatism and dedication to his goals but working to temper the harshness of those goals when it could. It was an echo of the gestalt feeling that governed the Irriol's life, and she and her kin found hope in it.

But what of the others? Tuvok asked. *Look at what they have done to you, and to us. Consider what they have forced you to become. Can you trust that this Jaza is anything more than an exception to the pattern?* He shared his own experiences of the Alliance—the deviousness and cruelty of his former master K'Tar, the sadism of intendants such as Kira and B'Elanna, the cruel tortures inflicted on the few other telepaths they had discovered. *Cooperate with them, and you will be reduced to living weapons, with no freedom even within your own minds.*

But they are too powerful, Orilly answered. *What can we do to fight them?*

You control a great power that they have given you: the biosphere of this planet. The animals you sent against us are formidable. Imagine what they could do against this outpost.

More would come and kill us.

This planet is remote from their territory. There are few Alliance personnel and ships here, and reinforcements are far away. He paused. *I do not claim that there would be no risk. Retaliation would be likely, and your people would surely suffer losses. But your only hope as a people is to continue resisting long and aggressively enough that they can no longer afford to exploit you. The resistance will help you—and in time, you may be able to help us more than I can say at this juncture.*

Despite his reticence, she sensed the subtext—something about a secret movement among the Vulcans, a plan to rise in force when the time was right. This was why preserving the secret of Vulcan telepathy was so urgent. But Orilly noted that he thought more of helping her people than soliciting their help for himself. Even with his outer coldness, he thought of the gestalt first. This was not something she sensed in any of the invaders save Jaza, and even in him it was muffled, restrained. True, she sensed no trace of it in the one Tuvok thought of as "Riker," but she could tell in Tuvok's thoughts that there were many others in the resistance who risked themselves for others. Including two good people who had died trying to save her—people she herself had helped to kill.

These are the ones we should be cooperating with, Orilly sent to her kinfolk. *They embody true gestalt. They wish to stand alongside us, not exploit us. And we have the power! We must act now to restore the proper order and expel those who disrupt it!*

She felt the others' resistance. They yearned for what she promised but were afraid to take the necessary steps. Several had already died or been deeply crippled in the mind when they exerted control too strongly or too often. The capture of the rebels had strained them severely; to use their power again so soon and so aggressively would probably burn them out. *We must not fear that!* Orilly told them. *It is worth our own sacrifice to protect the Whole. And if we die, then we deprive the invaders of the weapons they would use against us and others. We destroy the work they have done and leave them with nothing.*

Orilly had already decided that she would act, alone if necessary, no matter what the consensus was. But one by one, the others sent her their support, hesitant at first but getting stronger as their numbers grew. *We are with you,* she sent to Tuvok. *Now . . . what exactly do we do?*

As Najem and Ree discussed their plans for experimenting on the Vulcan, Christine became aware of Riker's relentless gaze upon her. She looked away and fidgeted, then caught herself and strode over to him, meeting his eyes. "You think you can intimidate me? Stare all you want. It's the only power you have."

"I'm just planning the best ways to make you suffer before you die."

"If you take comfort in that fantasy, go ahead."

He smirked. "You act like you've got a spine, but I know better. You're a craven traitor, too weak to stand up for yourself."

That made her laugh. "You have no idea. You think the way to improve your life is to scream and fight like a spoiled child? Has that actually gotten you anything other than danger and squalor and pain? I've made the system work for me. I live in comfort, I have an education, I get treated with respect and kindness. With luck, the children I bear for Najem will be able to pass as Bajoran and have an even better life."

Riker scoffed. "So you're a career girl. Just doing your duty."

"Yes, I am. I'm loyal to my master."

"You mean you bend over for anyone who owns you."

She shook her head, defying his contempt. "No. I'm loyal because he's *earned* it. Because he's a better man than anyone in your pathetic resistance will ever be." *Or anyone else in the Alliance,* she added silently, knowing better than to voice such sedition. If slavery was her lot in life as a Terran—and the resistance was foolish to think it had a chance of changing that reality in her lifetime—then she would make the best of it, do whatever she could to survive and prosper. Despite what she'd told Najem before, she would find a way to adapt and live on if she ever lost him. But life could never be as good or as safe for her without him as her master—and she was blessed that her best option for prosperity had brought her love and happiness as well.

So when the *monollir* and *navoliro* charged through the force field a moment later and began smashing up the lab, she rushed instantly to protect him, drawing her weapon and blasting at the stampeding beasts. She grabbed Najem's arm and pulled him behind a heavy console.

Ree was surrounded by the felinoids, but he was in full predator mode himself. He dodged one as it lunged with its tusk-claws clashing and caught it around its neck with his own fearsome jaws. Christine heard its neck snap even as Ree's tail swung and caved in another *navoliro*'s skull.

Meanwhile, the *monollir* were using their trunks to free the prisoners—both the rebels and the test subjects. "The Irriol!" Najem cried. "They're controlling the animals. I don't understand what prompted this change in behavior. The resistance must have gotten to them, but how?"

"Figure that out later, sir! We have to get to safety now."

"No, we can't let them destroy our work! If they do, all this suffering will have been for nothing."

The guards were arriving now, so there was no need for Christine and Najem to stay. But he had given her an order, so she did her duty and stayed to fight. Riker and Tuvok were free now, and the Vulcan was disconnecting the remaining Irriol from the equipment—though some were apparently dead already, burned out by their mental exertion. Christine fired at him. He dodged, but her beam grazed his flank, not a fatal blow but enough to fell him. A *monollir* moved to block her line of fire. She shot it, but its tough carapace absorbed most of the energy. "No!" Najem said. "It'll be too good an obstruction if you kill it. Drive it away." She fired in front of it, hoping its fear would override the Irriol's control.

Meanwhile, Riker was battling the guards, unconcerned by his comrade's injury. Despite his bulk, he moved with impressive speed, dodging the Klingon guard's disruptor blast and ducking around him, snatching his own *d'k tahg* from his belt and slashing his throat with it. Grinning savagely as he liberated the guard's *mek'leth* from its scabbard, Riker charged Ree from behind while the sauroid had his teeth buried in another *navoliro*'s neck. Christine called a warning and broke cover to run to his defense, but the Pahkwa-thanh took too long to get his head free and turned around. He managed to slash Riker's arm with a talon, too late to prevent the *mek'leth* from lodging itself in his neck. He screamed horribly and fell twitching to the floor, his convulsions jerking Riker around so much that Christine's phaser shot missed him.

She took aim again, but he swung the freed *mek'leth* at her, taking her by surprise. It sent the phaser flying and made a ruin of the hand that had held it. Christine screamed in pain as Riker pulled her toward him and held the sword against her neck. "Let me go or she dies!" he cried.

"Hold your fire!" Najem called to the guards, and Christine cursed her Terran stupidity for letting herself be taken and used against him.

Riker dragged her back toward the force field. "Mr. Riker!" Tuvok called from the floor.

"Save yourself if you can," Riker told him. "This mission's a bust. I'm getting out of here!" He took her out through the field, not sparing his comrade another glance.

"You really . . . don't care about anything . . . but yourself, do you?" she managed to get out.

"Oh, I care about you," he told her. "I care about the revenge I promised you."

"My master . . . will save me."

His breath was hot against her neck. "You'll be calling *me* master before you die."

Tuvok gave little thought to Riker's abandonment; it was only to be expected. What mattered was the success of the mission. With Ree dead and the equipment largely destroyed by the native animals, the research had suffered a major setback. The remaining priority was to ensure the escape of the surviving Irriol.

So when Orilly Malar and the other survivors came toward him, he told them, *Leave me! You must escape and organize resistance.*

No! Orilly sent back. *I will not leave you! Too many have died already!*

My death is by no means a certainty, he told her, though he kept the actual probability of his survival to himself. *Go! You, above all, should understand that the needs of the many outweigh the needs of the one.*

Finally, reluctantly, she turned and led her people out through the force field. The animals remained, continuing to attack the base personnel and impede pursuit. It was the best Tuvok could hope to achieve under the circumstances.

And so he allowed himself to succumb to oblivion, uncertain if he would ever awaken. His last conscious thought was of his wife and children.

At last, Riker thought as he stroked *Deanna*'s bulkhead. *You belong to me now.*

With escape being a priority, he hadn't been able to devote as much time as he'd wanted to dealing with the slave woman. At least he'd made sure it was memorable while it lasted. But whatever satisfaction he'd had to forgo with Vale was more than made up for by the thrill of finally stepping onto *Deanna*'s bridge and knowing it was all his. "Let's get out of here, fast," he told Bolaji.

"Where are the others?" she asked, wide-eyed.

"Dead. And we have to move if we don't want to end up the same way!" Bolaji was slow to move, wasting time with some useless feeling about the deaths of the others, so he flung her forcefully aside and took the helm himself. This ship was his now, so he should be the one controlling her.

She proved a bit rough to handle as he took her up. She had a lot of power, and she fought him, bucking like a bronco. But he rode her hard, knowing he could break her soon enough. The struggle to impose his will was so enthralling that he barely noticed they'd broken atmosphere until an alarm sounded. "They've sent a ship after us!" Sortollo cried.

"Let's see them try and catch this beauty," Riker said, and kicked in the warp drive.

But the ship lurched and squealed, and nothing happened. "What the hell?"

"We're too close to the gravity well, you idiot!" Bolaji said. "You forgot to recalibrate! It'll take over a minute to reinitialize warp!"

"Then we'll ditch them at impulse." He swung the ship around, down into the atmosphere. She bucked and shrieked in protest at the friction, but he pushed her forward, confident she could take it.

"She's coming in too steep!" Bolaji cried. The ship shuddered as a disruptor bolt detonated off their bow. "Give me the helm, Riker! You have no feel for her, you can't maneuver well enough in atmosphere! You're burning out the shields!"

"I'm through taking orders! She's mine now, and she goes where I tell her!"

Another bolt grazed them, the impact sending Bolaji and Sortollo to the deck. "Dammit, Riker, you'll get us all killed!"

"Speak for yourself," Riker said, forcing the ship to swerve hard to evade another bolt, fighting the friction. "I plan to live forev—"

He overcorrected, his swerve taking *Deanna* directly into another disruptor bolt. The shields had burned out a second before. Riker finally had his wish: *Deanna* would never belong to another, and he would never take orders from anyone again.

As soon as the animals had been subdued, Jaza led the surviving security forces after Christine. He ordered them to patch up the Vulcan—Tuvok, she had called him—and bring him along, willing to trade him for her if it came to that.

They soon reached the area where Christine had arranged for the rebel ship to land, but Jaza feared it might take too long to pinpoint it through the sensor interference. That fear was mooted when the ship rocketed off within eyeshot, replaced with a new fear that Christine was now in rebel custody. "Contact the patrol ship," he ordered. "Tell them to capture that vessel intact at all costs!" Still, he ran toward the takeoff site, hoping desperately that the Terran had let his hostage go once he'd reached his ship.

Then he began to find Christine's torn clothing strewn about, and his hope turned to dread. Moments later, he found her . . . what the Terran had left of her. He had laid her out carefully to make it clear exactly what he had done to her before ending her life.

Jaza didn't even remember screaming. He only became aware of himself kneeling over her body, dazed, his throat raw. The guards helped him to his feet, but he felt as if he were floating, detached from reality. How could he be part of the universe when the anchor of his existence was gone?

Then he caught sight of the Vulcan, and something within him felt tangible again. It was rage. "How could he do this to her?!" he screamed at the prisoner. "One of his own people! One who embodied the best of what Terrans were capable of being!" Tuvok only examined him stoically.

He caught sight of her again, the travesty that the terrorist had made of her perfection, and could stand it no longer. "Get her out of here," he ordered the guards. "Let her rest with some dignity."

"But, sir—"

"Leave him with me." He brandished his weapon, letting the guards know he would be all right. As they obeyed his instructions, he drew closer to the bound prisoner. "Is that why he did it?" he asked. "Because she was better than him? Because he couldn't stand the reminder of his own deficiency?"

"I did not know Mr. Riker well enough to speak with authority concerning his motives," the Vulcan said with infuriating calm.

"You knew he was Terran! Isn't that enough?" He sucked in breath through clenched teeth. "I thought she was proof that Terrans could be more than they are. That maybe there was some hope of redeeming the breed. But she was one of a kind, wasn't she? The rest, they're all like him! Killers and monsters! Their misbegotten race will never produce the likes of her again, because they'll destroy any good one that comes along before she even gets the chance. We might as well kill them all now and be done with it!"

Tuvok studied him closely. "You genuinely cared for her. Did you not?"

Jaza glared at him. "I loved her! Not that that's anything you'd understand, Vulcan."

"I understand that such empathy for a slave is a rare commodity within the Alliance. I submit that it would be a waste of that commodity if you allowed it to transform into hatred and vio-lence—commodities of which the Alliance already possesses an overabundance."

Struck by his words, Jaza fell silent. After a moment, he went on more calmly, "The Terrans have no shortage of those qualities themselves."

"That is the nature of hatred and violence. They tend to inspire equal hatred and violence in their victims. Thereby, a cycle of mu-tual retribution is created and perpetuated. Each side claims the other is innately corrupt due to its brutality—yet fails to recognize the contradiction as it embraces the same brutality in retaliation."

Jaza didn't want to admit that he'd had the same thoughts, had wondered whether the Alliance was provoking the violence with its hard-line tactics. He wanted to hate Riker and the Terrans for tak-ing Christine from him. "That's just making excuses. Any civilized species would find another way."

"Are you familiar with the alternate universe?"

Jaza frowned at the non sequitur. "Yes, I've read about the contacts."

"Then you should be aware that the alternate Bajor endured a brutal Cardassian occupation until less than a decade ago. That its people organized a resistance movement, employing whatever tac-tics were available to them. As with most resistance movements against vastly superior forces, these tactics included acts of terror-ism and random violence intended to demoralize the occupying population and diminish their support for the occupation. This tactic ultimately proved successful, but only after generations, and it naturally brought aggressive retaliation against the Bajorans. That Bajor suffered far worse under the Cardassians, and far more re-cently, than your Bajor did under the Terrans."

He took a step closer, though there was no threat in it. "If not for a twist of fate, Dr. Jaza, you yourself might have grown up in the same kind of conditions that produced Mr. Riker. And you might have turned out much as he did."

"What are you saying, Vulcan? Are you asking me to forgive him?"

"I am pointing out the illogic of vengeance. It does not bring justice or compensate for loss; it simply reproduces the same destructive impulses that create injustice and loss in the first place, guaranteeing greater injustice and greater loss. It is a waste of life and energy, nothing more.

"Consider, Dr. Jaza. You are a Bajoran who chose to reach out to a Terran and see the potential for a peaceful, mutually beneficial relationship with her. That is the way of thinking that can break the cycle of injustice and loss, if applied more broadly. Would that not honor Christine Vale's memory more than embracing the same vengeful mentality that killed her?"

Jaza pondered the question. He couldn't deny what Tuvok said about the Alliance. If they hadn't come here to exploit the Irriol, the rebels would never have come to sabotage the project. If he hadn't chosen to participate, he never would have brought Christine here into harm's way.

And if he had treated Christine as an equal from the start, if she had had the right to choose, perhaps she would not have been so willing to follow him to her own doom.

"I do—I did what I could to try to make a small difference. To lead a decent life in indecent times. But it wasn't enough. How could it be? I'm only one man."

Tuvok quirked an eyebrow. "You would be surprised at the power one man has to remake his society from within. If that man has the right strategy, the right resources, and the right allies."

Jaza studied him. "Are you offering yourself as the latter?"

"That depends upon your intentions."

For a long moment, he stared at the stained ground where Christine had lain. "We have to break the cycle," he muttered. "Or we'll all stay trapped in it together."

He moved behind the Vulcan and released his bonds. "As for my intentions . . . I think I will report to Governor Khegh that my Vulcan prisoner was devoured by wild animals. Then I will report that with Ree dead and the Irriol proving too hard to control or keep alive, the enhancement project is no longer feasible. That, at least, is not far from the truth."

A thought occurred to him. "Then I think I will persuade Khegh to sell me his Elaysian slave, to replace . . . the one I have lost. He'll probably be glad to get rid of her. Then I will take her with me on my private yacht . . . and I will beam you aboard and take you away from here. You can take the Elaysian with you, find her a nice low-gravity planetoid to live on."

He fell silent. "And then?" Tuvok prompted.

"Then . . . I will go home to grieve the woman I loved. After that . . ." He met Tuvok's eyes. "Understand—I am a patriot. I believe in the Alliance. It's simply lost its way. What I do, I will do to save it from its own worst impulses, not to destroy it. There are others like me, people I can organize. Scientific minds on whom the Alliance depends for its progress. We can exert pressure to improve the Alliance from within. To turn it away from slavery."

Tuvok frowned. "I am skeptical of your odds of success. However, I commend you for the undertaking. If it were to succeed, it would prevent much loss of life in the future."

"Yes," Jaza said. But all he could think was that no matter what he did, he could never bring back the one life that had mattered most to him.

You got what you wanted, Christine—to live your life without freedom. And this is where it led you. I wonder if, at the end, you understood.

For Want of a Nail

David Mack

HISTORIAN'S NOTE: *This tale takes place at the end of*
2376, approximately one year after the events of Saturn's Children *from*
Star Trek Mirror Universe: Obsidian Alliances *and prior to the*
events of Star Trek: Deep Space Nine—Warpath.

David Mack is the author of numerous *Star Trek* books, including *Wildfire, A Time to Kill, A Time to Heal,* and *Warpath*. With editor Marco Palmieri, he developed the *Star Trek Vanguard* literary series, for which he has written two novels, *Harbinger* and *Reap the Whirlwind*.

His other novels include the *Wolverine* espionage adventure *Road of Bones,* and his first original novel, *The Calling,* which is scheduled for publication in 2009 by Simon & Schuster. Other upcoming projects by David Mack include the as-yet-untitled fifth novel in the *Star Trek Vanguard* series, and *Promises Broken,* an original novel based on the TV series *The 4400*.

Before writing books, Mack co-wrote with John J. Ordover the *Star Trek: Deep Space Nine* fourth-season episode "Starship Down" and the story treatment for the series' seventh-season episode "It's Only a Paper Moon."

An avid fan of Canadian progressive-rock trio Rush, Mack has attended shows in all of the band's concert tours since 1982.

Mack lives in New York with his wife, Kara. Learn more about him and his work on his Web site, www.infinitydog.com, and on his blog, infinitydog.livejournal.com.

As soon as the Klingon sentry finished checking in with his base's security command center, K'Ehleyr reached down, out of the shadows and rain, and broke his neck with one brutal, twisting grab. His body dropped limply as his knees buckled. By the time his back struck the muddy ground, he was nothing but a sack of meat and bone.

The scouring downpour pelted his carcass. Lightning exposed the decrepit base's many buildings in a flash of electric-blue light, and then darkness returned with a crack of thunder.

Lowering herself headfirst, K'Ehleyr found the ground with her fingertips and gracefully cartwheeled to a standing position beside a nook of the base's perimeter wall, where she would be concealed from view. She reached out, grabbed the dead Klingon guard, and pulled him into the nook beside her.

"I'm in," she said, in a whisper that would be rendered with perfect clarity by her implanted subaural transceiver. "Sitrep."

Her tactical coordinator stuttered over the secure channel, *"You're th—thirty seconds slow. Her transport's l—landing already, on p—p—pad four."*

The heads-up display that had been built into the mask visor of K'Ehleyr's stealth suit lit up with a wireframe overlay of the base and directional guides to her target. "Got it," she said, and she started making her way across a narrow gap between the perimeter wall and the closest building. "Do they know who she is yet?"

"The whole b—b—base is on alert, and the c—commander is going to question her himself. So, yes, I think they know."

"Damn. That's not good."

K'Ehleyr halted as she noted a hint of motion beyond the building. She pressed her back to the wall and turned her head sideways. At the edge of her vision, she saw a hulking brute of a Klingon reach the corner, turn on his heel, and begin marching his patrol back the way he'd come. Unfortunately for him and for K'Ehleyr, his sentry line crossed back and forth in front of the section of a wall she needed to scale in order to sneak inside the base's detention facility.

She skulked up behind him in long strides. Though she was nowhere near equal in size to the guard, her half-Klingon, half-human ancestry had blessed her with greater than average height—most of it thanks to her long, lean legs. She didn't worry about the guard hearing her approach; whatever footfalls the stealth suit didn't muffle would be masked by the white noise of the storm that was soaking the base.

He reached the end of his patrol path, stopped, and turned back. K'Ehleyr plunged her *d'k tahg* through his larynx in a single thrust, and he pitched forward, silenced and bleeding. She caught his body as it fell and pulled her traditional Klingon dagger free of his throat. Then she dragged his ponderous dead weight to cover, between some empty fuel pods awaiting pickup for their return journey to some distant offworld refinery.

As she covered the body with a loose tarp, her tactical coordinator's voice nagged at her over the comm. *"We're l–l–losing time,"* he said. *"They're t–taking her to the detention center. If they p–put her in a m–m–mind-sifter—"*

"I know," K'Ehleyr cut in. "They could make her give up the entire movement." She found a handhold in a corner of the detention-center wall, near some pipes that would help her scale the building's exterior to a known vulnerable point on its roof. "That's why we're here—to get her out before that happens."

"But what if we're t–t–too late?"

"Then we do whatever it takes to contain the damage. Kill her, destroy this base, frag the planet—anything. Understand?"

"*Y–yes,*" he replied. "*I understand.*"

"Good." She took hold of one of the pipes and began a fast ascent of the building's wall. "Send me schematics for the crawl spaces." She knew that a solo assault on the base was a terrible risk, but there was too much at stake to play it safe any longer. If she failed, Memory Omega would be destroyed, and more than a century of hard-won achievements would be wasted.

Not today, K'Ehleyr vowed. *Not on my watch. Not ever.*

Wedged between his master control console, stacks of cross-wired equipment, and the computer core that housed the eponymous artificial intelligence of the reconnaissance vessel *Solomon,* Reginald Barclay could barely move his fingers fast enough to keep up with K'Ehleyr's demands for hard intel.

With a bit of help from the AI, he punched up a virtual three-dimensional schematic of the detention center's maintenance crawl spaces and patched it through to K'Ehleyr's stealth-suit visor. "Crawl space m–m–maps uploaded," he said, speaking softly into his slender headset microphone.

"*Just in time,*" K'Ehleyr replied. "*I'm on the roof. Breaching the heat vent in ten. Stand by to run interference.*"

"Check," Barclay said, already two steps ahead of her. He'd isolated the detention center's external security systems to prevent any alarms from being tripped by her entry, and he was making certain that the vent she was using would be flushed with clean air and then locked into standby mode. "G–good to go."

He wiped sweat from his high forehead. After more than fifteen years of working together, Barclay and K'Ehleyr now meshed with ease, like interlocking gears. They had been paired in their youth while growing up together in the Memory Omega headquarters hidden inside the Regula I planetoid, and they had been trained for much of their lives to function as a team.

The division of responsibilities had always been clear. K'Ehleyr was the field operative and mission commander. She set the agendas and called the shots. Barclay's job was to provide her with tactical support, impede their targets' security and communications, and arrange as many exit strategies for K'Ehleyr as he could, from his support center inside the *Solomon.*

The scrambled transceiver implanted in K'Ehleyr's ear canal kept Barclay aware of her position inside the detention facility while he raced to acquire the next set of floor plans and intel she would need. He muted his channel to K'Ehleyr and said to the AI, "Solomon, tap into the base's internal sensors, and give me positions of all personnel and prisoners inside the detention center, on screen three. I also need a tap on their internal communications regarding Alynna Nechayev."

"Operations in progress," the AI replied through an overhead speaker.

It was one of the cruel ironies of Barclay's life that the only time he didn't stutter was when he was talking to the AI. Real people made him nervous, but Solomon had always seemed nonthreatening. He had hoped that if he worked with K'Ehleyr for long enough, he might achieve the same degree of comfort with her, but so far, that day hadn't come. And so the trim, gray-haired tactician and engineer remained alone, sequestered inside the cramped aft cabin of their tiny cloaked recon ship.

"Level-by-level floor plans ready," Solomon announced as the diagrams appeared on one of Barclay's many monitors. *"And I have located General Nechayev."*

"Good work," Barclay said. "Put it on the big screen."

The master display changed to show a red dot, which stood for Nechayev, moving at a walking pace through the facility.

Reactivating his comm link to K'Ehleyr, Barclay uploaded the floor plans and Nechayev's position to her heads-up display. "F–f–found her," he said, wincing in private frustration at his uncontrollable stutter. "Sublevel six, section t–two-twenty."

"Can you tell if she has the device with her?"

"No, the b–base's internal sensors aren't set up to scan for that," he said. "Still no c–c–comm chatter, though. If the Klingons have it, they might not know what it is."

K'Ehleyr was descending quickly, moving in the spaces between the walls and floors and then down a turbolift shaft. *"Even if she dies, we need to get the device back,"* she said.

"I know," Barclay said, searching the base's records for any record of personal property that might have been taken from Nechayev when she was placed in Klingon custody. "L–looking for it now. Let you know if I f–f–find anything."

Barclay hoped they could save Nechayev in time. But he knew that her life didn't really matter. In the end, it was nothing.

The device, on the other hand, was *everything*.

A pair of gargantuan Klingon soldiers pushed Alynna Nechayev into the metal chair. Dull jolts shot up the trim, fiftyish human woman's tailbone. She bit down on her pain and fixed her glare on the pitted gray concrete wall in front of her.

The guards pulled her hands behind the back of the chair. Steel manacles snapped shut around her wrists, cold and tight. She shifted her weight to test the mobility of the chair; it didn't budge. *Must be bolted to the floor,* she realized.

Behind her, she heard the scuffle of boots on stone. The guards were keeping a close watch on her. She tilted her head back and squinted through a lock of her silver-blond hair at the naked light fixture that dangled above and slightly in front of her. With her eyes closed, she imagined she could feel the heat radiating from the bulb.

Outside the open door of the cell, she heard voices, a tense under-the-breath discussion. The corridor was dim compared with her circle of light, and the figures outside it were black shapes against a backdrop of shadow.

Then the debate ended, and a Klingon of medium build walked in and said to the two guards, "Get out."

The guards left. The new arrival shut the door after them. He pulled a communications device from his belt and keyed it on. "Computer, recognize my voiceprint."

"Acknowledged," a masculine voice replied in *tlhIngan Hol.*

"Deactivate all recording systems and internal sensors in this cell until I order otherwise," he said. "Authorization Duras-*SuD-cha'-Soch-vagh.*"

"Authorization confirmed. Internal sensors deactivated."

He grinned. "Now we can talk in private."

"A pleasure to make your acquaintance, General Duras," Nechayev said with an insinuating smirk.

His expression conveyed amusement and disdain. "Hmmph. No need for introductions, I see." He paced slowly to her left. "Whatever you have to say, you'll say only to me. Understand?"

"Perfectly," Nechayev said. "You want a monopoly on my intel. Probably to bolster your house's sagging fortunes."

Her verbal jab inflamed his temper. "What do you know of my family, you *petaQ*?"

"I know that you lost command of the *Negh'Var* to Kurn and that the higher his star rises beside Intendant Kira's, the farther yours falls." She made a show of looking around at the drab confines of her cell. "Though you couldn't have fallen much farther than *this,* could you? A worthless posting at the ass end of the Empire. Hardly a fitting billet for a warrior."

Duras reversed direction and plodded to Nechayev's right. "You're well informed about the Alliance's affairs," he said. "What I want to hear is what you know about the Terran rebellion. Their plans, resources, strongholds . . . everything."

"No," Nechayev said. "That's just what you *think* you want." Her smirk widened as she halted Duras's wanderings with a salacious gleam. "Let me tell you what you *really* want: the power *behind* the rebellion. The éminence grise that pulls the strings and sets the agenda. A secret society that's been plotting the fall of the Alliance and the return of the Terran Republic for more than a century."

Lowering his voice and leaning closer, Duras asked, "Does this mysterious cabal have a name?"

He gazed hard into her eyes and waited for an answer.

She met his unblinking stare with her own.

"Memory Omega."

The general had no visible reaction to her revelation. Then he snorted, stepped back, and shook his head. "And why should I believe a word of this outrageous story?"

"Because it will let you crush the Terran rebellion once and for all," Nechayev said.

He folded his arms and cast a suspicious look at her. "And why would you volunteer such vital information?"

She pinned her hopes on the truth.

"Because I want to defect."

Wedged in a gap between two walls, K'Ehleyr nearly fumbled her exosonic mic when she heard Nechayev utter the word *defect*.

Shock put a harsh note into her voice as she whispered, "Reg, did you hear that?"

"I heard it," Barclay replied over the subaural comm. *"Is it a d–d–disinformation scheme?"*

Through the clandestine listening device, K'Ehleyr picked up more snippets of Nechayev's discussion with Duras. "I don't think so," K'Ehleyr said. "She's telling him about the Vulcan sleeper agents. Dammit . . . she's telling him *everything.*"

"This is b–bad. If she talks about the MQT—"

"Then it's all over."

She knew that Barclay understood she wasn't exaggerating. If the Alliance learned that Nechayev had given them the master quantum transceiver, it would be in a position to wipe out all of Memory Omega, and the Terran rebellion with it.

The MQT was a gadget small enough to be hidden in one's hand. It contained fermions whose quantum-entangled matching particles were concealed in hidden Memory Omega bases throughout local space. With the right kind of hardware, they enabled the possessors of the two particles to communicate instantaneously across any distance, and in perfect privacy—there was no way to intercept such messages, because there was no transmission of the signal. When one entangled particle vibrated a certain way, its mate vibrated in perfect sympathetic harmony, as if they were one particle existing in two places at the same time.

It was an elegant solution to the problem of coordinating operations in secret and across vast distances. However, it had a vulnerability. The MQT could be used to send out pulses that would give away the location of every Memory Omega facility in the galaxy—and perhaps even remotely seize control of them and trigger their self-destruct sequences.

"Do you think she'd really g–g–give it to them?"

"It wouldn't make much sense for her to come this far and *not* hand it over," K'Ehleyr replied as she finished a virtual inventory of her weapons and gear. "We can't let that happen."

She shimmied toward a ventilation grate that led into a corridor a few intersections from Nechayev's holding cell. As she slithered over a bundle of power cables, Barclay's voice pestered her. *"K–K–Kay? What're you d–d–doing?"*

"Changing the mission profile," K'Ehleyr said. "New prime objective is kill Nechayev and anyone she's talked to. Soon as that's done, we confiscate the MQT and breeze outta here."

K'Ehleyr reached the grate and peeked through it. The corridor beyond was empty. She used a silent ion drill to weaken the screws that held it in place.

"M–maybe a less direct approach would b–b–be—"

"Save it, I can take these guys." She poked her fingers through slats in the grate and took hold of it. One push dislodged it from the wall. "Cut the chatter, I'm going in."

She tucked the grate behind her and slipped hands-first out of the ventilation shaft, into the corridor. Her visor's heads-up display guided her toward an intersection.

Heavy, plodding footfalls drew closer. *Two targets.*

K'Ehleyr eased her *d'k tahg* from its sheath. She struck at the first glimpse of her foes. Her blade sank into the closer guard's throat, a perfect kill, swift and silent.

The second guard reached for his disruptor pistol. He'd pulled his weapon halfway from its holster before K'Ehleyr caught him under the chin with a palm strike. With fluid grace, she snapped her dagger from the first guard's carotid artery and slashed it across the second guard's exposed throat.

Both bodies fell in a bloody jumble at her feet.

Then she saw four more guards at the end of the corridor, all looking back at her with expressions of intense surprise.

They reached for their sidearms.

She sheathed her *d'k tahg* with one hand and tossed out a handful of gas capsules with the other.

The corridor filled with thick black smoke, which was laced with an anesthetic compound tailored for Klingon biochemistry. Thanks to her stealth suit's visor, K'Ehleyr peered through the haze as if it weren't there, and the suit's breathing filter protected her from the sleeping gas she'd unleashed.

Meanwhile, her enemies choked and flailed helplessly. She dropped to the floor and crept forward, beneath their flurry of blind disruptor shots. She didn't want to use her own disruptor to fire back, for fear of giving away her position. Instead, she opened a packet of incendiary capsules and pitched them forward.

The capsules scattered like pebbles between the feet of the four dazed soldiers. Then an eardrum-shattering blast and a blinding flash reduced the hulking foursome to an insensate heap of scorched and broken limbs.

K'Ehleyr scrambled forward to the blast-proof gate that led to the maximum-security holding area, where Nechayev was being interrogated. "I'm in position," she said. "Hack the gate for me, fast."

"On it," Barclay said. *"C–c–company on your three."*

She glanced right. Back at the intersection from which she'd come, another Klingon guard had stumbled into the corridor full of blinding sleeping gas. He tried to aim his disruptor rifle but clearly had no idea what to shoot at.

In front of her, the lock on the gate released.

"Open," Barclay said.

"Thanks, Reg." She casually drew her sidearm and popped off a shot that struck the distant guard in his forehead. He fell backward, and K'Ehleyr smirked at her marksmanship. Then came the flash that slammed her against the wall and dropped her to the floor, stunned and shaking.

Consciousness faded quickly. "Reg, abort mission," she mumbled. "Reg, acknowledge . . ."

No answer came.

Then she lost hold of herself and had nothing more to say.

The general would be upset about having his interrogation interrupted, but Colonel Gowron didn't care. He quickened his pace down the dim corridor toward the secured holding cell.

As far as Gowron was concerned, Duras was a mediocrity who had traded on his family name instead of earning his own glory. One lucky break after another had seemed to land in Duras's lap. At least, until Martok had come to power, that was.

Regent Worf's capture by the Terran rebellion months earlier had come as a shock to almost everyone in the Alliance. The vacancy at the top of the Klingon government had represented a unique opportunity, but only General Martok had been poised to exploit it. Long a rival of Duras and an open foe of Gowron, Regent Martok had wasted no time marginalizing the two warriors.

Then had come the heroic rise of Worf's brother, Kurn. Not only had his victory at Empok Nor dealt a major blow to the Terran rebellion, but it had given Martok the opportunity to expel Duras and Gowron to a backwater world of the Empire, while he gifted Kurn with Duras's previous command, the *Negh'Var.*

Most galling of all for Gowron was being Duras's executive officer. The very thought of it made him spit sour bile.

He approached the holding cell's door. A pair of gigantic warriors with chiseled features flanked the portal like statues. Neither looked at Gowron as he stepped between them and pounded the side of his fist on the locked door. He waited.

The door slid open, revealing the furious mien of Duras. "What?" he shouted.

"We captured an intruder," Gowron said in a low voice.

"So?"

Gowron smirked. "An extremely well-equipped intruder," he elaborated. "Here, inside the detention center."

Duras stepped out of the holding cell, forcing Gowron to back-pedal away from him. The general looked at the two guards. "No one but me goes inside that room. Understood?" Both warriors nodded. He stepped away from the door, which shut and locked behind him. He nodded to Gowron to follow him down the corridor. They turned at the first corner. Duras ushered Gowron into an empty holding cell, followed him in, and shut the door.

"Quickly," the general said. "Details."

"A half-breed female," Gowron said. "Part Klingon, part human." He noted the wince of disgust on Duras's face and continued. "She emerged in the middle of a corridor on this level. Her weapons and equipment are very sophisticated."

The general frowned. "How sophisticated?"

"More advanced than anything known to the Alliance," Gowron said. "And far beyond the capabilities of the Terran rebellion."

Nodding, Duras asked, "Could they be of Romulan design?"

"Maybe," Gowron said. "The Romulan worlds *have* been funneling weapons to Calhoun and his people ever since the scouring of Romulus. But unless the Romulans have made a major leap forward in technology—"

"It wouldn't be the first time," Duras said. He paced the short distance to the rear of the cell and back. "Cloaking devices and their new warbird designs both came out of nowhere. They're the most likely source, so look into it."

Despite knowing that the devices were not even remotely Romulan in origin, and that the general was ordering him to waste his time, Gowron replied, "Yes, sir."

Duras opened the door and left the room. Gowron stayed close behind him as they walked back toward the holding cell where the general was holding the new human prisoner. "I'll let you know if the half-breed tells us anything interesting once we get her in the mind-sifter."

The general glanced sideways at Gowron while they walked. "Finish analyzing her equipment first," he said. "The more you learn on your own before you put her in the machine, the better you can target your questions, while she's still lucid enough to answer them."

"Yes, General," Gowron said, acquiescing to yet another squandering of his time and effort. They returned to the door flanked by the two brutes. "How goes your own interrogation?"

Turning back to face him, Duras said, "When there's a reason for you to know, I'll tell you. Dismissed."

Gowron bowed his head and slipped away. He heard the cell door slide open and shut behind him as the general retreated once more into seclusion. *Whoever that prisoner is, she knows something vital,* he concluded. *And the half-breed must know what it is—which is why he stalled my interrogation.*

It wasn't paranoia that made Gowron suspect the general was gathering intelligence for a new power grab.

It was common sense.

Barclay had helped K'Ehleyr put on her stealth suit countless times, but until now, he'd never had to don one himself. It was harder to do alone than he'd thought.

Fifteen years I've been a tac-support guy, he reflected, while struggling to attach various high-tech gadgets to the spare suit's equipment belt. *Fifteen years of sitting in the ship and pushing buttons.* He snapped on a packet of incendiary microrobotic munitions, which he and K'Ehleyr called "spiders." *What am I doing? I'm no field agent. I must be out of my mind.*

He checked the setting on his disruptor and calmed himself. It wasn't that he'd never been trained for field ops, but what experience he'd had was minimal and a long time ago. He couldn't be certain how much of his old instruction would come back to him when he needed it.

Standard procedure in a situation such as this was for him to do exactly what K'Ehleyr had told him to do, before her vitals tanked: abort the mission, and bug out. But there was nothing standard about this mess; too much was at stake for him simply to walk away.

Of course, Barclay might have done exactly that, anyway, and sought out a remote corner of the galaxy in which to hide himself, except for one thing: K'Ehleyr was still alive and in the hands of the enemy.

The coward in him wanted to retreat and call in a team to replace himself and K'Ehleyr. Some nobler spark of his nature refused to let him run. *I can't leave her,* he told himself.

In all the years they had worked together, he had never told K'Ehleyr how much he admired her, desired her, adored her as a woman and a heroine of Spock's movement. K'Ehleyr had never been one for sentimental declarations, and so no time had ever felt right for Barclay to bare his feelings. Though he knew his hope was irrational, he wondered if saving her life might one day give him a chance to confess his heart.

Focus, he reminded himself. *Live through today before you start day-dreaming about tomorrow.*

He pulled on the stealth suit's snug-fitting hood and put his heads-up-display visor and breathing mask in place. A tap on the control panel next to him activated the suit, and the visor snapped to life, rendering the aft cabin of the *Solomon* in frost-blue hues. "Solomon, do you read me?"

"Yes, Reg," answered the ship's AI through Barclay's subaural transceiver, which was now online.

"Transfer control of the tac-support system to my stealth suit, and get me a lock on K'Ehleyr's transceiver."

"Done," Solomon said.

Scads of tactical data flooded across Barclay's HUD, and he made some quick changes to limit it to immediately relevant scans and alerts. "I'll need the base layout and detention-center floor plans. Highlight K'Ehleyr's position, please."

"Uploaded. Range and direction on your visor, Reg."

"Thanks," Barclay said. He reviewed the tactical situation and was not encouraged. Since K'Ehleyr's capture, the entire base had been placed on a heightened state of alert. He couldn't see any low-engagement strategies that were open to him.

Thinking of the big picture, he asked, "Any luck finding out where they put Nechayev's personal effects?"

"Not yet," Solomon said. *"I'm running a new code-breaking algorithm, but I need to be careful not to trip their computer security alarms. As soon as I access the security system, I should be able to track down General Nechayev's belongings."*

Barclay powered up his suit's stealth circuits. "All right," he said as he watched his reflection fade from a deactivated monitor. "Give me a heads-up as soon as you do."

"Will do, Reg. Good luck."

"Thanks," he replied, musing darkly, *I'm gonna need it.*

He opened the side hatch of the cloaked ship and descended the ramp into the slashing rain and wind. Watching water pool on the *Solomon*'s invisible hull and run off in great torrents, he was grateful that he had taken the precaution of landing a short distance from the base, out of sight behind a rocky knoll.

Turning his back on the ship, he pressed on into the stormy gloom, keenly aware that he would either return with K'Ehleyr and the master quantum transceiver or not come back at all.

. . .

It was to General Duras's credit, thought Alynna Nechayev, that he knew when to shut up and just listen.

Since returning from their conversation's earlier interruption, he had let her talk freely. His questions had been few and to the point.

In less than an hour, she had told him in broad strokes about Spock's creation of Memory Omega; the disinformation campaign of the Vulcans' telepathic sleeper agents, who were now at large throughout the Alliance; the hidden archives of information preserved from the Terran Empire (and, later, the Terran Republic); and Memory Omega's caches of high technology, which included weapons, ships, medical devices, and much more.

Through it all, Duras had paid rapt attention to Nechayev's every word. His intense gaze had never left her eyes, even as he acknowledged her statements with solemn nods.

"And since then," she continued, "we've been embedding agents in the Terran rebellion, putting them in positions to advise and assist key leaders in growing their numbers and fomenting a massive civil uprising throughout the Alliance."

She looked up to gauge the general's reaction. Duras stood with one arm tucked against his armored chest and stroked his goatee with his free hand. He let out a pensive grunt and looked away from her. Then he let his arms drop as he paced around her.

"It sounds as if Spock's plan is proceeding quite successfully," he said. "With your organization so close to victory, why turn your back on it now?"

"Because they can't win," Nechayev said.

Duras stopped in front of her and cocked a curious eyebrow. "Why do you say that?"

"It's a simple matter of numbers," Nechayev said. "The Alliance has too many, and Memory Omega has too few."

"History is rich with tales of victory against overwhelming odds," Duras said. "Numbers don't always tell the story."

Nechayev rolled her eyes. "This is no adventure tale, General. My role in the organization was strategic planning. It was my job to know what we were capable of and advise the leadership accordingly. But they don't want to listen to me."

Folding his arms, he asked, "What have you told them?"

"That the Alliance is spread out across too vast a territory and has too many redundant safeguards in its command structure. No matter how deftly we coordinate our sleeper agents, we lack the resources and manpower to bring down the Alliance's government or military."

"A grim assessment," Duras said.

She sensed that he wasn't persuaded. "Do you want to know how dire the situation really is?" He nodded for her to go on. "The reason I'm even here is that we just abandoned our primary headquarters, because of *one* compromised operative."

"Was his knowledge of your operation *that* detailed?"

"Not enough to hurt us directly," Nechayev explained, "but our threat-assessment group decided that his capture had set in motion a series of events that would enable the Alliance to find our command center in less than a year." She shook her head and punctuated her story with a bitter chortle. "So we abandoned the safest base in the galaxy and blew it up."

Duras nodded. "A sensible precaution."

"Perhaps," Nechayev said. "But if we can't even protect our own headquarters, how are we supposed to win a war against the Alliance?"

The general's reserved smirk became a sneer. "So, rather than seek victory, you decided to surrender."

"Not surrender," Nechayev corrected him. "Change my allegiance and cast my lot with the obvious victors."

Duras stepped forward and loomed over her. "What makes you think the Alliance has any use for a traitor like you?"

"Because I'm here to help you rid the Alliance of the Terran rebellion and destroy Memory Omega."

That made him grin. "And how do you propose to do that?"

"By giving you the nail in their coffin," she said. "A device that

you can use to wipe out all of Memory Omega in one swift stroke—
and take the heart of the rebellion with it."

Her offer snared his attention; he was no longer grinning. He
asked, "And what do you want in return?"

"Freedom and a world to rule as my own," she said.

"You ask much."

"For wiping out the only serious threat to the Alliance's power
in local space? I think my terms are fair."

The general nodded. "Very well," he said. "Freedom and a
world to rule. I can give you those . . ." He leaned down until his
nose touched hers. "After you help me become regent."

Barclay had just perched at the top of the base's outer battlement,
like an invisible gargoyle staring into the storm, when a stiff wind
pushed him forward, off the wall.

Flailing to recover his grip, he felt himself tumbling. His hands
slipped on the wet, smooth concrete, and his gloved fingers clawed
wildly but found no purchase. He slid down the wall, palms pressed
against it, hoping that friction would slow his fall without damag-
ing his body suit's stealth fabric.

Impact. He slammed into a shallow puddle and rolled away
from the wall. Seconds later, he came to a stop, facedown in the
mud, bruised and winded.

Voices and running footfalls converged on his position. Harsh
beams of light slashed through the downpour and danced over the
rain-pocked ground on either side of him. Barclay remained still
and listened while a pair of Klingon soldiers lingered mere meters
away from him.

"Looks clear," said the first one, an older Klingon with a hoarse
rasp of a voice.

The younger warrior, whose baritone was rich and strong,
replied, "I know I heard something."

"Probably those scavenger birds again," the veteran said.

"It didn't sound like a bird."

Walking away, the older Klingon said, "Whatever it was, it's gone now. I'm going back to the post. If you want to stand in the rain, go ahead."

The young baritone continued to look around in frustration for a few seconds more, then he relented and followed the veteran back to someplace sheltered from the storm.

Alone once more, Barclay crawled across the muddy ground to the detention center and peeked around its corner. A new guard had been posted to walk a patrol along the north wall, where K'Ehleyr had made her ascent to the roof.

No way I can take him in hand-to-hand, Barclay admitted to himself. *Not that I'm in any shape to climb to the roof, anyway.* In a cautious whisper, he said, "Solomon, what's the base's security status?"

Like a voice inside his head, Solomon replied over the subaural transceiver, *"All forces have been placed on a state of heightened alert. Patrols have been doubled, and sentries have been deployed to the rooftops."*

He switched his visor between night-vision and thermal-vision settings. Within seconds, he had pinpointed the Klingon sentries lurking above him in the dark, on the rooftops. *So much for doing this quietly,* he realized.

"Solomon, show me a map of the base layout." The map appeared as a ghostly overlay of green lines and icons on his visor. "Pinpoint the command center, power generators, comm relays, and troop barracks." Yellow icons marked the locations he'd specified. "Mark those as targets," he said, detaching a pack of spiders from his belt.

Solomon asked with apprehension, *"Reg, what're you doing?"*

Activating the self-guided robotic munitions, Barclay grinned beneath his mask. "Making a mess," he said.

A stinging deluge of ice-cold water shocked K'Ehleyr back to consciousness. Shivering and coiled to react, she regarded her captors with a feral gleam.

The one in charge was short and slight, with crazy, bulging eyes. Behind him, looming over his shoulders, was a pair of standard-issue Klingon simpletons in matching suits of gray-black armor. One of them tossed aside an empty bucket.

"Good," the crazy one said to K'Ehleyr. "You're alive."

K'Ehleyr glanced at herself to assess her injuries and her options. She had been stripped of her stealth suit, weapons, boots, and equipment. All she had left were a loose pair of trousers and a shirt, both of which were now soaked with frigid water and clinging to her skin, leeching her body heat.

Crazy-eyes reached down and grabbed K'Ehleyr's chin. Lifting her face so he could aim his maniacal stare into her eyes, he said, "So, half-breed, what backwater rock were you born on?" K'Ehleyr shook her face from his grasp and growled. He flashed a toothy smile and continued, "Not an Alliance world, and definitely not an Imperial one. Abominations like you get drowned at birth. So, where do you come from?"

She thought of the now-destroyed hidden base at Regula, where her human mother, a Memory Omega agent, had given birth to K'Ehleyr after returning from a mission-gone-wrong in Alliance territory.

"No world you've ever heard of," K'Ehleyr said with a voice full of hate and eyes full of murder.

She looked past the three Klingons and scoped out the room. It was a typical Alliance chamber of horrors, stocked with torture devices ancient and modern, blunt and subtle. Pointed tips, sawtooth edges, and instruments glowing white with heat. Trays of hyposprays loaded with mind-breaking pharmaceuticals.

In the center of the room stood the most fearsome feature of all: a Klingon mind-sifter.

The madman slapped her face. "Pay attention," he said.

Fixing her gaze on him, she noted his rank insignia. He was a colonel. Recalling her premission briefing on the *Solomon,* she realized that he must be the base's executive officer. "As you wish," she said, adding with a snide note, "Gowron."

He punched her in the mouth, and she felt her bottom lip split open and spill warm blood down her chin. "You filthy whorechild! You dare speak my name?" She laughed at him. Enraged, he hit her again, snapping her head sideways and launching a stream of bloody spittle into the air.

She looked up at him and bared a facetious, bloody smile. "You hit like a *petaQ,* Gowron."

Gowron cocked his fist to strike again but stopped. "Who are you working for, half-breed?"

Before she could concoct an appropriately sarcastic answer, she heard Barclay's voice crackle inside her head: *"K'Ehleyr, it's Reg. I have a lock on your tr–transceiver, and I'm on my way in. Hold p–position till I trigger a d–d–distraction."*

K'Ehleyr smirked. The Klingons had failed to detect her sub-aural transceiver. She hadn't been certain the implanted device would get past their sensors; it had been designed to fool most Alliance scans, but there was never any guarantee that such precautions would actually work in the field.

A backhanded slap by one of Gowron's thugs got her attention but failed to knock the grin off her face.

"Who are you working for?" asked Gowron. He leaned closer in a failed effort to intimidate her. "Don't make me ask again."

"Or what? You'll torture me? You'll do that anyway."

He leered at her with a salacious grin. "Eventually." To his men, he barked, "Hold her!"

The two enlisted thugs pounced on K'Ehleyr and overpowered her with ease. Then they hauled her to her feet and slammed her backward against a bolted-down stainless-steel surgical table. Each warrior held one of her arms and pinned one of her legs.

Gowron cracked his knuckles as he walked toward her.

His first punch knocked the air from her lungs.

Her body was struggling to double over, but the soldiers holding her up refused to let her. Gowron landed a series of fast, hard jabs in K'Ehleyr's face. The third hit broke her nose. Dark crimson blood ran from her nostrils and dripped off her chin, speckling the floor between her bare feet.

"I'm tired of her face," Gowron said to his men. Off his nod, they pinned her arms behind her back and turned her away from him. She felt a large, powerful hand on the back of her head push her forward, bending her over the operating table. She thrashed but couldn't break free.

Despite having been trained by Memory Omega to withstand violation and torture, she felt her face burn with rage as Gowron grabbed her hair and twisted it while pressing himself against her. His foul breath was hot across her cheek. He grabbed her hip. "You like this, don't you, whorechild?"

"Not as much as you do, apparently." Angry tears rolled from her eyes—not for herself but for the suddenly conjured image of her sweet and loving mother suffering such a fate at the hands of monsters like these nearly four decades earlier.

Gowron seemed primed to indulge himself when the room trembled with the deep percussion of nearby explosions. A thunderous detonation turned the room pitch-black.

In the moment of confusion, the guards' grips on her arms relented by the slightest measure. K'Ehleyr jumped forward, launching herself over the operating table and pulling her foes with her. Agonizing pain blazed across her scalp as Gowron held fast to her hair, but one guard lost hold of her left arm.

She grabbed the edge of the table for leverage and kicked wildly, landing a few good hits with her heel in Gowron's face. He let go of her hair, stumbled backward, and fell on his ass.

The guard who still had her right arm tugged her toward him. Instead of resisting, she leaped toward him. She slammed into him and curled her left arm behind his head. As the lights flickered back on at half-strength, she grabbed his chin, gave it a savage twist, and broke his neck. He crumpled beneath her.

His partner charged at her. She plucked her victim's *d'k tahg* from its sheath and let it fly. It sank into the second warrior's throat, and he collapsed at her feet.

Gowron was back on his feet. He held a *d'k tahg* in each hand and prowled toward K'Ehleyr.

She lunged toward the surgical instruments so she could arm herself, but he was quicker and cut her off.

Empty-handed and injured, she backed away from him.

He was wiry and agile, and clearly an experienced killer. As he backed her into a corner, he sneered and said, "Time to die, half-breed."

He tested her responses with a rapid series of feints. Then he attacked in earnest, committed to the kill.

K'Ehleyr dodged the slashing of one blade and spun clear as he thrust the other at her heart.

She caught his wrist and turned it at an unnatural angle, breaking bones. His hand jerked open and dropped its weapon.

His other hand shot back in a blur. She barely blocked the slash at her throat. He swept her legs out from under her.

They collapsed together to the floor. He landed on top of her and pinned her with his knees on her chest and left arm.

Every second brought the tip of his dagger closer to her throat. She tried to shift her weight and throw him off but couldn't get the leverage she needed.

He was so close to her, his mad eyes looking into hers, yearning to see her life fade when his blade struck home. His putrid breath made her want to retch.

She felt the first sting of cold steel against her throat—

—and then the tip of Gowron's other *d'k tahg* erupted from his throat, thrust from behind and spraying K'Ehleyr's face with her foe's thick, pink blood. Gowron's eyes opened wider than she would have thought possible, then his face and body went slack.

With a simple push, she cast his corpse aside.

"Good timing," she said, ready to applaud Barclay for a well-executed rescue. Then she saw that it wasn't Barclay who had put the knife through Gowron's throat.

Duras loomed above her, offering her his open hand. "Come with me," he said. "There isn't much time."

Duras faced the door and stood guard while K'Ehleyr shimmied back into her stealth suit, which he had returned to her. He knew it was dangerous to turn his back on her, but the situation had become too volatile for him to indulge in paranoia.

As she dressed, she asked, "Why are you helping me?"

"Because we serve the same cause," Duras said. "I'm an ally of Memory Omega."

She chortled. "I find that hard to believe."

"My family has been prominent in the Empire's government for generations, but we've often clashed with its politics, and we've never been in favor of the Alliance," Duras explained. "My father, Ja'Rod, tried to forge a pact with the Romulan Star Empire to undermine the Alliance."

K'Ehleyr stepped into view beside him and pulled on her gloves, one at a time. "I'm guessing that didn't go well."

"No, it didn't. Mogh assassinated him on Khitomer before he could meet with the Romulan envoy." He handed her a disruptor pistol, which she accepted with a suspicious look. "But even though he failed to strike a deal with the Romulans, his sacrifice made Memory Omega take note of the House of Duras."

"Touching," K'Ehleyr said, holstering the borrowed weapon. "Assuming you're telling me the truth, why risk your cover now?"

He handed her the pullover mask for her stealth suit. "Because I can't let you fall victim to the mind-sifter any more than I can let Nechayev betray us by choice. That's why I shut off the security systems in her cell and banished the guards when I questioned her. My people think I did it for political advantage. I was really doing it to contain the damage of her defection." He nodded at the mind-sifter. "But if Gowron had put you in there, my efforts would have been for nothing."

She pulled the mask over her head and tucked it into the high collar of the suit. When the two pieces made contact, they seemed to fuse together into a seamless skin. "All right," she said. "What's our next move?"

"Cloak yourself. I'll lead you back to Nechayev's cell and find a reason to dismiss the guards. Once they're gone, you'll kill Nechayev and make your escape."

"What about her possessions?" asked K'Ehleyr, whose suit began to shimmer. "Where are they? I need to recover the master transceiver."

Duras tried to conceal his amazement as K'Ehleyr all but faded from view. "The secure locker in the cargo impound," he said. "Next to the landing pad."

"Got it," she said. "Let's move out."

He opened the door and checked the corridor. It was empty, but he heard voices and running footsteps echoing in the distance. "Clear," he said. "Follow me."

Moving at a quick step, Duras stole down the passageways, alert for any sign of trouble. Pausing at a corner, he looked back over his shoulder. He saw no sign of K'Ehleyr, and he realized he hadn't heard her footsteps, either. In a careful whisper, he asked, "Still with me?"

"Right behind you," she whispered back, into his ear.

Pressing on, Duras took the shortest route back to Nechayev's cell. Every step of the way, he pondered what ruse he would employ to get rid of the guards. Turning the final corner, he saw it was a moot point. The guards were gone, and the door of Nechayev's cell was open.

Duras rushed to the open cell. The two sentries were inside, on the floor. One's face had been blasted away. The other's throat was cut, and his disruptor was missing.

"Impossible," Duras muttered.

"Hardly," said K'Ehleyr, whose voice sounded as if it had come from in front of him. "She probably had half a dozen tricks hidden on her body that your scanners can't detect."

A clamor of running steps approached from the corridor they'd just left. "You need to go," Duras said. "Find her before she gets off the base. I'll stall my people as long as I can."

"Thank you, Duras," K'Ehleyr said.

He responded with a gruff tilt of his head. "Go."

Then he turned and waited for his men. He remembered having to celebrate Kurn's victory over the Terran rebellion at Empok Nor months earlier. Duras had done everything he could to thwart Kira's investigation of the rebels' activity in that sector, but once she'd involved Kurn, there had been nothing more Duras could do without drawing suspicion to himself.

It had galled him to hail Kurn as a hero of the Empire, and it hadn't saved him from Martok's spite or Kurn's wrath; he'd still ended up on this forsaken rock. Now, at least, he thought it might all have happened for a reason. His misfortune would serve a purpose.

A squad of warriors sprinted around the corner and halted in front of him. The lieutenant in charge saluted him. "General, Colonel Gowron is dead, and his prisoner has escaped!"

"So has mine," Duras said. "They must be working together. Deploy your men to secure the armory and the command center."

The lieutenant saluted again. "Yes, General!" He barked orders at his men and led them at a run past Duras while shouting more orders into his wrist comm.

Duras watched them go and heaved a growling sigh. He'd done all he could. He hoped it would be enough, because he had only one thing left to live for now: seeing Spock's plan fulfilled.

Until then, there would be no good days to die.

Nechayev stayed in the shadows as she skulked across the base.

Releasing the manacles that had bound her to the chair in her cell had been simple. A miniaturized signal emitter, embedded in her left palm and reachable by her index and middle fingers, had been designed to unlock a wide variety of Alliance security equipment, including cell doors.

She had decided to spring herself from custody as soon as Duras had left her to investigate the cause of the explosions rocking the base. Nechayev didn't need to wait for the answer. It was either an attack by the Terran rebellion, in which case she stood a significant risk of becoming collateral damage, or it was the work of a Memory Omega operative, which meant they had come either to rescue her or to kill her.

Another series of rumbling blasts had masked the sound of her cell door opening, and the sudden fall of darkness in the corridor had given her the distraction she needed. She'd plucked a *d'k tahg* from one of her guards and used it to cut the other's throat. As he'd sagged to the floor, she had snatched his disruptor and fired off a snap shot at the other guard, catching him in the face. All in all, killing them had been easy—at least, easier than dragging their bodies into her cell.

Now all that remained for her to do was to recover the master transceiver and steal herself some transport off this rock.

If Duras was too slow to strike a deal, that's his problem, she decided. *Because if he won't give me what I want, I'll just find another Klingon who will.*

K'Ehleyr crouched at the edge of the detention center's roof and searched for any sign of Alynna Nechayev on the ground below. Fierce gales pummeled the base with vast sheets of rain.

As if that weren't sufficient to occlude her vision, Barclay's demolitions handiwork was interfering with the enhanced settings of her stealth suit's visor. His spider-bomb assault had reduced several buildings to rubble and flames, and the blooms of heat that blanketed the camp also obscured the thermal signatures of anyone in their vicinity. Not only was she unable to track the Klingon soldiers who were scrambling to and fro, but she had no way of pinpointing the subtle variation of a human heat profile in all of that infrared noise.

Knowing that Barclay would be monitoring their open com-link on his subaural implant, she asked, "What's your status?"

"Hacking the g–g–gate on the impound locker now," Barclay said. *"J–just a few more seconds."*

"Watch your back in there," K'Ehleyr said, shimmying down an exposed pipe to ground level as she continued. "Nechayev probably wants two things right now, and you're next to one and blocking the way to the other."

She heard Barclay chuckle over the comm. *"Not for long,"* he said. *"I'm in the locker and s–sorting through her stuff now."*

"It'd be disguised," K'Ehleyr reminded him, "probably as something small and personal."

A troop of Klingons marched by her in formation, diagonally crossing the base's open parade ground. As the rear rank passed her, she slipped out from cover and fell into step directly behind them, in their shadow. Her footfalls were muffled by the rhythm of their marching and the roaring patter of the rain.

The squad proceeded down a narrow road between two low buildings, one of which was ablaze. K'Ehleyr ducked back under cover in a nook of the nonburning building and skulked along its foundation toward the still-distant cargo center.

She paused as Barclay's voice whispered in her ear, *"Got it! Y–you were right. It was small, and very . . . p–p–personal."*

"Please don't elaborate," K'Ehleyr said. "Just go back to the ship and wait for me. Once I take out Nechayev, we'll go."

"Ack—" The word caught in his throat. *"Acknowledged. I'm outta here."*

K'Ehleyr struggled to pierce the darkness, the rain, the fire, the smoke, and the mad activity of agitated Klingons, all to catch even one glimpse of Alynna Nechayev. *It won't take her long to find a way out of here,* K'Ehleyr fumed. *I can't let her get away. The next time she talks, she'll destroy us all.*

. . .

Barclay clambered like a monkey through a dense obstacle course of entwined pipes, which supplied fuel and other essential resources to the landing pad.

Squeezing through the gaps between the pipe clusters was awkward, but it seemed to Barclay like the only safe escape route; every other stretch of ground around the cargo center was teeming with Klingon soldiers looking for something to shoot at.

Rainwater trickled through several rows of piping over his head, and the droplets plunked erratically inside the maze, striking faint echoes from empty tubes. Crisscrosses of metal and polymer on all sides of him broke and bent the searchlights that were sweeping the camp in the wake of his earlier attack.

He neared a cross-shaped maintenance passageway that separated the tube maze into four equal quadrants. Once he was in the passage, he'd be able to stand and move normally again.

All I have to do is go out the south hatch, reach the outer wall, create another distraction, and I'll be home free.

Getting past the last obstacle entailed lying on his back and scuttling under a low, wide fuel main. For a moment, he feared he might have become stuck, but after a few seconds of panicked wriggling, he freed himself. He straightened, released another batch of spider bombs into the pipe maze, and sprinted for the south hatch, thirty meters away, past the intersection.

It was a foolproof plan, right up until the moment an arm shot out from behind the corner and clotheslined him.

He landed on his back in a greasy puddle, and all of the air was knocked from his lungs. Like a landed fish, he writhed while his body forced him to draw empty, futile gasps.

Nechayev emerged from behind the corner and pounced on him. She stuck a disruptor in his face as she yanked off the mask of his stealth suit, disabling its cloak. "Memory Omega," she said as Barclay shimmered into view.

"General N–Nechayev," Barclay said, barely able to breathe.

At first, she looked dumbfounded. Then her expression lit up with recognition. She smirked with scorn. "I know you," she said, never once shifting the aim of her weapon. "You're that stuttering twit who works with K'Ehleyr!" She touched her index finger to her temple, then snapped her fingers. "Broccoli!"

"B–B–Barclay," he protested meekly, trying to sit up.

She pressed the disruptor's muzzle against his nose. "That's what I said."

In his ear, Barclay heard K'Ehleyr say, *"Keep her talking, Reg, I'm heading for the west hatch."*

Nechayev eased herself back to her feet, keeping her weapon aimed at his face the entire time. "Tell you what, Broccoli. I need to go now. As long as you don't do something stupid, like get in my way, I'll let you live."

She inched past him, disruptor steady and on target, and moved toward the north hatch. Barclay recalled that the landing pad was at that end of the pipe maze. "General," he said, "I d–d–don't understand. We're here to r–rescue you."

She paused. "I was doing just fine without you." Evidently taking the bait, she lowered her weapon a few degrees.

"Well, if you're trying to reach the landing p–p–pad, don't take the n–north hatch. It's boobytrapped."

She turned her head to glance at the distant portal.

He drew his disruptor in half a blink.

She snapped hers back on target for his head.

Then she smiled. "Who do you think you're fooling, Broccoli?" She backed quickly down the passageway.

Barclay followed her, holding his disruptor level and maintaining his range and angle of fire. "Stop, General."

"Or what? You'll shoot me?" She shook her head and sneered as she continued backstepping.

"I'll d–d–do what I have to."

She was halfway to the north hatch. "No, you won't. You're no field agent, just a glorified button-pusher."

"D–d–don't make me shoot you," he said.

"Don't make me laugh. You've never pulled a trigger in your life." She was at the steps to the hatch. "I know your kind, Broccoli. You're a coward and a pacifist." Carefully, she climbed the few steps behind her. "Not that it's your fault—that's just what Memory Omega raised you to be: *weak*." From the top step, she added, "That's why it's going to lose."

Reaching blindly behind her, she found the hatch controls with her free hand. With a press of her thumb, the hatch unlocked and slid open behind her, filling the passageway with the whine of engine noise and the susurrus of the storm.

Barclay knew that if Nechayev reached the landing pad and made it into one of the Klingons' fueled and ready patrol shuttles, there would be almost no hope of catching her again before she inflicted irreparable harm on the movement.

She backed up to the hatch's threshold. "See ya, Broccoli."

His voice was as steady as his aim. "I can't let you leave."

Nechayev lowered her weapon and gave him a small shake of her head and a pitying smirk. "You don't have the balls to stop me." She turned and stepped through the hatchway.

He pulled the trigger.

The crimson pulse slammed into Nechayev's upper back and left a massive, circular scorch mark that burned through her clothes and deep into her flesh.

She staggered forward, dropped her disruptor, and fought to keep pulling herself up the stairs to the landing pad.

Barclay felt nauseated and dizzy as he took aim a second time. He'd never been a violent man, and certainly not a killer.

He fired again.

His second pulse struck the back of Nechayev's head and blasted away her coif of silver-blond hair, as well as her face and the top of her skull. Smoking and limp, her body pitched forward on the stairs, then tumbled back through the hatchway in a charred, lifeless heap.

Several seconds passed. Barclay no longer heard the noise from the landing pad or the surges of the storm; his ears were full of his pounding heartbeat and labored breathing. Something vile and hot forced its way up his esophagus. He holstered his disruptor just in time to fall to his knees and vomit a watery spew of acid on the muddy ground under his gloved hands.

He coughed and spat for a minute afterward, trying to expel the taste from his mouth. As he picked himself up and retrieved his mask, he saw a tall feminine form shimmer into view before him. K'Ehleyr peeled off her own mask and pressed a reassuring hand to Barclay's shoulder. "You all right?"

"Yeah," he said, sleeving sour flecks of spittle from his mouth and chin. "Fine."

She nodded toward Nechayev's body. "Looks like you didn't need me, after all." Lifting an eyebrow, she asked, "Still have the master transceiver?"

He patted a side pocket of his stealth suit. "Right here."

"Then we should get back to the ship," she said. "What's our exit strategy?"

"The armory and this fuel network are full of spiders."

K'Ehleyr grinned and put her mask back on. "Sounds like a plan." As she started to fade away, Barclay cast a final, regretful glance down the passageway at Nechayev. "Don't look so glum, Reg," said the now-invisible K'Ehleyr. "You just saved Spock's movement and the Terran revolution. You're a hero."

"I guess so," Barclay said, pulling his own mask back down over his face. On some level, he knew that what K'Ehleyr said was true, but it didn't make him feel any better about having taken a life or having shot a woman in the back.

He powered up his stealth suit. His HUD confirmed that he was once again transparent. He sighed and walked toward the south hatch. "Let's get the hell outta here."

The *Solomon* was two hours and half a light-year from the still-burning Klingon base, but Barclay's guilty feelings continued to weigh on his conscience. Though the tiny Memory Omega scout ship was cloaked from Alliance sensors, Barclay found nowhere to hide from his memory of pulling the trigger and watching Alynna Nechayev die in a flash of light and heat.

K'Ehleyr occupied the *Solomon*'s pilot's seat. She was relaxed behind the flight controls, guiding the ship toward its rendezvous with other Memory Omega teams at the movement's backup headquarters. She and Barclay had doffed their stealth suits and changed back into regular clothes as soon as the *Solomon* broke orbit, giving their quiet journey the ambience of a routine jaunt.

Barclay had been trying, with little success, to distract himself by studying the master quantum transceiver. Liberated from its disguise, it resembled little more than a plain metal cylinder, roughly equal in size to his middle finger.

"Amazing, isn't it?" he said, holding it up to the overhead light. "Thousands of quantum particles, vibrating in perfect harmony across unbreakable transdimensional strings with their sympathetic-twin partners, all over the galaxy."

"I should've known you'd see nothing but a fancy gizmo," K'Ehleyr teased with a grin.

He tucked the MQT back into a protective case. "I know it's more than just a gadget," he said. "It's *the* gadget."

"You still don't get it." Looking over her shoulder, she added, "That's not just the key to the revolution you're holding. It *is* the revolution."

Chastened, he contemplated how close they had come to letting everything slip away. A century of sacrifices and secrets had nearly been lost because of one woman's broken faith in the future. He rested his hand on the transceiver's case and permitted himself a moment of hopeful anticipation.

"We're going to live to see it, aren't we?" he asked.

K'Ehleyr grinned and kept her eyes on the streaks of stars outside the *Solomon*. "That's the plan, Reg. That's the plan."